The PHANTOM of the OPERA

also by Jean-Marc & Randy Lofficier
Arsène Lupin vs. Sherlock Holmes: The Hollow Needle
(*adapted from Maurice Leblanc*)

Doctor Ardan: The City of Gold and Lepers
(*adapted from Guy d'Armen*)

Doctor Omega
(*adapted from Arnould Galopin*)

Shadowmen: Heroes and Villains of French Pulp Fiction
(*non-fiction*)

Shadowmen 2: Heroes and Villains of French Comics
(*non -fiction*)

forthcoming from Black Coat Press:
Arsène Lupin vs. Sherlock Holmes: The Blonde Phantom
(*adapted from Maurice Leblanc*)

Harry Dickson: The Man in Grey
(*adapted from Arnould Galopin*)

available from iUniverse:
The Doctor Who Programme Guide
The Nth Doctor
Into the Twilight Zone

The PHANTOM of the OPERA

by
Gaston Leroux

adapted in English by
Jean-Marc & Randy Lofficier

with illustrations by
Hilary Barta, Juan Roncagliolo Berger,
Luciano Bernasconi, Stephen R. Bissette, Bret Blevins,
Mark Bodé, Fernando Calvi, Douglas Carrel, Caza,
Mike Collins, Gianluca Costantini, Rich Faber,
Seth Fisher, Gerald Forton, John Gallagher,
Manuel Garcia, John Heebink, Sam Hiti, Ladrönn,
David Lafuente, Steve Leialoha, Alfredo Macall,
Chris Malgrain, Mike Manley, Francesco Mattioli,
Mauricet, Paolo Ongaro, Fernando Pasarin,
Manuel Martin Peniche, Olivier & Stephane Peru,
Alberto Ponticelli, Paul Pope, Mike Ratera,
Edmond Ripoll, Denis Rodier, Steve Rude, Stan Sakai,
Eric Shanower, Jay Stephens, Ron Sutton, Dave Taylor,
Timothy II, Rick Veitch, Pete Von Sholly,
Mike Vosburg, Phil Yeh and Thomas Zahler

A Black Coat Press Book

Acknowledgements: We are indebted to every artist who contributed to this book, especially Dave Taylor, to Massimiliano Turco, and to David McDonnell for suggesting the concept and proofreading the typescript.

Visit our website at www.blackcoatpress.com

ISBN 1-932983-13-9. First Printing. October 2004. Published by Black Coat Press, an imprint of Hollywood Comics.com, LLC, P.O. Box 17270, Encino, CA 91416. All rights reserved. Except for review purposes, no part of this book may be reproduced or transmitted in any form or by any means, electronic or mechanical, including photocopying, recording or by any information storage and retrieval system, without permission in writing from the publisher. The stories and characters depicted in this book are entirely fictional. Printed in the United States of America.

To my older brother, Jo,
who is not a Phantom but is neverthless, like Erik,
a true Angel of Music.
Affectionately,
Gaston Leroux

Mike Collins

Steve Rude

Foreword

In which the author of this peculiar work tells the reader how he acquired the certainty that the Phantom of the Opera really existed

The Phantom of the Opera really existed. He was not, as has long been believed, the product of the imagination of the performers, of the superstition of the Directors, or the vapid creation of the overheated minds of the young ballerinas, their mothers, the usherettes, the cloak-room attendants or the concierge.

Yes, the Phantom was a creature of flesh and blood, even though he liked to assume the appearance of a real phantom, that is to say, a ghost.

When I began to rifle through the archives of the National Academy of Music, I was immediately struck by the remarkable correlation that existed between all the phenomena attributed to the so-called *Phantom* and the most mysterious and fantastic tragedy that I had ever come across in all my years as a Parisian journalist. It soon occurred to me that, perhaps, one might logically help explain the other.

The events that I am about to record occurred about 30 years ago.[1] Yet it would not be too hard to find in today's ballet community a number of old but respectable people, of unquestionable reputation, who still remember it as if it had all happened yesterday. You could ask about the mysterious and tragic events that surrounded the abduction of Christine Daae, the disappearance of the Vicomte de Chagny and the death of his elder brother Comte Philippe, whose body was found on

---

[1] circa 1880.

the banks of the underground lake which exists in the lower levels of the Opera on the side facing the Rue Scribe. But until now, none of the potential witnesses ever thought that there was any connection between these terrible occurrences and the mythical figure of the Phantom of the Opera.

The truth was slow to reveal itself to me. My investigation was constantly hampered by the discovery of events which, at first glance, seemed almost *supernatural* in nature. More than once, I was tempted to abandon this exhausting task in which I thought I was almost literally *chasing a phantom*. But finally, I uncovered proof that my initial instincts had been right. I was rewarded for all my efforts on the day I acquired indisputable evidence that the Phantom of the Opera was not a myth.

I had spent long hours that day poring over *The Memoirs of a Director*, the rather shallow autobiography of the all-too-skeptical Monsieur Armand Moncharmin who, during his entire tenure as Director of the Opera, not only understood nothing of the Phantom's cryptic behavior, but even made light of it. And he did so just as he was himself the victim of the bizarre financial transaction that became known as the "Magic Envelope."

I was at my wits' end, feeling extremely depressed when I left the library that day. Then, in the lobby, I met the delightful Director of the National Academy, who was chatting with a lively, little old man. The Director knew about my research, and how eager I was to locate the investigating magistrate who had been in charge of the notorious *Affaire Chagny*–a certain Monsieur Faure. Nobody seemed to know what had become of him, or even if he was alive or dead. As luck would have it, Monsieur Faure was the very man speaking with the Director, who was delighted to introduce me. As it turned out, the retired magistrate had spent the last 15 years in Canada and the first thing he had done, upon his return to Paris, was to call on the Director to inquire about getting free seats for the Opera!

Monsieur Faure and I spent a good part of the evening together and he told me everything he knew about the Chagny

8

case. For lack of any hard evidence, he had felt compelled to rule that the Vicomte had been temporarily insane and that his elder brother's drowning was an accidental death. Still, he remained convinced that another, terrible tragedy had occurred between the two brothers, a tragedy connected to the person of Christine Daae.

Monsieur Faure, however, did not know what became of Christine or the Vicomte. And when I cautiously mentioned the Phantom, he laughed. He, too, had heard of the strange events that hinted at the existence of some kind of supernatural being haunting the mysterious bowels of the Opera, and he knew the story of the *Magic Envelope*, but he had never found anything in it that required his attention as a magistrate. In fact, he had barely listened to the fanciful evidence given by a witness who had come forward of his own accord and declared that he knew the Phantom. That witness was a man known in various Parisian circles only as the "Persian." He certainly was well-known to every subscriber to the Opera at the time. But the worthy Monsieur Faure thought he was merely a harmless lunatic.

As you can imagine, I became immediately fascinated by the character of this "Persian." I desperately wanted, if there was still time, to locate the "harmless lunatic" who claimed to have known the Phantom. I was lucky to discover him, still alive, at the same address he had given to the magistrate at the time, a small apartment located on the Rue de Rivoli. I was doubly-lucky, in fact, since the Persian passed away only five months after my interview with him.

Like every good journalist, at first I was a bit skeptical of his story. But after the Persian, with a disarming, child-like candor, told me everything he knew about the Phantom, and even entrusted me with proof of his existence–including Christine Daae's remarkable letters!–I no longer doubted his word. It was true, the Phantom of the Opera was not a myth!

I know that some have told me that this correspondence could have been forged by the Persian himself, a man whose vivid imagination had been nourished by the most beguiling of tales. But, fortunately, I was able to locate a sample of Christine Daae's handwriting and compare it to that of the letters, and I can attest here that the correspondence is absolutely authentic.

I also meticulously researched the Persian's background and found that he was an honest man, unlikely to make up a story to pervert the course of justice.

This opinion, as I found later, was shared by every respectable person who, at one time or another, was involved in the Chagny case, or were friends with the Chagny family. I showed them all the documents I had painstakingly gathered and outlined my conclusions. All agreed with me and encouraged me to publish the results of my investigation. If I may, I shall quote from a letter I received from the famous General D*** on this very subject:

Dear Mr. Leroux:

I cannot urge you too strongly to publish the results of your inquiry. I remember very well that, a few weeks before the disappearance of the extraordinary Christine Daae, and the ensuing tragedy that upset all of the Faubourg Saint-Germain, there was a great deal of talk among the ballerinas of the Opera about the Phantom. *I believe that such talk only stopped* after *the whole tragic affair was over. If it is possible– and after hearing you, I believe it is–to explain this tragedy by exposing the role played by said Phantom, then I beg you to do so. Strange as the Phantom may seem to us, his presence will always be more palatable to me than the despicable version of the story that ill-intentioned people have spread, in which two brothers who loved each other all their lives were said to have killed each other.*

Sincerely,

General D***

Finally, my ever-thickening dossier under my arm, I returned to visit what had once been the Phantom's vast domain, the gargantuan edifice which he had made his personal kingdom, the Opera. Everything I saw with my own eyes exactly corroborated the Persian's statements.

A new, wonderful discovery finally crowned my labors in a most definitive fashion. You may remember that, recently, the Ministry decided to bury beneath the Opera, a time capsule containing phonographic recordings of some of the most celebrated singers of our time. While digging, the workers found a body. *I am convinced that this is the body of the Phantom of the Opera*! I even had the discovery authenticated by the Director of the Opera himself and, frankly, I could not care less that some newspapers continue to instead claim that the body is that of a victim of the Commune.

Serious historians know that all the poor wretches who were massacred in the vaults of the Opera under the Commune were not buried on the side where the excavation was being done. I will gladly point out where to find their remains, which is not far from the huge crypt that was used to stockpile food during the Siege of Paris. I came upon this information when I was looking for the body of the Phantom, which I would never have found if it had not been for the almost-predestined coincidence of burying the finest voices of our times!

I will return later to the matter of the body and what ought to be done with it. For now, I must conclude this necessary foreword by gratefully thanking all the people who were of invaluable assistance in my research: Monsieur Mifroid, who was the Police Commissioner in charge of the investigation into the disappearance of Christine Daae, Monsieur Remy, former Secretary of the Opera, Monsieur Mercier, former Director of the Opera, Monsieur Gabriel, former Chorus-Master of the Opera, and especially Madame la Baronne de Castelot-Barbezac, who was once "Little Meg" (and is not ashamed of it) and is now the most charming star of our admirable *corps de ballet* and is also the eldest daughter of the worthy Madame Giry, now deceased, who was the usherette of the Phantom's private box.

Thanks to all these wonderful people, I have been able, in the following pages, to relate in the most minute detail all these many hours of undiluted love and terror.[2]

Gaston Leroux

[2] Before embarking on this true and terrible story, it would be ungracious of me to omit my thanks to the present management of the Opera, which has so kindly assisted me in all my inquiries. Therefore, I particularly wish to acknowledge the help of Monsieur le Directeur Gabion, of Monsieur Messager and of that most amiable of men, the architect entrusted with the preservation of the building, who did not hesitate to lend me the original blueprints of its creator, Charles Garnier, although I'm sure he was quite certain that I would never return them. Lastly, I must pay public tribute to the generosity of my friend and former assistant, J.-L. Croze, who allowed me to borrow some of the rarest editions dearest to his heart from his splendid theatrical library. (*Note from the Author.*)

Stan Sakai

Pete Von Sholly

Chapter One
Is it the Phantom?

Our curtain rises on that evening of January 10, 18**, when Messrs. Debienne and Poligny, Co-Directors of the Opera at the time, gave a final gala performance to celebrate their retirement. The dressing-room of Mademoiselle Sorelli, the notorious dancer, had just been invaded by half-a-dozen young ladies of the *corps de ballet*, who had come up from the stage after dancing in *Polyeucte*. They exhibited great confusion, some with forced, nervous laughter, while others uttered small cries of terror.

Mademoiselle Sorelli, who wished to be alone to rehearse the praise-filled speech she was scheduled to give later in front of the departing Directors, looked angrily at the agitated and disorderly crowd. She inquired about the cause of such unusual commotion. It was Little Jammes–a small girl with a button nose, blue eyes, rosy-red cheeks and a lily-white neck–who gave her an explanation.

"It's the Phantom!" she exclaimed in a voice trembling with fear.

Then she promptly locked the door behind her.

Mademoiselle Sorelli's dressing-room was decorated with fitting, ordinary elegance. It featured the standard dressing table, sofa, chairs, screen and armoires. On the walls hung a few engravings, inherited from her mother who had known the glories of the old Opera on the Rue le Peletier: portraits of Vestris, Gardel, Dupont and Bigottini. But the room seemed like a palace to the brats of the *corps de ballet*, who were housed in communal dressing-rooms, where they spent most of their time singing, quarreling, berating their maids and hair-dressers and buying each other glasses of cassis, beer– even rum–until the call-boy rang his bell.

15

Mademoiselle Sorelli was extremely superstitious. She barely repressed a shudder when she heard Little Jammes speak of the Phantom.

"Silly little fool!" she blurted.

Yet, because she was a major enthusiast, in all matters supernatural in general and in the Phantom of the Opera in particular, she immediately pressed the girl for more details.

"Did you see him?" she asked.

"As plainly as I see you now!" said Little Jammes who dropped into a chair, moaning as her trembling legs gave way beneath her.

Little Giry–a girl with ink-black eyes, raven hair, a tawny complexion and unhealthy, thin skin stretched over small, weak bones–added:

"If that was the Phantom, he is horribly ugly!"

"Oh, yes!" cried the chorus of ballerinas.

And they all began to talk at the same time. The Phantom had appeared to them in the shape of a tall gentleman in a dinner jacket who had suddenly materialized in one of the corridors, They could not tell from where he had come. It was as if he had walked straight through the wall.

"Pooh!" said one of the girls, who had more-or-less kept her *sang-froid*. "You see the Phantom everywhere!"

That was unkind, but true. For the past several months, the only topic of conversation around the Opera was the ghost-like figure in a dinner jacket who wandered about the building, from top to bottom, like a lost soul. He spoke to nobody, nobody dared speak to him and he vanished as soon as he was spotted, no one knowing where or how. As any real phantom would, he made no noise when walking. At first, people had laughed and made fun of the notion of a phantom dressed like a gentleman–or an undertaker–but the legend soon grew to gargantuan proportions among the *corps de ballet*. All the girls claimed to have met the Phantom at least once, and to have fallen victim to his mysterious, but undoubtedly evil, wiles. Those who laughed the loudest were often the most afraid. When the Phantom did not actually appear, he betrayed his presence through small incidents, some humorous, others distressing, or at least the most superstitious people believed. If an accident occurred, a practical joke backfired or one of the girls misplaced her powderpuff, it was obviously the fault of the Phantom of the Opera.

In fact, who could honestly claim to have really seen him? One meets many fleet-footed men wearing dinner jackets at the Opera and none of them are phantoms. Truthfully, it was not the clothes that made the Phantom but what they covered– a frightful skeleton.

At least, so the ballerinas said.

And, of course, he sported a death's-head.

Was all this truly believable? The description of the Phantom as a walking skeleton was first given by Joseph Buquet, a chief stagehand who claimed to have actually seen him. He said he had had a close encounter–one might almost say a face-to-face if the Phantom had a face–with the ghost-like being on the small staircase by the footlights which leads directly to the vaults. He had seen him for no more than a sec-ond–for the Phantom had turned and fled–and that single en-counter had left Buquet with an indelible impression.

"He is abnormally thin," he said. "His jacket hangs on a skeletal frame. His eyes are so deep that you can hardly see the pupils. There are only two big, black holes, like a dead man's skull. His skin is stretched across his face tight as a drumhead and is not white, but a pasty yellow. His nose is so insignificant that you almost can't see it and *its very absence is too awful to behold.* The only hair I saw were three or four long dark locks on his forehead and behind his ears."

Monsieur Buquet had tried to chase after the Phantom but in vain. He had mysteriously vanished without leaving any trace of his presence.

The chief stagehand was a serious, reliable man with lit-tle imagination and was known for his sobriety. His story was met with a good deal of interest and amazement. Soon, others came forward to say that they, too, had met the skeleton in a dinner jacket.

When rational men heard the story, they first said that someone must have played a practical joke on Buquet and they even accused one of his assistants. Then, a series of bizarre, inexplicable incidents occurred and even the most determined skeptics began to feel uneasy.

For example, firemen are generally held to be brave men who fear nothing, least of all fire!

One day, Monsieur Papin, the fireman posted at the Opera had ventured a little farther than usual when making his usual rounds of inspection in the vaults... He suddenly appeared backstage, terrified, trembling, his face ashen, his eyes bulging out of their sockets and practically fainted in the arms of Little Jammes' proud mother. Why? Because advancing toward him, floating in the air at eye level, he had just seen a head of fire without a body![3] And yet, as I said, a fireman should normally not be afraid of fire.

The *corps de ballet* was thrown into disarray. First, that fiery head did not match the description that Joseph Buquet had given of the Phantom. The young ladies questioned the fireman, then interrogated the stagehand again, and finally came to the inescapable conclusion that the Phantom had more than one head, and could switch between them at will. Naturally, that only increased the danger in their minds. If a fireman could faint, then no one could possibly blame mere ballerinas for running away from dark corners and poorly lit corridors as fast as their slender legs could carry them.

In order to protect the Opera from the evil curse that might otherwise overtake it, at least as much as was humanly possible, Mademoiselle Sorelli herself, on the day after the incident with the fireman, ceremoniously walked to the concierge's vestibule, located next to the courtyard facing the aisle occupied by Management. She was accompanied by a gaggle of ballerinas that included even the children from dance class

---

[3] Monsieur Pedro Gailhard, former Director of the Opera, himself told me this anecdote and vounched for its authenticity. (*Note from the Author.*)

in their tiny leotards. There, on a table, she placed a blessed horseshoe. Anyone entering the Opera who was not a member of the paying public, was expected to rub it with their hand before setting foot on the first step of the grand staircase.

I did not make up the story of the horseshoe, any more than I have made up–unfortunately!–any other part of this tragic tale. The horseshoe is still there today, in the same place it has been ever since, in the concierge's vestibule, which one must pass through if one enters the Opera through the Cour de l'Administration.

This brief recap of past events enables us to better understand the state of mind of Mademoiselle Sorelli and her companions on the evening of January 10.

"It's the Phantom!" Little Jammes had exclaimed.

That decisive, yet all too believable, declaration had only increased the anxiety of the ballerinas. An agonizing silence reigned in the dressing-room. The only sound was that of the girls' gasping for air. Finally, Little Jammes flung herself upon the farthest corner of the wall and, her face filled with genuine terror, whispered that single word:

"Listen!"

Everybody did and they heard–or believed they heard–a faint rustling sound just outside the door. Not the sound of ordinary footsteps but a noise like that of silk lightly brushing against the wood panel. Then, there was nothing more.

Mademoiselle Sorelli tried to appear braver than her companions. She walked up to the door and, in a trembling voice, asked:

"Who's there?"

No one answered.

Feeling that all eyes were upon her, that her every move was being scrutinized, she redoubled her valiant effort and said more loudly:

"Is there any one behind the door?"

"Of course there is!" cried that little plum, Meg Giry, who bravely held Mademoiselle Sorelli back by the hem of her gauze skirt. "Whatever you do, please don't open the door!"

But Mademoiselle Sorelli paid her no notice. She was armed with a dagger that never left her person. She slowly turned the key and opened the door. All the dancers immediately retreated as one to the back of the dressing-room.

"Mum! Mum!" Little Meg Giry whimpered.

Mademoiselle Sorelli defiantly stepped into the corridor. It was empty. From behind its glass receptacle, the dancing flame of a gaslight cast an ominous, reddish light onto the walls, without quite managing to dispel the ambient darkness. The ballerina quickly slammed the door shut.

"No," she said with a relieved sigh, "there is no one there."

"Still, we all saw him!" Little Jammes insisted, returning with small, shy steps to take her place besides Mademoiselle Sorelli. "He must still be lurking out there somewhere. I'm not going back to the communal dressing-room alone. We should all go down to the foyer together. And after the speech, we can all come up together as well."

As she outlined her plan, the child reverently touched the small coral finger-ring which she wore as a charm against bad luck. Mademoiselle Sorelli discreetly made a St. Andrew's cross with the tip of her right thumb on the wooden ring which adorned the fourth finger of her left hand.

Mademoiselle Sorelli, wrote a famous chronicler, was a tall, beautiful ballerina with a sensual, grave face and a waist as pliant as a reed. It was often said of her that she was a "pretty thing." Her beautiful gold-spun blonde hair stood atop a noble forehead and two emerald eyes. Her head was elegantly balanced on a slender, delicate neck. When she danced, she moved her entire body in an indescribably graceful fashion, evoking, like no other dancer could, a feeling of overwhelmingly languid charm. When she raised her arms and leaned slightly forward before launching herself into a pirouette, thereby emphasizing the finely sculpted contours of her breasts and hips, it was said of that most delectable of women that she was enough "to make one shoot oneself in the head."

And speaking of heads, hers was not noted for its brain, but no one had ever seemed to mind that single flaw in an otherwise perfect creature.

So Mademoiselle Sorelli told the little ballerinas:

"Come, children, pull yourselves together! No one has ever really seen the Phantom."

"Yes, yes, we saw him–we saw him just now!" said the girls. "He wore his death's-head and dinner jacket, the same as when he appeared to Joseph Buquet!"

"And Gabriel saw him too!" added Little Jammes. "Only yesterday... Yesterday afternoon... In broad daylight too!"

"Gabriel, the Chorus-Master?"

"Yes! Didn't you know?"

"And he was wearing his dinner jacket, in broad daylight?"

"Who? Gabriel?"

"No! The Phantom!"

"Gabriel told me so himself," said Little Jammes. "The Phantom wore a dinner jacket. That's how he recognized him. He was in the stage manager's office. Suddenly, the door opened and the Persian walked in. You know the Persian has the evil eye..."

"Oh, yes!" answered all the little dancers together, warding off said evil eye by pointing their forefinger and little fingers while bending their second and third fingers against the palms of their hands and holding them down with their thumbs.

"And you all know how superstitious Gabriel is," continued Little Jammes. "But, he's always very polite. When he sees the Persian, he just puts his hand in his pocket and touches his keys. Well, as soon as the Persian walked into the room, Gabriel jumped up from his chair to grab the handle of the cabinet so he could touch iron! When he did that, he tore a piece of his coat on a nail. In the rush to get out of the room and escape the curse, he banged his head against a hat-rack, and got a huge bump. Dazed, he stepped back and scratched his arm on the decorative screen, near the piano. He tried leaning on the piano to catch his breath, but the lid fell on his hands and crushed his fingers. He stormed out of the office screaming like a madman, slipped on the stairs and fell down the whole of the first flight on his back. I know all of this because I was passing there with *Maman* and we helped him up. Poor Gabriel was all bloodied and covered with bruises. We were almost scared out of our minds. But he seemed happy and thanked God that he had gotten off so easily. That's when he told us what had really scared him. Behind the Persian, he had seen the Phantom–*the Phantom with the death's-head*! Just like Joseph Buquet described him!"

Little Jammes had told her wild story so quickly that one might have thought the Phantom himself was after her. She finished breathlessly, amongst the hushed whispers of her audience. A long silence followed. Mademoiselle Sorelli was nervously polishing her nails, always a sign of great anxiety. Finally, it was Little Giry, who remarked:

"Joseph Buquet should know better and hold his tongue."

"Why should he?" asked somebody.

"That's what my Mum says," replied Little Meg, lowering her voice and looking around her as if she feared she would be overheard by other ears than those present.

"Why does your mum say that?"

"Not so loud! Mum says the Phantom doesn't like being talked about."

"How would she know?"

"Because... because... nothing!"

That strange reluctance to elaborate only intensified the curiosity of the other young ladies who pressed Little Meg to explain herself. They all leaned forward side-by-side in a collective motion expressing both curiosity and fear. They shared their feelings of terror, taking a keen pleasure in feeling the blood chill in their veins.

"I swore not to tell!" whispered Little Meg.

But it was too late–the other girls left her no peace and, naturally, promised to keep the secret, until Meg, who all along had been burning to tell what she knew, began her tale, her eyes strangely fixated on the door of the dressing-room.

"It's because of the private box..."

"What private box?"

"The Phantom's box!"

"The Phantom has a box?"

The notion that the Phantom of the Opera might have his own private box sent the ballerinas into fits of gasps and shudders.

"Oh, do tell us, do tell us!" they begged.

"Not so loud!" said Meg. "It's Box No. 5, you know, the second box on the left, next to the stage."

"You're pulling our legs!"

"No I'm not! My Mum's in charge of it... You swear you won't say a word to anyone?"

"Of course!"

"Box No. 5 is reserved for the Phantom. No one has rented it in months. The Directors have given orders to never rent it to anyone."

"And the Phantom really sits there?"

"Yes."

"So what does he look like?"

"Well, the Phantom uses it–*but there's nobody there!*"

The young ballerinas exchanged puzzled glances. If the Phantom used the box, someone should certainly have noticed him since he wore a dinner jacket and a death's-head. They tried to explain that simple logic to Meg, but the little girl remained unmoved.

"That's just it! The Phantom can't be seen. He's got no dinner jacket and no death's-head! All that talk about that and the firehead is just plain nonsense! When he's inside the box, you can only hear him. My mum's never seen him, not once, but she's heard him. She knows it's true because she gives him his program."

That last detail was too much for Mademoiselle Sorelli who felt it was her duty to inject a semblance of credibility into the conversation.

"Little Meg, you're making fun of us!"

At that, the child began to cry.

"I shouldn't have told you a thing! If my mum ever finds out... But I'm right. Joseph Buquet shouldn't talk about things that don't concern him–it'll only bring him bad luck, you'll see. My mum said so last night..."

Suddenly, there was the sound of hurried, heavy foot-steps in the corridor.

"Cecile! Cecile! Are you there?" cried a woman almost out of breath.

"It's my mother's voice," said Little Jammes. "What's going on?"

She opened the door. A respectable lady, built along the lines of a Pomeranian grenadier, burst into the dressing-room and dropped, groaning, into a vacant armchair. Her eyes rolled madly in her cheerless, brick-colored face.

"How terrible!" she said. "How terrible!"

"What? What?"

"Joseph Buquet..."

"What about him?"

"Joseph Buquet is dead!"

The room was immediately filled with incredulous ex-clamations, horrified questions and frightened requests for an explanation.

"He was found hanging in the vaults, on the third level... But the most terrible thing," continued the poor woman, pant-ing, *the most God-awful thing, is that the stagehands who found his body said that they heard music that came from no-where surrounding the corpse... The music reminded them of the* Dance of the Dead!"

"It's the Phantom!" blurted Little Meg, almost in spite of herself. However, she corrected herself at once and, with her hands pressed to her mouth, kept muttering: "No, no! I didn't say that! I didn't say that!"

All around her, her panic-stricken companions repeated under their breaths:

"Yes... It's the Phantom! It's the Phantom!"

Mademoiselle Sorelli was very pale.

"I'll never be able to deliver my speech now," she said.

Little Jammes' Mother contributed her own opinion while downing a small bottle of liqueur she had found on a table. Yes, the Phantom had to be involved somehow. It was only common sense.

The truth, however, is that no one ever learned the cause of Joseph Buquet's death. The verdict at the inquest was suicide. In *Memoirs of a Director*, Monsieur Armand Moncharmin, one of the men who succeeded Messrs. Debienne and Poligny, described the incident as follows:

"*A regrettable accident spoiled the small party that had been organized to celebrate Debienne and Poligny's retirement. I was in the Director's office, when Mercier, one of the Assistant Directors, suddenly came rushing in. He seemed half out of his mind and told me that the body of a stagehand had been found hanging on the third level where some of the most elaborate sets were stored, between a country farm-house and scenery from* The King of Lahore.

" '*Let's go and cut him down!' I immediately said.*

"*But by the time we had rushed down the stairs and ladders to the third level, the man was no longer hanging and the rope was gone.*"

Monsieur Moncharmin seemed to have found that last detail quite normal. A man is found hanging at the end of a rope. When they go to cut him down, the rope is gone. But our Monsieur Moncharmin found a very simple explanation! Here's what he wrote:

"*It was right after the ballet and the dancers probably wasted no time in getting their hands on a notorious good luck charm.*"

There you have it! Picture the *corps de ballet* scurrying down precarious ladders in the dark to divide amongst themselves the rope of a hanged man! Simply preposterous!

On the other hand, when I consider the very spot where the body was found–the third level under the Opera–I ask myself whether *someone else* might not have had an interest in making that rope disappear after it had served its sinister purpose. Time will tell if I am wrong in this matter.

In any event, the awful news soon spread throughout the Opera, where Joseph Buquet was extremely well-liked. The dressing-rooms emptied. The ballerinas, huddling around Mademoiselle Sorelli like fainthearted sheep around their shepherd, made for the foyer through the poorly-lit corridors and stairways, trotting as fast as their tiny pink feet could carry them.

Mike Ratera

Ladrönn

Chapter Two
The New Marguerite

On the first landing, Mademoiselle Sorelli ran into the Comte de Chagny who was going upstairs. The Comte, normally a rather calm man, seemed greatly excited.

"Mademoiselle Sorelli! I was just coming to see you," he said, gallantly taking off his hat. "What an enchanting evening! And Christine Daae was a triumph!"

"Really?" said Little Meg. "Six months ago, she sang like a frog! But you've got to excuse us, Monsieur le Comte, we're in a hurry," continued the brat, with an exaggerated curtsey that was just short of insolence. "We're going to see the body of the poor man who was found hanging by the neck."

Just then, the Assistant Director came rushing by, but stopped dead in his tracks when he heard her remark.

"What!" he sounded upset. "You girls have already heard the news? Please, don't say anything to anyone, especially to Messrs. Debienne or Poligny. I don't want them distressed on their last day."

They all continued on to the foyer of the ballet, which was already full of people.

The Comte de Chagny had been right. No gala performance had ever equalled the one that had just occurred. Those lucky enough to have attended it still speak of it to their children and grandchildren with tears in their eyes. Gounod, Reyer, Saint-Saëns, Massenet, Guiraud and Delibes, each in turn had assumed command of the orchestra and conducted their own works. Faure and Mademoiselle Krauss were among the singers. And it was on that very night that Christine Daae was revealed to an astonished and enthusiastic audience, that same Christine Daae whose tragic destiny I recount in this book.

Gounod conducted the *Funeral March of a Marionette*; Reyer, his beautiful overture to *Sigurd*; Saint-Saëns, the *Danse Macabre* and a *Rêverie Orientale*; Massenet, an unpublished *Hungarian March*; Guiraud, his *Carnaval*; Delibes, the *Slow Waltz* from *Sylvia* and the *Pizzicati* from *Coppelia*. Mademoiselle Krauss sang the *Bolero* from the *Vespri Siciliani* and Mademoiselle Denise Bloch the *Brindisi* from *Lucrezia Borgia*.

But the real triumph was reserved for young Christine Daae, who had begun her performance that night by singing an aria from *Romeo and Juliet*. It was the first time she had sung this Gounod piece, which had not yet been produced at the Opera, having just been performed at the Opera Comique after a long run at the old Théâtre Lyrique (where it had first been sung by the notorious Madame Carvalho). One feels sorry for all who did not have the opportunity to hear Christine Daae's rendition of Juliet, who never beheld the beauty of her shy grace, who were never moved by her angelic voice, who never felt their souls fly away and soar above the tomb of the Lovers of Verona as she sang "*Lord! Lord! Lord! Forgive us!*"

And yet, even that performance was nothing compared to her sublime tones in the prison scene and the final trio from *Faust*, in which she replaced Mademoiselle Carlotta who was said to be indisposed. No one had ever heard or seen anything like it.

That night, Christine Daae revealed a new Marguerite, a radiant and splendid Marguerite who had never before been imagined.

The whole house rose to its feet, cheering and clapping, manifesting its indescribable excitement, while Christine, sobbing and fainting in the arms of her fellow singers, had to be carried back to her dressing-room. It was almost as if she had sung away her entire soul. A renowned critic, Monsieur P. de St. V., described the unforgettable events of that marvelous night in a chronicle he penned and justly entitled *The New Marguerite*. A perceptive and sensitive man, he wrote that this beautiful and gentle child had given more than her art that night at the Opera, she had given her heart. Every Opera aficionado knew that the 17-year-old singer's heart had remained pure and P. de St. V.'s keen intuition caused him to write that, in order to understand what had happened to Christine Daae, *"one had to believe that she had fallen in love for the first time."*

"I may be somewhat indiscreet," he added, *"but only love can explain such a miracle, such a prodigious transformation. I heard Mademoiselle Daae sing two years ago at the Conservatoire; she was then but a charming hope. From where did that night's sublime genius come?* If it did not float down from Heaven on the wings of Love, I am then forced to believe that it rose up from Hell, and that Mademoiselle Daae, like Master-Singer Ofterdinger, has signed a pact with the Devil! *Someone who has not heard Mademoiselle Daae sing the final trio from* Faust *has never before heard* Faust. *The exaltation of her voice and the holy rapture of her pure soul are beyond mortal understanding."*

Some of the Opera subscribers even complained. Why had such a great treasure been kept hidden from them for so long? Until then, Christine Daae had sung a decent Siebel to accompany Mademoiselle Carlotta's impressive, but rather earthy, Marguerite. If it had not been for her mysterious and inexplicable absence from the gala performance that night, Christine Daae could not have, at a mere moment's notice, shown her extraordinary talent in the part of the program normally reserved for the Spanish diva. When Mademoiselle Carlotta had suddenly withdrawn, why had Messrs. Debienne and Poligny assigned her the part of Marguerite? Did they know of her hidden genius? And if so, why had they kept it hidden until then? For that matter, why had *she*? Oddly enough, Mademoiselle Daae was not known to have a singing teacher. She had said many times that she preferred to practice alone. All in all, the whole affair smelled of mystery.

The Comte de Chagny had heard the frenzied applause, and, getting to his feet in his box, had taken part in it by loudly cheering the new revelation.

The Comte de Chagny (Philippe Georges Marie) was 41-years-old. He was a handsome, aristocratic man, above middle height, with attractive features, despite a harsh forehead and rather cold eyes. He was exquisitely polite to women and a little haughty to men, who often resented him for his success in society. Nevertheless, he had a kind and exacting conscience. After the death of Comte Philibert, he had become head of one of France's oldest and most distinguished families, which dated back to Louis X in the 14th century. The Chagny fortune was considerable and, when the old Comte, who was a widower, had died, the burden of managing the large estate had fallen squarely on Philippe's shoulders. His two sisters and his brother, Raoul, would not hear of dividing the estate and left its entire management to Philippe, as if the right of primogeniture was still in force. When the two sisters eventually married, on the same day, each received their respective portions of the estate from their brother, not as something that was rightfully theirs but as a dowry for which they thanked him profusely.

The Comtesse de Chagny—*née* de Moerogis de La Martyniere—had died giving birth to Raoul, born 20 years after Philippe. When the old Comte had passed away, Raoul was only 12. Philippe took an active part in the boy's education. He was greatly assisted in that task, first by his sisters, then by an old aunt, the widow of a naval officer, who lived in Brest and gave young Raoul his taste for the sea. Eventually, the young man served with honors aboard the navy training-ship *Borda* and made the customary trip around the world. Thanks to Philippe's powerful connections, he had just been appointed to join the official expedition of the *Requin*, which was to sail to the Antarctic to search for survivors of the previous *d'Artois* expedition, which had been lost for three years. Until the *Requin* was ready to sail, Raoul was enjoying a long, six-month leave in Paris. The dowagers of the Faubourg Saint-Germain, when they thought of all the terrible trials in store for the handsome, delicate young man, were already feeling sorry for him.

Raoul's shyness–I would be tempted to say his inno-cence–was remarkable. He seemed to have barely emerged from the folds of his mother's apron. Lovingly pampered by his two older sisters and his aunt, his purely feminine educa-tion had given him sincere and charming manners that nothing had been able to tarnish. He was just over 21 but looked barely 18. He had a small, fair mustache, beautiful blue eyes and a fine complexion.

Philippe spoiled Raoul. To begin with, he was very proud of him and was looking forward with pleasure to his younger brother's glorious future in the French Navy, in which one of their ancestors, the famous Chagny de La Roche, had served as Admiral of the Fleet. He took advantage of the young man's leave to introduce him to all the luxurious and artistic delights of Paris.

The Comte considered that, at Raoul's age, to be too well-behaved was not necessarily a good thing. Philippe him-self had a well-balanced personality, conducting himself with as much deliberation in his work as in his pleasures. His man-ners were always irreproachable and he could never have set a bad example for Raoul. He took him wherever he went. He even introduced him to the *corps de ballet*. I know it was ru-mored that the Comte was "on the best of terms" with Made-moiselle Sorelli, but that was hardly considered a crime for a gentleman who was still a bachelor and therefore had plenty of leisure. Since his sisters had married, Philippe liked to spend a few hours after dinner in the company of the famous dancer who, though not espercially witty, had the most beautiful eyes in Paris! Besides, there are several places where a true mem-ber of High Society, especially one with the rank of Comte de Chagny, must be seen, and at that time, the foyer of the *corps de ballet* of the Opera was one of those places.

Finally, perhaps Philippe would not have taken his brother backstage at the Opera if Raoul had not first asked him, repeatedly, with a gentle obstinacy which at a later date, the Comte was to remember all-too-well.

On that evening, Philippe, after profusely applauding Mademoiselle Daae, turned to Raoul and, to his surprise, saw that his brother had become quite pale.

"Can't you see that she's fainting," explained Raoul.

Indeed, on the stage, Christine had to be supported by her fellow singers.

"You look like you're about to faint, too," said the Comte. "What's wrong?"

But Raoul appeared to have recovered and stood up.

"Let's go," he said, his voice quivering.

"Go where?" asked Philippe who had never seen his younger brother in such a state.

"To see her! She never sang like that before."

The Comte gave his brother a second look, then a knowing smile appeared at the corners of his mouth.

"I see..." And he added right away: "Yes, of course, let's go and see her at once."

He was now immeasurably pleased.

They were soon standing at the door that led backstage, which was crowded by a mob of eager subscribers. While waiting to be let in, Philippe observed that Raoul was nervously tearing at his gloves, but he had too kind a heart to make fun of his younger brother's impatience. Now he understood why Raoul had recently been distracted and why he always tried to turn every conversation to the subject of the Opera.

At last they made their way backstage.

A crowd of gentlemen was hurrying toward the foyer and scurrying towards the artists' dressing-rooms. The shouts of the stagehands were drowned out by the haranguing of their supervisors. During an average intermission at the Opera, backstage is typically a beehive of a variety of chaotic activities: extras from the last scene rush out and collide with those of the next tableau, chair ladies dash about looking for refreshments, huge set pieces and trompe-l'oeils are hurriedly lifted up and down on cables by burly stagehands who bark their warnings to get out of the way with as much force as if they were trumpeting the second coming of Christ, last-minute repairs are effected by the carpenters with much hammering and yelling... The unwary visitor is constantly in danger of receiving a blow on the head, a shove in the back or a push on the side. The young man with his small, fair mustache, beautiful blue eyes and fine complexion was a complete stranger to the mysterious and wondrous world of the stage upon which Christine Daae had just triumphed–and below which the body of a man named Joseph Buquet had just been found hanging.

That night, more than usual, confusion reigned backstage. Still, Raoul had never been less shy. He pushed aside anything and anyone that stood in his way, paying no attention to complaints, not heeding the stagehands' recriminations. He only cared about seeing she whose magical voice had stolen his heart. For he now realized that his heart was no longer his. He had come to that understanding on the day when Christine, whom he had known as a child, had reappeared in his life. He had fallen in love with her, totally, madly, as soon as he had cast his eyes upon her.

At first, he had fought his passion, because he knew all too well that social conventions made it impossible for someone like him, a Vicomte de Chagny, to marry a mere Opera singer. He was far too honorable and upright to offer Christine anything less than marriage. But despite all his efforts to suppress his feelings, his desire was too strong. He experienced pains in his chest and shortness of breath, as if his heart had been ripped from inside him. He felt empty and soulless. He knew that the only thing that could restore happiness to his life was the love of she whom he worshipped. All these symptoms will be familiar to, and in truth can only be understood by, those who have experienced that strange phenomenon of human nature known commonly as "love at first sight."

Comte Philippe followed Raoul with some difficulty while continuing to smile.

At the back of the stage, past a set of double doors that opened on the stairs leading either down to the foyer or up to the dressing-rooms, Raoul was forced to stop by a mob of young ballerinas who blocked the corridor he was trying to take. Those charmingly painted lips shot him many flirtatious remarks, but he ignored them all. Finally, he was able to proceed and dove into the darkness of a corridor which echoed with the excited voices of the enthusiastic subscribers. The name "Daae! Daae!" was on everyone's lips.

Comte Philippe, rushing behind Raoul, remarked to himself, "The rascal already knows the way to her dressing-room," and wondered how that could be. Since he had never taken his brother to see Christine, he came to the conclusion that Raoul must have gone there by himself while he had stayed behind talking to Mademoiselle Sorelli in the foyer. The dancer often invited him to wait with her until it was time for her to go on stage. Sometimes, she also asked him to keep an eye on the little moccasins she put on to run down from her dressing-room, so that she could preserve the spotlessness of her satin ballet-slippers. Mademoiselle Sorelli had a valid excuse for such childish behavior: she had lost her mother, whose role it would otherwise have been to handle such menial tasks.

Comte Philippe, postponing his regular visit to Mademoiselle Sorelli, followed his younger brother down the corridor that led to Mademoiselle Daae's dressing-room. It had never been as crowded as it was that night. The whole theater seemed as excited by Christine's success as it was by her fainting fit. Since she had not yet come to, they had sent for the doctor. The latter had just arrived. He asked the crowd to step aside, unknowingly opening the way for Raoul who entered the dressing-room on his heels.

Thus, the doctor and the would-be lover found themselves together in Christine's presence. She received first aid from one, while opening her eyes in the arms of the other. Comte Philippe remained on the threshold, preventing the admiring crowd from invading the tiny chamber.

"Doctor, don't you think that all those gentlemen should leave?" asked Raoul with remarkable impudence. "There's hardly any space to breathe."

"You're absolutely right," said the doctor. And he ordered everyone to go, except for Raoul and Christine's chambermaid, who looked at the young man with undisguised astonishment, since she had never seen him before.

Yet, she dared not question him.

Thus, the doctor was led to believe that, if that young man acted as he did, it was because he had a right to do so. The Vicomte, therefore, was allowed to remain and watched Christine as she slowly regained consciousness, while the Co-Directors of the Opera themselves, Messrs. Debienne and Poligny, who had come to express their sympathy and congratulations, found themselves locked out in the corridor along with the rest of the crowd of admirers. The Comte de Chagny, who was one of those standing outside, laughed.

"Oh, the rascal, the cheeky rascal!"

And he added, under his breath: "I should know better than to trust today's youth with their school-girl airs and demure manners!"

He was absolutely beaming, and concluded: "So he's a de Chagny after all!" He then turned to go to Mademoiselle Sorelli's dressing-room, but ended up meeting her and her little troop of trembling ballerinas along the way, as we have already recounted.

Meanwhile, in her room, Christine Daae uttered a deep sigh, which was followed by a moan. She turned her head, saw Raoul and reacted with surprise. She looked at the doctor, smiled at him, then at her maid, then again at Raoul.

"Monsieur," she said, in a voice that was barely more than a whisper, "who are you?"

"Mademoiselle," replied the young man, kneeling on one knee and pressing a fervent kiss to the diva's hand, "*I'm the little boy who dove into the sea to rescue your scarf.*"

Christine again looked at the doctor and the maid and all three began to laugh.

Raoul turned bright red and stood up.

"Mademoiselle," he said, "since it pleases you not to recognize me, I'd like to say something to you in private–something very important."

"When I feel better, if you don't mind?" Her voice still shook. "You've been very kind."

"Indeed you have, but now you, too, must go," said the doctor to Raoul with his most pleasant smile. "Leave me to attend to Mademoiselle Daae."

"I'm not sick," said Christine suddenly, with a strange and unexpected burst of energy.

She rose and passed her hand quickly over her eyes.

"Thank you, doctor. I'd like to be alone now. Please go away–all of you. Leave me alone, please. I feel very tense and I need time to myself."

The doctor tried to convince Christine to change her mind, but noting the girl's visible agitation, he came to the conclusion that the best medicine was to agree with her wishes and leave. Once outside, he saw Raoul looking confused and said:

"She isn't herself tonight. She's usually so easygoing..."

Then, he said good night and Raoul was left alone.

That entire section of the Opera was now deserted. The farewell ceremony was scheduled to start in the foyer at any minute. Raoul thought that Christine might attend it, so he waited alone in the silence, taking refuge in the shadow of a doorway. He still felt a terrible pain in his heart and was eager to speak to the object of his adoration without delay.

Suddenly, the dressing-room door opened and the maid came out alone, carrying a bundle of clothes. He stopped her and asked how her mistress was. The woman laughed and said that she was quite well, but that he should not disturb her because she wished to be left alone. Then she rushed away. One thought filled Raoul's burning brain: of course, Christine wished to be alone–*for him*! Hadn't he told her that he wanted to speak to her privately? Wasn't that the reason she had asked everyone else to leave? Hardly breathing, he went over to the dressing-room. He was about to knock on the door and had leaned forward to better hear her whispered reply when, suddenly, his hand dropped.

He had just heard, from inside the room, a *man's voice* ordering: "Christine, you must love me!"

And Christine's voice, achingly painful, filled with tears, replied: "How can you say that? *When I only sing for you!*"

Raoul had to lean against the wall to ease the pain. The ache that he had previously felt in his chest was nothing compared to what he now experienced. It seemed to him that the whole corridor echoed the violent beating of his heart. His ears were deafened by the noise. Surely, if it went on making such a din, they would hear it inside the room. She would open the door and the young man would be turned away in disgrace. What a position for a de Chagny! To be caught eavesdropping outside a door! He grabbed his chest with both his hands, trying to force his heart to stop throbbing. But a human heart is not like a dog's muzzle, and even holding a dog's muzzle tightly does not stop the animal from growling.

The *Voice* spoke again: "Are you very tired?"

"Oh, yes. Tonight, I gave you my soul and I'm dead!" Christine replied.

"Your soul is a beautiful thing, child," replied the grave *Voice*, "and I thank you. No Emperor ever received so fair a gift. *The angels wept tonight.*"

Raoul heard nothing after the words: "*The angels wept tonight.*"

Still, he did not leave, but since he feared being caught in a compromising position, he returned to the darkened doorway, determined to wait for the man to leave. He had just simultaneously learned the true meaning of the words "love" and "hate." He knew that he loved. Now, he wanted to know whom it was that he hated. The door eventually opened, but to his surprise, only Christine appeared, wrapped in furs, her face hidden behind a lace veil. She closed the door behind her, but Raoul observed that she did not lock it. She passed by him without noticing his presence. He did not even follow her with his eyes, for these were fixed on the door–which did not open again.

When the corridor was once more deserted, Raoul rushed to the dressing-room and went inside, closing the door behind him. He found himself in absolute darkness, the gas lamps having been turned off.

"I know there's someone in here," he said in a quivering voice, his back to the door. "Why are you hiding?"

All was dark and silent. Raoul heard only the sound of his own breathing. He seemed to have passed the point where the unbelievable impropriety of his conduct bothered him at all.

"You won't leave here until I see you!" he shouted. "If you don't answer, you're nothing but a coward! I'll expose you!"

And he struck a match. The flame lit up the room. *It was empty*! Raoul, after having locked the door, relit the gas lamps. He then searched the closet, opened the cabinets, scutinized every inch of the room, felt the walls with hands dampened by perspiration. Nothing!

"I don't get it!" he said, aloud. "Am I going mad?"

He stayed in the empty room for a good ten minutes, listening to the soft sound of gas burning in the silence. Even though he loved Christine passionately, it did not occur to him to steal one of her ribbons, a memento to remind him of the perfume of the woman he adored. At last he left, not knowing what he was doing or where he was going. He wandered aimlessly backstage for a while, in a daze.

At one point, he felt an icy draft on his face and looked around to determine where he was. He was near a narrow staircase that went down into the vaults of the Opera. A procession of workmen were coming up it, carrying a stretcher covered with a white sheet.

"Could you tell me the way out?" he asked one of them.

"Straight ahead of you, you can see the door from here. But please, let us through."

Pointing to the stretcher, Raoul asked perfunctorily:

"Who's that?"

"That's the body of Joseph Buquet, who was found on the third level, hanging between a country farm-house and the scenery for *The King of Lahore*," the workman answered.

Raoul took off his hat, stepped aside to let the funereal procession pass, and left.

Chris Malgrain

Chapter Three
In which Messrs. Debienne and Poligny secretly inform the new Directors, Messrs. Moncharmin and Richard, of the true and mysterious reason for their resignation

Meanwhile in the foyer, the farewell ceremony was underway. I have already mentioned that this dazzling event had been organized to celebrate the retirement of Messrs. Debienne and Poligny, who were determined to "leave with a bang," as we would say today.

They had been ably assisted in the organization of this exquisite, though somewhat depressing, affair by everyone who was anyone in the dazzling, high society of Paris.

After the performance, all the guests had been asked to gather in the foyer, where Mademoiselle Sorelli awaited the arrival of the guests of honor with a glass of champagne in her hand and her prepared speech on the tip of her tongue. Behind her, the members of the *corps de ballet*, young and old, discussed the day's events in hushed whispers and exchanged discreet signals with their friends. A noisy throng already mobbed the buffet tables, which had been set up between Monsieur Boulanger's admirable painted sets for *La Danse Guerrière* and *La Danse Champêtre*.

A few of the ballerinas had changed into their street clothes, but most still wore their gossamer ballet skirts. Everyone bore a somber face, as required by the occasion; everyone, that is, except Little Jammes, whose 15 summers–happy age!– seemed to have enabled her already to forget the Phantom and the tragic death of Joseph Buquet. She laughed and babbled and prattled and joked, until an aggrieved Mademoiselle

Sorelli, having spotted Mrrs Debienne and Poligny arriving on the steps of the foyer, sharply told her to behave.

Everyone noticed that the retiring Directors looked cheerful, a fact which would have seemed out of place anywhere else in the country, but which was deemed to be good taste in Paris. To be a true Parisian, one must learn to always wear a mask of gaiety over one's sorrows and one of sadness, boredom or indifference over one's joys. If you learn that one of your friends is in trouble, don't bother trying to console him for he'll tell you it's not necessary. Should he meet with good fortune, don't bother trying to congratulate him, for he thinks it's so natural that he'll be surprised that you should even speak of it. Life in Paris is like a masquerade, and the foyer of the Opera was the last place where two men so wise in the ways of the world as Messrs. Debienne and Poligny, would have made the mistake of showing their grief, however genuine it might have been. In fact, one might have thought that they were overdoing it, smiling a bit too broadly at Mademoiselle Sorelli, who had begun to recite her speech.

Suddenly, the ever-exuberant Little Jammes uttered a cry, which shattered the two soon-to-be-ex-Directors' smiles so abruptly that the expressions of distress and dismay hidden beneath became apparent to all.

"The Phantom!"

Jammes yelled these words in a tone of unspeakable terror. Her finger pointed at a man who stood out amongst the well-dressed crowd. His face was so pallid, so somber and so ghastly, with two deep dark cavities under the prominent eyebrows, that it looked like a death's-head–and immediately attacted everyone's attention.

"The Phantom! It's the Phantom of the Opera!"

Everyone laughed–if somewhat nervously–and tried to get a better look. Some even wanted to offer the stranger a drink, but by the time they acted on the impulse, he was already gone. He had slipped through the crowd silently and vanished as mysteriously as he had appeared. While two older gentlemen tried to calm the hysterical Little Jammes, and while Little Giry stood screaming like a peacock, several guests looked everywhere for the mystery man–but in vain.

Mademoiselle Sorelli was incensed because she had not had time to finish her speech. Messrs. Debienne and Poligny had kissed her, thanked her and run away almost as fast as the Phantom himself. No one was particularly surprised by this, for everyone knew that the Directors were scheduled to attend another, identical ceremony on the floor above with the singers, and then a third one, reserved for personal friends, in the lobby outside their offices, where a more lavish supper was to be served.

It is at that last party that we rejoin them, in the company of their replacements, Messrs. Armand Moncharmin and Firmin Richard. The former Directors barely knew the new ones, but were nevertheless lavish in their display of mutual esteem, and in turn, received a thousand flattering compliments. Some of the guests, who had feared that the evening might turn out to be somewhat grim, were heartened and put on happy faces. The atmosphere was almost cheerful and many toasts were made. One, by a Deputy Minister, was so cleverly phrased, mingling past glories with future successes, that it spead much joy and felicity around the room. The retiring Directors had already handed over their powers to their successors in a simple ceremony the day before. Any pending questions regarding the transition between the two administrations had been ironed out before the Deputy Minister's watchful eyes in a spirit of frank and mutual cooperation. It was not, therefore, surprising to see all four Directors in such frankly good moods during the final dinner party.

Messrs. Debienne and Poligny had already handed over the two tiny master-keys which opened every door–and there were thousands of them–at the Opera. These little keys became the subject of everyone's curiosity and were passed from hand to hand, all marveling at their delicacy. Suddenly, the general attention was diverted by the discovery, at the end of the table, of the same strange man with the pallid face and hollow eyes, whom Little Jammes had greeted earlier with her cry of: "The Phantom!"

The Phantom–if it was he–sat at the end of the table as naturally and unobtrusively as possible–except that he neither ate nor drank.

Those who had initially smiled, as if the man's presence was some form of practical joke, now turned their heads away from him, fearful of a vision that evoked only the most sinister of thoughts. No one, absolutely no one, dared repeat the words that had earlier rung through the foyer, no one dared state:

"It's the Phantom of the Opera!"

The mystery man did not utter a word. His closest neighbors could not have stated precisely when he had sat down next to them. But everyone felt that, if the dead ever returned to sit with the living, they could not have cut a more terrifying figure. The friends of Messrs. Richard and Moncharmin thought that this macabre visitor was an acquaintance of Messrs. Debienne and Poligny, while the latters' believed him to be a guest of the formers'. The result was that everyone had an easy excuse not to talk to the foreboding stranger even to ask him who he was, and thus avoided any scene or unpleasantness that might have offended him.

A few of those present knew the legend of the Phantom of the Opera, and had even heard the description given by Joseph Buquet–although they were as yet unaware of his death– and thought, without really daring to believe it, that the man sitting grimly at the end of the table might easily have passed for him. Yet, according to the story, the Phantom had no nose, unlike the stranger. But Monsieur Moncharmin stated in his *Memoirs* that the mysterious guest's nose was *transparent*. "*Long, thin and transparent*," were his exact words. For my part, I will observe that this description might well fit a false nose, and that Monsieur Moncharmin might have mistaken *transparency* for what was only *shininess*. Everyone knows that orthopedic science can now make beautiful false noses for those who have, sadly, lost theirs naturally or as the result of an accident.

Did the Phantom really come uninvited and sit at the Directors' table that night? Can we really be sure that the Phantom was the mysterious visitor? Who can truly say? I described the incident at some length not because I want the reader to assume that the Phantom was systematically capable of acts of such great daring, but because, in final analysis, it is quite possible that it was he.

There is another reason why I believe the mystery man was the Phantom. In Chapter XI of his *Memoirs*, Monsieur Moncharmin wrote:

"*When I think back to that first night at the Opera, I cannot separate the secret confided to us by Debienne and Poligny in their office, from the presence at our table of that* phantom-like *person nobody knew.*"

These are the exact events to which he refers:

Messrs. Debienne and Poligny sat at the center of the table and had not yet seen the man with the death's-head when suddenly he began to speak.

"The ballerinas are right," he said. "The death of that poor man Buquet may not be as natural as some people think."

Messrs. Debienne and Poligny reacted in shock.

"Buquet is dead?" they exclaimed.

"Yes," replied the man, or what may have been the shadow of a man, quietly. "They found his body tonight, hanging on the third level between a country farmhouse and scenery from *The King of Lahore*."

The two Directors, or rather ex-Directors, stood up as one and stared at the visitor, aghast. They were more agitated than they should have been, that is to say, more agitated than the news of the suicide of a stagehand would normally have caused them to be. They looked at each other. They were whiter than the tablecloth. Finally, Monsieur Debienne made a sign to Messrs. Richard and Moncharmin. Monsieur Poligny muttered a few words of excuse to the guests and all four hurriedly entered the Directors' office. I'll let Monsieur Moncharmin take over the narration at this point, quoting again from his *Memoirs*:

"*Debienne and Poligny appeared to be quite concerned, as if they had an embarrassing revelation to make. First, they asked us if we knew the man sitting at the end of the table, who had told them the news of Joseph Buquet's death. After we said no, they looked even more concerned. They took the master-keys from us, stared at them for a moment, then advised us to have new locks made, in the greatest secrecy, for any room, cabinet or safe that we might want to be totally secure. They said it in such a conspiratorial fashion that we couldn't help laughing and asked if there were thieves at large at the Opera. They replied that there was something far worse—the Phantom! We started to laugh again, thinking that they were playing some kind of practical joke as part of our little soirée. But they asked us to take them seriously, so we decided to humor them and play along.*

"*They told us that they never would have mentioned the Phantom if they had not received specific instruction from said Phantom himself, to ask us to treat him well and to grant any request he might make. However, they felt so relieved at leaving the Opera, a domain in thrall to that mysterious and oppressive figure, that they had hesitated to do so until the very last moment. Besides, they thought that our skeptical minds would not be prepared to believe such a bizarre story. But the new of Joseph Buquet's death had served as a brutal reminder that, whenever they had in the past ignored one of the Phantom's orders, some freakish or disastrous occurrence had soon brought them back to accepting their own subservience.*

"*During these totally unexpected remarks, made in a tone better suited for a secret and momentous confidence, I looked at my friend, Richard. When he was still a student, he had acquired a great reputation for being a practical joker himself. He knew a thousand and one tricks to play on an unsuspecting victim, and the concierges of the Boulevard Saint-Michel still remembered him with dismay., He appeared to relish the dish that was being served up to him by our prede-*

cessors. He did not miss a morsel of it, though the seasoning was a little gruesome because of the stagehand's death. He nodded his head sadly while the others spoke, and his face wore the air of a man who bitterly regretted having taken over the Opera now that he knew it was haunted. I could think of nothing better to do than faithfully imitate his despondent attitude. However, in spite of our best efforts to hide our true feelings, we ultimately could not help but burst out laughing. Debienne and Poligny, who saw us go straight from complete gloom to insolent merriment, acted as if they thought we had gone mad.

"The joke becoming somewhat protracted and more than a little tedious, Richard finally asked, half-seriously, half in jest:

" *'But, after all, what does this Phantom of yours want?'*

"Poligny went to his desk and returned with the Official Rulebook of the Opera.

"It began as follows: 'The Directors of the Opera shall be obligated to stage productions of such quality as befit the premier lyric stage in France.' *And it ended with Article 98, which stated:* 'The foregoing privileges may be withdrawn under the following conditions: 1. In the event of any infringement by the Directors of any of the rules stipulated in the present rulebook.' *Thereupon followed three other conditions that might result in the removal of the Directors.*

"Poligny's copy was printed in black ink and, at first, looked entirely identical to that which the Deputy Minister had given us when we had agreed to take over the Opera. Poligny's copy, however, contained an additional subparagraph 5 at the end of Article 98, written in red ink in a strange and curiously labored handwriting, not unlike that of a child. It said, verbatim:

" '5. In the event of the late payment, by more than two weeks, of the stipend due to the Phantom of the Opera, said stipend to be fixed at 20,000 francs a month, or 240,000 francs a year.'

"*Poligny hesitantly pointed out this last clause, which unquestionably we had not expected to see.*

" '*Is this all? Is there anything else* he *wants?*' *asked Richard, with exagerrated coolness.*

" '*Yes, there is,*' *replied Poligny.*

"H*e turned the pages of the booklet until he arrived at Article 63*: 'Box No. 1 shall be reserved for all performances for the use of the President of the Republic. Box No. 20 on Mondays and Box No. 30 on Wednesdays and Fridays shall be reserved for all performances for the use of the Ministers of State. Box No. 27 shall be reserved for all performances for the use of the Prefect of Police of Paris.'

"*At the end of this clause, Poligny showed us that a line had been added, also in red ink*:

" 'Box No. 5 shall be reserved for all performances for the use of the Phantom of the Opera.'

"*When we saw this, we both felt that there was nothing else for us to do but rise from our chairs, warmly shake the hands of our predecessors and congratulate them on coming up with that precious little joke, which proved that the traditional French sense of humor would never become extinct. Richard added that he now understood why Debienne and Poligny were retiring. Business must have been impossible with such a demanding Phantom.*

" '*240,000 francs is certainly a great deal of money,*' *said Poligny, with a straight face. 'And losing Box No. 5 for every performance is also quite a burden. We couldn't rent it once. Worse yet, we had to refund its subscriber*! *It's just dreadful*! *Why should we slave to support the Phantom*? *That's why we decided to tender our resignations*!'

" '*Yes,*' *echoed Debienne. 'We'd rather leave. So it's goodbye*!'

"*And he stood up to leave.*

"*Richard then said*: '*If you don't mind my saying so, it seems to me that you were far too kind towards that Phantom. If I had such a bothersome intruder, I would have had him arrested.*'

" '*How? Where?*' *they exclaimed in chorus.* '*We've never seen him!*'

" '*How about when he was in his box?*'

" 'We've never seen him in his box!'

" '*Then why didn't you rent it?*'

" '*Rent the Phantom's box! Gentlemen, you're most welcome to try.*'

"*Thereupon we all four left the office. Richard and I had never laughed so much in our lives.*"

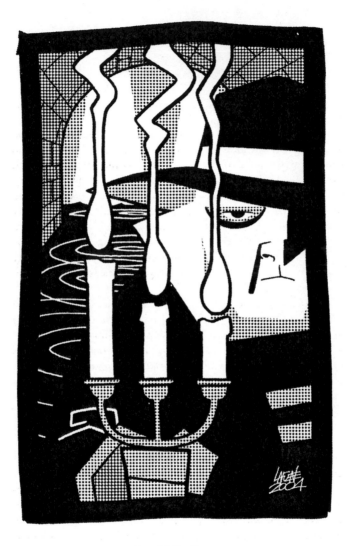

David Lafuente

Chapter Four
Box No. 5

Armand Moncharmin wrote such extensive *Memoirs* during his long period of co-directorship at the Opera that one could well ask when he actually found time to manage the theater. Monsieur Moncharmin did not know a note of music, but he was on a first-name basis with the Minister of Education and Fine Arts, had written a gossip column and was personally wealthy. Plus, as well as being a charming man, he was a smart one, and, as soon as he was appointed Director of the Opera, he looked for an experienced partner to effectively handle the day-to-day management of the theater. He had selected Firmin Richard.

Monsieur Richard was a distinguished composer and gentleman. Quoting from the biographical sketch published in *La Revue des Théâtres* at the time of his appointment:

"Monsieur Firmin Richard is a tall, sturdy man in his early fifties, in good physical condition. He carries himself proudly with distinction and speaks loudly. He sports a short beard and a crew cut that gives his face a melancholy expression,which is, however, at odds with his clear, honest gaze and charming smile.

"Monsieur Richard is a talented composer, a skillful organist and an experienced counterpointist. His compositions rarely lack grandeur. He has written a number of well-received pieces of chamber music, several piano sonatas, concertos and a highly original collection of melodies. His Death of Hercules, *performed last year at the Conservatoire, is an epic work reminiscent of Christoph Gluck, one of his avowed influences. Although a disciple of Gluck, Monsieur Richard is also a devotee of other masters, such as Fratelli Piccini, Giacomo Meyerbeer, whom he greatly admires, Domenico Cima-*

rosa, whose compositions he finds wildly entertaining and Carl Maria von Weber, whose genius he loudly proclaims. As regards Richard Wagner, Monsieur Richard declares that he was the first in France, perhaps the only one, to have understood him."

I believe that this rather lengthy quote shows that Monsieur Richard liked nearly every type of music and every sort of musician, and consequently felt that it was the duty of every sort of musician to also like Monsieur Richard. The only thing left to say to complete this quick portrait is to add that Monsieur Richard had what some generously call an "authoritarian nature," that is to say a nasty temper.

The two new Directors spent their first few days savoring the joy of being in charge of such a vast and magnificent theater as the Paris Opera. They had forgotten all about the fantastic story of its Phantom, when an incident occurred which proved to them that, if it was indeed a joke, it was not yet over.

That morning, Monsieur Richard arrived at his office at 11 a.m. His secretary, Monsieur Remy, handed him half a dozen letters which he had not opened because they were all marked "private and personal." One of the letters immediately caught the Director's attention not only because it had been addressed in red ink, but because he remembered having seen that handwriting before. It was the same child-like, red handwriting that had added new clauses to Monsieur Poligny's Opera Rulebook. He opened the letter and read:

Dear Director:

I apologize for having to bother you when you must surely be extremely busy deciding the fates of our Opera's most talented artists, renewing major engagements, signing new ones, all the while displaying a science and an understanding of theater, a knowledge of the public and its tastes, and a managerial skill that amazes even an old pro such as I.

I am well aware of your recent decisions regarding Mesdemoiselles Carlotta and Sorelli, Little Jammes and a few others, whose admirable qualities, talents–dare I say, genius?–you have recognized.

(Of course, you might have guessed that I am somewhat less than candid when bandying such words. Personally, I think that Carlotta clucks like a chicken and should never have left her street corner near the Café des Ambassadeurs, that Sorelli appeals mostly to dock workers and that Little Jammes dances like a drunken sailor. Conversely, Mademoiselle Daae's genius is unarguable, yet your singular lack of vision seems to prevent you from assigning her any major roles. Still, when all is said and done, you are free to manage your enterprise as you think best.)

All the same, I would like to take advantage of the fact that you have not yet fired Mademoiselle Daae, to hear her tonight in the part of Siebel, since you have not seen fit to give her Marguerite, even after her triumph of the other night. I shall also ask you to not rent my box today–or any other day. *For I must regrettably end this letter by telling you how unpleasant it has been to discover that my private box has been rented against my wishes–allegedly* according to your own instructions.

I have not yet registered a protest, because I dislike scandal. Also, it occurred to me that perhaps your predecessors, Messrs. Debienne and Poligny, who were always accommodating to me, might have neglected to inform you of our little arrangement before they left. I have now received a reply to my letter to those gentlemen asking for an explanation. It notifies me that you were informed of my additions to the Rulebook and that, consequently, by willfully ignoring them, you are treating me with out-and-out contempt. If you wish to live in peace, it is not wise to deprive me of my private box!

Despite these small grievances, I remain, Dear Director, Your Most Humble & Obedient Servant.

Ph. of the Opera

The letter was accompanied by a press clipping from the classified advertisements page of *La Revue Théâtrale*, which read:

"To P.O.: No excuse for R & M's conduct. We informed them and showed them the Rulebook. Regards. D&P."

Monsieur Richard had barely finished reading the letter when Monsieur Moncharmin entered, carrying a letter identical to the one received by his colleague. They looked at each other and burst out laughing.

"They're keeping up the joke," said Richard, "but I think it's wearing thin."

"What do you think it means?" asked Moncharmin. "Do they really believe that, because they were Directors of the Opera, we'll let them have a free box forever?"

There was no doubt in both men's minds that the letter and the advertisement were the products of their predecessors' fertile imaginations.

"I'm not in the mood to be the butt of their pranks," said Richard.

"It's harmless enough," observed Moncharmin. "What is it that they really want? A box for tonight?"

Monsieur Richard told his secretary to prepare two complimentary passes for Box No. 5 for the night's performance for Messrs. Debienne and Poligny, if it was not already rented. Since it was not, the tickets were sent to them by messenger. Debienne lived at the corner of the Rue Scribe and the Boulevard des Capucines; Poligny in the Rue Auber. When he examined the envelopes, Monsieur Moncharmin discovered that the two letters from the Phantom had been mailed from the Boulevard des Capucines.

"There! You see!" said Richard.

They shrugged and wondered how men of that age and distinction could possibly amuse themselves with such childish pranks.

"Still, they could have shown a bit more civility," complained Moncharmin. "Did you see what they wrote about Carlotta, Sorelli and Little Jammes?"

"I think they're consumed by jealousy. To think they even went to the expense of placing a small ad in *La Revue Theatrale*! Haven't they got anything better to do?"

"Did you notice?" asked Moncharmin. "They seem quite interested in that little Christine Daae... I wonder if..."

"I doubt it. She does have the reputation of being extremely easygoing," said Richard. "You know that as well as I do."

"Pfft! Reputations are easily made," replied Moncharmin. "Look at me: I've got the reputation of being knowledgeable about music and I don't know one key from another."

"Let me reassure you: you *don't* have that reputation," Richard retorted.

Thereupon, Monsieur Richard ordered his secretary to show in the various performers who, for the previous two hours, had been pacing up and down outside his office, looking anxiously at the door behind which awaited fame and fortune–or dismissal.

The rest of the day was spent discussing, negotiating, signing and cancelling contracts. That night–it was January 25–the two Directors, exhausted by a painful day of angry tirades, protests, threats, entreaties, declarations of mutual love or hatred, went to bed early without so much as sparing a glance for Box No. 5 to see whether Messrs. Debienne and Poligny were enjoying the night's performance. The Opera had been on double shifts since their arrival and numerous repairs and maintenance were being performed daily, while the program of performances continued uninterrupted.

The next morning, the two Directors each received a thank you card from the Phantom:

Dear Director:

Thank you. Charming evening. Daae exquisite. Choruses need stirring up. Carlotta a splendid but commonplace instrument. Will write you soon for the 240,000 francs, or rather 233,424. 70 francs, since Debienne and Poligny already paid me 6,575.30 francs. representing the first ten days of my stipend for the current year, their tenure having ended on Jan. 10.

Kind regards.

P.O.

However, there was also a letter from Messrs. Debienne and Poligny which read:

Dear Sirs:

We are grateful for your kind gesture, but you will obviously understand that even the prospect of hearing Faust *again, pleasant though it may be for ex-Directors of the Opera, cannot make us forget that we have no right to occupy Box No. 5, which is reserved exclusively for* him of whom we spoke *when we went through the Rulebook with you. Please refer to Art. 63, last sub-paragraph.*

Yours sincerely,

Debienne & Poligny

"Those two gentlemen are really starting to get on my nerves!" shouted Richard, throwing the letter away.

That evening Box No. 5 was rented out.

The next morning, when Messrs. Richard and Moncharmin arrived at their office, they were surprised to find a report from one of the supervisors relating an incident that had occurred the night before in Box No. 5. I quote below the essential part of the report, which was rather brief:

"*Tonight* (the Supervisor had written his report before leaving the Opera), *I was twice obliged to summon a policeman to clear Box No. 5 of its occupants, once at the beginning and once in the middle of the second act. The occupants arrived as the curtain rose on the second act and almost right away created a disturbance by laughing and talking loudly. At first, occupants of the neighboring boxes tried to get them to quiet down, but were unsuccessful. When the entire section of the theater began to complain, the usherette came to fetch me.*

I entered the box and gave them a warning. The occupants did not seem to be in their right minds and made some nonsensical remarks. I reiterated that, if there were any more disturbances, I would have no choice but to ask them to leave. As I stepped out, I heard laughter again and renewed protests from the house. So I returned with the policeman on duty who escorted them out. They then complained and refused to leave unless they got their money back. So I agreed to let them return to the box, under the strict condition that they would be quiet. But the laughter soon started again, so this time, I had them expelled for good."

"Send for the Supervisor," said Richard to his secretary, Monsieur Remy, who had already read and annotated the report with a blue pencil.

Monsieur Remy was 24-years-old, wore a thin mustache and was the model of elegance and distinction. (In those days, wearing formal dress was *de rigueur*.) Extremely intelligent, he was nevertheless shy and easily intimidated by Monsieur Richard. His long list of duties consisted of reading the newspapers and compiling press clippings, answering the mail, handling the delicate task of handing out complimetary passes, making appointments, entertaining any visitors waiting in the lobby, but also comforting sick performers, looking for extras, keeping the peace between rival factions of Opera workers and sundry other unwritten, yet crucial, chores. And for all that, he was paid the modest wage of 2,400 francs per year, taken directly from the Director's own salary, and could be let go at a moment's notice without indemnity.

So, the industrious Monsieur Remy had anticipated the Director's request and had already called the Supervisor. He entered the office looking somewhat concerned.

"Tell us what happened," asked Richard bluntly.

The Supervisor began to stammer and referred to his report.

"No, no, I want to hear what isn't in the report. For example, why were those people laughing?" asked Moncharmin.

"Well, Monsieur, I think they had already had a good dinner and more than one bottle of wine, if you see what I mean, because they were more interested in playing games than listening to good music. As soon as they entered the box, they called for the usherette. She came and asked them what they wanted. They told her, 'Look inside the box. It's empty, isn't it?' 'Yes,' she answered. 'Well,' they said, 'when we got in, we heard a voice saying that *the box was taken*!' "

Monsieur Moncharmin could not help smiling as he looked at Monsieur Richard, but his colleague was not smiling. He had been too much of a practical joker in his own youth to not recognize, in the Supervisor's candid tale, the earmarks of the kind of nasty joke which seems amusing at first, but often winds up driving its victims to fits of rage.

The Supervisor, seeking to curry favor with Monsieur Moncharmin, had thought it best to smile too. A most unfortunate choice! Monsieur Richard scowled at his subordinate, who immediately adopted a more contrite expression.

"I don't understand," roared Richard. "When those people arrived, the box was empty, wasn't it?"

"Yes, Monsieur! Not a soul in it, Monsieur! Nor in the box on the right, or on the left. I swear! Cross my heart! And that proves they were jokers, right?"

"What did the usherette say?"

"As far as she's concerned, it's simple. She said it was the Phantom of the Opera. Nonsense, of course!"

The Supervisor thought it judicious, at that stage, to grin. But he soon found out that he had made another mistake, for the words "*Phantom of the Opera*" had no sooner crossed his lips than Monsieur Richard's own expression turned from sour to positively furious.

"Send for the usherette!" he shouted. "I want to see her right this instant! Bring her to me! And get rid of all these people!"

The Supervisor tried to mollify his superior, but Monsieur Richard angrily ordered him to be silent. Then, after a minute during which the hapless man's lips seemed welded shut, the Director ordered him to open them once more.

"Who is this *Phantom of the Opera*?" he snarled.

By then, the Supervisor thought it prudent to not anger the mercurial Director any further and, instead of speaking aloud, he managed to convey, through a gesture of consternation, that he knew nothing about it, or rather that he did not wish to know.

"Have you ever seen him?"

By means of a vigorous shake of the head, the Supervisor denied it.

"Too bad!" said Monsieur Richard coldly.

The Supervisor's eyes almost bulged out of his head, as if asking why the Director had uttered that ominous "Too bad!"

"Because I'm going to fire anyone who has not seen him!" explained the Director. "Since the Phantom seems to be everywhere, I can't have people telling me that they haven't seen him. I don't want people with closed eyes working for me!"

Mauricet

Chapter Five
Box No. 5 (continued)

Having delivered his threat, Monsieur Richard stopped paying attention to the Supervisor. Instead, he began discussing various business matters with one of the Assistant Directors who had just entered the office. The Supervisor thought he had been dismissed and was inching away discreetly–extremely discreetly–walking backwards–towards the door, when Monsieur Richard figuratively nailed him to the floor with a thundering:

"You! Stay where you are!"

Meanwhile, the efficient Monsieur Remy had gone to fetch the usherette who, during the day, worked as a concierge on the Rue de Provence, near the Opera. It wasn't long before she arrived.

"What's your name?"

"Madame Giry. We've met before, Monsieur le Directeur. I'm the mother of Little Meg, do you remember?"

This was said in a grave and solemn tone that impressed Monsieur Richard. He took a second look at Madame Giry: she wore a faded shawl, worn shoes, an old taffeta dress and a soot-darkened bonnet. It was quite obvious from the Director's attitude that he did not, in fact, remember ever having met Madame Giry before, or Little Meg for that matter. But Madame Giry's pride was so great that the usherette imagined that everybody knew her. (She wasn't entirely wrong, for I believe that her name later became synonymous with gossip backstage at the Opera, as in "stop spreading such giries about me.")

"Never heard of her!" Richard finally declared. "But that's neither here nor there. What i'd like to hear from you, dear Madame, is precisely what happened last night to cause your Supervisor, who is obediently standing over there, to call the Police."

"I was just going to ask to see you, Monsieur le Directeur, and talk to you about it, so that you wouldn't have the same problems as Messrs. Debienne and Poligny. At first, they wouldn't listen to me either..."

"I'm not interested in what my predecessors did or didn't do. I want to know what happened last night."

Madame Giry turned purple with indignation. No one had ever talked to her like that before. She rose as if to leave, gathering the folds of her skirt and waving the feathers of her sooty bonnet with as much dignity as she could muster. Suddenly, she appeared to change her mind, sat down again and said, in a belligerent tone of voice:

"I'll tell you what happened. The Phantom was upset!"

Thereupon, as Monsieur Richard was about to explode, Monsieur Moncharmin judged it wise to intervene and took control of the situation. He discovered that Madame Giry thought it was entirely normal that a voice was heard to declare that the box was taken, even when there was nobody visible inside it. She was unable to explain this strange phenomenon, which had also occurred in the past, as having been caused by anything other than the intervention of the Phantom. Nobody could see him but everyone could hear him. She, herself, had often heard him and expected them to believe her, because she never lied. They could ask Messrs. Debienne and Poligny, or anyone else who knew her, and they would all tell them the same thing. They should also ask Monsieur Isidore Saack, whose leg had been broken by the Phantom!

"Really?" said Moncharmin, interrupting her. "The Phantom broke poor Isidore Saack's leg? How did that happen?"

Madame Giry opened her eyes wide, amazed and saddened by the extent of the Directors' ignorance. However, she deigned to enlighten the two unfortunates. The incident had occurred, also in Box No. 5, during Messrs. Debienne and Poligny's tenure and also during a performance of *Faust*.

Madame Giry coughed and cleared her throat. It was as if she was preparing to sing Gounod's entire score herself.

"It was like this, Monsieur," she said. "That night, Monsieur Maniera and his wife, the jewelers from the Rue Mogador, were sitting in the front of the box, with their friend, Monsieur Isidore Saack, sitting behind Madame Maniera. Mephistopheles was singing (at that point, Madame Giry burst into song herself) '...vous qui faites l'endormie.'[4] Right then, Monsieur Maniera heard a voice in his right ear–his wife was sitting to his left–whisper 'Ha! Ha! Julie's not playing at sleeping!' Julie was his wife. So, Monsieur Maniera turned around to see who was talking to him, but there was nobody there! He rubbed his ear and wondered if he wasn't hallucinating. Meanwhile, Mephistopheles was continuing with his song... I hope I'm not boring you two gentlemen?"

"No, not at all. Do go on."

"You're too kind," she replied, smirking. "Well, then, as Mephistopheles was singing (Madame Giry burst into song again) 'Catherine que j'adore–pourquoi refuser–à l'amant qui vous implore–un si doux baiser?'[5] Monsieur Maniera heard the same voice in his right ear saying: 'Ha! Ha! I bet Julie wouldn't refuse Isidore a sweet kiss!' So he turned around again, but this time towards his wife, and what did he see? Monsieur Saack had taken Madame Maniera's hand in his and was kissing it like this... (Here, she kissed the bit of palm left bare in the middle of her thread gloves.) I don't need to tell you that it started quite a row. Slap! Slap! Monsieur Maniera, who is big and strong like you, Monsieur Richard, slapped Monsieur Saack, who is small and delicate like you, Monsieur Moncharmin, with all due respect. There was quite an uproar. People in the theater shouted, 'Enough! Stop him! He's going to kill him!' Finally, Monsieur Saack managed to run away."

---

[4] '...while you play at sleeping.'

[5] 'Catherine, whom I adore–why deny–to the lover who implores you–such a sweet kiss?'

"So the Phantom didn't break his leg after all?" asked Moncharmin, a little peeved that his size had so unimpressed Madame Giry.

"He did so, Monsieur," replied the usherette contemptuously, well aware of the underlying sarcasm contained in the Director's question. "He broke it for him on the grand staircase, which Monsieur Saack ran down too fast. And he made such a good job of it, that it'll be a long time before that poor gentleman can go up those stairs again!"

"Was it the Phantom who told you what he said to Monsieur Maniera?" asked Moncharmin, with all the gravity of an investigating magistrate, while he was secretly enjoying his own performance.

"No, Monsieur, it was Monsieur Maniera himself, and..."

"But you've spoken to the Phantom, haven't you, dear Madame?"

"As I'm speaking to you now, Monsieur!"

"And he speaks to you, the Phantom... What does he say?"

"Well, he always tells me to bring him a footstool!"

This time, Monsieur Richard burst out laughing, as did Monsieur Moncharmin and Monsieur Remy. Only the Supervisor, who by now had learned his lesson, was careful not to laugh. Leaning against the wall, fiddling with the keys in his pocket, he couldn't help wondering how all this was going to end.

Madame Giry, who had made her last declaration with great solemnity, had turned to marble, but not just any kind of marble! No, she looked like Sarrancolin marble, a nasty yellow-colored marble with tiny red veins, like the kind used for the columns of the grand staircase.

The more confrontational Madame Gity became, the more the Supervisor feared a rekindling of his superiors' wrath. And now, he saw with horror that she was adopting a positively threatening attitude in response to the Directors' hilarity.

"Instead of laughing about the Phantom," she shouted, "you should do like Monsieur Poligny! He found out for himself..."

"Found out what?" asked Moncharmin, who had never been so entertained in his life.

"About the Phantom, what else? Look here..." She suddenly calmed herself, feeling that this was a momentous occasion. "*Listen*! I still remember it as if it was yesterday... They were playing *La Juive*... Monsieur Poligny had wanted to watch the performance from the Phantom's box... Mademoiselle Krauss had become a huge success. She had just started to sing the aria from the second act. (Thereupon Madame Giry began to sing):

> "*Près de celui que j'aime*
> *Je veux vivre et mourir,*
> *Et la Mort elie-même,*
> *Ne peut nous désunir.*" [6]

"Yes, yes, I'm familiar with it," said Moncharmin, with a dejected smile.

But Madame Giry continued *sotto voce*, the feather of her sooty hat bobbing up and down as she sang:

> "*Partons! Partons! Ici-bas, dans les cieux,*
> *Même sort désormais nous attend tous les deux.*" [7]

"Enough! We've got it!" shouted Richard impatiently. "What happened next?"

"At the point when Leopold cries, '*Let us fly!*' and Eléazar stops them, asking '*Whither go ye?*' Well, then, just at that moment, Monsieur Poligny–whom I was watching dis-

---

[6] "*Near the one I love / I want to live and die / And e'en Death itself / Cannot divide us.*"

[7] "*Go! Go! Here below or in Heaven / The same fate now awaits us both.*"

creetly from the back of the neighboring box, which was empty–Monsieur Poligny got up and walked out quite stiffly, like a statue. I barely had time to ask him 'Whither go ye?' like Eléazar, but he didn't reply. He was as pale as a corpse. I watched him go down the grand staircase, without breaking his leg of course, although he walked as if in a dream, a bad dream needless to say. And it was like he was lost, he who knew the Opera like the back of his hand!"

Thus was Madame Giry's tale, and after she was finished, she waited to see what impact it had had. But the story of Monsieur Poligny's strange behavior only made Monsieur Moncharmin shake his head in disbelief.

"That still doesn't tell us why the Phantom asked you to bring him a footstool," insisted the Director, looking the old usherette squarely in the eye, as we would say today.

"Well, after that night, no one ever tried to use the Phantom's private box again. The Directors gave strict orders that he was to have it for each performance. And whenever he came, he asked me for a footstool."

"Really, Madame! A phantom asking for a footstool! Is he a woman, then?"

"No, he is a man."

"How would you know if you can't see him?"

"Because he's got a man's voice, a lovely man's voice too! This is what happens: He usually arrives near the middle of the first act. He gives three little taps on the door of Box No. 5. The first time I heard them, when I knew the box was empty, you can imagine how baffled I was! I opened the door, listened, looked: nobody! And then, I heard a voice say, 'Madame Jules'–my late husband was named Jules–'could you please bring me a footstool.' If you don't mind my saying so, Monsieur, I almost wet myself. But the voice went on, 'Don't be afraid, Madame Jules, it's only I, the Phantom of the Opera!' I looked for the source of that voice that was so sweet and kind that I hardly felt frightened anymore. *It was sitting on the right corner chair in the front row*. I mean, even though there was no one sitting on that chair, you would have sworn that there was someone in it who spoke, and very politely, I might add."

"Was there anyone in the box to the right of No. 5?" asked Moncharmin.

"No, Monsieur. No. 7 and No. 3, on the left, were both empty. The curtain had just gone up."

"So what did you do?"

"I brought him his footstool. Of course, he didn't want it for himself, it was for his lady! But her, I never saw nor heard..."

"What are you saying? The Phantom has a lady-friend?"

The eyes of the two Directors traveled from Madame Giry to the Supervisor who stood behind her and was gesticulating to attract their attention. He was tapping his forehead with his forefinger to convey his opinion that the woman was very likely insane. Alas for him, that bit of pantomime only served to reaffirm Monsieur Richard's determination to, as soon as possible, get rid of a Supervisor who kept a madwoman on the payroll. Meanwhile, the good lady continued to talk about the Phantom, now praising his generosity:

"At the end of each performance, he always tips me 40 *sous*, sometimes a hundred, sometimes even ten francs when he hasn't been around for several days. It's only since people have begun to upset him again that he's stopped tipping me at all..."

"Excuse me, my good woman," said Moncharmin, who had been born with an inquisitive mind. (The feathers of Madame Giry's sooty hat shook, indicating her disapproval of the Director's continued familiarity.) "How does the Phantom manage to tip you?"

"Why, he leaves it on the little counter at the back of the box, of course. I find it there with the program, which I always bring him. Some nights, I've even found flowers in the box, a rose that must have dropped from his lady-friend's corsage... For he brings a lady with him sometimes. One day, I found a fan they'd left behind."

"The Phantom dropped a fan, did he? What did you do with it?"

"I gave it back to him the next night."

Here the Supervisor interrupted:

"That's a breach of the rules, Madame Giry. I'll have to fine you."

"Shut up, you idiot!" snapped Richard. Then, to the usherette: "You gave it back to him. What then?"

"Then, they took it away, Monsieur. It wasn't there at the end of the performance. But in its place, they left me a box of English sweets, which I'm very fond of. That's one of the Phantom's kindest thoughts."

"That will do, Madame Giry. You may go now."

After the usherette had bowed and let herself out, with the air of dignity that never seemed to desert her, the Directors told the Supervisor that they had decided to dispense with the services of such a crazy old woman. Then they asked him to leave.

After the Supervisor had gone, once again proclaiming his absolute devotion to the theater, the Directors instructed Monsieur Remy to pay the balance of his wages and let him go too. Finally alone, the Directors were able to speak out loud the idea they had simultaneously had, which was that they should personally look into that matter of Box No. 5.

We shall soon follow them there–but not quite yet.

Manuel Martin Peniche

Luciano Bernasconi

Chapter Six
The Magic Violin

Meanwhile, Christine Daae, who had been the victim of scheming of which I will give an account later, had not really benefitted from her triumphant night at the Opera. After the magnificent, gala production, she had sung only once, at the Duchess de Zurich's. There, she performed the best arias from her repertoire. This is what the renowned chronicler X.Y.Z., who was among the guests that night, wrote about her:

"*When you hear Mademoiselle Daae in* Hamlet, *you wonder if Shakespeare himself did not descend from the Elysian Fields to help her rehearse her Ophelia... Equally genuine is the feeling that, when she puts on the diadem of the Queen of Night, Mozart, too, must have departed from the Heavenly Choirs to listen to her. But, in truth, he does not have to leave his Celestial Residence, as the vibrant and glorious voice of the latest interpreter of his* Magic Flute *must have reached him in the Great Hereafter as effortlessly as it made the transition from a humble farmhouse in Skotelof to the gold and marble halls of the palace erected by Monsieur Garnier.*"

Her performance at the salon of the Duchess de Zurich was the last occasion on which Christine Daae was heard in high society. Indeed, she refused all invitations and turned down many attractive offers. She even refused, without giving any excuse, to appear at a charity concert to which she had previously committed. She behaved as if she was no longer in control of her fate and as if she feared any new triumph.

She knew that the Comte de Chagny, to please his brother, had actively interceded on her behalf with Monsieur Richard. She wrote to him to thank him and request that he stop. No one ever learned the exact reasons for her strange attitude. Some claimed that it was due to arrogance; others, to unabashed modesty. In my experience, performers rarely feel pangs of modesty. No, I think it was all due to fear. I believe that Christine Daae was frightened by what had happened to her. I have a letter she wrote during that period (it was given to me by the Persian), which in fact suggests that she was in thrall to an emotion far more powerful than mere fright, something more akin to *absolute terror*:

"I no longer recognize myself when I sing," wrote the poor, gentle, kind-hearted child.

Christine Daae did not appear anywhere in public. Raoul tried to see her, but in vain. He finally sent her a letter, asking for permission to visit her. He despaired of receiving a reply when unexpectedly, one morning, the following note arrived:

Dear Sir:

I have not forgotten the little boy who dove into the sea to rescue my scarf. Today, I am traveling to Perros to fulfill a sacred duty. Tomorrow is the anniversary of the death of my poor father, whom you knew and who was very fond of you. He is buried there, with his violin, in the graveyard of the small church, at the bottom of the hill where we used to play as children, next to the road where, when we were a little older, we said goodbye for the last time.

As soon as he read this note, the Vicomte de Chagny hurriedly consulted a railway guide, dressed as quickly as he could, wrote a few lines for his butler to take to his brother and jumped into a cab which took him to the Gare Montparnasse just in time to see the morning train pulling away from the station.

He spent a discouraging day and his spirits only recovered when he was safely aboard the night train later that evening. He read Christine's note over and over again, smelling its perfume, recalling the sweet memories of his childhood, and spent the rest of that long night in feverish dreams that began and ended with Christine Daae.

He arrived at Lannion at dawn, then rushed to take the coach to Perros-Guirec. He was the only passenger. He questioned the driver and learned that, the previous evening, a young lady who looked "Parisian" had traveled to Perros and was staying at the Sunset Inn. It had to be Christine, and she was alone. He would finally be able to talk to her in peace, without risk of being disturbed. He felt for her a passion stronger than any emotion he had ever felt before. The young man who had traveled the entire world was as helpless in the face of his first love as an unarmed man confronting a tiger.

The nearer Raoul came to Christine, the more fondly he remembered her life story, the fairy tale of a young Swedish singer who had made good. Most of the details are still unknown to the public today.

Once upon a time, there was a farmer who lived with his family in a small market-town not far from Uppsala. He toiled in the fields during the week and sang in the choir on Sundays. This farmer had a daughter whom he had taught to read music before she even knew her alphabet. Christine's father–for it was he–was a great musician, though he did not realize it. There was no better fiddler anywhere in Scandinavia. His reputation grew by leaps and bounds and he was invited to play at many weddings and fairs. When Christine entered upon her sixth year, her mother, who had been sick for a long time, finally died. Then her father, who cared only for his daughter and his music, sold his farm and moved to Uppsala in search of fame and fortune. Alas, he found nothing but poverty.

So he returned to the country, wandering from fair to fair, playing his Scandinavian melodies, while his daughter, who never left his side, listened to him adoringly or sang as he played. One day, at a fair in Ljungby, the famous Professor Valerius heard them and took them to Göteborg. He thought that Christine's father was one of the best violinists he had ever heard and that his daughter had the makings of a great singer. The Professor provided her an education and she made rapid progress, charming everyone with her beauty, grace and genuine desire to please.

When Professor Valerius and his wife decided to resettle in France, they took the Daaes with them. Madame Valerius treated Christine as if she had been her own daughter. But her father soon felt homesick. While in Paris, he never ventured outside, living in a kind of daze nurtured by his music. He remained in his bedroom for hours, fiddling and softly singing with his daughter. Sometimes Madame Valerius would listen to them from behind the door, wipe away a tear and tiptoe downstairs again. She, too, longed for her native Scandinavian skies.

Daae only seemed to recover his spirit when the whole family went on vacation for the summer in Perros-Guirec, a remote corner of Brittany ignored by most Parisians. There, he loved the ocean which, he said, was the same color as in his own country. Often, he would play his saddest tunes on the beach and pretend that the sea stood still to listen to them. Finally, he convinced the Valeriuses to indulge one of his whims.

During the weeks when the Bretons held their various religious celebrations, festivals and dances, Daae toured the country with his daughter and his fiddle, just like in the old days. The villagers never tired of hearing them, for the Daaes gave them enough musical memories to last them for a year. At night, they slept in barns, turning down offers of beds at the local inns, preferring to lie close to each other on the straw, just like when they were so poor in Sweden.

They were always neatly dressed, never asked for any money and politely refused any that was offered to them. The villagers were confused by the behavior of this foreign fiddler who wandered the country roads with a pretty child who sang like an angel in tow and did not seem to want anything in return. Soon, people began following them from village to village.

One day, a little boy from the big city, who was out with his governess, forced her to walk with him all day, for he could not tear himself away from the little girl with the pure, enchanting voice. They came to the seashore and a creek called the Trestraou, which at the time was nothing more than a place where the sky met the sea and golden sand. It was a windy day and Christine's scarf was blown out to sea. The little girl cried out and tried to catch the precious scarf as it flew away, but it was already too late. Soon the scarf was floating away on the waves. Then she heard a voice say:

"Don't cry, Mademoiselle. I'll go and fetch your scarf."

And she saw a little boy quickly running into the sea, despite the loud and indignant warnings of a lady in black. The boy bravely dove into the waters, fully-dressed, and brought her scarf back. Naturally, both boy and scarf were soaked through. The lady in black made a great fuss, but Christine laughed joyfully and kissed the little boy. We now know, of course, that he was none other than the Vicomte Raoul de Chagny, who was staying in Lannion with his aunt.

During the season, Raoul and Christine saw each other and played together almost every day. At his aunt's request, supported by Professor Valerius, Monsieur Daae agreed to give the young Vicomte some violin lessons. Thus, Raoul learned to love the same music that had bewitched Christine's childhood.

They both had the same quiet and imaginative minds. The only thing they seemed to love was listening to old Breton legends, and their favorite pastime was to go door-to-door and ask the locals, like beggars:

"Dear Madame, or Gentle Sir, would you please tell us a story?"

And it was seldom that they did not have one handed to them, as nearly every old Breton grandmother has, at least once in her life, seen the korrigans dance by moonlight on the moors.

But their great treat was when, in the evening, in the great silence of the night, after the Sun had set in the sea, Monsieur Daae came and sat down with them on the roadside. There, in a low voice, as though he feared he might frighten the very ghosts whom he evoked, he told them the great legends of the Northlands. Some were as beautiful as Andersen's Tales; others were sad as the songs of the great poet Runeberg. And the moment he stopped, the children would beg for more.

There was one such tale that began thus:

"A King sat in a small boat on one of those deep, still lakes that open like a bright eye in the midst of the Norwegian mountains..."

And another:

"Little Lotte thought of everything and nothing. A true bird of summer, she glided in the golden rays of the Sun, her blonde hair adorned with the crown of Spring. Her soul was as clear and blue as her eyes. She cajoled her mother, was kind to her doll, took great care of her dress, her little red shoes and her fiddle, but most of all she loved, when she went to sleep, to hear the Angel of Music..."

While the old man told this story, Raoul looked at Christine's blue eyes and golden hair. And Christine thought that Little Lotte was very lucky to hear the Angel of Music when she went to sleep. The Angel of Music played a part in all of Monsieur Daae's stories, and the children kept pestering him for endless explanations, always wanting to know more about the Angel. Monsieur Daae maintained that every great musician, every great artist, received a visitation from the Angel at least once in his life. Sometimes, the Angel leaned over their cradle, as had happened to Little Lotte, and that was why there were child prodigies who could play the fiddle at six better than men of 50, which, one must admit, is rather extraordinary. Sometimes, the Angel came much later, because the children were naughty and wouldn't learn their lessons or practice their scales. And sometimes, he never came at all, because one did not have a pure heart or a guilt-free conscience...

No one ever sees the Angel, said Monsieur Daae, but those who are meant to hear him can do so. He often comes when they least expect him, when they are sad and disheartened. Then, their ears suddenly perceive a celestial harmony, a

78

divine voice, which they will remember all their lives... Those who are visited by the Angel are seared by the experience. They tremble with a passion unknown to the rest of mankind. And they can no longer touch any instrument, or open their mouths to sing, without producing sounds that put all other human sounds to shame. People who do not know that the Angel has visited those persons say that they have genius.

Little Christine asked her father if he had ever heard the Angel of Music. But Monsieur Daae shook his head sadly. Then, his eyes lit up and he said: "You will hear him one day, my child! When I am in Heaven, I will send him to you!"

It was around that time that Monsieur Daae began to cough frequently.

Fall came and signaled the end of the summer holidays. Thus, Raoul and Christine were separated.

Three years later, they met again in Perros. They were much grown up by then. Raoul never forgot that encounter. Professor Valerius was dead, but his widow remained in France where she still had responsibilities. Monsieur Daae and Christine continued to play the violin and sing, extending their harmonious, dream-like existence to their kind patroness, who now seemed almost to live on music alone.

Raoul had gone to Perros on a lark, and had headed straight to the house where his friend used to live. He first saw Monsieur Daae, who got up from his chair and, with tears in his eyes, hugged the young man, all the while telling him they had never forgotten him. In fact, hardly a day had gone by when Christine had not mentioned Raoul. Monsieur Daae was still speaking when the door opened and his daughter appeared, carrying a tea-tray. She recognized Raoul and put the tray down. Her beautiful face flushed slightly at the sight of her old friend. She remained hesitant, silent. Her father looked at them, a twinkle in his eye. Finally, Raoul went up to Christine and kissed her. She did not seek to avoid the kiss, asked him several questions, prettily performed her duties as hostess, again picked up the tray and left the room.

Then, she ran outside and took refuge on a bench in the solitude of the garden. For the first time in her young life, she felt a rush of conflicting emotions in her heart. Raoul followed her and they shyly talked till evening. They were so different now, each not recognizing in their self-important new facades, the people they had once been. They were as cautious as diplomats and spoke of things that had nothing to do with their feelings. When they took leave of each other at the side of the road, Raoul placed a small, proper kiss on Christine's trembling hand.

"Mademoiselle," said the young man, "I shall never forget you!"

He walked away full of regret, because he knew that a girl like Christine Daae could never become the wife of a Vicomte de Chagny.

As for Christine, she went back to her father and said:

"Didn't you find that Raoul wasn't as nice as he used to be? I don't think I like him anymore."

She tried to put him out of her mind, but wasn't always successful. As a result, she devoted herself, body and soul, to her art. She made astonishing progress and those who heard her predicted that she would someday become the greatest singer in the world. Then, her father died and it seemed that buried along with him were her voice, her soul and her genius. She had barely enough of them left to enable her to just manage to gain entry to the Conservatoire, where she did not particularly distinguish herself. She attended her classes without enthusiasm and won a prize only to please old Madame Valerius, with whom she continued to live.

The first time that Raoul saw Christine at the Opera, he had been charmed by her beauty and the sweet memories of his youth that it evoked, but at the same time, was rather surprised by her conspicuous lack of artistry. She seemed detached from everything. He returned to listen to her and followed her backstage. He waited for her behind a piece of scenery. He tried to attract her attention. More than once, he followed her to the very door of her dressing-room, but she never seemed to notice him. In fact, she did not seem to notice anyone else either. She was indifference personified. Raoul suffered, for she was very beautiful and he was shy and dared not confess his love, even to himself. Then came the thunderstorm, the bolt of lightning that had been the gala performance. The Heavens had been torn asunder and the voice of an angel had been heard upon the Earth for the delight of Mankind–and the utter conquest of his heart.

And then, there had been that *Voice* behind the door. "*You must love me!*" Yet, there was no one in the room.

Why did she laugh when he had told her, as she opened her eyes, "*I'm the little boy who dove into the sea to rescue your scarf?*" Why had she not recognized him? Why had she never written to him?

The highway Raoul was on seemed to go uphill forever. He passed the Cross of the Three Roads... Then the deserted moors, the frost-covered briar, the immobile landscape beneath a milk-white sky... The sound of the windows shaking with every bump hammered at the young man's ears. Why was such a noisy coach traveling so slowly? He recognized the small houses, the fields, the hills, the trees alongside the road... Then, they took the last curve before the long downhill slope that led to the sea and the great bay of Perros.

He recalled that Christine was staying at the Sunset Inn. Of course! There was no other inn in Perros. And besides, it was a comfortable place. He remembered that, long ago, they had heard many a fine story there... His heart beat violently. How would she react when she saw him?

The first person Raoul saw when he walked inside the inn's smoky parlor was Old Mother Tricard. She recognized him at once and showered him with compliments. Then she asked him what had brought him to Perros. He blushed a little and said that he had had some business to transact in nearby Lannion and had felt like making a detour to Perros to say hello to all his old friends there–herself being first on the list, of course. Mother Tricard offered him lunch but Raoul politely declined. "Later," he said. He was waiting for something—or someone.

Suddenly, the door opened. He jumped to his feet. It was her! He tried to speak but no words would come. Christine, on the other hand, stood before him, smiling and showing no surprise. Her face was very lightly flushed, like the pale color of a strawberry that grew in the shadows, perhaps because she had to walk uphill to reach the inn. Her loyal heart beat softly in her chest. Her eyes, clear pools of pale azure, like the ever-still, dream-like lakes of her native North, offered him only the tranquil reflection of his own honest soul. Her fur jacket was only partially buttoned up, revealing her thin waist and the graceful, elegant curves of her body.

Raoul and Christine looked at each other in silence for a long time. Mother Tricard knew when discretion was called for and left the room.

"So you've come," she said at last. "I'm not surprised. I knew I would find you waiting for me when I came back from Mass. *Someone* at the church had told me so. Yes, *someone* had told me you'd come.

"Who?" asked Raoul. She let him take her delicate hand in his.

"Why, my poor father, who is dead."

There was another long silence. Then, Raoul asked:

"Did your father tell you that I love you, Christine, and that I can't live without you?"

Christine blushed deeply and turned her head away. In a trembling voice, she said:

"Me? That's ridiculous, my dear!"

She let out a tiny laugh, putting on airs to avoid showing her true feelings.

"Don't laugh, Christine. I'm serious."

She replied gravely: "I didn't ask you to come here to tell me things like that."

"Yet, you did ask me to come here for a reason, Christine. You knew very well that your letter would touch me and that I would rush to Perros. How could you believe all that, if you didn't also believe that I loved you?"

"I just thought you would remember the fun we had here when we were children... And that my father shared so much of it with us... To be honest, I'm not really sure what I was thinking when I wrote to you... Maybe I was wrong to do it... Your sudden appearance in my dressing-room the other evening brought back happy memories of our time together so long ago... I felt like writing to you as the little girl that I was then, who would find comfort in her moment of sadness and solitude to once again have her old friend by her side..."

They both fell silent. It seemed to Raoul that there was something about Christine's attitude that felt wrong, yet he could not put his finger on what it was. He did not feel that she was hostile, far from it. The sad tenderness he saw shining in her eyes made that clear. But why was her tenderness mixed with so much sadness? That was what he wanted to know— and it irritated him that he was so far unable to discover its cause.

"When you saw me in your dressing-room, was that the first time you'd noticed me, Christine?"

She was incapable of deception.

"No," she said. "Several times I'd noticed you in your brother's box. And once or twice backstage."

"I thought so!" said Raoul, pursing his lips. "But, when you saw me there, sitting at your feet, reminding you of the day I rescued your scarf from the sea, why did you act as if you didn't know me? And why did you laugh at me?"

Raoul's tone was so cruel and unexpected that Christine stared at him in shock, unable to reply. The young man himself was taken aback by the sudden violence of his words when he had resolved to speak only of tenderness, love and his devotion to Christine. A husband, a lover perhaps, who might feel entitled, would speak thus to a wife or mistress who had offended him. He was annoyed at his own clumsiness and stupidity, but saw no way out of his embarrassment other than to continue behaving with indignation.

"Are you unable to answer?" he asked angrily, feeling even more unhappy. "Then, I will answer for you. It was because there was someone else in that room, Christine. Someone else whose presence embarrassed you and whom you didn't wish to know that you could possibly be interested in anyone else!"

"If there was anyone embarrassing me that evening, my dear," Christine broke in coldly, "it was you. That's why I told you to leave!"

"Yes! So that you could be alone with another man!"

"What are you saying, Monsieur?" asked the girl, growing agitated. "Who do you mean?"

"The man to whom you said, '*I only sing for you! Tonight, I gave you my soul and I'm dead*!' "

Christine seized Raoul's arm and grabbed it with a strength no one would have suspected in such a frail creature.

"You were listening behind the door?"

"Yes, because I love you... I heard everything..."

"What did you hear?"

The young girl, strangely calm again, released Raoul's arm.

"He said, '*Christine, you must love me*!' "

At these words, a deathly pallor spread over the poor girl's face. Dark circles appeared under her eyes. She staggered and would have fallen if Raoul had not stepped forward and caught her in his arms. Christine eventually recovered and said in a faint, almost inaudible voice:

"Go on! Tell me everything you heard!"

Raoul looked at her, hesitated, at a loss for words.

"Go on!" she begged. "Can't you see that you're torturing me?"

"After you said you'd given him your soul, I heard him reply, '*Your soul is a beautiful thing, child, and I thank you. No Emperor ever received so fair a gift. The angels wept tonight.*' "

Christine put her hand to her heart. She stared at Raoul, visibly in the grip of some unspeakable emotion. Her expression was so wild, so frantic that it could have been that of a lunatic. Raoul was struck with fear when he looked at her. Suddenly, her eyes moistened and two large tears, like brilliant pearls, rolled down her ivory cheeks.

"Christine!"

"Raoul!"

The young man tried to take her in his arms again, but she pulled away and fled in great distress.

While Christine remained locked inside her room at the inn, Raoul couldn't stop blaming himself for the brutality he had shown her. Still, jealousy burned hot in his veins. For the girl to react with such anxiety at the notion that someone had discovered her secret, the latter must have been inordinately important to her. In his heart, despite what he had overheard, Raoul was unable to doubt the purety of Christine's intentions. He knew her reputation for keeping to herself. He was also wise enough in the ways of the world to realize that it is sometimes necessary for an aspiring singer to fake words of love to further her career. Yes, she said she had given her soul, but it was obviously in the context of her singing and music. If that was the case, why, then, was she feeling so agitated? Raoul was profoundly unhappy. If he could have seized the *Voice* by the throat, he would have forced him to explain his intentions.

Why had Christine fled? Why wouldn't she return?

Raoul refused breakfast. He was concerned and bitterly saddened to see the hours he had hoped to find so sweet, slip away without Christine's presence. Why wouldn't she wander with him through that countryside which held so many shared memories? Why did she linger in Perros instead of returning to Paris? She had nothing more to accomplish, and was, in fact, doing nothing while she remained,? He had learned that she had had a Mass said for the repose of her poor father's soul and spent a long time praying in the small church and beside the old fiddler's tomb.

Dejectedly, Raoul walked towards the cemetery near the church. He pushed the old iron gate and entered, where he wandered, alone among the tombs, reading the inscriptions. As he moved behind the apse, he was suddenly struck by the dazzling note created by the vibrantly colored flowers that spilled over from the granite slab and sprawled across the white ground. Their sweet smell permeated this small corner of icy Breton winter. They were marvelous red roses that looked as if they had bloomed in the snow that very morning. They brought a speck of life to the dead, and death was all around him. Like the flowers, it too spilled across the ground, which had heaved up its overabundance of corpses. Hundreds of skulls and skeletons were heaped against the church's wall, held their only by a fine wire mesh that left the gruesome stack somberly visible. Dead men's heads, arranged in rows like bricks, held together by the bleached-white bones, were the buttress upon which the walls of the sacristy had been built. Its door opened in the middle of that ossuary, as is often the case with ancient Breton churches.

Raoul said a prayer for Monsieur Daae. Then, painfully shaken by so many eternal smiles frozen on the mouths of the skulls, seemingly staring at him, he left the cemetery. He walked up the hill and sat down on the edge of the moor overlooking the sea. The wind roared over the sands, chasing the pale, timid rays of the Sun until they were forced to flee and became barely a silver line on the horizon. Then the victorious wind quieted and evening came. Raoul was surrounded by icy shadows but did not feel the cold. His thoughts, his memories, wandered over the desolate, deserted moor. It was here, on this very spot, that he had come with little Christine to watch for Korrigans dancing in the light of the rising Moon. He had never seen any, though his eyesight was good, whereas Christine, who was a little nearsighted, claimed she had seen many. He smiled at the thought then, suddenly, turned around. A shape had appeared out of nowhere, without any noise to betray its approach, and now it stood beside him. It said:

"Do you think the Korrigans will come tonight?"

It was Christine. He tried to speak, but she closed his lips with her gloved hand.

"Hush! Listen to me, Raoul. I've decided to tell you something important, very important!"

Her voice was shaking. He waited for her to continue.

She did, almost panting from the effort.

"Do you remember the legend of the Angel of Music?"

"Of course, I do!" he exclaimed. "I believe we were right here when your father first told it to us."

"And it was here, too, that he said to me, 'When I am in Heaven, my child, I will send him to you.' Well, Raoul, my father is in Heaven and I have been visited by the Angel of Music!"

"I have no doubt of it," replied the Vicomte gravely, for it seemed to him that his friend was piously connecting the memory of her father with the glory of her recent triumph at the Opera.

Christine seemed taken aback by the matter-of-fact way that Raoul reacted to the news of her visitation by the Angel of Music.

"What do you mean, Raoul?" she asked, her pale face in the dark coming so close to his that he could have thought she was going to kiss him, when she only wanted to read the answer in his eyes.

"I mean," he replied, "that no human being can sing as you sang the other night without some miraculous or Heavenly intervention. No professor on Earth could have taught you such timbre. Yes, I believe you have heard the Angel of Music, Christine."

"I have," she said solemnly, "*in my dressing-room.* That's where he comes to give me my daily lessons."

The tone with which she uttered these words was so profound and strange that Raoul looked at her with worry, as one would look at someone who had just said something utterly unbelievable or recounted an insane vision, believing in its reality with every fiber of a fevered brain. She stepped back and was now but a motionless shadow in the night.

"*In your dressing-room?*" he echoed stupidly.

"Yes, that's where I heard him. And I wasn't the only one who did."

"Who else heard him?"

"Why, you, my dear."

"I? I heard the Angel of Music?"

"Yes, the other night, it was he who spoke to me when you were listening behind the door. It was he who said, '*You must love me*!' I thought I was the only one who could hear his voice. Imagine my surprise when you told me, this morning, that you, too, could hear him!"

Raoul laughed. Just then, the darkness seemed to melt as the first rays of the Moon began to bathe the deserted moor and shroud the two young people in their silvery light. Christine turned towards Raoul with a hostile glare. Her eyes, usually so gentle, flashed fire.

"Why are you laughing? Do you think it was just any voice that you heard?"

"Well..." said the young man who felt confused by Christine's aggressive attitude.

"And of all people, Raoul, how can you say such a thing? You, an old childhood friend! My father's friend! The only thing I can say is that you must have changed a great deal since then. How could you believe such a thing of me? I'm a decent girl, Monsieur le Vicomte, I don't lock myself inside my dressing-room with strange men. If you'd opened that door, you would have seen that there was nobody else but me inside the room!"

"That's true... I did open the door, after you'd gone, and I didn't see anyone in the room..."

"There! So what do you have to say now?"

Raoul summoned up all his courage.

"What I say, Christine, is that I think someone is playing tricks on you."

She made a pained cry and ran away. He ran after her, but, in a tone of fierce anger, she shouted back at him: "Leave me! Leave me!"

Then, she disappeared. Raoul returned to the inn, feeling weary, discouraged and sad.

He was told that Christine had gone to her room, saying that she would not be down for dinner. He inquired if she had taken ill. Mother Tricard replied ambiguously that if she was, it was nothing too serious. Since the old woman believed the young couple had separated because of a lover's quarrel, she went away shrugging and muttering under her breath about young fools who weren't smart enough not to waste the few hours of happiness the Good Lord had given them to spend on this Earth in silly arguments.

Raoul dined alone near the fireplace, feeling justifiably gloomy. After, he went to his room and tried to read, but in vain; then, he went to bed and tried to sleep, with similar success. No sound came from the room next to his–Christine's room. What was she doing? Was she asleep? And if she wasn't, what was she thinking about? What was *he* thinking about? He would have been at pains to say. The strange conversation he'd had with the young girl still troubled him greatly. He wasn't as much thinking *of* Christine as *about* Christine. And that *about* was such a mysterious, incomplete picture that he couldn't help but feel a peculiar sense of apprehension.

The hours crawled by. It was around 11:30 p.m. when he distinctly heard someone moving in the next room. It was a light, furtive step. Had Christine not gone to bed? Without thinking about what he was doing, Raoul dressed, taking care not to make any noise, and waited. Waited for what? He had no idea? But his heart thumped in his chest when he heard Christine's door moving slowly on its hinges. He wondered where she could be going at such a time of night, when everyone else in Perros was fast asleep? Softly opening his own door, in the moonlight he clearly saw Christine's pale, white form slip along the corridor. She went down the stairs and he leaned over the bannister above her.

He heard two voices in rapid, whispered conversation. He caught one sentence: "Don't lose the key." It was Mother Tricard's voice.

The door facing the sea was opened and locked again. Then all was still. Raoul ran back to his room and over to the window. He opened the shutters and saw Christine's white form standing on the deserted pier outside.

The inn's first floor was built fairly low and a tree growing against the wall tempted an impatient Raoul with its branches. The young man struggled through the window and used it to climb down to the ground, so that Mother Tricard had no suspicion that her guest had gone out. The next morning, therefore, the landlady's amazement was all the greater when the young Vicomte was brought back to the inn, half-frozen, more dead than alive. She learned that his body had been found stretched out on the steps of the altar of the small church. She quickly ran to tell Christine, who hurried down and, with Mother Tricard's help, did her best to revive Raoul. He soon opened his eyes and recovered when he saw his friend's lovely face leaning over him.

What had happened during the night? Police Commisioner Mifroid had the opportunity of questioning the Vicomte de Chagny a few weeks later, when the tragedy at the Opera compelled the intervention of the Public Prosecutor's office. He asked him about the events of that night in Perros and I quote here *verbatim* the questions and answers given in the official transcript of that interview, pp. 150 et seq.:

Question. *"Did Mademoiselle Daae see you climb down from your room by the rather unorthodox means you took?"*

Answer. *"No, Monsieur, she did not. To be honest, when I went after her, I didn't even try to hide the sound of my footsteps. In my heart, I wanted her to turn around and notice me. I knew that it was totally improper for me to follow her that way, and that my constant spying on her was unworthy of me. But she seemed not to hear me and acted as if I wasn't there. Silently she left the pier and quickly walked up the road. The church bell struck a quarter to twelve. I thought the sound of it* caused her hurry, as if she was late for something, as it seemed she almost began to run. Then she arrived at the cemetery."

Q. "*Was the gate open?*"

A. "*Yes, Monsieur. That surprised me, but it didn't seem to surprise Mademoiselle Daae.*"

Q. "*Was there anyone inside?*"

A. "*I didn't see anyone. If someone had been there,, I would have seen them. The light of the Moon was extremely bright and there was snow everywhere. It reflected the light and made everything totally visible.*"

Q. "*Could it have been possible for someone to hide behind the tombs?*"

A. "*No, Monsieur. They are small graves. They were mostly buried beneath the snow, and their crosses barely stood above ground level. The only shadows were ours and those of the crosses. The church stood out clearly. I've never seen such a brilliant night. It was fine, translucent and extremely cold. It was the first time I'd been in a cemetery at night. I never thought one could see so much light there*—a light that seemed to float."

Q. "*Are you superstitious?*"

A. "*No, Monsieur. I am a good Catholic.*"

Q. "*What was your state of mind?*"

A. "*Normal and peaceful, I assure you. Yes, Mademoiselle Daae's strange behavior in going out at that hour of the night had worried me at first. But, as soon as I saw her go to the cemetery, I thought she meant to fulfill some pious duty at her father's grave and I considered this so natural that I became totally calm. The only thing that surprised me was that she had not heard me following her, for my footsteps were quite audible on the hard snow. But she must have been completely absorbed by her prayers and I resolved not to disturb her. When she reached her father's grave, I remained a few feet behind her. She knelt down, made the sign of the cross and began to pray. At that moment, the bell tolled midnight. As the last stroke still rang in my ears, I saw Mademoiselle*

Daae lift her eyes to the sky and stretch her arms towards the Moon. She seemed to be, as far as I could tell, in a state of near-ecstasy. I was still wondering what the reason for her sudden and strange condition might be, when I, too, felt compelled to raise my head. I cast a look of panic around me. My entire being felt drawn towards something that could not be seen–something invisible that played the most beautiful music in the world! *Both Christine and I recognized that music. We had heard it as children. But old Monsieur Daae had never played it on his fiddle with such divine talent. In that moment, I could only remember what Christine had told me earlier about the Angel of Music. I didn't know what to believe. If that unforgettable music was not coming down from Heaven, it also could not have been originated on Earth. There was no visible violin, nor any visible hand holding a bow. I still recall that wonderful melody. It was* The Resurrection of Lazarus, *which old Monsieur Daae used to play to us in his hours of melancholy and faith. If Christine's Angel existed, he could not have played better than he did that night. The invocation from Jesus to Lazarus tore at us and I almost expected to see Monsieur Daae's grave open and the old man return. I also thought that he might have been buried with his violin and was playing from within his grave... Truth to tell, in that macabre yet shining moment, in that small, God-forsaken provincial cemetery, surrounded by the grim smiles of all those grinning skulls, I no longer knew the boundaries of my fevered imagination. When the music finally stopped, I was at last able to recover my senses. I thought heard a noise coming from the wall of skulls in the ossuary."*

Q. *"So you heard a noise in the ossuary?"*

A. *"Yes. It was as though the skulls were chuckling. I couldn't repress a shudder."*

Q. *"Didn't it occur to you that your invisible musician could have been hiding behind that very stack of bones?"*

A. *"It was the one thought that did occur to me, Monsieur, so much so that I did not follow Mademoiselle Daae when she stood up and silently left the cemetery. She was still* so absorbed that I am not surprised that again she did not notice my presence. I remained where I was, staring at the ossuary, determined to discover the truth and reach the end of this incredible journey."

Q. "What happened that caused you to be found in the morning lying half-dead on the steps of the church's altar?"

A. "It all happened very fast. First, a skull rolled at my feet... Then another... and another... It was as if I were the target of some macabre game of bowling. Then, I thought that perhaps a misstep by the invisible musician had upset the precarious balance of the ossuary behind which he had been hiding. This seemed to be confirmed when suddenly I saw a shadow appear on the brightly-lit sacristy wall.

"I ran towards it. The shadow had already pushed open the door of the church and gone inside. The shadow wore a cloak. I ran like the devil and I was fast enough to catch hold of its edge. At that moment, we both stood, the shadow and I, directly in front of the altar. Moonbeams fell straight upon us through the stained-glass windows of the apse. Since I would not release its cloak, the shadow turned and its cape slipped open. Then, Monsieur, I saw, as clearly as I see you now, a terrible death's-head which stared at me with eyes that burned with the very fires of Hell! I felt as if I had come face-to-face with Satan himself! In the presence of such a ghastly apparition, my heart failed me, my courage failed me... And I remember nothing more until I regained consciousness at the Sunset Inn."

Edmond Ripoll

Chapter Seven
A Visit to Box No. 5

When we last saw Messrs. Firmin Richard and Armand Moncharmin, they were about to personally look into the matter of Box No. 5.

They took the main stairs, which lead from the waiting-room outside their offices to the backstage area, then they crossed the stage, exited through the small door reserved for subscribers and entered the theater itself from the first corridor on the left. Once there, they made their way through the front rows of the orchestra seats to look at Box No. 5. It was impossible for them to get a good view of it, however, because it was half-shrouded in darkness and seat covers had been flung over the red velvet railing of its balcony.

They were almost alone in the huge, dark house and a great silence surrounded them. At that hour, most of the stage-hands usually went out for a drink.

The staff, too, was momentarily gone from the stage, leaving a scene half set. A few rays of light–a wan, gloomy light that seemed to have been stolen from a dying star–trickled in through some opening or other, and fell upon an old tower that raised its papier-mâché battlements on the stage. Everything in this phony darkness, or rather this deceptive light, took on alien shapes. The protective sheets covering the orchestra seats resembled an angry sea, its squalid waves suddenly frozen into place by a secret command from the Storm Giant who, as everyone knows, is called Adamastor. Messrs. Moncharmin and Richard stood there like shipwrecked mariners in a static tempest made of painted fabric. They headed for the boxes on the left, pushing their way through like sailors forced to abandon ship and struggle to shore.

Eight great, polished columns stood in the darkness like enormous pylons supporting a massive cliff that was threatening to collapse. Its sediment layers were the semi-circular, parallel and wavy lines of the balconies of the first, second and third tiers of boxes. At the very top of that "cliff," lost in Monsieur Lenepveu's magnificent copper ceiling, stood grinning and grimacing figures that seemed to laugh and jeer at Messrs. Richard and Moncharmin's concern. Normally, these figures would have been extremely serious. Their names were Isis, Amphitrite, Hebe, Pandora, Psyche, Thetis, Pomona, Daphne, Clytie, Galatea and Arethusa. Yes, Arethusa herself and Pandora, whom everyone remembers because of her box, looked down upon the two new Directors of the Opera. They had finally reached a kind of "island" and, from there, stared silently at Box No. 5.

I said that they were concerned. At least, I suppose that was so. Monsieur Moncharmin, at least, admitted that he was intimidated. To quote his own words from his *Memoirs*:

"*The sinking boat of an Opera into which Debienne and Poligny had so cleverly lured us* (what style!), *especially all that nonsense about the Phantom, may have begun to affect my imagination and possibly even my visual faculties. Or it may have been that the unique surroundings in which we stood, in the midst of overwhelming silence, intimidated us to an extraordinary extent. Or perhaps, we were merely the victims of an hallucination caused by the semi-darkness of the theater and the obscurity that shrouded Box No. 5? In any event, I saw, and Richard saw as well, a* shape *in that Box. Richard said nothing, and neither did I. But we spontaneously grabbed each other's hand. We stood like that for a few minutes, motionless, our eyes fixed on the Box. But the figure had vanished. We left the place immediately, and, once in the lobby, shared our impressions of that* shape. *The sad thing was that my* shape *was not at all like Richard's! I had seen a thing like a death's-head resting on the edge of the box, whereas Richard had seen the shape of an old woman who looked like Madame Giry. So we came to the conclusion that we had in-*

96

deed been the victims of an hallucination. We ran, laughing like madmen, to Box No. 5, and went inside where, naturally, we didn't find a shape of any kind."

Now, it is time for us, too, to enter Box No. 5.

It is exactly like all the other grand boxes of the first tier. To be honest, there is nothing to distinguish it from any of the others.

Mrss. Moncharmin and Richard, ostensibly amused and laughing at each other, moved the furniture around, lifted the seat covers and paid particularly close attention to the *right corner seat in the front row* where Madame Giry had said *the Voice used to sit*. But they saw that it was a normal chair just like any other, with nothing magical about it at all. Altogether, Box No. 5 was the most ordinary box in the world, with its red curtains, its chairs, its carpet and its railing covered in red velvet. After having examined the carpet in the most thorough manner possible, and discovering nothing more there or anywhere else, the two Directors went down to the box located just below Box No. 5, on the pit tier next to the first exit from the stalls on the left. They found nothing worth mentioning there either.

"All those people are making fools of us!" Firmin Richard finally exclaimed. "On Saturday, we'll play *Faust*. And we'll both watch the performance from Box No. 5!"

Gerald Forton

Chapter Eight
In which Messrs. Richard and Moncharmin
dare stage Faust *in a* cursed theater
and the terrible events which ensued

On Saturday morning, upon reaching their office, the two Directors found, waiting for them, identical letters from "P.O." spelling out his terms:

Dear Directors:

Have you decided it is to be war between us?

If you still desire peace, here is my ultimatum.

It consists of the following four conditions:

1. You must give my private box back to me–and it is henceforth to remain entirely at my disposal.

2. Tonight, the part of Marguerite *shall be sung by Christine Daae. Don't worry about Carlotta; she will be indisposed.*

3. I absolutely insist upon the good and loyal services of Madame Giry, my usherette, whom you will immediately reinstate in her previous position.

4. Let me know by a letter that you will hand over to Madame Giry, who will see that it reaches me, that you accept, as your predecessors did, the conditions stated in the rulebook relating to my monthly stipend. I will inform you later how you are to pay me.

If you refuse, tonight, Faust *will be staged* in a cursed theater.

A word to the wise is sufficient!

P.O.

"He's getting on my nerves! He's really getting on my nerves now!" shouted Richard, raising an angry fist into the air and slamming it on his desk.

Just then, Mercier, one of the Assistant Directors, entered the room.

"Lachenal would like to see one of you gentlemen," he said. "He says it's urgent and he seems quite upset."

"Who's Lachenal?" asked Richard.

"He's your senior lad."

"What do you mean, my senior lad?"

"Well, Monsieur le Directeur," explained Mercier, "there are several lads working at the Opera and Lachenal is in charge of them."

"And what does this 'senior lad' do?"

"He takes care of our stables."

"What stables?"

"Why, yours, Monsieur, the stables of the Opera."

"We have stables at the Opera? My word, I had no idea. Where are they?"

"In the vaults, near the Rotunda. It's a very important department. We have 12 horses."

"Twelve horses! What for, in Heaven's name?"

"Well, we need them for the processions in *La Juive*, *The Prophet* and so on. The horses must be strage-trained and it's the lads' job to train them. Lachenal is very good at it. He used to be in charge of the stables at Franconi's."

"Interesting... Well, what does he want?"

"I don't know. I never saw him in such a state."

"Best show him in then!"

Lachenal came into the room, carrying a riding-crop with which he nervously struck his right boot.

"Good morning, Monsieur Lachenal," said Richard, impressed in spite of himself. "To what do we owe the honor of your visit?"

"Mr. Director, I've come to ask your permission to get rid of the entire stable."

"What? Why do you want to get rid of our horses?"

"I'm not talking about the horses, just the lads."

"How many do you employ, Monsieur Lachenal?"

"Six!"

"Six? That's at least two more than we should have."

"They are 'sinecures,' Monsieur," interrupted Mercier. "Jobs created at the special request of the Under-Secretary of the Ministry of Fine Arts and filled with protegés of the Government. If I may be so bold..."

"I don't give a damn about the government!" roared Richard. "We don't need more than four lads to take care of 12 horses."

"Eleven," said the senior lad, correcting him.

"Twelve," repeated Richard.

"Eleven," repeated Lachenal.

"But the Assistant Director told me that we have 12 horses?"

"We did have 12, but now, we only have 11 because Caesar was stolen."

Lachenal smacked his boot hard with the crop.

"Someone stole Caesar?" cried Mercier. "The white horse from *The Prophet*?"

"There's only one Caesar," replied the senior lad grimly. "I worked for Franconi for ten years and I've seen plenty of horses in my time. But in all that time, there's only been one Caesar. Or there was, because now he's been stolen."

"How?"

"I don't know. Nobody knows. That's why I've come to ask you to let me kick them all out."

"What do the lads say?"

"Nothing but rubbish. Some are accusing the extras. Others think it's the concierge..."

"The concierge? He's as honest as I am!" protested Mercier.

"But, Monsieur Lachenal," said Richard, "you must have some idea about what happened..."

"I do," Lachenal declared. "I've got an idea and I'll tell you what it is. As far as I'm concerned, there's no other possibility." He walked up to the two Directors and whispered in their ears: "*The Phantom did it*!"

Richard made a face.

"What? Not you too!"

"What do you mean, not me too? You make it sound like I'm mad..."

"No, Monsieur Lachenal, not at all, but..."

"After what I saw, it would be mad not to tell you what I think, wouldn't it?"

"What did you see?"

"As clearly as I see you now, I saw a black shadow riding a white horse that looked just like Caesar!"

"Did you chase them?"

"Of course I did. I shouted too, but they were too fast for me. They disappeared into the darkness."

Monsieur Richard rose.

"All right, Monsieur Lachenal. You can go now. We'll file your complaint against the Phantom."

"And kick out my stable?"

"Certainly! Goodbye."

Lachenal bowed and withdrew.

Richard foamed at the mouth.

"Settle that idiot's account and fire him at once," he told Mercier.

"He's a close friend of the Under-Secretary," the Assistant Director ventured to say.

"And he takes his *apéritif* every day at Tortoni's with Lagrène, Scholl and Pertuiset, the big game hunter," added Moncharmin. "We'll have the whole press against us! He'll tell his story about the Phantom and everyone will laugh at us! Don't they say, 'Better to be dead than a laughing stock!' "

"Fine, we won't mention it again," said Richard, whose mind had already moved on to other concerns.

Just then, the door opened. It must have been left unguarded because Madame Giry walked in holding a letter in her hand and, without the usual formalities, said hurriedly:

"I beg your pardon, gentlemen, but this morning I got a letter from the Phantom. He told me to come here to pick up something that you..."

She did not complete her sentence. She saw Firmin Richard's face and it was a terrible sight. The honored Director of the Opera looked as if he was ready to explode. The fury that knotted him inside was now manifest through the purplish color of his irate face and the malevolent fire in his eyes. He said nothing, as he was incapable of uttering a single word. However, he was able to act! His left arm lashed out to seize the unfortunate Madame Giry, then forced her to turn around with such an unexpected motion that she uttered a small cry of panic. The honored Director's right foot followed his action, and imprinted its mark on the back of Madame Giry's black taffeta skirt, which had certainly never before been visited with such outrage.

This had all happened so suddenly, that Madame Giry found herself back in the waiting-room, bewildered and not having fully understood what had occurred. But, eventually, understand she did, and the entire Opera rang with her screams of indignation, her violent protests and assorted threats. It required three stagehands to remove her from the building and two policemen to escort her home.

About that same time, Mademoiselle Carlotta, who lived in a small hotel on the Rue du Faubourg-St.Honoré, rang for her maid, who brought the day's post to her in bed. Among it was an anonymous missive, which read:

"If you sing tonight, a great misfortune will befall you... a misfortune worse than death."

The letter was written in *red ink*, in strange and curiously labored handwriting, not unlike that of a child.

After reading the letter, Mademoiselle Carlotta's appetite for breakfast vanished. She pushed away the cup of steamy chocolate prepared by her maid, sat up in bed and thought furiously. It wasn't the first letter of this kind that she had ever received, but the others had not been phrased in such a threatening manner.

In those days, she sincerely believed that she was, indeed, the target of a thousand jealous plots and often said that she had a secret enemy who had sworn to ruin her. She swore that a wicked scheme was being hatched against her, a cabal that would come to a head one of these days; but she added that she was not the type of woman to be easily intimidated.

To be frank, if there was a cabal of any kind, it was led by Mademoiselle Carlotta herself and directed against poor Christine, who suspected nothing. The older woman had never forgiven the young girl for her triumph when taking the diva's place at the last minute.

When Mademoiselle Carlotta had heard of the astounding reception bestowed upon her understudy, she found herself immediately cured of an incipient attack of bronchitis and a bad fit of sulking against Management. She lost the slightest inclination to leave her job and, from that moment, used all her considerable influence to "smother" her rival, enlisting the services of powerful friends to persuade the Directors not to give Christine any new opportunities for glory. Newspapers which had begun to praise the young singer's talent suddenly switched to covering only Mademoiselle Carlotta's latest successes. Finally, inside the Opera, the famous diva made the most scandalous remarks about Christine and tried to cause her endless minor difficulties.

Mademoiselle Carlotta had neither heart nor soul. She was but an instrument, albeit a beautiful one. Her repertory included every opera that might test an ambitious singer, from the German masters to the Italians and French. Never had anyone ever heard her sing off-key, nor lack the power in her voice to do justice to any aria in her immense repertory. As an instrument, she had range, she was powerful and finely-tuned. But no one would have told Mademoiselle Carlotta what Rossini once said to Mademoiselle Krauss after she sang for him in German, his *Dark Forest* from *William Tell*: "You sang with your soul, my dear, and it is a beautiful soul!"

Where was Mademoiselle Carlotta's soul when she danced in Barcelona's taverns of ill-repute? Where was it, later, when she sang lurid music-hall ballads on the small, pitiful stages of Paris? Where was her soul when she sang for her future patrons as they gathered at the homes of one of her many lovers, displaying the flexible voice that could sing equally well, and with the most sublime indifference, a song about the purest of loves or a ribald, orgiastic ballad? If Mademoiselle Carlotta had ever had a soul, and had merely lost it, she could have reclaimed it when she sang Juliet, El-vire, Ophelia or Marguerite. For there were many who started from the lower depths but were redeemed by the combination of their art–and love.

To be fair, when I recall all the small insults and indigni-ties that Christine Daae suffered because of Mademoiselle Carlotta, I can hardly contain my anger. It is not altogether surprising, therefore, that I occasionally digress about art in general, and singing in particular, in a way that the admirers of Mademoiselle Carlotta may not find to their liking.

When Mademoiselle Carlotta had finished pondering the threat contained in the mysterious letter, she got up.

"We shall see," she said, adding a few oaths in her native Spanish with a determined air.

However, when she looked out her window, the first thing she saw was a hearse. The sight of it–a dire omen–cou-pled with the letter convinced her that she was running the greatest of risks if she did indeed sing that night. She gathered all her supporters, told them that she had been threatened by a cabal undoubtedly organized by Christine Daae and declared that they must strike back by filling the house with her own admirers. She had no lack of them, had she? She relied upon them to be prepared for any eventuality and to silence her enemies if, as she feared, they were intent on creating a public disturbance.

Monsieur Richard's private secretary, who had called to inquire about the diva's health, returned to the Opera with the assurance that she was perfectly well and that, "were she dy-ing," she would sing the part of Marguerite that night. As the secretary had urged her, on the Directors' behalf, to commit

105

no imprudence, to remain home for the rest of the day and to avoid drafts, Mademoiselle Carlotta could not help, after he had left, but make a connection between this rather unusual and unexpected advice and the threats contained in the letter.

It was 5 p.m. when the post brought a second anonymous letter in the same handwriting as the first. It was short and said simply:

"*You have a cold. If you are wise, you will realize that it is madness to try to sing tonight.*"

Carlotta sneered, shrugged her beautiful shoulders and sang two or three notes to reassure herself.

Her friends were as good as their word. They all went to the Opera that night, but looked in vain for the cabal of conspirators they were supposed to fight. There were a few *irregulars*, respectable bourgeois whose placid faces showed nothing but their desire to hear for the umpteenth time a piece of music which had long ago conquered their hearts. The *regulars* were subscribers whose fine, elegant and dignified manners rendered absurd any possibility of public disturbance. The only unusual thing was the presence of Messrs. Richard and Moncharmin in Box No. 5. The diva's admirers thought that, perhaps, the Directors had gotten wind of the cabal themselves and had decided to be present in the theater in person in order to nip any scandal in the bud. But, as we know, this was not the case at all. Messrs. Richard and Moncharmin were thinking only of the Phantom.

> "*Rien! En vain j'interroge, en mon ardente veille*
> *La Nature et le Créateur.*
> *Pas une voix ne glisse à mon oreille*
> *Un mot consolateur!*" [8]

---

[8] "*Nothing! In vain do I call, in my ardent vigil / On Nature and the Creator / Not a voice slips into my ear / A word of consolation!*"

The famous baritone, Carolus Fonta, had barely finished Doctor Faust's first appeal to the Powers of Darkness, when Monsieur Firmin Richard, who was sitting in the Phantom's own seat–*the right corner seat of the front row*–leaned over to his associate and, in a good mood, asked him:

"Has a *Voice* whispered in your ear yet?"

"Patience! Don't be in such a hurry," replied Monsieur Armand Moncharmin, using the same cheerful tone. "The performance has just begun and you know that the Phantom doesn't usually arrive until the middle of the first act."

The whole first act passed without incident, which did not surprise Mademoiselle Carlotta's admirers, since Marguerite does not sing in it. As for the Directors, when the curtain fell, they looked at each other, smiling,.

"One down!" said Moncharmin.

"Yes, the Phantom appears to be late," replied Firmin Richard.

"It's not a bad house," said Moncharmin, "for a *cursed theater*."

Richard smiled and pointed to a fat, somewhat common woman, dressed in black, sitting in the middle of the auditorium, flanked on either side by two men in cheap frock-coats.

"Who on Earth are those wretches?" asked Moncharmin.

"Those *wretches*, as you call them, my dear fellow, are my concierge, her husband and her brother."

"You gave them tickets?"

"I did. My concierge had never been to the Opera–this is her first time–and since she is now going to be working here every night, I wanted her to have a good seat before she spends her evenings showing other people to theirs."

Moncharmin asked what he meant and Richard answered that he had persuaded his concierge, in whom he had the greatest confidence, to take over Madame Giry's position as usherette.

"Speaking of Madame Giry," said Moncharmin, "did you know that she plans to file a complaint against you."

"With whom? The Phantom?"

The Phantom! Moncharmin had almost forgotten him. And, in fact, that mysterious person was presently doing nothing to attract the Directors' attention.

Suddenly, the door of their box opened as a bewildered stage manager entered.

"What's the matter?" they both asked, amazed to see him there right before the beginning of the second act.

"I've just heard there's a plot against Carlotta started by Christine Daae's friends. Carlotta's furious."

"What now?" said Richard, furring his brows.

But the curtain rose on the feast at the beginning of Act II and Richard signaled that the stage manager should leave.

When the two were again alone, Moncharmin leaned over to Richard:

"Daae has friends?" he asked.

"Yes, she has."

"Who?"

Richard discreetly pointed at another box on the first tier with only two occupants.

"The Comte de Chagny?"

"Yes. He spoke to me on her behalf with such enthusiasm that if I didn't know him to be La Sorelli's friend..."

"Hmm... And who is the pale young man sitting next to him?"

"That's his brother, the Vicomte."

"He should be in bed. He looks ill."

Meanwhile, the stage rang with an ode to wine, a cheerful song celebrating drunkenness:

> "*Vin ou bière,*
> *bière ou vin,*
> *Que mon verre*
> *soit plein!*" [9]

---

[9] "*Wine or beer, / beer or wine, / May my glass / be full!*"

Students, bourgeois, soldiers, girls and matrons whirled light-heartedly in front of an inn with the sign of Bacchus above its doors. Siebel made her entrance.

Christine Daae looked charming in boy's clothes. Her fresh youth and melancholy grace were irresistibly seductive. Mademoiselle Carlotta's admirers expected to hear her greeted with an ovation that would have enlightened them as to the intentions of her friends. Of course, if there really were those with evil intentions, such an ovation would have been a foolish and clumsy move. But nothing happened.

In fact, what occurred when Marguerite crossed the stage and sang the only two lines given her in this second act was unexpected:

> "*Non, messieurs! Je ne suis demoiselle ni belle,*
> *Et je n'ai pas besoin qu'on donne la main!*" [10]

It was Mademoiselle Carlotta who was greeted with enthusiastic applause. It was so out-of-proportion and uncalled for, that those who knew nothing about the plot looked at each other and wondered what was happening. That act also ended without incident.

Everyone said: "Of course, it will be during the next act." Some, who claimed to be better informed than the rest, declared that the "row" would begin with the ballad of the *King of Thule* and rushed to the subscribers' entrance to warn the diva.

The Directors left their box during the intermission to find out more about the so-called cabal about which the stage manager had warned them, but they soon returned to their seats, shrugging their shoulders and dismissing the whole affair as nonsense. The first thing they saw, on entering the box, was a small carton of English candy on the little shelf. Who had put it there? They asked the usherettes, but no one had

---

[10] "*No, my lord, not a lady am I, nor yet a beauty, / And I do not need an arm to help me on my way!*"

seen anything. They went back inside the box and this time, next to the candy, they found an opera glass. They looked at each other. This time, they had no desire to laugh. Everything Madame Giry had told them came back into their thoughts... They began to feel a strange draft around them... They sat down in silence, truly mystified.

The scene now showed Marguerite's garden:

> "*Faites-lui mes aveux,*
> *Portez mes voeux...*" [11]

As Christine sang her first two lines, a bunch of roses and lilacs in her hand, she raised her head and saw the Vicomte de Chagny in his box. After that, her voice became less sure, less pure, less crystal-like than usual. Something seemed to deaden and dull her singing. Someone who knew her, might have detected an undercurrent of fear...

"How strange she is!" said one of Carlotta's admirers in the orchestra, almost loud enough to be overheard. "The other night, she was divine, and tonight she's simply bleating. No experience, no training."

> "*C'est en vous que j'ai foi,*
> *Parlez pour moi.*" [12]

The Vicomte put his head in his hands and wept. Behind him, the Comte viciously chewed the ends of his mustache, shrugged his shoulders and frowned. Normally a calm, controlled man, betraying his inner feelings in such a fashion was a sign of extreme anger. And angry he was. He had seen his brother return from his sudden, mysterious journey in an alarming state. Raoul's explanation had not made the Comte feel any more reassured and, wishing to find out once and for all where Christine stood, he had requested an appointment to

---

[11] "*Give her my confession, / Carry my wishes...*"
[12] "*It is in you that I have faith, / Tell her from me.*"

see her. She, in turn, had had the audacity to reply that she would not see either him or his brother. At first, he thought it was some devious scheme of hers. He could not forgive Christine for making Raoul suffer, but even more, he could not forgive Raoul for suffering over Christine. What had possessed his brother to become interested in a minor singer whose single triumph still remained incomprehensible to all?

> *"Que la fleur sur sa bouche*
> *Sache au moins déposer*
> *Un doux baiser."* [13]

"The shameless hussy!" growled the Comte.

He wondered what she really wanted. What she hoped for... Rumor had it that she was virtuous, had no friend, no "protector" of any kind... This angelic girl from the North must be very cunning, he thought...

Raoul, behind the curtain of his hands that hid his child-like tears, was thinking only of the letter he had received upon his return to Paris, Christine having fled Perros like a thief in the night and having reached the capitol before him. It read:

My Dear Old Friend:

You must have the courage to never see me again, to never speak to me again... If you love me just a little, do this for me, for the girl who will never forget you, my dearest Raoul. And above all, never again enter my dressing-room! *My life depends upon it. Your life depends upon it.*

Your Dear Christine

Suddenly, there was thunderous applause. Mademoiselle Carlotta had just made her entrance.

The scene in the garden unfolded as it always did. After Marguerite had finished singing the ballad of the *King of*

---

[13] *"May the flower on her mouth / Try at least to deposit / A sweet kiss."*

Thule, she was loudly cheered. And again when she reached the end of the famous jewel song:

> *"Ah! Je ris de me voir*
> *Si belle en ce miroir..."* [14]

Sure of herself, sure of the friends who sat in the house, sure of her voice and of her success, fearing nothing, Mademoiselle Carlotta flung herself whole-heartedly into the part with energy, enthusiasm and overindulgence... Her art was without modesty nor shame. She no longer played Marguerite, instead, she was closer to Carmen. She was applauded all the more. Her duo with Faust seemed ready to bring her a new height of success, when suddenly... a truly dreadful thing happened. Faust was kneeling before her, singing:

> *"Laisse-moi, laisse-moi contempler ton visage,*
> *Sous la pâle clarté*
> *dont l'astre de la nuit, comme dans un nuage,*
> *Caresse ta beauté!"* [15]

And Marguerite sang back:

> *"O silence! O bonheur! Ineffable mystère!*
> *Enivrante langueur!*
> *J'écoute! Et je comprends cette voix solitaire*
> *Qui chante dans mon coeur!"* [16]

---

[14] *"Ah my beauty past compare, / These jewels bright I wear..."*

[15] *"Let me, let me gaze on your face, / Under the pale light / Of the star of night which like a cloud, / Caresses thy beauty!"*

[16] *"Oh silence! Oh happiness! Ineffable mystery! / Intoxicating languor! / I listen! I understand this lonely voice / Which sings inside my heart!"*

Just then, at that very moment, the thing happened... The truly dreadful thing...

The entire audience rose from their seats like a single entity. The two Directors in their box could not suppress their exclamations of horror. Spectators looked at each other as if asking themselves how such an entirely unexpected thing could have happened. Mademoiselle Carlotta's face expressed only the most intense pain; her eyes were haunted by a look of madness. The poor woman stood at the center of the stage, her mouth still half-open from having just sung "...*Cette voix solitaire qui chante dans mon coeur*," but she was not singing any more. *She did not dare sing a note or even utter a single word*!

That mouth which had been born for music, that supple instrument that nad never before failed, that magnificent organ which had produced the most wonderful sounds, handled the most difficult harmonies, the softest tremolos, the most fiery cadences, that sublime human singing machine that only needed Heavenly fire to become a goddess, to raise souls and move hearts... That amazing mouth had uttered...

That amazing mouth had let out...

...*A croak*!

Ah! The awful, hideous, horrid, ghastly, repulsive, dreadful, frightful, shocking croak!

How could it have happened? Had it been dangerously lurking behind the diva's vocal chords, lying in wait for its opportunity to treacherously escape her mouth and... croak!

Croak! Croak! Ah! The dreadful thing!

It was almost as if an invisible toad had leaped from the diva's throat. No one could see the wretched beast, but all could hear it. Croak!

The audience was aghast. Never had any frog on any lily pad shatterered the silence of the night as effectively as that awful croak.

And it was such a wholly unexpected sound, too. Mademoiselle Carlotta could believe neither her larynx nor her ears. Lightning crashing down from the skies to her feet could not have surprised her more than the full-throated croak that had just spilled from her mouth.

And lightning would not have destroyed her so utterly, whereas the croak spelled the end of her career. Some singers had even been known to die from such humiliation.

Dear God! Who could have imagined such a thing! She was so beautifully singing "*Et je comprends cette voix solitaire qui chante dans mon coeur,*" effortelessly, as always, with the same ease as you or I would have had saying "Good Morning, Madam, how are you today?"

One cannot deny that there are arrogant singers who make the mistake of overestimating their talent and, in their pride, try to use the mediocre voice God gave them to reach heights and sing notes that have been denied them since birth. To punish them, God causes them to croak when they attempt such follies. Everyone knows this to be the case. But no one thought that Mademoiselle Carlotta, who could easily have reached two octaves higher, was one of those unfortunate singers.

No one had forgotten her strident *contre-fa*s, her incredible *staccati* in *The Magic Flute*. Everyone remembered her *Don Juan* where she sang Elvire and achieved the most amazing triumph when, one night, she sang the *bemol* that her colleague who sang Doña Anna could not reach. So, then, why this incomprehensible croak at the end of that insignificant, complacent, trifling "*voix solitaire qui chante dans mon coeur?*"

It was unnatural. There to be some kind of devilry behind it. That croak smelled of brimstone. Poor miserable, wretched, despairing, crushed Carlotta!

The uproar in the house was indescribable. If that thing had happened to anyone but Mademoiselle Carlotta, she would have been booed off of the stage. But everyone knew how perfect her voice was, and therefore, there was no anger, only horror and dismay, the sort of dismay that men must have felt when they witnessed the catastrophe that broke the arms of the

Venus de Milo... And at least they saw the blow... Understood its effect...

But here? The croak was utterly incomprehensible!

So much so that, after a few seconds spent in asking herself if she had really heard that note—was it a note, that sound? —could one even call it a sound, for isn't a sound still part of music?—that infernal noise that had escaped her throat, Mademoiselle Carlotta tried to persuade herself that it had not, and that instead she had been the victim of an audible hallucination and not of a treasonous act on the part of her larynx...

On the verge of panic, she cast her eyes around, looking for a refuge, some kind of protection, or more likely the reassurance that her voice was still untainted. Her fingers were clutched her throat in an unconscious gesture of defense and protest. No! No! That croak could never have been hers! It seemed that her singing partner, Carolus Fonta, shared her opinion for he looked at her with an indescribable expression of childlike stupefaction. He had stood next to her when *that* had happened. He had not left her side. Perhaps he might explain what had happened? But no, he could not. His eyes were firmly rooted on Carlotta's mouth in the way that a child stares at a magician's hat, waiting for the rabbit to pop out. It was as if they were saying, "How could such a tiny mouth release such an enormous croak?"

All of this: the croak, the emotion, the terror, the audience in turmoil, the confusion on stage and backstage as well—where some second roles wore utterly astonished faces— all this, as I have described it, took mere seconds at most.

But those mere seconds seemed endless to Messrs. Moncharmin and Richard in Box No. 5. The two Directors had turned exceedingly pale. This extraordinary and inexplicable catastrophe filled them with a dread which was even more powerful since they had also just had to deal with the direct presence of the Phantom.

They had felt his breath. Moncharmin's hair had stood on end. Richard had wiped the perspiration from his forehead. Yes, the Phantom was there. He was around them, behind them, beside them... They felt his presence without seeing him. They heard his breath, close, so close to them! *One always knows when someone else is present...* Well, now they knew someone was! *They were sure there were three people in the box!* They trembled. They thought of running away, but they dared not... They dared not make a move or exchange a word that would have told the Phantom that they knew he was there! What might happen next? What *would* happen next?

The croak happened!

Their joint cry of horror was heard above all the other sounds in the theater. *They felt the Phantom's strike!* Leaning over the edge of their box, they stared at Mademoiselle Carlotta as if they did not recognize her. The blasted woman may have unwittingly given the signal for another impending catastrophe. Yes, they were waiting for that catastrophe! The Phantom had promised they would have it! The theater was cursed! The two Directors gasped and their chests ached from the weight of the impending catastrophe that was bound to come. Richard's strangled voice was heard calling to Mademoiselle Carlotta:

"Well, go on!"

But the diva did not go on. Instead, bravely, heroically some might say, she started at the beginning of the fatal *couplet* at the end of which. the croak had previously emerged.

A dreadful silence succeeded the uproar. Carlotta's voice alone again filled the stage:

"J'écoute..."

The audience also listened, but not without trepidation...

"...Et je comprends cette voix solitaire croak!
croak! *Qui chante dans mon* croak!"

The croak was back—more powerful than ever!

The theater erupted into a wild tumult. The two Directors collapsed in their chairs and dared not even turn around. They no longer had the strength. The Phantom was chuckling behind their backs! And, at last, they distinctly heard *his* Voice in their right ears, the impossible Voice, the bodyless Voice, that said:

"*Tonight, her singing is bad enough to bring down the chandelier!*"

In tandem, they raised their eyes to the ceiling and uttered a terrible cry. The chandelier, the immense mass of the chandelier, was sliding down, falling towards them at the sound of that diabolical voice. Released from its hook, it dropped from the ceiling and came crashing down in the middle of the orchestra, amidst a thousand screams of horror. It was terrifying. Everyone ran towards the exits. My purpose here is not to retell what is now an historical event. Anyone curious to learn more can check the papers of the day. There were many injured and one dead.

The chandelier had fallen straight down upon the head of the unfortunate woman who had come to the Opera for the first time in her life–the woman whom Monsieur Richard had appointed to replace Madame Giry, the Phantom's own usherette! She died on the spot. The next day, one of the morning papers ran this headline:

"*Five hundred pounds lands on a concierge's head!*"

That was her only epitaph.

Juan Roncagliolo Berger

Chapter Nine
The Mysterious Carriage

The evening was a tragedy for everyone. Mademoiselle Carlotta fell ill immediately after. Christine Daae disappeared following the performance. For the next two weeks, no one saw her, either at the Opera or anywhere else.

That first disappearance, which was not considered scandalous, should not be confused with her later abduction, which happened under mysterious and heartbreaking circumstances.

Naturally, Raoul was the first to be shocked by the diva's absence. He had sent her a letter in care of Madame Valerius and had received no reply. That hadn't particularly surprised him, since he knew Christine's state of mind and her determination to no longer see him, even though he did not understand her reasons.

However, his grief increased and he became seriously alarmed when Christine's name never appeared for any of the performances. *Faust* was put on without her. Around 5 p.m. one afternoon, he went to the Directors' office to inquire about her whereabouts. He thought the two men appeared extremely preoccupied. Even their closest friends barely recognized them: they had lost all their gaiety and spirit. They were seen crossing the stage, heads held low, brows furrowed, faces pale, as if they were haunted by some unspeakable knowledge or had become the victims of one of those abominable twists of fate that, once it takes hold of a man, never lets him go.

The crash of the chandelier had created massive liabilities, but it was hard to get them to talk about it.

The investigation came to the conclusion that it was nothing more than an accident, caused by wear and tear of the chain that suspended the chandelier from the ceiling. Arguably, it was the duty of either the old or new Directors to have looked into such things, thus remedying them in time to prevent any catastrophe.

I feel bound to add that, at that time, Messrs. Richard and Moncharmin seemed so changed, so distracted, so mysterious, so incomprehensible, that many of the subscribers thought that some other event, even more awful than the crash of the chandelier, had affected their states of mind.

In day-to-day business, they were as impatient as ever, except with Madame Giry, who had been reinstated to her functions. With this knowledge, it is not difficult to picture their reception of the Vicomte de Chagny when he came to inquire about Christine. They merely told him that she was taking a few days off. When he asked how many days, they replied curtly that they had no idea, Mademoiselle Daae having requested a personal leave of absence for health reasons.

"Then she's ill!" he cried. "What's wrong with her?"

"We don't know."

"Didn't you send the Opera's doctor to see her?"

"No. She didn't ask for him. And, since we trust her, we took her word."

The whole business seemed rather odd and Raoul left the Opera feeling even more depressed. He decided that whatever embarrassment it might cause, he had no choice but to call on her at the home of Madame Valerius. He remembered the strong words in Christine's letter, forbidding him to try to see her. But all that he had seen in Perros, all that he had heard from behind her dressing-room door, the conversation he had had with her on the moors, all of it caused him to suspect that whatever scheme was afoot, devilish as it appeared, it still had to be the product of a human mind. He thought of Christine's highly strung imagination, her tender and credulous soul, the simple education she had received which had nurtured her childhood with a constant stream of fairy tales, her ever-present obssession with her late father and, above all, the state of sublime ecstasy that she seemed to fall into when she heard music manifest itself in certain exceptional conditions, such as those at the Perros cemetery. All this, to him, seemed to constitute a too fertile a ground for the nefarious designs of some unknown, sinister entity. But of whom was Christine the victim? This was the clearly rational question which Raoul asked himself as he hurried off to visit Madame Valerius.

Indeed, Raoul did have a rational mind. True, he was something of a poet, loved music for its lyrical glory and was fond of the old Breton folk tales where korrigans danced in the moonlight. And, of course, he loved Christine Daae, his dear, northern sprite. Still, for all that, he did not believe in the supernatural, outside of religion, and the most fantastic tale in the world would never have made him forget that two plus two make four.

What would he learn from Madame Valerius? His hand shook as he rang the bell of her small apartment in the Rue Notre-Dame-des-Victoires.

The same maid whom he had seen coming out of Christine's dressing-room that fateful night answered the door. He asked to speak to Madame Valerius. He was told that she was ill, in bed and unable to see visitors.

"Please take her my card," he asked.

He did not have long to wait. The maid returned and showed him into a small, scantily furnished drawing-room, on the walls of which, facing each other, hung portraits of Professor Valerius and old Monsieur Daae.

"Madame begs Monsieur le Vicomte to excuse her," said the maid. "She can only see him in her bedroom, because she can no longer stand on her poor legs."

Five minutes later, Raoul was ushered into a poorly-lit room where, in the semi-darkness of an alcove, he at once recognized the good, kind face of Christine's benefactress. Madame Valerius' hair was now entirely white, but her eyes had not aged in the least. On the contrary, their expression had never been so bright, so pure, so child-like.

"Monsieur de Chagny!" she cried gaily, holding out both her hands to her visitor. "Ah, Heaven must have sent you to me! I can at last talk about *her*!"

This last sentence sounded rather ominous to the young man's ears. He immediately asked:

"Dear Madame... where is Christine?"

The old lady calmly replied:

"She is with her guardian angel!"

"What guardian angel?" exclaimed poor Raoul.

"Why, the *Angel of Music*!"

Appalled, the Vicomte collapsed into a chair. Could it be? Christine with the *Angel of Music*? And there was Madame Valerius lying in bed, smiling, happy, her finger to her lips, asking him to keep it all secret!

"You mustn't tell anyone!" she added.

"You can rely on me," said Raoul. He hardly knew what he was saying. His notions about Christine's predicament, already confused, were becoming ever more tangled. It seemed as if everything was spinning around him: the room, this wonderfully kind woman with white hair and eyes blue and empty as the sky. "You can rely on me," indeed.

"I know! I know!" she said, with a happy laugh. "Now come closer. Sit next to me like you used to do when you were a boy! Give me your hand, like when you told me the story of Little Lotte, which my poor husband taught you. You know, I'm very fond of you, Raoul. And Christine is, too!"

"Is she?" sighed the young man. He found it difficult to collect his thoughts and reconcile Madame Valerius' "guardian angel," the Angel of Music that Christine had so strangely mentioned to him, the *death's-head* which he had seen in his nightmarish vision in the little church in Perros–and the *Phantom of the Opera*, whose reputation had come to his attention one night when he was visiting backstage and overheard several stagehands repeating the ghastly description of it that Joseph Buquet had made just before his mysterious death.

"What makes you think that Christine is fond of me, Madame?" he asked in a low voice.

"She used to talk about you every day."

"Really? And what did she say?"

"She said that you had proposed to her!"

And the kind, old lady began laughing heartily, showing all her pearly white teeth which she had proudly managed to keep. Raoul sprang from his chair, red as a beet, suffering to the core of his being.

"What? Where are you going? Sit down, please! You don't think I'd let you go like that? You're angry with me for laughing? I'm sorry. After all, what happened isn't your fault. You couldn't know. You were young. You thought Christine was free..."

"Is she engaged?" the unfortunate Raoul asked, in a choking voice.

"No! Of course, not! You know as well as I do that Christine couldn't marry, even if she wanted to!"

"No! I don't know anything of the kind! Why can't she marry?"

"Because of the *Angel of Music*, of course!"

"The Angel..."

"Yes! He's forbidden her!"

"He's forbidden her! The Angel of Music has forbidden her to marry!"

Raoul leaned over Madame Valerius, his jaws clenched so tightly he could barely speak. Had he meant to attack the poor old woman, he could not have looked at her with a fiercer gaze. Sometimes, too much innocence can seem so monstrous that it becomes an object of hatred. And Raoul thought Madame Valerius was far too innocent.

She remained unaware of the terrible stare that loomed above her and continued on as if what she was saying was the most natural thing in the world.

"Well, he's forbidden her without really forbidding her... He just told her that, if she got married, she would never hear him again. That's all! And that he would go away forever! So, you understand, she can't let the *Angel of Music* go. It's quite natural."

"Yes, yes," echoed Raoul breathlessly, "it's quite natural."

"Besides, I thought Christine had told you all this when she saw you in Perros, when she went there with her guardian angel."

"I see. So she went to Perros with her guardian angel, did she?"

"Not quite. He had arranged to meet her in the cemetery, at Monsieur Daae's grave. He promised to play *The Resurrection of Lazarus* on her father's violin!"

Raoul de Chagny rose and, with impressive authority in his voice, asked:

"Madame, will you be kind enough to tell me where this guardian angel lives?"

The old lady did not seem the least surprised by this rather rude question. She raised her eyes and replied:

"In Heaven!"

Such naivete baffled him. Her candid and innocent faith in an angel who came down nightly from Heaven to visit the dressing-rooms at the Opera left him speechless.

He now understood the state of mind of a girl who had been brought up by a superstitious fiddler and an old woman prone to angelic visions, and shuddered when he thought of the consequences.

"Is Christine still virtuous?" he could not keep himself from asking.

"I swear it on my soul!" exclaimed the old woman, who, for the first time, seemed indignant. "And, if you doubt it, Monsieur, I don't know why you are here!"

Raoul tore at his gloves.

"How long has she known this guardian angel?"

"About three months... Yes, it's been just over three months since he began to give her singing lessons."

The Vicomte threw his arms in the air in a great gesture of angry despair, then, feeling crushed, let them fall back to his sides.

"So the guardian angel gives her singing lessons! Where?"

"Now that she has gone off with him, I can't say. But until two weeks ago, it was in her dressing-room. It would have been impossible in this small apartment. The whole house would have heard them. Whereas, at the Opera, at 8 a.m., there's no one about, you see?"

"Yes, I see! I see!" cried the Vicomte.

And he hurriedly said goodbye to Madame Valerius, who was left wondering if the young nobleman wasn't a little wrong in the head.

When he crossed the drawing-room, Raoul again saw the maid and, for a brief moment, wanted to question her as well, but he thought he saw a strange, fleeting smile on her lips. He feared she might make fun of him and practically ran out the door. Besides, what more did he need to know? He had sought information and he had found it. What else was there to find? He walked home to his brother's house in a pitiful state.

He could have struck himself, banged his head against the walls! To have believed in such innocence, such purity! He had tried to make sense of it because of her naivete, her simple faith, her immaculate candor... But the *Angel of Music*! He knew who he was now! He could almost see him! He was undoubtedly some handsome tenor, a good-looking ruffian who leered as he sang! He felt he had reached the point where he was as ridiculous and miserable as he could possibly be. "Oh, what a wretched, insignificant, silly young man the Vicomte de Chagny had become!" thought Raoul, enraged. And what a brazen and damnably cunning creature Christine had become!

Nevertheless, the long walk through the streets of Paris had helped him to calm down a little. When he went to his room, all he wanted was to collapse onto the bed and soak it with his tears. But his brother was there, waiting for him. Raoul fell into his arms, like a child. The Comte consoled him, without asking for any explanation. In any event, Raoul would have hesitated to tell him the story of the *Angel of Music*.. There are things one does not brag about, and others which are simply too embarrassing to whine about.

The Comte took Raoul out for dinner at a popular cabaret. Overcome as he was with despair, Raoul would almost certainly have refused to go if Philippe had not told him, as an inducement, that the lady of his heart had been spotted, the previous night, in company of a man in the Bois de Boulogne. At first, Raoul refused to believe him, but he heard so many details that at last he had no choice but to accept it. It turned out to be the most banal of stories. She had been seen in a carriage with the window down. She merely seemed to be taking in the icy night air. There was a glorious Moon shining. She was recognized beyond any doubt. As for her companion, only his shadowy outline was seen leaning back against the seat in the dark. The carriage was moving at a leisurely pace on a lonely road just behind the grandstands of Longchamp.

Raoul dressed in frantic haste, prepared to forget his grief by throwing himself entirely into a "whirlwind of pleasures," as people say. Unfortunately, he was exceedingly poor company that night, and leaving his brother early, at 10 p.m., found himself inside a cab passing behind the Longchamp race track.

It was bitterly cold. The road appeared to be deserted and all was bright under the moonlight. He told the driver to wait for him at a nearby corner and, hiding himself as well as he could, he waited, stamping his feet to keep warm.

He had been indulging in this odd exercise for about a half-hour, when a carriage coming from the direction of Paris turned the corner and drove quietly in his direction, at a leisurely pace.

He immediately thought: "it's her!" His heart began thumping in his chest, the same heavy beats that he had felt in the corridor when he heard the *Voice* behind her dressing-room door. God! How he loved her!

The carriage was approaching. He dared not move an inch. He waited. If it was she, he was prepared to jump into the carriage and have a face-to-face confrontation with the *Angel of Music*!

A few yards more and the carriage would be right next to him. He had no doubt that it was her. Indeed, he saw a woman's head leaning out of the window.

Suddenly, the Moon shed a pale gleam over her features.

"Christine!"

The sacred name of his love had sprung from his heart to his lips. He could not stop it. He would have leaped forth to call it back if he could, for that name, uttered in the stillness of the night, became the signal for the carriage to begin a mad rush, causing it to accelerate past him before he could react. The carriage window had been closed and the girl's face had disappeared. He ran towards the cab, but the carriage was already no more than a small black spot on the white road.

He called out again: "Christine!" No reply. He stopped, swallowed by the silence.

He stared up at the sky, looking at the cold stars in despair. He beat his chest. He was the epitome of unrequited love.

With a melancholy gaze, he looked at the cold, desolate road and the pale, dead night. But nothing could be colder, nor more dead than his own heart. He had loved an angel and now he despised a woman!

"Raoul, that dear Northern sprite has mocked you!" he thought. How could one with such a fresh, innocent face, shy and all-too-ready to wear the blush of modesty, spend the night alone in carriage with a mysterious lover? Shouldn't there be some limits to hypocrisy and deception? Had she any right to have pure, child-like eyes when she had the soul of a courtesan?

She had fled without answering his cry.

But then, why had he felt it necessary to hunt her down and almost jump in front of her carriage?

What right did he have to pursue her so when all she had asked was for him to forget her?

"Go away! Leave! You're nothing to her!"

He wanted to die, and he was only 21-years-old!

In the morning, his valet found him sitting on his bed. He had not undressed, and at the sight of his despairing face, the servant feared that some horrible disaster had occurred. Raoul snatched the letter the man had brought for him. He had recognized Christine's paper and her handwriting. She wrote:

Dear Raoul:

Two nights from now, go to the masked ball at the Opera. At midnight, be in the little salon behind the fireplace in the grand foyer. Stand next to the door that leads to the Rotunda. Don't mention this rendezvous to anyone. Wear a white domino cloak and be well-masked. If you love me, make sure no one recognizes you.

Christine

Seth Fisher

Sam Hiti

Chapter Ten
The Masked Ball

The envelope was spattered with mud and unstamped. It bore the words "To be delivered to Monsieur le Vicomte de Chagny," with the address written in pencil. It must have been thrown outside in the hope that a passer-by would pick it up and hand-deliver it, which was just what had happened. The letter had been found on the sidewalk in the Place de l'Opera. Raoul read it yet again with fevered eyes.

Nothing else was needed to revive his shattered hopes. His newly conceived dark image of a Christine who had forgotten her morals and self-respect was replaced by his original notion of an innocent and unfortunate child who was the victim of her carelessness and overly emotional personality. But to what extent, exactly, was she a victim? And of whom? Into what kind of disaster had she been dragged? He asked himself these distressing questions, but the pain they caused was bearable compared to the fury he had experienced when contemplating the notion of a lying, deceitful Christine. What had happened? Under whose influence was she? What kind of monster had carried her off and how had he succeeded?

The answer to this last question could be nothing other than music! The more he thought about it, the more he was convinced that music held the key to the mystery. He still remembered the fervor in her voice when, in Perros, she told him she had been visited by the *Angel of Music*. He would need clues to help him dispel the darkness that shrouded this whole matter. He knew the deep despair Christine had felt after her father's death, and the aversion she had developed for daily life, including her art. She had gone through the Conservatoire like a wretched, singing automaton. Then, suddenly, she was reborn, as if through some kind of Heavenly intervention. The *Angel of Music* had come! She had sung Marguerite in *Faust* and triumphed!

The *Angel of Music*!... Who was impersonating him for Christine's benefit? Who, knowing the folk tale dear to Monsieur Daae's heart, had used it so fiendishly well that the girl had become putty in his hands, malleable to his every wish?

Raoul knew that a similar incident had occurred once before. He remembered a story about the Princess Belmonte of Naples, who had lost her husband and whose immense despair had progressed to stupor. For a month, she was unable to either speak or even cry. Her physical and moral inertia had grown worse with every passing day and the slow disintegration of her sanity would not have taken long to bring about her own death. Every day her servants carried her to the Gardens, but she barely seemed aware of her surroundings. Meanwhile, Raff, the great German singer was visiting the city and wanted to see its famous Gardens, celebrated far and wide for their beauty. One evening, one of the Princess' ladies-in-waiting had the inspiration of asking the artist if he would sing for her mistress, while he remained hidden behind a bush. The German tenor agreed and sang a simple melody that the Princess had often sung with her husband during the early days of their marriage. It was a beautiful and moving song. The melody, the words, the artist's admirable voice, everything combined to break through the Princess' despair. Tears suddenly appeared in her eyes! She was finally able to weep! She was saved and became persuaded that her late husband, that evening, had come down from Heaven to sing "their" song.

"That evening," thought Raoul. "Yes, a single evening perhaps, but such a masquerade could not have endured without a repeat of the exact, same conditions..."

The unfortunate, grieving Princess Belmonte would have eventually discovered Raff hiding behind the bush if she had returned to the Gardens every night for three months.

Yet, for three months the *Angel of Music* had been giving Christine singing lessons... Clearly, he was a most devoted teacher! And now, he was taking her for drives in the Bois de Boulogne!

Raoul's fingers clutched at his flesh, above his jealous heart. He even drew a few droplets of blood. Being inexperienced in love, he now asked himself with terror what game the girl was playing, inviting him to a masked ball? How far would an opera singer go to make a fool of a lovesick young man? O misery!

Thus did Raoul's thoughts vacillate between extremes. He no longer knew whether he should pity Christine–or hate her. So he pitied and hated her in turn–but just in case, he also bought a white domino.

Finally, it was the hour of the rendezvous. With his face hidden behind a mask trimmed with long, thick lace, looking like a pierrot in his white makeup, the Vicomte thought he appeared perfectly ridiculous. A man of the world did not disguise himself to go to the Opera! He was laughable. Only one thought consoled him: no one would be likely to recognize him! The costume had another advantage: he would be able to move about freely, with his heavy heart and sad soul, without needing to pretend he was happy. He had no need to compose his face into a mask, since he was already wearing one!

This Opera ball was an exceptional affair, given just before Mardi-Gras in honor of the birthday of a famous artist, a student of Gavarni whose pencil had immortalized the figures of Carnival and the drunken procession from Belleville that was known as the *descente de la Courtille*. Thus, it was expected to be much more joyful, noisier and more Bohemian than an ordinary masked ball. Numerous performers had arranged to be there, escorted by a huge entourage of models and dandies who, by midnight, would be making quite a ruckus.

Raoul walked up the grand staircase at 11:55 p.m. He did not linger to stare at the colorfully costumed guests parading themselves on its marble steps against one of the world's most magnificent stages. He did not let any facetious mask engage him in banter. He did not respond to any jokes and ignored the overly familiar invitations of several couples who had already become a trifle too convivial. After crossing the grand foyer and managing to escape a *farandole* of dancers which had almost caught him, he finally stepped inside the room described in Christine's letter. He found it crammed, for it was the intersection where those going to supper at the Rotunda met up with those who were returning from having had a few glasses of champagne. The excitement was intense and euphoric. He thought that Christine had chosen this place for her mysterious rendezvous because they would be less noticed there amongst all the commotion than in an isolated, lonely corner.

Raoul leaned against the door and waited. He did not wait long. A black domino glided by and gave the tips of his fingers a quick squeeze. He understood that it was her and followed:

"Is that you, Christine?" he whispered, between clenched teeth.

The black domino quickly turned back and touched her finger to her lips, undoubtedly warning him to not mention her name again.

Raoul continued to follow her in silence.

He was afraid of losing her, after meeting her again in this peculiar fashion. His anger was gone. It was clear to him now that she had nothing for which to reproach herself, no matter how bizarre and inexplicable her behavior had been. He was ready to make any act of forgiveness, contrition—or humiliation. He was in love. And he was sure he would soon receive complete justification for her unexplained absence.

The black domino turned back from time to time to see if the white domino continued to follow her.

As Raoul again crossed the grand foyer, this time led by his masked guide, he could not help noticing the presence of a small crowd gathering amongst the larger crowd... Amidst all the extravagantly disguised guests, one group had assembled around a character whose costume's originality and rather macabre appearance was causing a sensation.

It was a man dressed entirely in scarlet, with a large feather-brimmed hat sitting atop a death's-head. Ah! What a wonderfully realistic death's-head it was too! The dandies pressed around him to congratulate him, praise him for his accomplishment, asking him which shop, what masterly makeup artist, obviously one of Hades' own assistants, had made him up, painted him, applied on him such a marvelous death's-head! The Grim Reaper himself must have served as his model.

The man with the death's-head, the feather-brimmed hat and the scarlet attire dragged an immense red-velvet cloak, which hung from his shoulders and trailed along the floor behind him as if he was a king. Embroidered in gold letters on the cloak were the following words, which everyone read and repeated aloud: "*Do Not Touch Me*! *I Am The Red Death Stalking The Land*!"

Despite the words, one guest did try to touch him... but a skeletal hand shot out of a crimson sleeve and violently seized the fool's wrist; and he, feeling the grip of naked bones, the fierce grasp of Death who would never let him go, uttered a cry of pain and terror. When the Red Death eventually released him, the man ran off like a madman, pursued by the jeers of the other guests.

It was at that exact moment that Raoul passed in front of the macabre character, who had just happened to turn in his direction. He nearly exclaimed:

"The death's-head from Perros-Guirec!"

For he had recognized him! He wanted to dart forward, forgetting Christine, but the black domino, who also seemed under the spell of some strange sensation, caught him by the wrist and pulled him away from the grand foyer, away from the hellish crowd that was being stalked by the Red Death...

The black domino was constantly looking behind her and, twice, appeared to see something that terrified her, for she quickened her pace, dragging Raoul behind her, as if she feared they were being pursued.

They went up two floors. There, the stairs and corridors were almost deserted. The black domino opened the door of a private box and gestured to the white domino to follow her inside. Then, Christine (whom Raoul now recognized by the sound of her voice) closed the door behind them and warned him, in a whisper, to remain at the back of the box and not show himself. Raoul took off his mask, but Christine kept hers on. As the young man was about to ask her to remove it, he was surprised to see her put her ear to the wall and listen for any sounds that might be coming from the box next to theirs. She then opened the door slightly and looked out into the hallway. In a hushed whisper, she said:

"He must have gone upstairs, to the Blindmen's Box..." Suddenly, she exclaimed: "No! He's coming down!"

She tried to shut the door, but Raoul stopped her. He had seen, at the top of the stairs that led to the floor above, *a scarlet-clad foot*, followed by another... Slowly, majestically, the Red Death appeared before his eyes. Again, he recognized the death's-head he had seen in Perros-Guirec.

"It's him!" Raoul exclaimed. "This time, he won't get away!"

But Christine succeeded in shutting the door before Raoul could rush out. He tried to push her aside.

"What do you mean, *him*?" she asked, in a changed voice. "Who's not going to get away?"

Raoul tried to overcome the girl's resistance by force, but she fought him off with a strength which he would not have suspected her of possessing. He understood, or thought he did, and suddenly lost his temper.

"Who?" he repeated angrily. "Why, *him*! The man who hides behind that hideous death mask! The evil figure I saw in the Perros cemetery! The Red Death! In a word, your friend— your so-called *Angel of Music*! But I'll rip that mask from his face as well as the one from mine and, this time, we'll look at each other, without any disguises or lies between us! I'll find out whom you love and who loves you!"

He broke into an insane laugh, while Christine made a small, painful whimper behind her velvet mask.

With a tragic gesture, she flung her arms wide, creating a barrier of pale flesh against the door.

"For the sake of our love, Raoul, do not go!"

He stopped. What had she just said? "For the sake of our love?" She had never before admitted that she loved him, even though she had had plenty of opportunities. She had watched him, miserable, in tears before her, begging for a word of kindness, which she had not uttered. She had seen him sick, almost dead of terror and cold after the mysterious night in the Perros cemetery. Had she stayed by his side then, when he needed her the most? No! She had fled back to Paris! And now, she said she loved him, spoke of "our love?" Bah! Her only goal was to delay him for a few precious seconds! She wanted to give the Red Death time to escape. "Our love?" She was lying!

So, in a tone of childish petulance, he said:

"You lie, Mademoiselle! You don't love me and you never have! What a naive fool I must be to allow you to mock and ridicule me as you have! Your behavior towards me in Perros, the joy I thought I saw in your eyes, even your very silence, all that gave me reason for hope. An honest hope, as befits an honest man talking to someone whom he believes is an honest woman. Why, Mademoiselle? Was your intention always to deceive me? Well, in that you have succeeded! You have deceived us all, even taking shameful advantage of the naive affections of your benefactress, who continues to believe in your sincerity while you run around the Opera with a man dressed as the Red Death! I despise you!"

He then burst into tears. She had stood by as he insulted her because she thought of only one thing: preventing him from leaving the box.

"Someday you'll beg my forgiveness for all the ugly things you've just said, Raoul, and on that day, I will forgive you!"

He shook his head. "No! No! You've driven me insane! When I think that all I wanted in this life was to give my name to an opera singer..."

"Raoul! My poor Raoul!"

"I'll die of shame!"

"No, dearest Raoul, you must live!" said Christine in a voice that had suddenly become dreadfully grim. "Goodbye, Darling!"

"Goodbye, Christine!"

"Goodbye, Raoul!"

The young man stepped forward, staggering as he moved. He dared one more barb:

"You must permit me to come and applaud you from time to time!"

"I shall never sing again, Raoul!"

"Indeed?" he replied, even more sarcastically. "So he's taking that good care of you? Congratulations! Perhaps we'll meet again in the Bois, one of these nights!"

"Not in the Bois nor anywhere else, Raoul. You won't ever see me again."

"May I at least ask to what dark world you will be returning? For what Hell–or Paradise–are you leaving us, mysterious lady?"

"I had planned to tell you that tonight, darling, but now I can't... I don't think you would believe me, because you've lost your faith in me, Raoul. It's over!"

She had spoken, "It's over!" with such despair that the young man was utterly shaken and began to feel remorse for his earlier cruelty.

"I don't understand!" he cried. "Why can't you tell me what you mean? You're free, without ties. You move about Paris freely. You put on that domino to come to the ball. Why can't you just go home? What have you been doing for these last two weeks? What's that story about the Angel of Music that you told Madame Valerius? Has someone deceived you, taken advantage of your trusting nature? I saw it for myself in Perros. But, you know better! You're no fool, Christine. You know what you're doing. Think of poor Madame Valerius, waiting for you at home, believing you're still with that Angel of yours! Explain yourself, Christine, I beg you! Anyone can be deceived. What is this farce?"

Christine took off her mask and said: "It's no farce, but a tragedy, dearest Raoul!"

When the young Vicomte saw her face, he was unable to suppress a cry of surprise and terror. The fresh complexion she'd always had was gone. A deathly pallor now enveloped her features, which had once been so charming and delicate, reflecting her serene grace and guilt-free conscience. How tormented she now looked! Despair had imprinted small, merciless lines on her face and traced dark, unutterably sad circles under her eyes. Those clear, beautiful eyes that had once been like Little Lotte's, the image of the lakes of her Northern lands, were now bottomless, inky pools of misery.

"My dearest love! I'm so sorry!" he moaned, holding out his arms. "You promised to forgive me..."

"Perhaps! Someday, perhaps!" she said, putting her mask back on. Then, she left, forbidding him to follow her with a gesture.

He tried to run after her, but she turned around and repeated her gesture of farewell with such authority that he dared not try again.

He watched her until she disappeared from sight. Then, he went back downstairs to mingle with the crowd, hardly aware of what he was doing. His head throbbed and his heart ached. As he crossed the dance floor, he asked if anybody had seen the Red Death. They asked: "Who is the Red Death?" and he replied: "A man with a death's-head and a great, scarlet cloak." Everyone told him the Red Death had just gone past, dragging his cloak behind him, but Raoul could not find him anywhere. At 2 a.m., he decided to go backstage to the corridor that led to Christine's dressing-room.

His steps took him to the place where he had first known pain. He knocked at the door, but there was no answer. He went inside, just as he had gone inside when he had been looking everywhere for the *Voice*. The room was empty. A gas lamp was burning, low. He saw some writing paper on a small desk. He thought of composing a letter for Christine, but he heard footsteps in the corridor. He had just enough time to hide in an alcove, which was separated from the rest of the dressing-room by a simple curtain. A hand opened the door. It was Christine.

He held his breath. He desperately wanted to discover her secret! To learn the truth! Something told him that he was at last about to unveil some of the mystery and would perhaps understand what was going on...

Christine entered, removed her mask and, with a weary gesture, dropped it on the table. She sighed and let her pretty head fall into her hands. What was she thinking about? Was she thinking of him? No, for Raoul heard her whisper: "*Poor Erik!*"

At first, he thought he was mistaken. He firmly believed that, if anyone deserved her pity, it was he, Raoul. It would have been quite natural, after what had just taken place between them, if she had said, "Poor Raoul!" But instead, shaking her head, she repeated: "*Poor Erik!*" What did this *Erik* have to do with Christine's suffering and why was she pitying him when he, Raoul, was so unhappy?

Christine then began to write in a calm, deliberate manner, so gracefully that Raoul, who was still shaking from the effects of the tragedy that had torn them apart, was sullenly impressed.

"What coolness!" he said to himself.

She continued to write, filling two, three, then four sheets. Suddenly, she lifted her head and hid the sheets inside her blouse. She seemed to be listening for something. Raoul, too, listened. From where came that strange sound, that faraway music? A faint song seemed to emanate from the very walls... Yes, it was as if the walls themselves were singing! The music grew louder. The words were now distinguishable. He heard a voice, a beautiful, soft, enthralling voice. But, for all its softness, it was the *Voice*, a man's voice, not a woman's... The voice came closer and closer... It came through the wall itself... It was here... *The Voice was in the room*, in front of Christine. Christine rose and addressed the *Voice*, as if she spoke to someone physically standing in front of her:

"Here I am, Erik," she said. "I'm ready. You're the one who is late."

Raoul, who was cautiously peering from behind the curtain, could not believe his eyes–which saw nothing.

Christine's face lit up. A smile of happiness appeared upon her bloodless lips, the smile of someone struck with a deadly disease who first learns there is the hope of recovery.

The disembodied voice continued to sing, bringing together in the same tempo and the same breath the extremes of harmony. Never before in his life had Raoul heard anything more absolutely and intrepidly sweet, more gloriously insidious, more powerfully delicate, more delicately powerful, in short, more irresistibly triumphant. It masterfully contained a set of absolute ideals which, by the mere effect of hearing them, helped raise the ideals of those mere mortals who felt for, loved and expressed themselves through music. It was a pure and serene source of harmony from which the faithful could calmly drink, confident that they drank from the very essence of musical grace. And their own talent, having touched the divine, was also transfigured. Raoul listened to the voice in a fever and at last began to understand how Christine Daae was able to appear one evening, in front of a stupefied audience, singing with a glorious resonance previously unknown, with superhuman exaltation, clearly under the influence of her mysterious and invisible master. And he understood that enormous event even more effortlessly by listening to the voice singing not something exceptional, but something quite ordinary. From vile lead it had been spun into gold. The banal verses, the flamboyance–one might almost say the vulgarity–of the melody appeared even more beautifully transformed when sung by a voice that caused them to soar to un-

141

precedented heights on the wings of passion. For the Heavenly voice was lending its glory to a most profane song.

The voice was singing the wedding night aria from *Romeo and Juliet*.

Raoul saw Christine stretch her arms out to the *Voice* as she had done to the invisible violin playing *The Resurrection of Lazarus* in the Perros cemetery.

Nothing could describe the passion with which the *Voice* sang:

"Fate links thee to me for ever and a day!"

The strains sliced through Raoul's heart. Struggling against the spell that seemed to rob him of his will-power and energy–and of almost all his clarity at a time when he needed it the most–he succeeded in pulling back the curtain that hid him. He walked towards Christine. She herself was moving towards the back of the dressing-room, the whole wall of which was taken up by a great mirror that reflected her image, but not his, for he was just behind her and entirely hidden by her.

"Fate links thee to me for ever and a day!"

Christine walked towards her reflection in the mirror, as her reflection walked towards her. The two Christines–the living one and its image–finished by touching each other. Raoul reached out with his arms to grasp the two in a single embrace.

But, by some kind of dazzling miracle that sent him reeling backwards, the young man was suddenly flung back, while an icy blast swept over his face. He saw not two, but four, eight, 20 Christines spinning around him, laughing at him and fleeing so swiftly that he could not grasp any of them.

At last, everything was again still. He saw himself in the mirror, alone. Christine had vanished.

He rushed up to the mirror. He banged at the walls. Nobody! Though the room still echoed with the sounds of far-off, passionate singing:

"*Fate links thee to me for ever and a day!*"

With his hands, he wiped the sweat from his fevered brow. He pinched himself. He stumbled through the room and turned the gaslight to its full power. He was positive that he was not dreaming. He was at the center of some kind of terrible, powerful, almost supernatural game, a game for which he had no clues and which might end up destroying him. He thought of himself as a daring prince who had crossed into a forbidden land in a fairy tale, and therefore shouldn't be surprised at finding himself the victim of a magical phenomena which he has thoughtlessly unleashed because of his love and which must somehow be conquered...

Where had Christine gone? How would she return?

Would she ever return? Had she not told him that *it was over*? And hadn't he heard the *Voice* repeating: "*Fate links thee to me for ever and a day!*"

To me? To whom?

At last, worn out, beaten, empty-headed, Raoul sat down on the chair that Christine had just left. Like her, he let his head fall into his hands. When he raised it, tears were rolling down his cheeks, real, heavy tears like those of a jealous child, tears that expressed the mundane sorrow all-too-common to every lover on Earth. Suddenly, he said aloud:

"Who is Erik?"

Thomas Zahler

Chapter Eleven
"You Must Forget the Name of the Voice!"

The day after Christine had vanished in a manner so incredible that he was still doubting the evidence of his own eyes, the Vicomte de Chagny called on Madame Valerius. He walked in on a charming sight.

Christine herself was making lace, seated next to the old woman, while the latter was propped up against her pillows, knitting. Never had a more enchanting face, purer features, softer eyes worked on such delicate stitching. The color had returned to the young girl's cheeks. The dark rings under her eyes had gone. Raoul no longer recognized the tragic face of the day before. If the young man had not been able to still detect the melancholy veil that continued to overlay her lovely features–which, to him, represented the only remaining evidence of the bizarre drama in which the enigmatic girl was involved–he would have sworn that Christine had played no part in the events at all.

Emotionless, she rose and offered him her hand. But Raoul's confusion was so great that he stood there, dumbfounded, without moving or saying a word.

"Why, Monsieur de Chagny," exclaimed Madame Valerius, "don't you recognize our dear Christine? Her guardian angel sent her back to us!"

"Mama!" the girl interrupted quickly, while a deep blush rose to her face. "I thought that we agreed we wouldn't discuss this again! You know very well that there's no such thing as the Angel of Music!"

"But, child, he gave you lessons for three months!"

"Mama, I gave you my word that I would explain everything to you soon, and I will... But you promised me that until then, you wouldn't say anything about it, or ask me any questions!"

"If only you would vow never to leave me again! Will you vow that, Christine?"

"Mama, I'm sure this is terribly boring for Monsieur de Chagny."

"On the contrary, Mademoiselle," said the young man, in a voice which he tried to keep firm and brave, but which trembled nevertheless. "Anything that concerns you interests me greatly. I can only hope that you will one day understand how greatly. I can't deny that my surprise at finding you here with your adopted mother equals my joy. After what happened between us yesterday, after what you said and what I saw with my own eyes, I hardly expected to see you again this soon. I would be the first to celebrate your return, if you were not so intent on keeping a secret that could well prove fatal... I have been your friend for far too long not to feel alarmed, just as Madame Valerius does, at your part in some sinister intrigue. It will no doubt remain dangerous, at least until we unravel its threads and I fear you will end up as its victim, Christine."

At his words, Madame Valerius thrashed about on the bed.

"What do you mean?" she cried. "Is Christine in danger?"

"Yes, Madame," said Raoul boldly, firmly ignoring the signs Christine directed towards him.

"My God!" exclaimed the kind, simple old woman, gasping for breath. "You must tell me everything, Christine! Why did you try to reassure me? And what is this danger, Monsieur de Chagny?"

"A charlatan is taking advantage of her good nature."

"Is the Angel of Music a charlatan?"

"She told you herself that there is no Angel of Music."

"But then who is he, in Heaven's name?" begged the old woman. "You will be the death of me!"

"There is a terrible mystery surrounding all of us, Dear Madame, you, me and Christine. A very rational mystery that is far deadlier than any phantom or angel!"

Madame Valerius turned her terrified face towards Christine, but the young girl had already run to her adopted mother and taken her in her arms.

"Don't believe him, Mama, don't believe him," she repeated. She tried to reassure her with her kisses, while the old woman made a series of deep, heart-breaking sighs.

"Then tell me that you will never again leave me," implored the widow.

Christine remained silent, so Raoul continued:

"You must promise, Christine. It's the only thing that will reassure your mother and me. We will agree to not ask you a single question about the past, if you promise to remain under our protection in the future."

"That is something which I haven't asked of you and a promise that I refuse to make!" said the young girl, fiercely. "I am my own woman, Monsieur de Chagny. You have no right to tell me what to do, and I'm asking you to stop interfering in my life. As to what I have or have not done during the past two weeks, only one man in the world would have the right to demand an account of my actions: my husband! Well, I have no husband and I shall never marry!"

She gestured with her hands to emphasize her words and Raoul turned pale, not only because of what she had said, but because he had caught sight of a plain gold ring on Christine's finger.

"You have no husband and yet you wear a wedding-ring?"

He tried to seize her hand, but she swiftly drew it back.

"It's a gift!" she said, blushing again and unsuccessfully trying to hide her embarrassment.

"Christine! Since you have no husband, that ring can only have been given to you by one who hopes to marry you! Why continue to deceive us? Why torture me further? That's an engagement ring! It must mean you've accepted a proposal of marriage!"

"That's what I said!" exclaimed the elderly woman.

"And what was her answer, Madame?"

"That's none of your business," said Christine, driven to exasperation. "Don't you think, Monsieur, that this cross-examination has lasted long enough? As far as I am concerned..."

Raoul was afraid to let her finish in case she was about to officially break things off with him. So he interrupted her:

"I humbly beg your forgiveness for speaking as I did, Mademoiselle. You know I'm only meddling out of the purest of intentions. I'm sure you believe that what we've just discussed has nothing whatsoever to do with me. But at least allow me to tell you what I saw–and I saw more than you suspect, Christine–or what I thought I saw, for, to tell you the truth, on several occasions I have been inclined to doubt the evidence of my own eyes."

"Well, what did you see, Monsieur, or think you saw?"

"I saw your ecstasy *at the sound of the Voice*, Christine. The *Voice* that came from the wall or possibly from the room next to yours... Yes, *your ecstasy!* And that is what makes me fear for you... You are under some kind of dangerous spell. And yet, you seem to be aware of the pretense, because today you say *that there is no Angel of Music*! In that case, Christine, why did you follow him? Why did you stand up, with a radiant face, as if you really were hearing an angel? Yes, it is a very dangerous *Voice*, Christine, for when I heard it myself, I was so under its spell that you vanished before my eyes without me even being able to tell how it had happened! Christine, Christine, in the name of Heaven, in the name of your father who is in Heaven now and who loved you so dearly, and who loved me too, Christine, tell us, tell your benefactress and me– *to whom does the Voice belong*? If you do, we will save you in spite of yourself. Come, Christine, tell us the name of that man! The name of the man who had the audacity to put a ring on your finger!"

"Monsieur de Chagny," the girl declared coldly, "that you shall never know!"

Thereupon, seeing the hostility with which the Vicomte had addressed her darling adopted daughter, Madame Valerius suddenly took Christine's side.

"And, if she does love that man, Monsieur le Vicomte?" she said in a bitter voice. "What business is it of yours?"

"Alas, Madame," Raoul humbly replied, unable to control his tears, "I do believe that Christine loves him! Everything proves it! But that is not the only thing which drives me to despair... That about which I am not certain is, whether the man whom Christine loves is worthy of her love?"

"I am the best judge of that, Monsieur!" said Christine, looking Raoul angrily in the eyes.

"When a man," continued Raoul, who felt himself weakening, "adopts such lurid tricks to entice a young girl's affections..."

"...The man must be either a villain, or the girl a silly little fool. Is that it?"

"Christine!"

"Raoul, why do you condemn a man whom you have never seen, whom no one knows and about whom you yourself know nothing?"

"No, Christine! I do know at least one thing: the name that you meant to keep from me for ever. The name of your Angel of Music is–Erik!"

Christine immediately betrayed herself. She turned as white as a sheet and stammered: "Who told you?"

"You did!"

"What do you mean?"

"You were feeling sorry him, the other night, the night of the masked ball. When you returned to your dressing-room, you said, '*Poor Erik*!' Well, Christine, there was also a poor Raoul who overheard you."

"That's the second time that you listened behind my door, Monsieur de Chagny!"

"I wasn't actually behind the door... I was in your dressing-room, behind the curtain in the alcove, Mademoiselle."

"Oh, my God!" moaned the girl, showing every sign of unspeakable terror. "You fool! Do you want to die that badly?"

"Perhaps."

Raoul uttered words with so much love and despair in his voice that Christine could not hold back a sob.

She took his hands and looked at him with all the pure love of which she was capable. Under her gaze, Raoul felt his heart heal as if by magic.

"Raoul," she said, "*you must forget the name of the Voice*! You must never try to fathom its mystery."

"Is it so terrible?"

"There is nothing more awful on this Earth. Swear to me that you will make no attempt to learn more," she insisted. "Swear to me that you will never again come to my dressing-room, unless I send for you."

"Then you promise to send for me sometime, Christine?"

"I promise."

"When?"

"Tomorrow."

"Then I swear I'll do as you ask."

He kissed her hands and left, cursing Erik and resolving to be patient.

Rick Veitch

John Heebink

Chapter Twelve
Above the Trap-doors

The next day, Raoul visited Christine at the Opera. She was still wearing the plain gold ring, was gentle and kind to him, talking to him about his plans, his future, his career.

He told her that the date of his Polar expedition had been moved forward and he would leave France in three weeks or a month at the most.

She suggested, almost merrily, that he should look upon the voyage with happiness, as a prelude to his inevitable fame. When he replied that fame without love meant nothing to him, she treated him as a child whose sorrows are always short-lived.

"How can you speak so lightly of such serious things?" he asked. "It may be that we'll never see each other again! I could die during this expedition."

"As could I," she said simply.

She was no longer smiling or joking. She seemed to be thinking of some new notion that had entered her mind for the first time. Her eyes burned with it.

"What are you thinking about, Christine?"

"I've just realized that we'll never see each other again."

"That's the realization that is making you so radiant?"

"In a month, we'll have to say goodbye to each other forever!"

"Unless we pledge our devotion and agree to wait for each other till the end of time!"

She put her hand over his mouth.

"Hush, Raoul! You know that can't be... We can never marry! That was understood!"

Suddenly, she seemed almost unable to contain an over-powering joy. She clapped her hands with childlike glee. Raoul, concerned, stared at her with incomprehension.

"Even if we can't be married," she continued, holding out her hands to Raoul, or rather giving them to him as if she had resolved to make him a present of them, "nothing prevents us from being engaged! Nobody has to know except us, Raoul. There have been plenty of secret marriages, so why not a secret engagement? Let's say we're engaged, dearest Raoul–for a month! After that, you'll leave me and I can be happy with the memories of that month for the rest of my life!"

She was thrilled with her idea. Then, she became serious again.

"*This*," she said, "*is a happiness that will harm no one.*"

Raoul understood. He jumped at the idea. He wanted to act on it immediately. So he kneeled at Christine's feet and, with touching humility, said:

"Mademoiselle, may I have the honor of asking for your hand?"

"But you already have both of them, my dear fiancé!" she replied, smiling. "Oh, Raoul, how happy we're going to be! We'll play future husband and wife all day long."

Raoul was thinking to himself: "Such a child! A month, will give me time to make her forget, or at least uncover and destroy the mystery of, the *Voice*. In a month, she'll agree to become my wife for real. In the meantime, I'm willing to pretend!"

It was the sweetest game in the world and they enjoyed it like the children that they still were. Oh, the flowery speeches they made to each other! The eternal vows they exchanged! The notion that, in four weeks' time none of this would matter, freed them even as it left them feeling on edge, a condition they enjoyed with guilty pleasure. They alternated non-stop from laughter to tears. They played with their love as other children played with balls, flinging it back and forth, practicing at catching it each time without letting it drop.

However, on the eighth day after they had begun their game, Raoul could no longer take it and he stopped playing, uttering these frantic words:

"I've decided not to go to the Pole!"

Christine, who, in her innocence, had never considered this possibility, suddenly realized the inherent danger of her game and bitterly reproached herself. She said nothing to Raoul and went straight home.

The conversation had happened in the afternoon in the singer's dressing-room, where they met every day, dining on cookies and port across a table decorated with a vase of violets.

That evening, Christine didn't sing and Raoul didn't receive his usual letter, even though they had agreed to write to each other every day during "their" month. The next morning, he ran to see Madame Valerius, who told him that Christine had gone away for two days. She had left at 5 p.m. the day before, saying that she would not be back until the following day.

Raoul became distraught. He hated Madame Valerius for giving him such terrible news with such amazing serenity. He tried to pry more information out of her, but it was clear that the elderly lady knew nothing further. Her answer to each of his frantic questions was, "It's Christine's secret!"

As she said it, she raised her finger to indicate both discretion and an attempt to convey reassurance.

"Christine's 'secret!' Indeed!" Raoul raged, rushing down the stairs like a madman. "With a chaperone like Madame Valerius, a young girl could elope twice a week and no one would be any the wiser!"

Where had his Christine gone? Two days. Two fewer days of happiness in a month that was already too short! He knew it had all been his fault! Wasn't it clearly agreed between them that he would leave? And even if he had decided not to go on his expedition, what had possessed him to tell her so soon? He berated himself for his clumsiness and was the most unhappy of men for the next 48 hours, until Christine's homecoming.

Her return was triumphant. She finally reprised her extraordinary success of the gala performance. Since the incident of the "croak," Mademoiselle Carlotta had been unable to appear on stage. Terror at the mere thought of a new "croak" filled her heart and deprived her of all her abilities. The scene that had been the cause of her incomprehensible disgrace had become odious to her and she had managed to break her contract. Christine had been asked to temporarily fill the now-vacant position. She received thunderous applause when she sang in *La Juive*.

The Vicomte, who, of course, was there that night was the only one to suffer on hearing the myriad echoes of this new triumph, for he saw that Christine still wore the plain gold ring. A faint inner voice whispered in the young man's ear:

"She still wears that ring tonight and it's not yours, it's *his*! She gave her soul again, but it wasn't to you, it was to *him*!"

The inner voice added: "If she won't tell you what she did these past two days, if she hides the location of her retreat, then you must ask... Erik!"

He ran backstage and intercepted her as she made her way back to her dressing-room. Christine saw him at once for her eyes had been searching for him. She said: "Quick! Quick! Come!" Then she dragged him inside, not the least bit bothered by all the admirers of her young glory, who stood outside her closed door, whispering: "What a scandal!"

Raoul immediately fell to his knees before her. He swore to her that he would go on his expedition and begged her to never again subtract a single hour from the happiness she had promised him. She let her tears flow. They hugged each other like a grieving brother and sister who have just been struck by a common loss and come together to mourn a dead parent.

Suddenly, she broke away from the young man's soft, shy embrace, seeming to listen to something only she could hear and, quickly, pointed at the door. When Raoul stood on the threshold, she said to him, in a voice so low that the Vi-comte guessed at more than heard her words:

"Tomorrow, my dear fiancé! And be happy, Raoul: I sang for you tonight!"

He returned the next day.

Alas! Those two days of absence had broken the charm of their once-delightful game. They looked at each other in her dressing-room with sad eyes, barely exchanging a word. Raoul had to restrain himself to keep from crying out: "I'm jealous! I'm jealous! I'm jealous!" Christine heard him all the same.

She said: "Come for a walk, dear Raoul. The air will do you good."

The Vicomte thought she was proposing a stroll in the country, far from the Opera which he now hated as a prisoner hates his prison–a prison with a jailer whose presence he could feel within its very walls... a jailer named Erik. Instead, she took him on stage and had him sit on the wooden edge of a papier-mâché fountain, in the dubious peace and coolness of the first piece of scenery set up for that night's performance. On another day, they held hands while wandering through the deserted paths of a garden the vines of which had been care-fully arranged by a skillful set dresser. It was as if real sky, real flowers and real earth were forever forbidden to her and she had been condemned to breathe no air other than that of the Opera. The young man hesitated to ask her the least ques-tion, as it was obvious that she could not answer them and would only suffer needlessly.

From time to time, a fireman passed them, watching their melancholic idyll from afar. Sometimes, she bravely tried to delude herself, as well as him, about the deceptive charms of a scenery that was nothing more than an illusion created for the public. Her ever-lively imagination credited it with colors so magnificent that, as she pointed out, nature herself could not match it. She grew emotional while Raoul, slowly, took her fevered hand. She said: "Look, Raoul! See these walls, these woods, these rocks, these painted backgrounds, all of them have witnessed the most sublime of loves and passions sung by the greatest poets, a hundred times more powerful than normal. Tell me that our own love isn't perfectly set off by them, since it, too, is a mere fabrication and–alas!–an illusion!"

Since he was too troubled to answer, she continued:

"Our love is too sad for this Earth; let's take it up to the Heavens! See how simply we can do that here!"

And she would drag him up above the painted clouds, into the magnificent chaos of the rafters, where she loved to make him feel dizzy by running ahead of him along the delicate beams, among thousands of cables fastened to pulleys, spools and rollers, in the midst of a genuine aerial forest of ropes and masts. If he hesitated, she said, with an adorable pout on her lips:

"I thought you were a sailor!"

Then, they returned to *terra firma*, that is to say, to some solid corridor that led them to sounds of laughter, dancing and youth being admonished by a severe voice saying: "Deeper, Ladies! Pay attention to your position!" It was the dancing-school for the youngest girls, where brats between six and ten, already dressed in decolletéd tutus, white slips and pink tights, tirelessly and painfully practiced their steps, hoping they would be allowed to join the quadrille, then the *corps de ballet*, become chorus girls and, one day perhaps, prima ballerinas, covered with diamonds while men lay prostrated at their feet. While they waited, Christine gave them sweets instead.

Another day, she showed him a vast room in her "palace," filled with garish uniforms, knightly armor, lances, shields and standards, and reviewed with him ghostly regiments of silent, motionless soldiers, covered with dust. She said a few kind words, promising them that they would again, some day, see the limelight of the stage and parade to the sound of thundering trumpets.

She took him through her entire empire, which, although fake was immense, covering 17 stories from ground floor to roof and inhabited by an army of subjects. She moved among them like a popular Queen, encouraging them in their labors, sitting amongst them in the workshops, offering words of advice to the seamstresses whose hands hesitated to cut into the rich cloth that would soon dress heroes. There were tradesmen of every kind in her realm. There were cobblers and goldsmiths. All had come to know her and love her, for she always took an interest in their problems and way of life.

She even knew of a forgotten cubbyhole that was secretly occupied by an elderly couple. She knocked on their door and introduced Raoul as the Prince Charming who had asked for her hand. Then, the two lovers, sitting on a worm-eaten prop, listened to legends of the Opera, just as they had once listened to old Breton tales when they were children. The old couple remembered nothing outside the Opera. They had lived there for countless years. Past Managements had forgotten them, revolutions had ignored them, French history had run its course without them and nobody even remembered their existence.

The precious days sped by in this way. Raoul and Christine faked an incongruous interest in outside matters, as they awkwardly tried to hide from each other what was really in their hearts. One thing was certain: Christine, who, for the most part, had shown herself as the stronger of the two, suddenly became incredibly nervous. On their expeditions, she would start running for no reason, or she would suddenly stop, her hand, turning ice-cold in an instant as she held Raoul back. Sometimes, her eyes seemed to focus on imaginary shadows. She would cry out, "This way" and "That way," as she laughed breathlessly, even though she ultimately broke down and wept. Raoul tried to speak up and question her, despite his resolution not to do so. But before he could even get a word out, she answered feverishly:

"It's nothing. I swear it's nothing."

Once, when they passed next to an open trap-door on the stage, Raoul stopped over the dark void and said:

"You've shown me the upper levels of your empire, Christine, but I've heard strange stories about its lower ones. Why don't we go down?"

159

When she heard this, she grabbed him in her arms as if she feared he would be swallowed whole by that black maw and, in a trembling voice, she whispered:

"Never! Don't ever go down there! I forbid it! Besides, it's not part of my empire... *Everything underground belongs to him*!"

Raoul looked her in the eyes and said roughly:

"So *he* lives down there, does *he*?"

"I never said that! Who told you such a thing? Come on! You know, sometimes, I wonder about your sanity, Raoul. You say such foolish things. Come on! Come on!"

And she literally dragged him away, for he was obstinate and wanted to remain by that trap-door, that dark hole that attracted him so strangely.

Suddenly, the trap-door was shut so quickly that they did not even see the hand that did it. It was so brutal that they were both totally dazed.

"Perhaps *he* did it," Raoul said, at last.

She shrugged, but did not seem reassured.

"No, no, it must have been a *trap-door-closer*. That's their job, you know, opening and closing trap-doors, for no particular reason... They're like the *door-closers*, they've got to keep busy somehow."

"But what if it was *him*, Christine?"

"No! It can't be *him*! *He*'s shut himself up! *He*'s working!"

"Oh, really! *He*'s working, is *he*?"

"Yes! Even *he* can't work and close trap-doors at the same time. We're alone."

She shivered as she said this.

"What is *he* working on?"

"Oh, something terrible! But that's good for us. When *he*'s working like that, *he* sees nothing; *he* doesn't eat, drink or breathe for days and nights... *He* becomes a living dead man and doesn't have time to play with trap-doors."

She shivered again. She leaned forward towards the trap-door and listened. Raoul was letting her speak and act. He remained silent, fearing that even the sound of his voice disturbed her concentration and broke the fragile thread of her confessions.

She was still holding him in her arms. At last, she sighed and said:

"But what if that was *him*?"

"Are you afraid of *him*?" Raoul asked, warily.

"No... Of course not," she replied.

Involuntarily, the young man became patronizing, as one might towards someone who is prey to imaginary fears. His entire being seemed to scream: "You have nothing to fear, for I am here!" His gestures became overly protective. Christine looked at Raoul's courage and virtue with surprise and seemed to honestly appreciate his chivalrous, yet futile, display of bravado. She kissed him as a sister would her younger brother, to thank him for having used his little fists to defend her against life's everyday dangers.

Raoul understood her gesture and blushed with embarrassment. He found himself as weak as she. He thought: "She says she isn't afraid, but she ran away from that trap-door trembling." And, of course, he was right.

The next day and all the days after, they kept their chaste love amongst the rafters, far away from any trap-doors. Christine's agitation increased as the hours passed. Finally, one afternoon, she arrived extremely late, her face so desperately pale and her eyes so horridly red, that Raoul immediately resolved it was time for extreme measures, and shouted that "*he would not go to the Pole unless she first told him the secret of the Voice!*"

"Hush! In Heaven's name, hush! What if *he* heard you, my poor Raoul!"

And, wildly, Christine stared all around her.

"I'll take you away from *his* power, Christine! I swear it! And you won't have to think of *him* anymore."

"Is that possible?"

She allowed herself this doubt, which was an encouragement, while dragging the young man to the uppermost

161

story of the Opera, "up in the air," far, very far, from the trap-doors.

"I'll take you to some unknown corner of the world, where *he* won't ever come looking for you. You'll be safe; and then, I'll leave, since you've sworn never to marry."

Christine seized Raoul's hands and squeezed them with glorious rapture. Then, suddenly, alarmed again, she turned her head away.

"Higher!" was all she said. "Higher still!"

And she dragged him towards the summit.

He had difficulties following her. They were soon under the very roof of the Opera, in the maze of its timber-work. They slipped through the buttresses, the rafters and the joists; they ran from beam to beam as they might have run from tree to tree in a forest.

Still, despite the care which she took to keep constant watch behind her, she failed to see a shadow which followed her like her own shadow, which stopped when she stopped, which started again when she started and which made no more noise than any normal shadow should. As for Raoul, he saw nothing either; for, when Christine was in front of him, nothing behind him held any interest at all.

Alberto Ponticelli

Stephen R. Bissette

Chapter Thirteen
Apollo's Lyre

In this way, they eventually reached the roof of the Opera. Christine glided across it, light as a swallow. Their eyes swept the empty spaces between the three domes and the triangular facade. She reveled in the breathtaking view of Paris, watching as it labored at their feet. She looked trustingly at Raoul and asked him to join her in walking side-by-side along the roof's zinc streets and lead alleys. They beheld their twin reflections in the rain water collected inside the huge tanks where, during the hottest days of summer, the 20 or so small boys of the *corps de ballet* learned to swim and dive.

The shadow had followed behind them, hugging their steps, occasionally flattening itself against the roof, silently stretching its black shape over the intersections of the iron lanes, hiding behind cisterns, stealthily moving around the domes and not once did the two young lovers suspect its presence. After a while, they sat down, feeling protected by the statue of mighty Apollo, who, with a powerful gesture, lifted his mammoth bronze lyre into the heart of the fiery sky.

It was a glorious spring evening. The setting Sun had tinged the clouds with a gossamer veil of gold and purple. As these drifted slowly above their heads, Christine said to Raoul:

"You'll be leaving me soon. You're going to travel farther and faster than those clouds, to the very edge of the world, and we'll probably never see each other again... But if a propitious moment comes when you can carry me away, Raoul, I want you to do it. And, if I refuse to go with you of my own will–well, then you must force me!"

She said this with such force, seemingly all directed at herself, all the while nervously huddling closer to him, that the young man was struck by her determination.

"Why? Are you afraid that you might change your mind, Christine?"

"I don't know," she said, shaking her head sadly. "He is such a demon!"

She shivered and nestled, moaning, in his arms.

"I'm afraid of going back to live with him... below ground!"

"Why are you forced to go back?"

"If I don't, terrible things will happen!... But I can't do it anymore! I just can't! I know one ought to feel sorry for someone who has no choice except to live below ground, but he's too horrible! And yet the time is almost here! I only have a day left. And if I don't go, he'll come after me, with his *Voice*. He'll drag me back to his home, underground. He'll kneel before me, with his hideous death's-head. He'll tell me that he loves me–and he'll cry! Oh, Raoul, those tears oozing out of the twin, dark eye-sockets of his ghastly death's-head! I cannot stand to see those tears flow again!"

She wrung her hands in anguish, while Raoul, victim of her contagious despair, pressed her against his heart.

"No! No! You'll never again hear him tell you that he loves you! You won't see his tears! Let's run away, Christine! Let's run away right this minute!" And he tried to drag her away, then and there.

But she stopped him.

"No," she said, shaking her head sadly. "Not now! It would be too cruel. Let him hear me sing one last time tomorrow night and then we'll go. Come to my dressing-room at the stroke of midnight, exactly. That's when he'll be waiting for me in his dining room by the lake. We'll be alone and you can take me away... Promise me that, Raoul! Even if I refuse to go, you must take me away by force. I'm afraid that if I go back to him one more time, I may never return."

She added: "You can't understand..."

Then, she sighed–and it seemed to her that from behind her, an echoing sigh replied.

"What was that?" she said. "Did you hear something?"

166

Her teeth chattered.

"No," said Raoul. "I didn't hear anything."

"It's horrible," she confessed, "to always live in fear this way! And yet, up here, we run no danger. We're in my element now: the sky, the open air, the light. The flames of the Sun still burn and the birds of night cannot stand to gaze upon them. I've never seen him by daylight–but it must be horrible!" She turned to look at Raoul with fevered eyes. "The first time I saw him!... I thought *he* was going to die."

"Why?" asked Raoul, now truly frightened by the strange and terrifying nature of her secret. "Why did you think that *he* was going to die?"

"*Because I had seen him!*"

"..............."

This time, Raoul and Christine both turned at the same time:

"Did you hear that? It sounded like someone in pain," said Raoul. "Maybe someone is hurt..."

"I can't be sure," Christine confessed. "*Even when he is not with me, my ears are always full of his horrible moans.* Still, if you think you heard something..."

They stood up and looked around, but it seemed as if they were completely alone on the immense lead roof. They sat back down and Raoul said:

"Tell me about the first time you saw him."

"I had been hearing him for three months but hadn't seen him at all. The first time I heard him, like you, I thought that that wonderful voice came from another dressing-room. So I went out and looked everywhere... But, as you know, Raoul, my dressing-room is fairly isolated, and I couldn't find any sign of where it came from. As soon as I walked outside of my room, it seemed to disappear, while I could hear it steadily inside. And it not only sang, but it also spoke to me and answered my questions, like a real person's voice. The difference was that it was as beautiful as the voice of an angel. I couldn't find any explanation for such a mystery. I had never stopped thinking about the Angel of Music, whom my poor father had promised to send to me as soon as he got to Heaven... I'm not embarrassed to tell you all this, Raoul, because you knew my father. He loved you and you, too, believed in the Angel of Music when we were children. So I know you won't laugh at me. My soul was still as sweet and gullible as Little Lotte's and living with Madame Valerius probably didn't help. I carried that tiny white soul between my naive hands and candidly offered it to the *Voice*, believing him to be the Angel. My poor adopted mother was partially to blame as well. When I told her about the mysterious phenomenon, she immediately said:

" 'It must be the Angel of Music! In any event, there's no harm in asking him.'

"So that's what I did. The *Voice* replied that, yes, he was the Angel of Music whom I'd been expecting and who my father had promised to send from Heaven. From that point on, the *Voice* and I grew very close and I trusted it unconditionally. It told me it had come down to Earth to help me share in the pleasures of the eternal art and asked my permission to give me music lessons every day. Naturally, I enthusiastically agreed and never missed any of the appointments it gave me in my dressing-room, when the rest of the Opera was totally deserted. I can't even begin to tell you how wonderful those lessons were! Even you, who heard the *Voice*, can't imagine what they were like."

"No, of course, I can't imagine," said Raoul a little peevishly. "How were you accompanied?"

"Some music that I didn't know came from behind the wall of my room. It was always perfectly flawless. The *Voice* seemed to know exactly where my father had left off when he taught me and what natural methods he had used. I remembered, or rather my larynx remembered, all of my past lessons and, with the help of the new ones, in a few weeks' time, I'd made prodigious progress. Progress like that would have normally taken years. If you remember, I used to have a rather immature voice. I had almost no range in the lower notes and some difficulty reaching the higher ones. In general, I lacked power. My father had struggled with all those problems and made some progress, but the *Voice* conquered them all. Little by little, I gained strength on a scale that my former imperfection would never have allowed me to achieve. I learned to control my breathing and, even more useful, the *Voice* also taught me the secret of singing soprano using one's chest. But, more importantly it was able to stoke the sacred fires of my inspiration; it awakened in me a fiery, all-consuming, sublime flame. By permitting me to hear it, the *Voice's* power raised me to its level. It allowed me to vibrate on its same harmony. Its very soul inhabited my being and breathed its own music into it.

"After a few weeks, I hardly knew myself when I sang. I even became frightened by it. I was afraid there was some kind of spell behind it all; but Madame Valerius reassured me. She said that she knew I was much too good a girl to enable the Devil to take control of me.

"My progress was kept secret, known only to the *Voice*, Madame Valerius and me. It was so strange–outside my dressing-room, I sang with my ordinary, everyday voice and no one was the wiser. I did everything the *Voice* asked me to do. It told me: 'Wait! You'll see! We'll surprise all of Paris!' So I waited. I lived in a kind of ecstatic dream ruled by the *Voice*. Then, one night, for the first time, I saw you in the theater. My joy was such that it never occurred to me to hide it when I returned to my dressing-room. Unfortunately, the *Voice* was already there and it soon noticed, by my manner, that something had happened. It asked me what had happened and I saw no reason to conceal our story or lie about the place you occupied in my heart. Then the *Voice* fell silent. I called to it, but it wouldn't reply. I begged and entreated, but in vain. I was terrified that it was gone for good. If only... That night, I went home in tears. I threw myself into Madame Valerius' arms, saying: 'The *Voice* is gone! It may never return!' And she was as frightened as I was and asked me to tell her everything, which I did. Then, she said: 'Why, of course, the *Voice* is jealous!' And that, dearest Raoul, is how I first realized that I loved you."

Christine stopped for a moment and rested her head on the young man's shoulder. They sat like that for a while, in silence. Their emotions were such that they did not see, nor feel, the movement, mere feet away, of the creeping shadow of two great black wings, a shadow that skulked on the roof so near them, that if it had enshrouded them, it might have suffocated them.

"The next day," continued Christine, with a deep sigh, "I returned to my dressing-room, pondering over what had happened. The *Voice* was back! It spoke to me with great sadness. It told me firmly that, if I were to bestow my heart on Earth, it would return to Heaven. It said this with such a note of *human* sorrow that I should have begun to suspect, then and there, that I was victim of my own deluded senses. But my faith in the *Voice*, combined with the memory of my poor father, remained unshaken. What I most feared was that I might never hear it again! I had also given some thought to the love I felt for you and realized how dangerous that could be. To be honest, I was not even sure if you remembered me at all. No matter what my feelings, I thought that your social position made it impossible for us to marry. So, I swore to the *Voice* that you were–and would ever be–nothing more than a brother to me, and that my heart was devoid of any Earthly love. And that, Raoul, is why I pretended to not recognize or even see you when you tried to attract my attention backstage or in the corridors.

"Meanwhile, the hours during which the *Voice* taught me were spent in a divine exhilaration, until, at last, it said to me: 'Now, Christine! Now you can give man a small taste of the music of Heaven!'

"Why that night, that gala night, Mademoiselle Carlotta who was supposed to sing, failed to show up, I will never learn. Nor do I know why I was called upon to sing in her place... But sing I did, with a sense of elation I had never before known. I felt as buoyant as if I had wings and for a moment I felt as if my fiery soul had left my body!"

"Oh, Christine," said Raoul, whose eyes teared when remembering that prodigious night. "My heart quivered with every lilt of your voice. I saw tears stream down your pale cheeks and I wept with you. How could you sing, sing like that, while crying?"

"All my strength suddenly left me," said Christine, "I closed my eyes. And when I opened them, you were by my side in my dressing-room. But the *Voice* might have been there, too... I was afraid for your safety, so, again, I pretended not to recognize you and laughed when you reminded me that you were *the little boy who dove into the sea to rescue my scarf*!

"Alas! The *Voice* was not fooled! It recognized you and became jealous! For the next two days, it was one horrible scene after another. It told me: 'You love him! If you didn't love him, you wouldn't be avoiding him! You would shake his hand and treat him the same as any old friend! If you didn't love him, you wouldn't be afraid of being alone in your dressing-room with him–and with me! If you didn't love him, you wouldn't send him away!'

" 'Enough!' I finally said to the *Voice* angrily. 'Tomorrow, I'm going to Perros-Guirrec to pray on my father's grave and I'll ask Monsieur de Chagny to come with me.'

" 'Do as you please,' replied the *Voice*, 'but know that I, too, shall be in Perros, for wherever you are, Christine, I am also there! And if you are still worthy of me, if I see that you have not lied to me, I will play *The Resurrection of Lazarus* at the stroke of midnight on your father's grave, on your father's own violin.'

"That, dearest Raoul, is why I wrote the letter that brought you to Perros. How could I have been so easily duped? How was it that, when I saw how selfish the *Voice* truly was, I did not suspect some impostor? But I was no longer in control of myself– I had become its puppet! Its powers were so beguiling that it easily held sway over the child I was!"

"But if you learned the truth," cried Raoul, interrupting Christine when she seemed to be crying over having fallen prey to her own innocence and gullibility, "why didn't you try to escape from that monstrous nightmare?"

"Learned the truth? Escape from that nightmare? My poor Raoul, I entered that nightmare, as you call it, only when I *did* learn the truth! Hush! Let me speak! I've barely begun my tale... You must now follow me underground... Oh, pity me, Raoul, pity me!... It was that terrible night... That night when so many horrible things happened... You remember, when Mademoiselle Carlotta began croaking on stage like a regiment of frogs, when the chandelier came crashing to the floor? So many people were injured that night, as the entire Opera rang with their terrified screams...

"My first thought, after that catastrophe, was for you and for the *Voice*, because both of you claimed, at that time, equal halves of my heart. I was immediately reassured about your well-being, because I remembered seeing you in your brother's box and I realized that you were out of danger. But the *Voice* had told me it would be attending the performance and I was afraid, yes, really afraid for it, just as if it had been an ordinary human being, capable of dying. I thought: 'My God! Maybe the chandelier crushed the *Voice*.' I was on stage when the horrible thing happened and I was about to run into the orchestra to look for the *Voice* among the dead and injured, when it occurred to me that, if the *Voice* was safe, it would surely be in my dressing-room, where it would reassure me as to its fate. I rushed back to my room, but the *Voice* wasn't there. I locked my door and, with tears in my eyes, beseeched it, if it were still alive, to manifest itself to me. The *Voice* did not reply, but suddenly, I heard a long, beautiful wail which I knew well. It was the complaint of Lazarus when, at the sound of Jesus' voice, he begins to open his eyes and sees the light of day. It was the cry of my father's violin. I recognized its music; it was the same music which he used to enchant us when we were children, Raoul, and the same music which we heard on that magical night in the Perros cemetery.

"Then the *Voice* began to sing exultantly over the sound of that invisible and eloquent instrument. It was a song of life, of sovereign power that could not be denied: 'Come!' it said. 'Believe in me! Those who believe in me, even though they die, will live! Come forth! Those who live and believe in me will never die!' I can't even begin to explain to you the effect that music had on me. It sang about eternal life, even as the poor wretches who had been crushed by that awful chandelier, lay broken and bleeding in the theater. It seemed to command me, too, to come forth, to stand up and walk! It retreated and I went with it. 'Come! Believe in me!' I believed and I followed, and that was the most extraordinary thing–as I stepped forward, my dressing-room seemed to grow longer... Clearly, it was some trick of the mirror, because I was standing in front of the wall mirror... Yet, suddenly, without knowing how, I was outside the room!"

Raoul interrupted the young girl. "What do you mean, without knowing how? Were you dreaming, Christine?"

"No, I wasn't dreaming, my dearest Raoul, all I can tell you is that I suddenly found myself outside my room with no idea of how I had gotten there. You, yourself, saw me disappear from my dressing-room–can you explain it? I cannot. I can only tell you that, suddenly, the wall mirror was gone and so was my dressing-room. I looked for them, ahead and behind me, but they had disappeared. I was standing in a dark corridor. I was scared and I cried out.

"Everything around me was dark, except for a faint red glow on far along the wall. I called out but my voice was the only sound I heard, for the singing and the violin had stopped. Suddenly, in the dark, I felt a hand on mine... Something cold and bony that caught my wrist and didn't let go. I screamed. Then, an arm seized me by the waist and lifted me off the ground. I struggled in the midst of my terror, feeling my fingers scrape against the damp stone walls; then, I simply gave up. I stopped moving and thought I would die of my fear. I was being carried toward that distant red light. There, by its glow, I saw that I was in the arms of a man wrapped in a large, black cloak, and wearing a mask that hid his entire face. I made one last effort; my limbs stiffened, my mouth opened again to scream in horror, but a hand closed over it, a hand the touch of which I felt on my lips, on my skin–a hand that reeked of death. I fainted.

"How long did I remain unconscious? I'll never know. When at last I opened my eyes, we–the man in black and I– were still surrounded by darkness. A small lantern, placed on the ground, lit a small bubbling fountain. The water that splashed out of the wall, disappeared, almost at once, beneath the floor on which I was lying. My head rested in the lap of the man in black. That silent wraith sprinkled water on my temples with a care, an attention and a delicacy that seemed more dreadful to bear than the earlier brutality of his kidnapping. His hands, as gentle as they were, continued to reek of death. I tried to push them away, but lacked the strength. Apprehensively, I asked:

" 'Who are you? Where is the *Voice*?'

"His only answer was a sigh. Suddenly, I felt hot breath on my face. In the darkness, I saw a white shape next to the man's black shape. The black shape lifted me and set me on top of the white shape. A happy neighing greeted my astounded ears and I whispered: 'Caesar!' The animal quivered beneath me. Believe it or not, Raoul, I was lying half back on a saddle, but I had recognized the white horse from *The Prophet*, which I had so often fed sugar and treats! I remembered hearing a rumor whispered around the Opera that a horse had disappeared; that it had been stolen by the Phantom. I believed in the *Voice* but I had never believed in the Phantom. But now, I began to tremble and wonder if he wasn't my captor. I called from the deepest core of my being for the *Voice* to come rescue me, for it had never crossed my mind that it and the Phantom could be one and the same. You have heard about the Phantom of the Opera, haven't you, Raoul?"

174

"Yes, Christine, but tell me, what happened after you ended up on that white horse from *The Prophet*?"

"I kept still and let him take the lead. Little by little, a strange torpor was replacing the fear and anguish I had felt till then throughout the terrifying ordeal. The black shape held me up and I made no effort to escape. A curious feeling of peace had come over me–I thought that perhaps I was under the calming influence of some strange elixir. I was in full possession of all my senses; my eyes became accustomed to the darkness, which here and there was broken by small lights. I thought that we were inside a narrow, spiraling passageway, probably circling the Opera, which beneath ground is immense. I had once–only once, mind you!–been down inside those unbelievable vaults, but had gone no further than the third level, not daring to go deeper underground, even though there are two additional levels, lower still, each large enough to contain an entire village. But the things I had seen there caused me to flee. There are demons down below, entirely black, standing in front of boilers, wielding shovels and pitchforks, stoking fires and stirring up flames. If you get too near them, they'll try to scare you away by suddenly opening the scarlet jaws of their furnaces...

"On that nightmarish night, while Caesar quietly carried me on his back, I saw those black demons in the distance, quite far away, looking very small in front of the red flames of their furnaces, as if I was looking at them through the wrong end of a spyglass. They appeared, disappeared, then appeared again, as we continued along our winding way. At last, they disappeared altogether. The shape was still holding me up while Caesar walked on, unled and sure-footed. I could not tell you, even approximately, how long that night ride lasted. I only know that we seemed to twist and turn, traveling ever deeper in an endless spiral into the very bowels of the Earth–and even that feeling may well have been caused by the spinning of my head. But I don't think so... No! My mind was crystal clear. At one point, Caesar flared his nostrils, sniffed the air and quickened his pace a little. I felt dampness in the air, then Caesar stopped. The darkness had lightened. A sort of bluish-glow surrounded us. We were at the edge of a lake, the leaden waters of which stretched far into the distant darkness. The blue light illuminated the shore and I saw a small boat fastened to an iron ring on a pier!

"Of course, I had heard about the lake beneath the Opera, I knew that it was real and that there was nothing supernatural about the pier and boat. But think of the amazing circumstances that had brought me to its shore! The souls of the dead must have felt the same anguish when they set foot on the banks of the Styx. Charon could not have been more grim or silent than the dark shape that led me onto that boat. Perhaps the effects of the elixir had worn off? Or was the coldness of the place responsible for bringing me to my senses? Whatever the reason, my torpor disappeared and I began to struggle again, although weakly, under the power of my terror. My sinister escort noticed, and with one quick gesture, he dismissed Caesar; the horse ran off into the darkness of the gallery and I heard his hoofs pounding up some invisible stairs. Then, the man jumped into the boat, untied the cable that held it and seized the oars. He rowed with quick, powerful strokes. His eyes, under his mask, never left me. I felt the weight of his ghastly stare upon me. The lake around us was deathly still. We glided across the water through the blue light which I mentioned, then were again surrounded by complete darkness. That was when I felt the boat touch shore. The man once again lifted me into his arms. I felt that some of my strength had returned and I cried out. Then, suddenly, I fell silent, dazzled by the light...

"For I had been set down in the middle of a brilliant light. I felt like myself again. I sprang to my feet and looked around. I was in the middle of a drawing-room that seemed to be decorated, adorned and furnished with nothing but flowers, flowers both magnificent and absurd, because of the silk ribbons that tied them to baskets that could have come from any shop on the boulevards. They were common flowers, like the ones I used to find in my dressing-room after a first night.

And, in the midst of all those flowers, stood the black shape of the masked man, his arms crossed over his chest. He said:

" 'Don't be afraid, Christine; you are in no danger.'

"*He was the Voice*!

"My anger now competed with my bewilderment. I rushed to him and tried to snatch off his mask, so that I could at last see the face of the *Voice*. But then he said:

" 'You are in no danger–as long as you do not remove this mask.'

"So saying, he took me gently by the wrists and pushed me into a chair.

"Then, he got down on his knees before me and said nothing more!

"His self-effacing manner helped me to regain some of my courage. The bright light that defined my surroundings once again reminded me of the reality of life. However extraordinary my adventure was, here were visible, tangible things. The tapestries on the walls, the furniture, the candles, the vases and all those flowers in their golden baskets, the origins and price of which I could almost have guessed, all helped rein in my imagination and reinforced the awareness that I was in an ordinary drawing-room, the only peculiarity of which, was that it was located somewhere in the vaults below the Opera. I was dealing with a man, a terrible, eccentric man undoubtedly, who, in some mysterious fashion, had managed to make his residence there, as others had, by need, with the silent complicity of Management. He had found a permanent refuge below that modern Tower of Babel where, above ground, people lived, sang in every language and loved in every tongue.

"Then, the *Voice*, the *Voice* which I had recognized beneath the mask, *was the man on his knees before me*!

"I no longer thought about the horrible situation in which I was, I no longer wondered about what would happen to me, and what mysterious, dark and tyrannical scheme that had led me to be as caged in that drawing-room as a prisoner in a cell or a slave in a harem. No! I only thought: 'So that is what the *Voice* is: *a mere man*!' and I began to cry.

"That man, still on his knees, must have understood the cause of my tears, for he said:

" 'It's true, Christine! I'm not an Angel, nor am I a phantom! I am only Erik!' "

Here, Christine's narrative was again interrupted. The two young lovers thought that an echo behind them had repeated the word: "Erik!" But what caused the echo? They both turned around and noticed that night had fallen. Raoul made a movement as if to rise, but Christine kept him beside her.

"Don't go," she said. "I want to tell you everything *here*!"

"Why *here*, Christine? I'm worried that you'll catch cold."

"We have nothing to fear except the trap-doors, dearest Raoul, and here we are at the opposite end of his world... I'm not allowed to see you outside the theater. This is not the time to upset him. We must not arouse his suspicion."

"Christine! Christine! Something tells me that we are wrong to wait till tomorrow night... We ought to run away right now!"

"I've told you that if he doesn't hear me sing tomorrow, it will cause him infinite pain."

"It's difficult to both not cause Erik any pain but still leave him for good."

"You're right about that, Raoul...I'm sure he'll die if I go..." Then she added in a muted voice: "But that cuts both ways, because he might kill us before we succeed."

"Does he love you that much?"

"He would kill for me."

"But it's possible to find out where he lives, to go in search of him. Now that we know Erik is no phantom, we can speak to him, force him to answer!"

Christine shook her head.

"No, no! There's nothing anyone can do against Erik– except to run away!"

"Then why, when you were able to run, did you choose to go back to him?"

"Because I had to. You will understand that when I tell you how I left him."

"I hate him!" cried Raoul. "And you, Christine, tell me, I need you to tell me so that I can calmly listen to the rest of your outrageous love story, do you hate him, too?"

"No," said Christine simply.

"No, of course not... It's clear that you love him! Your fear, your terror, all of it is just love, love of the most intense kind, the kind that people don't admit, even to themselves," said Raoul sulkily. "The kind that gives you shivers when you think of it. And why not? A man who lives in an underground palace!" He laughed bitterly.

"Do you prefer that I return to him?" said the young girl sharply. "Take care, Raoul. I told you: I will never go back down there!"

There was a frightful silence amongst the three of them: the two who spoke and, behind them, the shadow who listened.

"Before I answer that," said Raoul, speaking very slowly, "I would like to know what feelings he inspires in you, since you said you don't hate him."

"Horror!" she said, with such power that her words covered the terrible sighs in the night behind them.

"That's the terrible thing about it," she said with growing passion. "He fills me with horror, yet I can't hate him. How could I, Raoul? Imagine Erik at my feet, in his house by the lake, deep below ground. He accuses himself, he curses himself, he begs my forgiveness!

"He confessed his deception. He loves me! He lay his immense and tragic love at my feet. He abducted me for love! He imprisoned me with him, underground, for love! But he showed me respect: he crawled, he moaned, he wept! And, when I stood up, Raoul, and told him that I could not respect him in return if he did not, then and there, give me back my freedom... he offered it to me! I was free to leave! He said he would show me the way... Take me back... But... But... He stood, too, and I was forced to remember that, if he wasn't an angel or a phantom, in spite of everything, he was the *Voice*– for he started singing...

"And I listened... and stayed!

"That night, we didn't exchange another word. He took up a harp and with his angelic voice, began to sing the romance of Desdemona. The memories I had of having sung the part myself made me feel ashamed. There is a virtue in music, dearest Raoul, that makes you ignore the existence of the outside world when your soul listens to its harmonies. I forgot all about my extraordinary adventure. Only the *Voice* existed for me and I followed it on its underground journey. I had become like Orpheus' flock! I felt Desdemona's pain and pleasure, her martyrdom, despair, exuberance, death and, finally, wedding day. I listened breathlessly while he sang. He also sang compositions which I had never heard before, a new music that conveyed sweetness, dreaminess and repose... A music which, after raising my soul, made it feel at peace and slowly led me to the Land of Dreams. At last I fell asleep.

"When I woke up, I was alone, lying on a bed in a small, simply furnished bedroom, with an ordinary mahogany bedstead, a Jouy tapestry hanging on the wall, all lit by a lamp standing on the marble top of an old Louis-Philippe chest of drawers. Where was I? I passed my hand over my eyes as if to dispel a bad dream... Alas! I soon realized that I wasn't dreaming! I was a prisoner and the only exit from my room led to a very comfortable bathroom, with hot and cold running water.

"When I returned to the bedroom, on the chest of drawers I saw a note, written in red ink, which told me everything I needed to know and removed any doubts I might still have had about all that was happening to me:

" '*My dear Christine, you should not be concerned about your fate. You have no better nor more respectful friend in the world than myself. You are alone, at present, in this home, which is yours. I am going out shopping for all the things that you will need.'*

" 'Oh My God!' I said to myself. 'I've fallen into the hands of a madman. What will become of me? How long does that lunatic think he can hold me in his underground prison?'

"I searched my small apartment like a madwoman, looking for some way of escape, which I wasn't able to find. I bitterly reproached myself for my childish superstition and I felt a morbid sense of pleasure in deriding the innocence with which I had previously greeted the Voice of the Angel of Music through the walls of my dressing-room... When one is that gullible, I thought, one should be prepared for the worst catastrophes–and deservedly so, too! I could have hit myself! I felt like both laughing and crying at my fate at the same time. That was my state of mind when Erik returned.

"After three small knocks on the wall, he quietly walked in through a hidden door that I had failed to discover and which he left open. His arms were full of boxes and packages. He calmly arranged them on the bed while I screamed insults at him and ordered him to remove his mask, if he at least cared enough to show me the face of an honest man.

"He replied serenely:

" 'You will never see Erik's face.'

"Then he gently admonished me for not being dressed at that time of day–he was good enough to tell me that it was 2 p.m. He said he would give me a half-hour to get ready. While he spoke, he rewound my watch and set it for me. After which, he asked me to come to the dining room, where a good lunch was waiting for us.

"I realized how hungry I was, so I slammed the door in his face and went to the bathroom. I took a bath, after having placed within reach of my hand a large pair of scissors with which I was determined to defend myself–or kill myself–if after behaving like a madman, Erik decided to stop conducting himself like a gentleman. The refreshing bath helped me feel better.

"When I again saw Erik, I had made the sensible decision of not getting upset or being irritating. but rather to try to flatter him in order to quickly regain my freedom. He mentioned his plans for me first, to reassure me, he said. He was too happy to be in my company to deprive himself of it right away, as he had promised me the day before, when he saw the expression of terror on my face. I needed to understand, he said, that there was nothing about him to fear. Yes, he loved me, but he would only tell me so if I allowed it, and the rest of our time together would be devoted to music.

" 'What do you mean, the rest of our time?' I asked.

"He replied firmly:

" 'Five days.'

" 'And after that, I'll be free?'

" 'Yes you will, Christine, because after those five days, you'll have learned not to fear me. Then, from time to time, you'll return to see your poor Erik!'

"The tone he used when he spoke these last words moved me deeply. It seemed to me that they contained such honest, pitiful despair, that for the first time I looked upon his masked face with a degree of sympathy. I couldn't see his eyes, because they, too, were masked and I still felt uncomfortable and unexpectedly queasy talking to a featureless piece of black silk, but near the edges of the mask, I thought I saw the glistening of one, then two, then three and four tears.

"Silently, he pointed to a chair opposite him, next to a small table at the center of the room where, the night before, he had played the harp. I sat down, feeling greatly perturbed. Nevertheless, I managed to eat a few shrimp and the wing of a chicken. I also drank half a glass of tokay, which he had himself, he told me, brought from the wine-cellars of Konigsberg that legends say were once patronized by Falstaff himself. Erik didn't eat or drink. I asked him what his nationality was and if the name Erik was a clue to a Scandinavian origin. He told me that he had no name nor country and that he had taken the name Erik *by accident*. I then asked him why, since he claimed he loved me, he had found no better way to show it than to kidnap me and imprison me underground.

" 'It's very difficult to love anyone when you're trapped inside a tomb,' I said.

" 'One lives where one can,' he replied in a rather forbidding tone.

"Then, he rose and took my hand, saying he would like to show me his home, but I quickly snatched it away, while crying out. What I had touched was cold, damp and bony; and I remembered that his hands reeked of death.

" 'Please, forgive me!' he moaned.

"He opened a door before me.

" 'This is my bedroom,' he said. 'It is rather interesting, if you would care to see it?'

"His manners, his words, his attitude made me trust him and I entered without hesitation. I also felt I should not show fear.

"It was as if I had entered a mortuary. The walls were covered with black hangings, but instead of the white embroidery that usually adorns funereal decoration, there was an enormous music staff with the notes of the *Dies Irae* repeated over and over. In the middle of the room was a canopy, from which hung red brocade curtains, and, under it, an open coffin.

"Upon seeing that, I stepped back.

" 'That is where I sleep,' said Erik. 'One must get used to everything in life, even eternity.'

"The grim display so upset me that I turned my head away. Then, I saw the keyboard of an organ which filled an entire wall. On its stand was a music book covered with scrawled notes in red ink. I asked his permission to look at it and, on the first page, I read: *Don Juan Triumphant*.

" 'Yes,' he said, 'sometimes, I also write music. I began that composition 20 years ago. When it's finished, I'll take it into that coffin with me and never wake up again.'

" 'Then you must work on it as seldom as you can,' I said.

" 'On the contrary. I sometimes work on it for two weeks straight, days and nights, during which I live on nothing but music. Then, I put it aside for years at a time.'

" 'Will you play me something from your *Don Juan Triumphant*?' I asked, thinking that would please him as well as help me overcome the repugnance I felt at staying in that room of death.

" 'You must never ask me that,' he said, in a somber voice. 'My *Don Juan* was not written to follow the words of a Lorenzo d'Aponte; he is not motivated by wine, trivial affairs and petty vices, before finally being punished by God. I will play you Mozart, if you like, which will only make you weep and think pleasant, pure thoughts. But my *Don Juan*, Christine, burns–yet he is not struck by the fire from Heaven!'

"Thereupon, we returned to the drawing room we had just left. I noticed that there were no mirrors anywhere in the entire place. I was about to remark upon this, but Erik had already sat down at the piano. He said:

" 'You see, Christine, there is some music that is so horrifying it consumes all those who hear it. Fortunately, you have not yet discovered that kind of music, for if you had, you would lose your pretty colors and no one would recognize you when you return to Paris. Let's sing something from the Opera instead, Christine, something from the Opera.'

"He spoke those last words as if he was flinging an insult at me.

"But I had no time to think about his meaning. We immediately began the duet from *Othello* and already catastrophe loomed in the air. I sang Desdemona with a sense of despair, a heartfelt fear that I had never displayed before. Instead of robbing me of my abiliities, the company of such a grim partner inspired a magnificent sense of terror in me. The events of which I had become the victim, brought me closer to the Bard's thoughts and I found a proficiency deep within myself that would have astonished all of my former music teachers. As for him, his voice thundered forth, his vengeful soul emphasized every note, prodigiously magnifying its power. Love, jealousy and hatred burst around us in his harrowing cries. Erik's black mask naturally made me think of the Moor of Venice. He had become Othello. I truly felt he was going to strike me, that I would die beneath his blows... And yet I did not run from his fury, like shy Desdemona. Quite the opposite. I moved closer to him, attracted and fascinated, finding a new charm in Death amidst such passion... But before I died, I wanted to carry with me, as I took my last breath, the sublime image of his unforgettable features, transfigured by the fires of eternal art. I wanted to know the *face* of the *Voice*. Suddenly, with a movement which I was utterly unable to control, for I no longer was in control of myself, my fingers hurriedly tore away the mask...

"Oh, the horror, the horror, the horror!"

Christine stopped at the thought of the ghastly vision that had so terrified her that she fruitlessly tried to push away its memory with her two trembling hands. Behind them, the echoes of the night that had earlier repeated the name of Erik, now thrice moaned the cry:

"The horror, the horror, the horror!"

Raoul and Christine, brought even closer by the frightful nature of her tale, clutched each other and raised their eyes to the stars that shone in the clear, peaceful sky.

Raoul said:

"It's strange, Christine, that this night, which is so calm and sweet, should be so full of lamentations. It's almost as if it is sharing our pain."

She replied:

"When you know *his* secret, Raoul, your ears, like mine, will be full of lamentations."

She took Raoul's protecting hands in hers and, with a deep shiver, continued:

"If I live to be a hundred, I'll always hear the superhuman cry that he uttered, a cry of pain and hellish rage, when that–thing–appeared before my eyes, eyes widened with horror. My mouth stood open in a silent scream and I was powerless to close it.

"Oh! Raoul! That thing! How could I ever forget it? My ears cannot forget his cries, anymore than my eyes his face! What a vision! How can I forget it and still convey its horror to you? Raoul, you have seen death's-heads after they have become dried and withered by the centuries. Perhaps, if you were not the victim of a nightmare, you saw *his* death's-head that night in the Perros cemetery. And you saw the Red Death during the masked ball at the Opera. But those death's-heads were inanimate; their silent horror was not alive. But imagine, if you can, the mask of the Red Death suddenly coming to life to express with the four dark pits of its eyes, its nose and its mouth, a stupendous rage, the mighty fury of a demon. *And there was not a single light coming from those dark sockets*, for, as I found out later, you cannot see his blazing yellow eyes except in total darkness. I fell back against the wall, as much the image of terror as he was of hideousness.

"He came over to me, grinding his awful, lipless teeth. I fell upon my knees. He hissed mad, incoherent words and curses at me. Words of furor and frenzy. I remember none of them! I don't wish to remember! Then, leaning over me, he shouted:

" 'Look! You wanted to see me! Then look at me! Feast your eyes, glut your soul on my accursed ugliness! Look at Erik's face! Now you see the face of your sainted Voice! You could not be satisfied with merely listening to me, eh? You also had to know what I looked like! Oh, you women are ever too prying!'

"He laughed insanely, repeating: 'Women are ever too prying!' A thunderous, abrasive, angry, frightful laugh. He continued in that vein, saying:

" 'Well, are you satisfied now? Aren't I a handsome fellow? When a woman has seen me, as you have, she is mine. She loves me forever. I am a kind of Don Juan, you know!'

"Drawing himself up to his full height, his hand on his hip, his other fist in the air, he shook the hideous thing that was his head and roared:

" 'Look at me, I tell you! *I am Don Juan triumphant*!'

"And when I turned my head away, begging for mercy, he turned it to him, brutally twisting his dead fingers in my hair."

"Enough! Enough!" cried Raoul. "I will kill him. In Heaven's name, Christine, tell me where to find his *house by the lake*! I will kill him!"

"Please, Raoul, let me finish!"

"Yes, I want to know why you went back to him! That's the secret I still need to find out! But, mark my words, Christine—no matter what, I will kill him!"

"Dearest Raoul! If you want to know, listen to me! He dragged me by my hair and then... And then... Oh, it is too horrible!"

"What? What else did he do?" exclaimed Raoul fiercely. "Quick! Tell me!"

"Then he hissed at me:

" 'So, I frighten you, do I? You don't say! Perhaps you think that I'm wearing a mask? And that, this—my head—is just another mask? Well,' he roared, 'tear it off as you did the other! Come on! Come on! Again! Again! I insist! Your hands! Your hands! Give me your hands! If they're not enough, I'll lend you mine! And we'll both tear off this horrid mask!'

"I squirmed at his feet but he managed to grab my hands, Raoul, and he pushed them into the horror that was his face. With my own nails, he ravaged his flesh, tore his awful dead flesh!

" 'Know, know,' he shouted from deep within his throat that throbbed like a furnace, 'know that I am made up of death, from head to foot! And that it is a corpse who loves you, adores you and will never, never leave you! I will get a bigger coffin, Christine, for both of us, for the day when our love has run its course... Look, I am not laughing now, I am crying—crying for you, Christine, because you have torn off my mask and therefore you can never leave me again! As long as you believed I was handsome, you might have returned to me... Yes, I know you would have returned to me... But now that you have seen my hideousness, you will run away forever. So I shall keep you with me here! Oh, why did you want to see me? Poor, mad Christine who wanted to see me! When my own father never saw me! And my own mother, so as not to see me, cried when she gave me my first mask!'

"At last, he had released me and was instead thrashing on the floor, uttering terrible sobs. Then he crawled away like a snake, went into his room, closed the door and left me alone to my fear and my thoughts. A formidable silence, the very silence of the grave, had succeeded that tempest of emotions and I at last had time to consider the terrible consequences of my foolish gesture. The Monster's final words had told me what they were likely to be. I had imprisoned myself forever and my own insatiable curiosity was solely responsible for my misfortune. He had given me ample warning, told me that I would be totally safe as long as I did not touch his mask. But I had torn it off. I cursed my recklessness and could not help thinking that he had been right. Yes, I would have returned if I had not seen his face... He had already moved me, interested me enough, awakened my sympathy with those glistening tears that I saw behind his mask, that I would not have remained insensitive to his requests. Nothing could make me forget that he was the *Voice* who had breathed some of his genius into me, and I would not have been ungrateful. I would have returned. But now, once free of those catacombs, I would never return. *No one would return to share a tomb with a loving corpse!*

"Judging from the way he had looked at me, or rather brought those two dark pits of his invisible eyes close to my face during that unforgettable scene, I had taken the measure of his passion. The fact that he had not ravaged me while I was powerless in his arms showed that perhaps there was, after all, an Angel lurking inside the Monster... Maybe he *was* the Angel of Music, in some fashion, and he could have been so more fully if God had chosen to clothe him in handsome flesh instead of dressing him in festering rot.

"Panicking at the thought of the fate he had promised me, terrified by the perspective of seeing the door to the coffin room open, and to again see the Monster without his mask, I found refuge in my own room. I grabbed the scissors and was contemplating putting an end to my own, miserable destiny... when suddenly I heard the sound of the organ...

"It was then, dearest Raoul, that I began to understand Erik's earlier contempt when he had spoken of Opera music. What I now heard was utterly different from anything I had heard before that day. His *Don Juan Triumphant* (for I had no doubt that he had rushed to his masterpiece to forget the horror of the moment) at first sounded like one long, awful, magnificent sob in which poor Erik had poured all his accursed misery.

"I remembered the music book covered with the scrawled notes in red ink and I easily imagined that those notes had been written in his own blood. The music took me through every agonizing detail of his martyrdom. It showed me every nook and cranny of the abyss, the abyss where the *hideous man* lived. It portrayed Erik painfully bumping his poor, repulsive head against the sinister walls of his personal hell, until he found refuge where he would no longer frighten ordinary beings. I stood, stunned, breathless, pitiful and defeated by the eruption of those formidable chords that turned *his Pain itself* into something divine. Then, the sounds that rose from the abyss suddenly gathered into a huge, threatening flight, rising up into the air like an eagle climbing towards the Sun. That triumphant symphony decisively set the whole world aflame and I understood it was over, that Ugliness transported on the wings of Love had dared look Beauty in the face! I was almost intoxicated. The door that separated me from Erik yielded to my touch. Erik rose as I entered, *but dared not turn in my direction.*

" 'Erik,' I cried, 'show me your face without fear! I swear that you are the most unfortunate and sublime of men; and if ever I temble again when I look upon you, it will be because I am thinking of the magnificence of your genius!'

"Then Erik turned around, for he believed me, and I, too–alas!–had faith in my words. He raised his bony hands towards Destiny and fell at my feet, with words of love... With words of love coming from his dead mouth... And the music stopped...

"He kissed the hem of my dress and did not see that I had closed my eyes.

"What more can I tell you, dearest Raoul? You now know the full extent of the tragedy. It went on for two weeks– two weeks during which I lied to him. My lies were as hideous as the Monster who inspired them, but they were the price of my freedom. I burned his mask. I was so convincing that, even when he was not singing, he would try to catch my eye, like a dog hungry for its master's approval. He was my faithful slave and offered me endless small courtesies. Gradually, I made him so confident that he ventured to take me walking along the banks of the lake and to row me in the boat on its leaden waters. Near the end of my captivity, at night he let me out through the gates that close the underground tunnels and lead to the Rue Scribe. There, a carriage awaited us and took us to the Bois de Boulogne.

"The night when we encountered you proved nearly fatal to me, for he is terribly jealous of you and I had to tell him that you were leaving soon... Finally, after two horrible weeks of captivity, during which I was, in turns, filled with pity, en- thusiasm, despair and horror, he believed me when I told him: '*I will come back!*' "

"And you did go back, Christine," groaned Raoul.

"Yes, darling, but I must tell you that it was not his terri- ble threats when he set me free that convinced me to keep my word, but the tormented wail which he made on the threshold of the tomb... That wail," repeated Christine, agonizingly shaking her head, "bound me to his unfortunate soul more than I suspected when I said goodbye to him. Poor Erik! Poor Erik!"

"Christine," said Raoul, rising, "you told me that you love me, but hardly had you recovered your freedom than you returned to Erik! Remember the masked ball!"

"That was part of our agreement, Raoul. Those few hours, I've spent with you... filled with much danger for both of us."

"I doubted your love during those hours."

"Do you doubt it now, Raoul? You must understand that each of my visits to Erik increased my horror of him. For each of those visits, instead of reassuring him, as I had hoped, made him even more insanely jealous! And now, I'm frightened, so very frightened!"

"You're frightened of him, but do you love me? If Erik was handsome, would you still love me, Christine?"

"Poor Raoul! Why tempt fate? Why ask me for answers that I keep buried deep in my soul like the darkest sins?"

She rose and put her two trembling arms around the young man's neck.

"Oh, my darling betrothed for a day," she continued, "if I did not love you, I would not thus give you my lips! Take them, for the first time—and the last."

He kissed her lips. But suddenly, the night that enveloped them was rent asunder by thunder and lightning. They fled the approach of the storm. And before they returned to the attics of the Opera, they saw with eyes, still filled with the fear of Erik, high up above them, the huge shape of a giant night creature that stared at them with blazing eyes, seemingly clinging to the strings of Apollo's lyre.

Caza

Chapter Fourteen
The Trickster's Master Stroke

Raoul and Christine ran as fast as they could. They fled from the roof and the glowing eyes that appearead only in the darkest night. They did not stop until they got to the eighth floor on their way down. There was no performance at the Opera that night and the corridors were empty.

Suddenly, a strange character stood in front of them and blocked their path:

"No! Not this way!"

He pointed to another corridor which they could use to reach the backstage area.

Raoul wanted to stop and ask for an explanation.

"Hurry! Hurry!" said the man, who wore a long frock-coat and a foreign-looking hat.

Christine was already dragging Raoul, forcing him to run faster.

"Who was that? Who is that man?" asked the young man.

Christine replied: "It's the *Persian*."

"What's he doing here?"

"Nobody knows. He's always somewhere around the Opera."

"What you're making me do is cowardly, Christine," said Raoul, who was extremely upset. "You're forcing me to run away; it's the first time in my life I've done that."

"Pah!" said Christine as she began to recover her calm. "Maybe we've only been running away from a shadow, a product of our imaginations."

"If we really did see Erik up there, what I should have done is nail him to Apollo's lyre, just like they nail owls to the walls on the farms of Brittany. We would have been finished with him for good that way!"

"But, darling Raoul, you would have had to climb all the way up to the lyre. That's no easy matter."

"His glowing eyes were there!"

"Hah! You're getting to be like me now! You see him everywhere! What we thought were his glowing eyes were probably just a couple of stars shining through the strings of the lyre."

Christine moved down another floor and Raoul followed her.

"Since you've made up your mind to leave, Christine, I really think it would be better to go now. Why wait for tomorrow night? He may have heard us tonight."

"No, no! I told you! He's been working on his *Don Juan Triumphant* tonight. He hasn't been thinking of us."

"If you're so sure of that, why do you keep looking behind you!"

"Let's go to my dressing-room."

"Wouldn't it make more sense for us to leave the Opera?"

"No! Not until I'm ready to go for good! It would bring us all kinds of trouble if I didn't keep my word. I promised him that I would only see you there."

"It was very kind of him to allow you to do even that," said Raoul bitterly. "I suppose it was rather daring of you to play our game of being engaged?"

"No. He knew all about it. He said to me: 'Christine, I trust you. Monsieur de Chagny is in love with you and will be going abroad soon. When he leaves, I want him to be as unhappy as I am.' "

"What's that supposed to mean?"

"I should be the one asking you that. Are people so unhappy when they're in love?"

"Yes, they are, Christine, when they love and are not sure they are loved in return."

"Are you talking about Erik?"

"About Erik–and myself," said the young man, shaking his head, looking pensive and sad.

They finally arrived at Christine's dressing-room.

"Why do you think that we're safer here than anywhere else in the theater?" asked Raoul. "You heard him through the walls, which means he can also hear us."

"No. He gave me his word that he wouldn't lurk behind the walls of my dressing-room and I trust Erik's word. This room and my bedroom in *the house by the lake* are for me alone, exclusively, and that is sacred to him."

Raoul looked speculatively at the giant mirror on the wall.

"How could you have gone from this room to that dark corridor, Christine? Maybe we should try to duplicate your movements?"

"That would be dangerous, darling. The mirror might take me away again and, this time, instead of running away, I would have to follow the secret passage all the way to the lake and then call for Erik."

"Would he hear you?"

"Erik will hear me wherever and whenever I call him. He told me so. He's a very strange genius. You mustn't think, Raoul, that he's just a man who likes living underground. He does things that no other man could do. He knows things that no one else in the world knows."

"Take care, Christine! You're turning him into a phantom again!"

"No, he isn't a phantom, he's a man, a man of both Heaven and Earth, that's all."

"A man of both Heaven and Earth, that's all! That's an interesting way of thinking of him! You're sure that you're still intent on running away?"

"Yes, tomorrow night."

"Do you want me to tell you why I'd like you to run away with me tonight?"

"Yes, my darling."

"Because by tomorrow night, your resolve will be gone!"

"Then, Raoul, you'll have to carry me off by force. Isn't that what I asked of you?"

Raoul sighed with resignation.

"I'll be here at exactly midnight tomorrow night," he said somberly. "No matter what happens, I'll keep my promise. You said that, after listening to the performance, he'll go and wait for you in the *dining room by the lake*?"

"Yes. That's where he told me to meet him."

"But how are you supposed to get there, if you don't know how to use the mirror trick to leave your dressing-room?"

"I'm supposed to take the long way around."

"Going down through each of the vaults? Taking the same stairs and corridors that engineers and service employees use? But you would never be able to keep that a secret, Christine! Everyone will see you and a crowd will follow you all the way to the lake!"

Christine opened a box, took out an enormous key and showed it to Raoul.

"What's that?" he asked.

"The key to the gate that closes the underground passage that leads to the Rue Scribe."

"Ah! Now I understand! It leads straight to the lake. Give me that key, Christine!"

"Never!" she said energetically. "That would be dis-loyal!"

Suddenly, all the color drained from Christine's face. A mortal pallor spread over her features.

"Oh my God!" she cried. "Erik! Erik! Have pity on me!"

"Hush!" said Raoul. "Didn't you just say he would hear you call to him!"

But the singer's manner became increasingly mysterious. She wrung her fingers, repeating distraughtly:

"Oh my God! Oh my God!"

"What is it? What's wrong?" Raoul implored.

"The ring!"

"What ring? Please, Christine, tell me what's upsetting you!"

"The gold ring he gave me."

"Ah! So it was Erik who gave you that thing!"

"You know he did, Raoul! But what you don't know is that, when he gave it to me, he said:

" 'I give you back your freedom, Christine, on the condition that this ring will always be on your finger. As long as you wear it, you'll be protected against any danger and Erik shall remain your friend. But woe to you if you ever part with it, for Erik will have his revenge!'

"My God! My God The ring is gone! Woe to us both!"

They both searched frantically for the missing ring, but could not find it. Christine would not calm down.

"It must have happened when I kissed you earlier on the roof," she said, shaking. "The ring must have slipped from my finger and dropped to the street! We'll never be able to find it. What troubles are in store for us now! We must run away!"

"Yes. Tonight!" Raoul insisted, once more.

She hesitated. He thought that she was going to say yes. But then her bright pupils dimmed and she said:

"No! Tomorrow night!"

And she left him hurriedly, looking still troubled and wringing and rubbing her fingers as if she hoped that would bring the ring back.

Raoul went home, greatly perturbed by all that he had learned.

"If I don't save her from the hands of that monster," he said aloud as he went to bed, "she's lost. But I will save her."

He put out his lamp and, irrationally, felt the need to insult Erik in the dark. Three times, he shouted: "Monster! Monster! Monster!"

Suddenly, he propped himself up on his elbow. A cold sweat broke out on his forehead. Two eyes, like blazing coals, had appeared at the foot of his bed. They stared at him fixedly, terrifyingly, in the blackness of the night.

Raoul was no coward, yet he trembled. He reached a shaking, hesitant, fumbling hand towards his nightstand. Having found the matchbox, he lit a candle. The eyes disappeared.

Still ill at ease, he thought to himself:

"She told me you could only see *his* eyes in the dark... His eyes may have disappeared in the light, but *he* may still be here."

He got up and carefully searched the room. He looked under his bed, like a child. Then he thought the whole thing was utterly ridiculous. He said aloud:

"What should I believe? What not to believe, with such a fairy tale? Where does reality end and fantasy begin? What did she really see? Or what was it that she thought she saw?"

He added, with a shiver:

"And what did I see myself,? Were those glowing eyes really there? Or did they glow only in my imagination? Now I'm not sure about anything! And I wouldn't even swear to the reality of those eyes."

The young man got back into bed and blew out the candle. Everything went dark again.

The eyes reappeared.

"Oh!" sighed Raoul.

He sat up and stared back at them with all the bravery he possessed. After a long silence, which he used to muster his courage, he cried:

"Is that you, Erik? Man, angel or phantom, is it you?"

Then, he reflected:

"If it's him, he must be on the balcony!"

Still in his night-shirt, he ran to a chest of drawers in which he knew he would find a revolver. He groped for the gun. Once armed, he opened the balcony window. The night was bitterly cold. He looked out, saw nothing and closed the window again. He returned to bed, shivering and put the revolver on the table within easy reach.

Once more, he blew out the candle.

The eyes were still there, at the foot of the bed. Were they between the bed and the window, or behind the window, that is to say, on the balcony?

Raoul wanted to know. He also wanted to know if those eyes belonged to something human. He wanted to know everything.

Patiently, calmly, *without disturbing the darkness that enveloped him*, he seized the revolver and took aim.

He aimed at the two yellow stars that still stared at him with their strange, fixed gaze.

In fact, he aimed slilghtly above the twin stars. For if they were eyes, and if above those eyes there was a forehead, and if he was not too clumsy...

The shot made a terrible racket in the silence of the slumbering house. As footsteps came hurrying along the corridors, Raoul sat up with his arm stretched out, ready to fire again. He peered into the night.

This time, the two stars had disappeared.

Servants appeared, carrying lights. Comte Philippe burst into the room, terribly concerned:

"What happened?"

"I think I must have been dreaming," replied the young man. "I fired at two stars that were keeping me from sleeping."

"What are you raving about? Are you mad? For God's sake, Raoul, tell me what happened?"

The Comte grabbed the revolver.

"No, no, I'm not raving... Besides, we'll soon see..."

The young man got out of bed, put on a dressing-gown and slippers, took a light from the hands of a servant and, opening the window, stepped out onto the balcony.

The Comte saw that the window had been pierced by a bullet at the height of a man's head. Raoul was leaning over the balcony holding out his candle:

"Aha!" he said. "Blood! Traces of blood! Here, there, more blood! Good! A phantom who bleeds is much less dangerous!" he said wryly.

"Raoul! Raoul! Raoul!"

The Comte shook him as if he was trying to awaken a sleepwalker from his deadly trance.

"But, my dear brother, I'm not asleep!" Raoul protested impatiently. "You can see the blood for yourself. I thought I might have been dreaming and firing at two stars. But I wasn't! It was Erik's eyes–and there is Erik's blood to prove it!"

Then, he added, suddenly very concerned:

"Maybe I was wrong to shoot at him. Christine may never forgive me... Ah! All this wouldn't have happened if I'd drawn the curtains before going to bed."

"Raoul, have you gone mad? Wake up!"

"What, you still think that I'm asleep? You'd do better, brother, to help me find Erik... Because a phantom who bleeds can always be found."

The Comte's valet interrupted:

"The young Vicomte is correct, Monsieur le Comte. There is blood on the balcony."

The other servant brought another lamp and with its added light they could examine the balcony carefully. The blood went along the railings, reached the gutters and then trailed up them to the roof.

"My dear brother," said Comte Philippe, "I think you shot a cat."

"The sad thing," said Raoul, with a grim snigger that pained his brother when he heard it, "is that it's quite possible. With Erik, one can never be certain. Was it Erik? Was it a cat? Was it the Phantom? Was it substance or shadow? No, with Erik, one can never be certain!"

Raoul kept making odd remarks in the same vein, which, to him, closely and reasonably reflected his apprehension, based on Christine's strange account of the very real, yet fantastic, experience that she had undergone. But to other people, his mutterings sounded as if the Vicomte was losing his sanity. The Comte, himself, came to that conclusion and, later, so did the Investigating Magistrate when he read the report of the Police Commissioner.

"Who is Erik?" asked the Comte, pressing his brother's hand.

"He is my rival. And if he's not dead, it's a shame."

He dismissed the servants with a wave of his hand and the two Chagnys were left alone. But the men had not yet moved out of earshot when the Comte's valet heard Raoul say, distinctly and emphatically:

"I'm going to take Christine away tonight."

That phrase was later repeated to Monsieur Faure, the Investigating Magistrate. But no one ever knew exactly what else was said between the two brothers after they were left alone that night.

The servants testified that this was not their first quarrel. Their voices penetrated the wall. And the object of their argument was a singer named Christine Daae.

At breakfast–an early morning breakfast which the Comte took in his study–Philippe sent for his brother. Raoul arrived silent and low-spirited. There was another, brief confrontation between the two brothers. The following report of their conversation was later entered into evidence:

Comte Philippe (handing his brother a copy of the paper L'Epoque *and pointing to an article). "Read that!"*

Vicomte Raoul (reluctantly). "The latest news on the Boulevards is of the engagement between the notorious Opera singer, Mademoiselle Christine Daae, and the Vicomte Raoul de Chagny. If the gossips are to be believed, Comte Philippe de Chagny is said to have sworn that, for the first time on record, such a promise shall not be kept. But love conquers all–at the Opera more than anywhere else–and one wonders how Comte Philippe intends to stop his brother from leading his new *Marguerite* to the altar. The two brothers are said to be very close, but we think the Comte is severely mistaken if he imagines that brotherly love will triumph over pure, romantic love."

Comte Philippe (sadly). "You see, Raoul, you've made us the object of ridicule! That girl has turned your head with her tales of the Phantom."

(One would infer from this that Raoul had repeated Christine's story to his brother during the night.)

Vicomte Raoul. "Goodbye, Philippe."

Comte Philippe. "Have you made up your mind? You're really leaving tonight?"

No reply.

Comte Philippe. "With her? Surely you wouldn't do anything so foolish?"

No reply.

Comte Philippe. "I'll find a way to stop you, you know!"

Vicomte Raoul. "Goodbye, my brother!"

He exits the room.

That conversation was reported to the Investigating Magistrate by Comte Philippe himself, who did not see Raoul again until that night at the Opera, a few minutes before Christine's disappearance.

Raoul devoted the whole day to preparations for his flight with Christine.

The horses, the carriage, the driver, the food, the luggage, the money required for the journey, the itinerary–he had decided not to go by train so that it would be more difficult for Erik to track them down–all this had to be organized and it occupied him until 9 p.m. that evening.

At 9 p.m. sharp, the selected carriage, a *berline* with its curtains drawn, was parked near the Rotunda outside the Opera. It was pulled by two powerful horses driven by a man whose face was almost entirely concealed in the long folds of his scarf. Parked in front of this carriage were three other coaches. Later, the Investigating Magistrate discovered that they belonged, respectively, to Mademoiselle Carlotta, who had suddenly returned to Paris, Mademoiselle Sorelli and, at the head of the line, Comte Philippe de Chagny. No one left the *berline*. The driver remained on his seat, as did the three other drivers.

A witness reported seeing a shadowy figure dressed in a long black cloak and wearing a soft black felt hat walking along the sidewalk between the Rotunda and the three carriages. They claimed that the figure seemed extremely interested in the *berline*, even going over to take a closer look at the horses and its driver, then moving away without saying a word. The Magistrate later believed that this shadowy figure was Vicomte Raoul de Chagny. I don't agree, since that night, like every other night, the Vicomte was wearing a top hat, which, indeed, was found later. I am far more inclined to think that the shadowy figure was none other than the Phantom, who knew everything about the whole affair as the reader will soon discover.

That night, as luck would have it, they were playing *Faust* before a full house. Paris' High Society was magnificently represented. In those days, the Opera subscribers did not sub-lease or share their boxes with the world of commerce and finance, or foreigners. Today, one is just as likely to find in Marquis ***'s box–often referred to as such since said Marquis is contractually the lessor of that box–a wealthy trader in salted pork, which mind you, is quite appropriate since, after all, it's that good tradesman who makes the Marquis' lease payments. But in those days, such a transaction was virtually unknown. The boxes of the Opera were the salons where High Society congregated and, occasionally, enjoyed some music.

All these people knew each other, without necessarily being close. But they were able to put names on faces and, that night, the face of Comte de Chagny was known to everyone.

The article in the morning's *Epoque* had already produced its effect, for all eyes were turned towards the box in which Comte Philippe sat alone, apparently indifferent to everyone around him and not exhibiting a single sign of concern. The women in this sparkling assemblage were understandably puzzled. The Vicomte's conspicuous absence gave rise to much whispering behind their fans. Christine Daae, when she appeared on stage, received a rather cold reception. That particular audience could not forgive her for setting her sights so far above her station.

The singer noticed this rather hostile attitude on the part of the audience and was upset by it.

The regulars of the Opera, who claimed to know the truth about the Vicomte's affair, exchanged meaningful gazes during certain passages in Marguerite's part. They made a show of turning and looking at Philippe de Chagny's box when Christine sang:

> *"Je voudrais bien savoir*
> *Quel était ce jeune homme;*
> *Si c'est un grand seigneur,*
> *Et comment il se nomme."* [17]

The Comte sat with his chin on his hand and appeared to take no notice of these demonstrations. He kept his eyes fixed on the stage–but was he truly watching it? His thoughts seemed far away.

Christine increasingly lost her confidence. She began to shake. She was on the verge of a catastrophe... Carolus Fonta, the tenor, wondered if she was ill and if she could remain on stage until the end of the Garden Act. In the theater, people had not forgotten that it was at the end of that very act that Mademoiselle Carlotta had experienced her own catastrophe–that historic *croak* which had temporarily put her Parisian career on hold.

Just then, Carlotta made her entrance in a box facing the stage–a sensational entrance. Poor Christine raised her eyes towards this latest perturbation. She recognized her rival. She

---

[17] *"I would really like to know / Who that young man was; / If he is a great lord, / And what is his name?"*

thought she saw a sneer on her lips. That saved her. She forgot everything, in order to once again triumph.

From that moment, the diva sang with all her heart and soul. She tried to surpass all that she had done until then–and she succeeded. In the last act, when she began the invocation to the angels and rose up above the Earth, she made the entire audience tremble and feel as if they, too, had wings.

During that superhuman plea, a man had stood in the center of the threater and remained standing, facing the singer, as if he, too, was ready to depart this Earth. It was Raoul.

"Anges purs! Anges radieux!" [18]

And Christine, her arms outstretched, her throat filled with fire, her glorious hair cascading over her bare shoulders, uttered the divine lines:

"Portez mon âme au sein des cieux!" [19]

It was at that very moment that the stage was suddenly plunged into darkness. It happened so quickly that the spectators barely had time to cry out their surprise, for the lights came back up almost immediately.

But Christine Daae had vanished! What had become of her? What was this phenomenon? All and sundry looked at each other uncomprehendingly. Excitement spread and grew throughout the audience. Emotions ran just as high backstage. Stagehands rushed to the spot where only a minute before, Christine had been singing so gloriously. The performance was interrupted amidst the greatest chaos.

Where? Where had Christine gone? What spell had spirited her away before the eyes of hundreds of enthusiastic onlookers, from the arms of Carolus Fonta himself? It was as if

---

[18] *"Pure angels! Radiant angels!"*
[19] *"Carry my soul to the bosom of Heaven!"*

the angels had heard her supplication and really had carried her up "to rest" body and soul.

Raoul, still standing in the orchestra, had uttered a cry. Comte Philippe, in his box, had sprung to his feet. People looked at the stage, at the Comte, at Raoul, and wondered if this mysterious event was in any way connected with the article in that morning's paper. But Raoul hurriedly left his seat, the Comte disappeared from his box and, as they lowered the curtain, the subscribers rushed to the door that led backstage. The rest of the public waited for an announcement amidst an indescribable racket. Everyone spoke at the same time. Everyone offered his own explanation for the extraordinary event. Some said: "She fell through a trap-door." Others said: "She was lifted up to the rafters too fast; the poor girl is the victim of some kind of new special effect." Yet others said: "It's foul play; the fact the lights went out just as she vanished is proof enough."

At last, the curtain slowly rose. Carolus Fonta stepped to the conductor's desk and, in a sad, grave voice, said:

"Ladies and gentlemen, something unprecedented has just occurred, and has thrown us all into a state of great alarm. Our dear colleague, Christine Daae, has disappeared before our very eyes–and no one knows how or why!"

Gianluca Costantini

Jay Stephens

Chapter Fifteen
The Curious Incident of the Safety Pin

There was indescribable chaos backstage. Artists, stagehands, dancers, bit players, extras, chorus-girls, subscribers, everyone was asking questions, shouting and bustling. "What happened to her?" "She ran off." "The Vicomte de Chagny took her." "No, his brother the Comte did." "What about Mademoiselle Carlotta–she did it!" "No, it was the Phantom!"

A few laughed, especially as a careful examination of the trap-doors and stage-boards had ruled out the possibility of an accident.

Amidst this noisy throng, one could have noticed three men talking in low voices but gesticulating in a panicked manner. They were Gabriel, the chorus-master, Mercier, one of the Assistant Directors and Remy, the Directors' secretary. They stood in a remote corner, next to the corridor leading from backstage to the foyer. There, they argued, partially hidden behind a pile of large props.

"I knocked at their door. No one answered. Maybe they're not in the office? At any rate, I can't tell because they took the keys with them."

That was Monsieur Remy and "they" were obviously the two Directors, who had given orders, during the last intermission, that they were not to be disturbed for any reason whatsoever. "They were not in for anybody."

"All the same," exclaimed Gabriel, "a singer doesn't pull a vanishing act onstage every day!"

"Did you try shouting that through the door?" asked Mercier.

"No, but it's worth a try. I'll do it now," said Remy, rushing back towards the Directors' office.

Just then, the stage manager arrived.

"Well, Monsieur Mercier, are you coming? What are you two doing here? You're needed, Monsieur."

"I refuse to say or do anything until the Police arrive," declared Mercier. "I've sent for Commissioner Mifroid. We'll wait until he gets here!"

"I think you should go down to the 'organ' immediately."

"Not until the Police arrive."

"I've already been down to the 'organ' myself."

"And, what did you see?"

"Nobody, at all! Do you hear me? Nobody!"

"So, what do you want me to do about it?"

"Well," said the stage manager, frantically running his hands through his rebellious hair. "My thought was that, if there'd been someone at the 'organ,' he might have been able to tell us who turned off the lights. Because I can't find Mauclair anywhere. Do you see now?"

Mauclair was the head gaffer responsible for manufacturing day and night, as necessary, on the Opera's stage.

"You can't find Mauclair anywhere?" repeated Mercier, taken aback. "What about his assistants?"

"There's no Mauclair and no assistants! No one at the lights at all!" roared the stage manager. "That girl didn't disappear on her own! It was a conspiracy! We've got to find out what happened. Why aren't the Directors here? What can they be doing at a time like this? I gave orders that no one was to go near the lights and I posted a guard next to the 'organ.' Did I do the right thing?"

"Yes, yes, absolutely! But now we should just wait for the Police."

The stage manager walked away shrugging and unhappy, muttering insults about the lily-livered bureaucrats who preferred hiding quietly in a corner while the rest of the theater was thrown into chaos.

But, as a matter of fact, Messrs. Gabriel and Mercier were not quiet at all. Indeed, they had received an order that prevented them from acting. The two Directors had been most explicit that they were not to be disturbed *for any reason whatsoever*. Remy had tried to ignore that order but had met with no success.

The secretary returned, with a strange, puzzled look on his face.

"Well, did you see them this time?" asked Mercier.

"Moncharmin finally opened the door," Remy replied. "His eyes were bulging out of his head. I thought he was going to strike me. I couldn't get a word in. Guess what he shouted at me?

" 'Do you have a safety pin on you?' he asked.

" 'No!' I said.

" 'Then, get out of here!' he shouted back at me.

"I tried to tell him that something unprecedented had just happened onstage, but he kept screaming: 'A safety pin! I need a safety pin at once!' An office boy heard him–he was bellowing like a bull–ran up with a safety pin and gave it to him. At which point, Moncharmin slammed the door in my face, and here I am!"

"Couldn't you have said, 'Christine Daae...' "

"I would have liked to see you try! He was foaming at the mouth. He wasn't thinking of anything but his damned safety pin. I honestly believe that if that boy hadn't brought him one then and there, he would have had a fit! None of this is right! The Directors have gone crazy!"

Monsieur Remy was deeply unhappy. He continued in the same tone:

"It can't go on like this! I'm not used to being treated that way!"

Suddenly, Gabriel whispered:

"What if it was another trick of–*P.O.*?"

Remy snickered. Mercier sighed and seemed about to say something, but meeting Gabriel's eye, kep quiet.

Still, the Assistant Director felt that his responsibility increased as the minutes ticked by without the Directors' appearing. Finally, he wasn't able to stand it any longer.

"OK! I'll go and get them myself!" he said.

Gabriel, suddenly became quite gloomy and serious and stopped him.

"Be careful, Monsieur Mercier! If the Directors have locked themselves in their office, it may be because they have no choice! *P.O.* has more than one trick up his sleeve!"

But Mercier shook his head.

"Thanks, but I'm going! If they'd listened to me before, we would have told the Police everything long ago!"

He left.

"*Everything*?" asked Remy immediately. "What should we have told the Police? Why won't you answer me, Gabriel? Ah, so you do know something! You'd better tell me, if you don't want me spreading it around that you're all going mad! Yes, that's what you all are: mad!"

Gabriel feigned a stupid look and pretended not to understand the secretary's unseemly outburst.

"What is it that I'm supposed to know?" he said. "I don't know what you're talking about, Monsieur Remy."

Remy began to lose his temper.

"Tonight, Richard and Moncharmin were acting like lunatics here, during the intermission."

"I didn't notice anything unusual," muttered Gabriel, looking noticeably embarrassed.

"Then you must be the only one! Do you think that I didn't see them? Or that Monsieur Parabise, the Director of the Crédit Central, didn't notice it either? Or that Monsieur de La Borderie, the ambassador, doesn't have eyes to see? All the subscribers were staring at the Directors!"

"What were they doing that was so strange?" asked Gabriel, putting on his most innocent air.

"What were they doing? You know better than anyone what they were doing! You were there! You watched them, you and Mercier! And you were the only two who didn't laugh."

"I don't have any idea what you're talking about!"

Gabriel, very coldly, crossed his arms, intending to convey that this subject of conversation no longer held any interest for him. But Remy wouldn't let it go:

"What was the meaning of their bizarre new behavior? *Why didn't they want anyone going near them?*"

"What do you mean, *they didn't want anyone going near them?*"

"*They didn't want anyone to touch them!*"

"Really? You thought that *they didn't want anyone going near them?* I agree. That would have been very odd indeed!"

"Oh, so now you admit it! Finally! Then, *they walked backwards!*"

"Backwards? You saw the Directors *walk backwards?* Why, I thought that only lobsters walked backwards!"

"Don't laugh, Monsieur Gabriel! Don't you dare laugh!"

"I'm not laughing," protested Gabriel, trying to look as solemn as a judge.

"Then perhaps you can tell me this, Monsieur Gabriel, since you're such a close friend of the Directors. When I went up to see Monsieur Richard outside the foyer, during the Garden intermission, as I was approaching him with my hand held out, why did Monsieur Moncharmin rush towards me, pull me back and whisper: 'Go away! Go away! Whatever you do, don't touch Monsieur Richard!' Do I have some kind of infectious disease?"

"That's incredible!"

"Then, a little later, when Monsieur de La Borderie went to talk to Monsieur Richard, didn't you see Monsieur Moncharmin step between the two of them? Didn't you hear him cry out, 'Please, Monsieur l'Ambassadeur, don't touch Monsieur Richard'?"

"That's unbelievable! And what was Monsieur Richard doing at the time?"

"What was he doing? Why, you saw him! He turned around. *He bowed, as if he was greeting someone, although there was nobody there, then he withdrew, walking backwards!*"

"Backwards?"

"And Moncharmin, behind Richard, also turned around, that is, he made a semicircle behind Richard and *he walked backwards as well*! And that's how they moved to the staircase leading back to their office: *backwards*, *backwards*, *backwards*! If they're not mad, can you tell me what it all meant?"

"Perhaps they were rehearsing some kind of new ballet step?" suggested Gabriel, without much conviction in his voice.

The secretary became furious at such a pitiful attempt at an explanation while such dramatic events were occurring. He knit his brows and pursed his lips. Then he leaned towards Gabriel and whispered in his ear:

"You think you're clever, don't you, Gabriel? But there are things going on here for which you and Mercier may be partially responsible."

"What are you saying, Monsieur Remy?" asked Gabriel.

"Christine Daae may not be the only one who disappeared tonight."

"Nonsense!"

"There's no nonsense about it. Maybe you can tell me why, when Madame Giry came down to the foyer earlier, Mercier took her by the hand and rushed off with her?"

"Did he?" said Gabriel, "I didn't notice."

"You did more than notice it, Monsieur Gabriel! You went to his office with him and Madame Giry. Since then, we've seen you and Mercier, but no one has seen Madame Giry."

"Do you think we killed and ate her?"

"No! You've locked her up in the office. Anyone who passes by can hear her screaming, 'Scoundrels! Scoundrels!' "

As their curious conversation reached this point, Mercier returned, totally out of breath.

"It's worse than I thought!" he said, in a depressed sounding voice. I shouted: 'Open the door! It's me, Mercier! Something grave has happened!'

214

"I heard footsteps. The door opened and Moncharmin appeared, he was extremely pale. He said: 'What do you want?'

"I answered: 'Someone has abducted Christine Daae.'

"What do you think he said? 'Good for her!'

"Then, he slammed the door in my face, after dumping this in my hand."

Mercier opened his hand. Remy and Gabriel looked.

"The safety pin!" cried Remy.

"Odd! Very odd!" muttered Gabriel, who could not repress a shiver.

Suddenly, a voice caused all three of them to turn around.

"I beg your pardon, gentlemen. Could you tell me where Christine Daae is?"

Despite the gravity of the circumstances, the absurdity of the question would have made them all burst out in laughter, had they not caught sight of a face so stricken with despair that they were immediately seized with pity.

The questioner was the Vicomte Raoul de Chagny.

Olivier & Stephane Peru

Chapter Sixteen
"Christine! Christine!"

Raoul's first thought, following Christine's incredible disappearance, was to blame Erik. He no longer doubted the quasi-supernatural powers of the *Angel of Music* in the Opera, where he had so diabolically created an empire.

Therefore, Raoul had rushed backstage, in a mad fit of love and despair. "Christine! Christine!" he moaned, calling to her as he felt that she must be calling to him from the depths of the dark pit to which the Monster had carried his prey, who still trembled under the power of her divine exaltation and was still wrapped in the white shroud in which she had offered herself to the angels of Heaven.

"Christine! Christine!" Raoul continued to cry. And it seemed to him that he could hear her screams through the thin floorboards that separated the two of them. He bent forward, he listened, he wandered across the stage like a madman. Ah, to descend into that abyss of darkness, which was now closed to him!

The thin slats of woods that ordinarily slid so easily, could reveal the depths where he knew the object of his love had been taken. Those slats, which creaked beneath his feet, creating sounds which echoed through the gargantuan vaults below, now seemed more than simple, inert objects. They had become truly unyielding. It was as if they were an obdurate force, refusing to disclose their secrets to him. And even the very stairs that led below were forbidden to everyone!

"Christine! Christine!"

People pushed him aside, laughing. They made fun of him. They thought the young man's mind had become unhinged!

In what frenzied rush, through which dark, mysterious passages known to him alone, had Erik managed to drag that pure, soulful girl back to his awful lair, with its Louis-Philippe bedroom and drawing-room opening onto the hellish underground lake?

"Christine! Christine! Why don't you answer me? Are you still alive? Or did you surrender your last breath in a wave of overpowering terror when you felt the Monster's burning breath?"

Hideous thoughts flashed through Raoul's congested brain.

Of course, Erik must have discovered their secret, must have found out that Christine had betrayed him. How dreadful might his vengeance be?

What would the Angel of Music do, having had his pride crushed? Christine, alone in the all-powerful clutches of that Monster, would surely be lost!

Raoul thought back to the twin blazing stars that had appeared the night before on his balcony. Why had he not made sure his shot had done its work?

There were some men's eyes that dilated in the darkness and shone like stars or cats' eyes. (Some albinos, who appeared to have rabbits' eyes during the day, have cats' eyes at night: everyone knows that!)

It was undoubtedly Erik upon whom he had fired. Why had he not killed him? The Monster had escaped up the rainspout, like a cat or a burglar who–everyone knew that, too– could scale the very skies with only a rainspout for support.

No doubt Erik was, even then, plotting some nefarious scheme against Raoul himself, but he had been wounded and had fled, forced to strike at poor Christine instead.

Such were the cruel thoughts that haunted Raoul as he ran to the singer's dressing-room.

"Christine! Christine!"

Bitter tears burned the young man's eyes as he saw, scattered around the room, the very clothes which his beautiful fiancée was to have worn for their flight. Oh, why had she refused to leave sooner? Why had she toyed with impending calamity? With the Monster's heart? Why, in a final gesture of pity, had she insisted on throwing, as a last sop to that demon's soul, her divine song:

> *"Anges purs! Anges radieux!*
> *Portez mon âme au sein des cieux!"*

Raoul, his throat heavy with sobs, oaths and insults, awkwardly fumbled at the great mirror that had previously opened before his very eyes, to let Christine travel to the somber world that lay below. He pushed, pressed, groped around, but the mirror seemed to obey no one but Erik... Perhaps actions were insufficient with a mirror of that kind? Perhaps he was expected to utter a magical phrase? When he was a boy, he had heard about magic mirrors that responded only to spoken words!

Suddenly, Raoul remembered something about a gate that opened onto the Rue Scribe, an underground passage that ran straight from the lake to the street... Yes, Christine had mentioned it to him... And after discovering that the great, iron key was–alas!–no longer in its box, nevertheless the young man ran directly to the Rue Scribe.

Once in the street, he ran his trembling hands over the huge stones of the Opera, felt for secret passages, examined openings sealed with iron bars... Could this be the entrance he sought? Or that one? Or could it be that grate instead? He peered uselessly through the bars and saw only darkness! He listened and heard only silence! He went around the building and came across a huge gate, with bigger bars, at the entrance to the Cour de l'Administration.

Raoul rushed into the concierge's lodge.

"I beg your pardon, Madame... Could you tell me where to find a gate or a metal door, with bars, iron bars, that opens into the Rue Scribe and leads to the lake? You know which lake I mean? The underground lake–beneath the Opera."

"Yes, Monsieur, I know there is a lake somewhere under the Opera, but I don't know which door leads to it. I've never been there!"

"But the Rue Scribe, Madame, the Rue Scribe... Surely you've been to the Rue Scribe?"

The woman laughed, huge peals of laughter as if he was making a joke! Raoul couldn't stand it any longer and left, filled with powerless rage. He ran upstairs, then downstairs, rushed through the entire management wing only to find himself once more back on stage.

There, he stopped, his heart thumping in his chest. He wondered if Christine had perhaps been found? He saw a group of men and asked:

"I beg your pardon, gentlemen. Could you tell me where Christine Daae is?"

And that is when Messrs. Mercier, Remy and Gabriel laughed.

Suddenly, the stage buzzed with a new rumor. A gentleman had just made his entrance, surrounded by men in black coats, all talking and gesticulating together. The newcomer seemed quite calm and sported pleasant features, a chubby face with a rosy complexion, crowned by curly blond hair and lit up by a pair of wonderfully serene blue eyes. Mercier pointed him out to Raoul and said:

"This is the gentleman to whom you should put your question, Monsieur le Vicomte. This is Police Commissioner Mifroid."

"Ah, Monsieur le Vicomte de Chagny," said the Commissioner. "I'm delighted to meet you, Monsieur. Would you mind coming with me? And now, where are the Directors? Where are the Directors?"

Mercier did not answer. Remy volunteered the information that the Directors were locked in their office and that, as yet, they knew nothing of what had happened.

"Really? Take me to their office at once!"

Then, Monsieur Mifroid, followed by an ever-growing crowd, proceeded towards the management wing. Meanwhile,

Mercier, taking advantage of the confusion, slipped a key into Gabriel's hand.

"This isn't going well," the Assistant Director whispered. "You'd better let Madame Giry out."

And Gabriel quickly went off to do just that.

The Commissioner soon arrived at the Directors' door. Mercier was asked to knock on it, which he did in vain: it remained closed.

"Open up, in the name of the law!" ordered Mifroid finally, in a loud and somewhat uneasy voice.

Finally, the door was opened. Everyone rushed into the office, right on the Commissioner's heels.

Raoul was the last to enter. As he was about to follow the crowd, a hand was laid on his shoulder and these words were spoken in his ear:

"*Erik's secrets are nobody's business!*"

He turned around and stifled an exclamation. The hand that had touched him on the shoulder now held a finger to the lips of a man with a dark complexion, jade-green eyes and who wore an astrakhan hat: the Persian!

The stranger kept up the gesture that mimed discretion then, just as the astonished Vicomte was about to ask him the reason for his mysterious intervention, bowed and disappeared.

Fernando Pasarin

Chapter Seventeen
The Amazing Revelations of Madame Giry
about her personal relationship
with the Phantom of the Opera

Before following Commissioner Mifroid into the Directors' office, first I need to tell the reader about the amazing events that took place there earlier. You remember that both Messrs. Remy and Mercier had vainly tried to gain entrance and that Messrs. Richard and Moncharmin appeared to have locked themselves inside for a purpose so far unrevealed. It is my historical duty–or, I should say, my duty as an historian–without further delay to enlighten the reader about what happened therein.

I stated before that, lately, the Directors' moods had undergone an unhappy transformation and explained that this transformation was not entirely due to the crash of the chandelier on that other memorable night.

Now, it's time to inform the reader–despite the fact that the Directors would wish this to remain undisclosed–that they had paid the Phantom his first 20,000 francs. There had, of course, been much wailing and gnashing of teeth, but it had still happened as simply as could be.

One morning, the Directors found a pre-addressed envelope on their desk. It just said: "*To P.O. (personal)*" and was accompanied by a note from said "*P.O.*" which read:

"*The time has come to carry out the terms set forth in the Rulebook. Please put 20 1,000-franc notes into this envelope, seal it well and hand it to Madame Giry who will do what is required of her.*"

The Directors jumped at what they saw as a golden opportunity to catch the blackmailer. They wasted no time asking themselves how the mysterious missive could have landed on their desk, in an office which they were careful to lock every night. Instead, after confiding in Gabriel and Mercier, and swearing both of them to secrecy, they put the 20,000 francs into the envelope. They then handed it to Madame Giry, who had been reinstated in her position. The old usherette showed no surprise, but, of course, she was closely watched!

Madame Giry went straight to the Phantom's box and deposited the precious envelope on the little shelf mentioned earlier. The two Directors, as well as Gabriel and Mercier, remained in hiding throughout, but in such a way that they did not lose sight of the envelope for a single second during the entire performance, and even afterwards. The envelope had not moved, so those who watched it did not move either. Madame Giry eventually went home while the Directors, Gabriel and Mercier were still secretly watching. Finally, they grew tired of waiting. They went to the box, grabbed the envelope and opened it, after checking that the seal had not been broken.

At first, Richard and Moncharmin thought that the bank notes were still inside. But upon closer examination, they realized that they had been had! The 20 genuine notes were gone and had been replaced by 20 notes of play money! At first, the Directors were enraged, then they were struck with consternation.

"It's a trick worthy of Robert Houdin," said Gabriel.

"But a lot more expensive," remarked Richard.

Moncharmin wanted to send for the Police right away, but Richard objected. He thought he had a plan.

"Let's not look ridiculous," he said. "All of Paris will laugh at us. *P.O.* won the first game; we'll win the next."

He was obviously already thinking of the next month's stipend.

Nevertheless, they had been so totally tricked that, during the following weeks, they began to feel rather despondent. It wasn't hard to understand why. One reason that they had not immediately called the Police, was that, in the back of their minds, they held on to the idea that this mysterious incident might still be part of some elaborate practical joke devised by their predecessors. They were afraid that, if they divulged it before they could get to the bottom of it, they would look foolish indeed. Even that notion was sporadically superceded in Monsieur Moncharmin's mind by a mild suspicion directed towards his co-Director, Richard himself. After all, the man was known for his occasional flights of fancy... So, the Directors chose to wait, ready to act should the opportunity present itself, keeping an eye on Madame Giry all the while.

Richard thought it unwise to question her at this stage. "In any case, if she's an accessory," he explained, "it won't do anything to help us get the money back. That's long gone. But in my opinion, she's nothing but an old fool."

"She's not the only fool in this affair," reflected Moncharmin.

"Who would have thought it?" moaned Richard. "But don't worry! Next time, I'll take every precaution!"

"Next time" happened to be the very day that Christine Daae disappeared. In the morning–in the same mysterious fashion–the Directors received a note from the Phantom reminding them that his stipend was due. It read:

"*Do just as you did last time. Things worked perfectly. Place the 20,000 francs in the envelope and hand it to the admirable Madame Giry.*"

The note was accompanied by a pre-addressed envelope that was an exact duplicate of the previous one. All they needed to do was insert the bank notes.

Which they did that very night, approximately half-an-hour before the curtain rose on *Faust*. It is at that moment, therefore, that we shall rejoin the Directors in their office.

First, Richard showed the envelope to Moncharmin. Then, he counted the twenty notes–genuine bank notes, drawn from the bank that very afternoon–right in front of him. Finally, he placed the notes inside the envelope, but did not seal it.

"Now," said Richard, "let's call Madame Giry."

They sent for the old woman. She walked in and made a sweeping curtsy. She still wore her old taffeta dress, the color of which was rapidly turning to rust, and her soot-darkened bonnet. She seemed in good humor and said at once:

"Good evening, Messieurs! I suppose it's for the envelope?"

"Yes, Madame Giry," said Richard, most amiably. "For the envelope–and something else besides."

"At your service, Messieurs, at your service. What is the other thing that you need?"

"First of all, dear Madame, I have a small question to put to you."

"By all means, Monsieur. I'll be delighted to answer."

"Are you still on good terms with the Phantom?"

"Excellent terms, Monsieur; couldn't be better."

"Wonderful, we're delighted... Look here, Madame Giry," said Richard, changing his tone to one of sharing an important confidence. "We may just as well come out and say it straight... We know you're no fool!"

"Why, Monsieur le Directeur!" exclaimed the usherette, causing the two black feathers of her bonnet to nod in accord. "I can assure you that no one has ever doubted that!"

"Then we're all in agreement and we'll all be able to understand one another. This entire Phantom business is all an elaborate joke, isn't it? Seriously, just between the three of us, it's lasted long enough."

Madame Giry looked at the Directors as if they had spoken to her in Chinese. She stepped closer to Richard's desk and asked, rather anxiously:

"What do you mean? I don't understand."

"Oh yes you do, you understand me quite well. And, if not, you'd better understand, and fast... First of all, tell us his name."

"Whose name?"

"The name of your accomplice, Madame Giry!"

"Me? The Phantom's accomplice? In what, exactly?"

"You do everything he wants."

"That! He doesn't ask much, you know."

"Does he still tip you?"

"I can't complain."

"How much does he pay you to bring him that envelope?"

"Ten francs."

"Really? That's not much, is it?

"Why?"

"I'll tell you later. But right now, Madame Giry, we're curious to know what extraordinary reason has caused you to give yourself body and soul, to this Phantom... I suspect one doesn't buy that kind of friendship and devotion for a measly five or ten francs."

"That's true enough... I'll be happy to tell you the reason, Monsieur. There's no shame in it. Quite the reverse, in fact!"

"We're listening, dear Madame."

"Well, it's like this... It's just that, normally, the Phantom doesn't like it if I talk about his business..."

"Indeed?" sneered Richard.

"But I suppose this is a matter that concerns only me... I was in Box No. 5 one night, when I found a letter addressed to me, a sort of note written in red ink. I don't need to read it to you, Monsieur, because I know it by heart, and I'll never forget it if I live to be a hundred!"

And Madame Giry, drawing herself up, recited the letter aloud with touching eloquence:

Madame:

1825. Mademoiselle Ménétrier, lead dancer of the ballet, became Marquise de Cussy.

1832. Mademoiselle Marie Taglioni, a dancer, became Comtesse Gilbert des Voisins.

1846. Mademoiselle Sota, a dancer, married a brother of the King of Spain.

1847. Mademoiselle Lola Montes, a dancer, became the morganatic bride of King Louis of Bavaria and was made Countess of Landsfeld.

227

1848. Mademoiselle Maria, a dancer, became Baronne d'Herneville.

1870. Mademoiselle Theresa Hessier, a dancer, married Dom Fernando, brother to the King of Portugal.

Richard and Moncharmin listened to the old woman, who, as she enumerated all these glorious weddings, seemed to expand, became braver and, finally, illuminated, like an oracle of ancient times, in a voice bursting with pride, uttered the last sentence of the prophetic letter:

1885. Meg Giry, Empress!

Exhausted by this supreme effort, the usherette fell into a chair, saying:

"Gentlemen, the letter was signed, *Phantom of the Opera*. I had heard a lot about the Phantom over the years, but only half believed in him. From the day he announced that my little Meg, the flesh of my flesh, the fruit of my womb, would become Empress, I believed in him totally."

To be honest, it wasn't necessary to study Madame Giry's excited features closely to understand what sway the two words "Phantom" and "Empress" would have held over such a first-rate intellect!

But who pulled the strings of such an incongruous puppet? That was the question.

"You've never seen him, but he speaks to you and you believe every word he says?" asked Moncharmin.

"Yes. First, it's because of him that my little Meg was promoted to the chorus. I said to the Phantom: 'If she is to become Empress in 1885, there's no time to lose; she must be part of the chorus right away.' He said: 'Consider it done.' He had only a word to say to Monsieur Poligny and the thing was done."

"So Monsieur Poligny saw him!"

"No more than I did; but he heard him. The Phantom whispered a word in his ear, you know, that night when he left Box No. 5 looking so dreadfully pale."

Moncharmin sighed heavily.

"What a business!" he groaned.

"I always thought there were certain secrets between the Phantom and Monsieur Poligny," Madame Giry continued. "Anything that the Phantom asked, Monsieur Poligny gave to him. He couldn't refuse the Phantom anything."

"You hear, Richard: Poligny didn't refuse the Phantom anything..."

"Yes, yes, I heard!" said Richard. "Poligny is a friend of the Phantom. Madame Giry is a friend of Poligny, and that's that! But I don't give a damn about Poligny," he added rudely. "The only person whose fate really interests me right now is yours, Madame Giry. Do you know what's inside this envelope?"

"Of course not," she said.

"Then look."

The usherette looked into the envelope, at first squinting with suspicion, but her eyes opened wide as soon as she saw the contents.

"Thousand-franc notes!" she cried.

"Yes, Madame Giry! Twenty thousand francs to be exact! And you knew!"

"I, Monsieur? I swear I didn't..."

"Don't swear, Madame Giry! And now, I'll tell you the other reason that I sent for you. I'm going to have you arrested!"

The two black feathers on the soot-darkened bonnet, which usually looked bent like two question marks, suddenly straightened into exclamation points. The bonnet itself trembled frightfully atop the old woman's bun. Little Meg's mother manifested her surprise, indignation, protest and dismay through a series of vehement gestures that were meant to symbolize her offended virtue. It brought her right under Richard's nose, making him fall back into his chair.

"Arrested!"

As she shouted, her mouth seemed to spit the three teeth that it had left right into the Director's face.

But Richard behaved heroically. He did not retreat. Instead, his threatening forefinger was already pointing out the hapless usherette of Box No. 5 to an invisible tribunal of judges.

"Yes, Madame Giry! I am going to have you arrested! As a thief!"

"Say that again!"

And Madame Giry gave the Director a mighty slap in the face before Moncharmin had time to intervene. But it was not the irate old crone's withered hand that hit the directorial cheek; it was the very envelope that had been the cause of all this trouble, the "magic envelope" that suddenly broke open, scattering bank notes which fell like a fantastic whirl of giant butterflies.

The two Directors yelled in unison and the same thought made them both scurry about on their knees, feverishly picking up the precious scraps of paper. They hurriedly examined them.

"*Are they still real?*" asked Moncharmin.

"*Are they still real?*" asked Richard.

"Yes, they're still real!"

Above them, Madame Giry's three teeth rattled a litany of hideous imprecations. But all that could be clearly heard was the leit-motif:

"Me, a thief? Me, a thief?"

She was choking with rage. Finally she shouted:

"I'm completely bowled over!"

Suddenly, she ran under Richard's nose again.

"In any case," she barked, "*Monsieur Richard, you should know better than I where those 20,000 francs went!*"

"I?" asked Richard, astounded. "How would I know?"

Moncharmin, looking grim and unhappy, immediately asked the woman to explain herself.

"What do you mean, Madame Giry?" he inquired. "Why do you say that Monsieur Richard should know *better than you* where the 20,000 francs went?"

Richard, who felt himself turning red under Moncharmin's accusing gaze, grabbed the usherette's wrist and shook it violently. In a voice that growled and rolled like thunder, he yelled:

"Why should I know better than you where the 20,000 francs went to? Why?"

"Because they went straight into your pocket!" gasped the old woman, now looking at the Director as if he was the Devil incarnate.

This time, it was Richard's turn to be stunned, first by the entirely unexpected declaration, then by Moncharmin's increasingly suspicious glare. As a result, he lost all the strength that he needed in such a difficult moment to defend himself against the contemptible accusation.

Thus, the most innocent among us sometimes appears to be guilty when the sudden blow that hits them causes them to grow pale or turn red, to tremble or stand fast, to sweat profusely or remain too dry, to speak when they should stay silent, or stay silent when they should speak.

Moncharmin stayed Richard's avenging hand, for the innocent Director would have struck Madame Giry if he could have. Instead, Moncharmin pressed her with more questions, that he delivered in a gentler tone of voice:

"Come now, Madame Giry! How could you suspect my partner, Monsieur Richard, of pocketing 20,000 francs?"

"I never said that," declared the usherette, "seeing that I was the one who put the money into Monsieur Richard's pocket."

Then, she muttered under her breath: "There! I said it! May the Phantom forgive me!"

As Richard began yelling anew, Moncharmin ordered him to be silent.

"Please! Please! Please! Let the woman explain herself. Let me question her." And he added: "I find it strange that you would overreact in such a fashion! We're just about to solve the entire mystery and you have a fit! You should be more like me. I'm enjoying myself immensely."

Madame Giry, playing the martyr that she thought she was, raised her head, her face beaming with her belief in her own innocence.

"You told me there were 20,000 francs in the envelope which I put inside Monsieur Richard's pocket, but I'm telling you again that I knew nothing about it—nor Monsieur Richard either for that matter!"

"Ah!" said Richard, suddenly assuming a swaggering air which Moncharmin did not like. "So I knew nothing either! You put 20,000 francs in my pocket and I knew nothing about it! I'm very glad to hear it, Madame Giry!"

"Yes," the indomitable usherette confirmed. "Yes, it's true. Neither of us knew anything. But eventually, you, you must have found out!"

Richard would certainly have devoured Madame Giry alive if Moncharmin had not been there to protect her from his partner's wrath. He resumed his questions:

"What sort of envelope did you put inside Monsieur Richard's pocket? Was it the one which we gave you? The one which you took to Box No. 5 before our very eyes? That's the one which contained the 20,000 francs."

"I beg your pardon, Monsieur. The envelope which you gave me was indeed the one which I slipped inside Monsieur Richard's pocket," explained Madame Giry. "The one which I took to the Phantom's box was another envelope, just like the first, which the Phantom had given me beforehand and which I had kept hidden up my sleeve."

So saying, Madame Giry took from inside her sleeve an already prepared envelope that was similarly pre-addressed and which looked just like the one containing the 20,000 francs. The Directors took it. They examined it and saw that it was sealed with the same seals which they themselves used to conduct Opera business. They opened it. It contained 20 notes of play money, just like those which had astounded them the previous month.

"How simple!" said Richard.

"Yes, how simple!" repeated Moncharmin.

"The most fantastic tricks," replied Richard, "always have the simplest explanations. All that you need is a straw-man..."

"...Or a straw-*woman*," continued Moncharmin, with his eyes fixed upon Madame Giry, as if he was trying to hypnotize her.

"So it was the Phantom who gave you this second envelope and told you to replace it with the one which we gave you? And it was the Phantom who also told you to put the first envelope into M. Richard's pocket?"

"Yes, it was the Phantom."

"Then would you mind giving us a demonstration of your legerdemain? Here is the envelope. Act as if we know nothing."

"Whatever you say, Monsieur."

Madame Giry took the envelope with the 20 bank notes inside it and made for the door. She was just about to leave the office when the two Directors rushed at her:

"Oh, no! Oh, no! We're not going to be tricked a second time! Once bitten, twice shy!"

"I beg your pardon, Messieurs," said the old woman apologetically, "but you told me to act as if you knew nothing. Well, if you knew nothing, I would have left with your envelope!"

"I see. So when would you slip it into my pocket?" asked Richard, whom Moncharmin fixed with one eye, while he kept the other on the usherette–a demanding feat for his eyesight, but Monsieur Moncharmin was prepared to undergo any sacrifice to uncover the truth.

"I'm supposed to do it when you least expect it, Monsieur. You know that I always go backstage during the night, sometimes to visit my daughter in the *corps de ballet*, as I've got the right to do, being her mother. I bring her shoes or whatever little accessories she needs... In fact, I pretty much come and go as I please... The subscribers also come and go– and so do you, Messieurs... There are lots of people around at that time... I go behind you and slip the envelope inside the tail-pocket of your jacket... There's no witchcraft about that!"

"No witchcraft!" growled Richard, rolling his eyes like Zeus about to unleash his thunder. "No witchcraft! Why, I've just caught you in a lie, you old witch!"

The attack against her veracity offended Madame Giry more than the insult. She faced him down, bristling, her three teeth poking out of her mouth.

"I didn't lie!"

"You did! Because I spent the whole of that night watching Box No. 5 and the phony envelope which you'd put there. I didn't set foot into the foyer, not for a second."

"That's right, Monsieur, and that's why I didn't slip you the envelope that night, but during the next performance... The following night when the Under-Secretary of the Ministry of Fine Arts..."

At her words, Richard suddenly interrupted Madame Giry:

"Yes, that's true! I remember now! The Under-Secretary went backstage. He asked for me. I went down to the foyer for a short time. I was on the steps; the Under-Secretary and his assistant were in the foyer itself. Suddenly, I turned around... You had just walked behind me, Madame Giry... It felt like you'd brushed against me... There was no one else behind me at the time. Yes, I can still see you, I can still see you!"

"That's it, Monsieur! That's it. That's when I slipped the envelope inside your pocket! That pocket of yours is very handy, Monsieur!"

And Madame Giry once again proved true to her word. She walked behind Richard and slipped the envelope into the pocket of one of the tails of his expensive jacket so deftly that Moncharmin himself was impressed.

"Of course!" exclaimed Richard, looking a little pale. "It's very clever of P.O. The problem he had to solve was this:

how to do away with any dangerous intermediaries between the one giving the money and the one receiving. Absolutely the best thing he could hit upon was to come and take the money from my own pocket, without me noticing it, since I had no idea it was there. It's brilliant!"

"Oh, brilliant, no doubt!" Moncharmin agreed. "Only, you seem to forget, my dear Richard, that I contributed half of those 20,000 francs–and nobody put anything in *my* pocket!"

Mike Vosburg

Chapter Eighteen
The Curious Incident of the Safety Pin
(continued)

Moncharmin's last sentence so clearly expressed the suspicion he now felt towards his fellow Director that it was bound to cause a violent argument. In the end, it was agreed that Richard would do everything that Moncharmin asked in order to find the villain who was persecuting them.

It was now the intermission of the Garden Act, during which the observant Monsieur Remy first noticed the two Directors' strange behavior. Knowing what had transpired, it is now easy to explain such outrageous conduct, so far removed from the proper decorum one would legitimately expect of a Director of the Opera.

Messrs. Richard and Moncharmin's actions were the direct result of the discoveries they had just made, i.e.: 1. Richard was, that night, supposed to repeat the exact movements he had made on the night of the disappearance of the first 20,000 francs; 2. Moncharmin would not, at any time, lose sight of Richard's tail pocket, inside which Madame Giry had deposited the second 20,000 francs.

So Richard went and stood at the very spot where he had greeted the Under-Secretary, while Moncharmin took up his position a few steps behind him.

Madame Giry walked by, brushed up against Richard, stashed the 20,000 francs in his tail pocket and walked away...

Or rather, she was taken away. In accordance with the instructions received from Moncharmin a few minutes earlier, Mercier took the old usherette and locked her up in his office, thus making it impossible for her to communicate with the Phantom. In any case, she had willingly cooperated, for Madame Giry had become a hapless figure, her feathers plucked, her eyes rolling in fear, behaving like a panicked chicken whose crest frantically bobs up and down as she runs to escape from the farmer–in this case, the Police, whose steps she already thought she heard, coming to take her away. She uttered a series of moans that were so loud it seemed they would shatter the marble columns of the grand staircase.

Meanwhile, Monsieur Richard was bending and bowing and walking backwards, just as if he had that high and mighty civil servant, the Under-Secretary of the Ministry of Fine Arts, standing before him.

These displays of civility would have gone entirely unnoticed had the Under-Secretary, in fact, stood before Monsieur Richard. But since there was no one in front of the Director, they became the source of considerable surprise for those who watched a seemingly unnatural and totally inexplicable scene.

Monsieur Richard bent before no one, bowed to no one and walked backwards to let no one pass!

And, several steps behind him, Monsieur Moncharmin did the same thing!

He pushed Remy away and begged Monsieur de La Borderie, the ambassador, and Monsieur Parabise, the Director of the Crédit Central, "not to touch Monsieur Richard."

Moncharmin, who was now suspicious of his own partner, did not want Richard to come to him later, after the 20,000 francs had disappeared, and say: "Perhaps it was the ambassador, the Director of the Crédit Central or Remy."

This strange display was particularly important because Richard had said that, the first time, he had not met anyone in that section of the theater after Madame Giry had brushed up against him. Therefore, he could not be allowed to come into contact with anyone that night, since he was supposed to repeat the very same movements as had taken place then.

Having begun by walking backwards after bowing to the invisible Under-Secretary, Richard continued to do so out of caution until he reached the corridor leading to the Directors' office. Throughout, he was constantly watched by Moncharmin from behind, while he, himself, kept an eye on anyone approaching from the front.

As I mentioned, this novel method of walking the corridors of the Opera, adopted by the Directors of our National Academy of Music, was likely to attract considerable attention.

And that it did.

Messrs. Richard and Moncharmin were lucky that, while their curious pantomime was taking place, the younger members of the *corps de ballet* were all in their communal dressing-rooms near the attics.

For the girls would have been mercilessly lampooning the two Directors. But the gentlemen in question thought only of their 20,000 francs.

Upon reaching the darkened corridor leading to their office, Richard said to Moncharmin, in a low voice:

"I am sure that nobody has touched me. Now, we should keep a little distance between us, but continue to watch me until I come to the door of our office. Better not arouse any more suspicions. We'll see if anything happens."

But Moncharmin replied:

"No, Richard, no! You walk ahead and I'll be *right behind* you! I'm sticking to you like glue!"

"If you do that," exclaimed Richard, "they'll never be able to steal the money!"

"Indeed, I should hope not!" declared Moncharmin.

"But then what we're doing is pointless!"

"No. We're doing exactly what we did last time. If you remember, last time, I joined you as you left backstage and I followed *close behind you* down this corridor."

"That's true!" sighed Richard, shaking his head and obeying Moncharmin without any further argument.

Two minutes later, the two Directors had locked themselves back in their office.

Moncharmin himself put the key in his pocket and said:

"Last time, we stayed locked up like this until you left the Opera to go home."

"That's right. And no one came to talk to us, if I recall?"

"No one."

"Then," said Richard, who was trying to remember the details, "I must have surely been robbed on my way home from the Opera."

"No," said Moncharmin in a drier tone than ever, "that's impossible. I took you home in my own cab. *The money disappeared at your place.* There can't be a shadow of a doubt about that."

And, that was what Moncharmin now assumed.

"I can't believe it!" protested Richard. "I am sure of my servants... Besides, if one of them had done it, he would have been long gone by now."

Moncharmin shrugged, as if to indicate that he did not wish to worry about the details of the scheme.

Thereupon, Richard began to think that Moncharmin was treating him in a rather insufferable fashion.

"Moncharmin, I've had enough of this!"

"Richard, I've had too much of it!"

"How dare you suspect me!"

"I do–of a silly joke."

"One doesn't joke when 20,000 francs are at stake."

"I agree with you," replied Moncharmin, unfolding his newspaper and ostentatiously studying its contents.

"What are you doing?" asked Richard. "Are you planning to read the paper?"

"Yes, Richard, until I take you home."

"Like last time?"

"Yes, just like last time."

Richard snatched the paper from Moncharmin's hands. Moncharmin stood up, more irritated than ever, and found himself confronting an equally exasperated Richard, who, crossing his arms on his chest–a gesture of defiance since the dawn of time–said:

"Look here, *I'm thinking of what I would be thinking* if, like last time, after spending the evening alone with you, you take me home... What if, when we part, I suddenly discover that the 20,000 francs are missing from my pocket–like last time?"

"And what would you be thinking then?" asked Moncharmin, crimson with rage.

"I would be thinking that, since you never left my side, and since, according to your own wishes, you've been the only one to come into contact with me, *just like last time*, I would be thinking that, if the money is no longer in my pocket, it would stand a very good chance of being in yours!"

Moncharmin leapt up, aghast at the suggestion. Then, he shouted:

"Fine! What we need is a safety pin!"

"What do you want a safety pin for?"

"To fasten you with! A safety pin! A safety pin!"

"You want to fasten me with a safety pin?"

"Yes, to fasten you to the 20,000 francs! That way, whether it's here, or on the drive home, or inside your home, you'll feel the hand that tries to pull it out of your pocket–and you'll see if it's mine! So, *you're* suspecting *me* now, eh? Well, a safety pin will take care of that!"

And that was the moment when Moncharmin opened the door and shouted to Remy:

"Do you have a safety pin on you?"

We now know that the secretary didn't have one, but an office boy heard the Director screaming and fetched him the pin he so much desired.

Moncharmin then slammed the door and locked it again.

Afterwards, this is what happened.

First, Moncharmin knelt down behind Richard.

"The notes are still there, I hope," he said.

"So do I," said Richard.

"The real ones?" asked Moncharmin, determined he wouldn't be tricked a second time.

"Look for yourself," said Richard. "I refuse to touch them."

Moncharmin took the envelope from Richard's pocket and drew out the bank notes with a trembling hand. This time, in order to be able to check on the presence of the real notes, they had not sealed or even licked the envelope. The Director felt reassured on discovering that they were all there and quite real. He put them back inside the envelope, and the envelope back inside the pocket and very carefully pinned them in place.

Then he sat down behind Richard and kept his eyes fixed on the back of his jacket, while Richard, sitting at his desk, did not stir.

"A little patience, Richard," said Moncharmin. "We've only got a few minutes left to wait. The clock will soon strike midnight. That's when we left last time."

"I'll be as patient as can be!"

The time passed, slowly, ponderously, stifling and fraught with mystery. Richard tried to laugh.

"I'm almost ready to believe in this all-powerful Phantom," he said. "Just now, don't you find something uncomfortable, disquieting, even alarming, hanging in the air of this room?"

"You're absolutely right," said Moncharmin, who was genuinely intimidated.

"The Phantom!" continued Richard, in a low voice, as if he feared being overheard by invisible ears. "The Phantom! What if it was a phantom who left the magic envelopes on this desk, who spoke in Box No. 5, who killed Joseph Buquet, who unhooked the chandelier–and who is robbing us! Because, after all, there's in this room but you and I! If that money disappears again, and neither you nor I had anything to do with it, well then, we're forced to believe in the existence of the Phantom... in the Phantom."

Just then, the clock on the mantlepiece gave a warning click and struck the first stroke of midnight.

The two Directors shuddered. A powerful feeling of fear gripped them–they could not identify its source, nor could they fight it off. Beads of sweat ran down their foreheads. The twelfth stroke resounded strangely in their ears.

When the clock stopped, they both sighed and rose from their chairs.

"I think we can go now," said Moncharmin.

"I think so, too," agreed Richard.

"Before we go, do you mind if I look inside your pocket?"

"But, of course, Moncharmin, you must!"

"Well?" asked Richard, as he felt Moncharmin feeling at the pocket.

"I can still feel the pin."

"Of course, you can feel the pin. It's just as you said. We can't be robbed without my noticing it."

But Moncharmin's hands were now fumbling about the jacket.

"I can feel the pin, *but I can't feel the notes*!" he yelled.

"No! Don't joke, Moncharmin! Not now!"

"See for yourself!"

Richard tore off his jacket. The two Directors turned the pocket inside out. *It was empty*!

The strangest thing was that the safety pin was still stuck in the exact same place.

Richard and Moncharmin turned deathly pale. They no longer doubted there was some kind of sinister sorcery at work.

"The Phantom!" muttered Moncharmin.

But Richard suddenly sprang upon his partner.

"No! You're the only one who touched my pocket! Give me back my 20,000 francs! Give me back my 20,000 francs!"

"On my soul," sighed Moncharmin, who looked ready to faint. "On my soul, I swear that I haven't got it!"

Then someone knocked at the door.

Moncharmin walked to it like an automaton and opened it. He barely recognized Assistant Director Mercier. He exchanged a few words with him, without really understanding what the other was saying. Then, with an unconscious movement, he deposited the now-useless safety pin into the hands of his bewildered subordinate.

Steve Leialoha

Chapter Nineteen
The Police Commissioner, the Vicomte and the Persian

Police Commissioner Mifroid had barely entered the Directors' office before he inquired about the missing singer.

"Is Christine Daae here?"

He was, as I mentioned, followed by a sizeable crowd.

"Christine Daae here?" replied Richard. "No. Why would she be?"

As for Moncharmin, he no longer had enough strength to even utter a word. His state of mind was far more despondent than Richard's, for if the latter could still suspect Moncharmin, the former could no longer suspect Richard. He faced the ultimate mystery, one that has kept mankind in the thrall of fear since the dawn of time: the power of the Unknown.

For the benefit of the Commissioner and the crowd which continued to observe an impressive silence, Richard repeated his question:

"Why would you ask if Christine Daae is here, Monsieur?"

"Because she's missing, gentlemen," declared the Commissioner rather solemnly.

"What do you mean, she's missing? Do you mean to say she's disappeared?"

"Right in the middle of the performance!"

"Right in the middle of the performance? But that's unbelievable!"

"Isn't it? And it's also unbelievable that you're only learning about it now and from me!"

"Indeed," agreed Richard, taking his head in his hands and muttering. "What's happening around here? It's enough to make a man hand in his resignation!"

He distractedly pulled a few hairs out of his mustache, completely unaware that he had done it.

"So she disappeared right in the middle of the performance?" he repeated, as if in a daze.

"Yes. She was taken during the Prison Act, just as she was singing to invoke the help of Heaven. But I doubt she was carried off by an angel."

"And I'm just as sure that she was!"

Everybody turned around. A pale young man, trembling with excitement, repeated:

"I'm sure of it!"

"Sure of what?" asked Mifroid.

"That Christine Daae was carried off by an angel, Monsieur le Commissaire. And I can even tell you his name."

"Ah-ha, Monsieur le Vicomte de Chagny! So you argue that Mademoiselle Daae was carried off by an angel–an angel of the Opera, no doubt?"

Raoul looked around. He was clearly looking for someone. At that moment, when it seemed necessary for him to call on the Police to help him rescue his fiancée, he wished that he would again see the mysterious stranger who, earlier, had suggested discretion. As he was nowhere to be found, he had no choice but to speak alone. Still, he was reluctant to do so in front of a crowd that stared at him with such insalubrious curiosity.

"Yes, Monsieur, by an angel of the Opera," he told Midfroid. "I'll happily tell you where to find him when we are alone."

"Good idea, Monsieur."

Then, the Police Commissioner, after offering Raoul a seat, cleared the room of all the other spectators, with the exception of the two Directors, who made no protest, so overwhelmed were they by the extraordinary turn of events.

At last, Raoul spoke:

"Monsieur le Commissaire, the angel is named Erik; he lives beneath the Opera *and calls himself the Angel of Music!*"

"The *Angel of Music*! Really! That is extremely interesting! The *Angel of Music*!"

Turning to the Directors, Mifroid asked:

"Do you have an '*Angel of Music*' on the premises, gentlemen?"

Richard and Moncharmin shook their heads, without even bothering to smile.

"But," said the Vicomte, "these gentlemen have heard of the Phantom of the Opera. I am in a position to state that the Phantom of the Opera and the Angel of Music are one and the same–and his real name is Erik."

Mifroid rose and looked at Raoul attentively.

"I beg your pardon, Monsieur, but are you attempting to make fun of the law?"

"Of course not!" protested Raoul painfully, all the while thinking: "Yet someone else who won't believe me."

"If not, what's all this nonsense about a Phantom of the Opera?"

"I am certain that these gentlemen have heard of him."

"Gentlemen, do you know a Phantom of the Opera?"

Richard rose, with the few remaining hairs from his mustache still in his hand.

"No, Monsieur le Commissaire, no, we do not *know* him–but we wish we did, because this very night, he stole 20,000 francs from us!"

And Richard looked intensely at Moncharmin, clearly saying: "Give the money back or I'll tell the whole story."

Moncharmin understood the meaning of the look for, with resignation, he said:

"Go ahead! Tell him everything and be done with it!"

As for Commissioner Mifroid, he looked in turn at the Directors and Raoul, wondering if he had accidentally strayed into a lunatic asylum. Distractedly, he ran his hand through his hair.

"A Phantom," he finally said, "who, on the same night, abducts a singer and steals 20,000 francs is a busy Phantom indeed! If you don't mind, we'll take things in order. The

247

singer first, the money after. Please, Monsieur de Chagny, let us try to discuss this seriously. You believe that Mademoiselle Daae was abducted by an individual called Erik. Do you know this person? Have you seen him?"

"Yes."

"Where?"

"In a cemetery."

Mifroid gave a start and again looked quizzically at Raoul.

"Of course!" he said. "That's where phantoms are usually found! But what were you doing in that cemetery?"

"Monsieur," said Raoul, "I understand how strange my answers to your questions are, and how odd all this must sound to you. But I beg you to believe that I am in full possession of my faculties. The safety of the person dearest to me in the world, other than my brother Philippe, is at stake. I would like to convince you in as few words as possible, because time is of the essence and every minute counts. Unfortunately, if I don't tell you the strangest story that you will ever hear from the beginning, you won't believe a word I say. I'll tell you everything I know about the Phantom of the Opera, Monsieur le Commissaire. Regrettably, I don't know all that much!"

"Never mind, go ahead!" exclaimed Richard and Moncharmin, suddenly greatly interested.

Unfortunately, their hopes of learning some detail that could put them on the trail of their deceiver was crushed as soon as they came to the sad realization that the Vicomte de Chagny had completely lost his head. His story about Perros-Guirec, death's-heads and magic violins could only have been invented inside the deranged mind of a young man who was unlucky in love.

It was obvious that Commissioner Mifroid shared their views. The policeman would have liked to cut short the Vicomte's tangled story–which we have recounted in the earlier portion of this book–if circumstances had not conspired to interrupt it.

The door opened and in walked an oddly dressed man. He wore a long, black coat and a tall hat that came down to his ears and which was both shabby and shiny. He walked over to the Commissioner and whispered a few words in his ear. The others assumed he must be an agent of the Sûreté who had come to report the results of some urgent errand.

During their conversation, Monsieur Mifroid did not take his eyes off Raoul.

At last, he addressed him:

"Monsieur le Vicomte, we've spent enough time talking about the Phantom. I think it's time for us to talk a little bit about you, if you don't mind. You were supposed to take Mademoiselle Daae away tonight?"

"Yes, Monsieur le Commissaire."

"After the performance?"

"Yes, Monsieur le Commissaire."

"Were all your arrangements made?"

"Yes, Monsieur le Commissaire."

"The carriage that brought you here tonight was ready to take both of you away. The coachman had his instructions. The itinerary had been decided. Indeed, there were already fresh horses waiting for you at every stop."

"That is all true, Monsieur le Commissaire."

"Yet, that carriage still sits outside, near the Rotunda, awaiting your instructions, is that right?"

"Yes, Monsieur le Commissaire."

"Did you know that there were three other cabs waiting next to yours?"

"I didn't pay the least bit of attention."

"They were the carriages of Mademoiselle Sorelli, who could not find room to park in the Cour de l'Administration, Mademoiselle Carlotta and your brother, Monsieur le Comte de Chagny..."

"That's quite possible..."

"What is certain, however, is that your carriage, Mademoiselle Sorelli's and Mademoiselle Carlotta's are all still there, by the Rotunda. On the other hand, the Comte de Chagny's is gone."

"What does that have to do with anything?"

"I beg your pardon. Wasn't Monsieur le Comte opposed to you marrying Mademoiselle Daae?"

"That is a private matter of no concern to anyone but my family."

"You've answered my question: he was opposed to it. And that was why you decided to take Mademoiselle Daae away, out of your brother's reach. Well, Monsieur de Chagny, I'm sorry to have to inform you that your brother beat you to the post. He is the one who abducted Christine Daae!"

"That's impossible!" moaned Raoul, pressing his hand to his heart. "Are you sure?"

"Immediately after her disappearance, which was managed through a series of circumstances which we still have to clarify, he jumped into his carriage and drove straight across Paris at a hellbent pace."

"Across Paris?" asked poor Raoul, in a hoarse voice. "What do you mean by across Paris?"

"Across Paris and out of Paris."

"Out of Paris? Where did he go?"

"He was reportedly seen taking the road to Brussels."

The devastated young man made a raspy scream.

"Oh," he cried. "I swear I'll catch them!"

So saying, he rushed out of the office.

"Make sure you bring her back to us safely!" shouted the Commissioner jovially. "What do you think of that? Wasn't that bit of news more interesting than what the young man told us about the Angel of Music?"

Turning towards the dazed Directors, Commissioner Mifroid delivered a mild lecture on good, old-fashioned police technique.

"Gentlemen, I have no idea if the Comte de Chagny has really abducted Christine Daae or not, but I want to learn more about it and I believe that, right now, no one is more eager to tell us than his own brother, the Vicomte. At this very moment, he's running, I would say almost flying, in pursuit of him! He's virtually become my chief assistant! This, gentlemen, is the art of police work, which is often thought to be greatly complicated, but which, in reality, consists merely of getting things done by people who don't work for us at all!"

However, Police Commissioner Mifroid would not have been quite so satisfied with himself if he had known that his newest "assistant" had been stopped dead in his tracks at the entrance of the very first corridor outside the office. It was deserted, the crowd of onlookers having long since scattered away.

A tall, shadowy figure had blocked Raoul's way.

"Where are you going in such a hurry, Monsieur de Chagny?" the shadow asked.

Impatiently, Raoul raised his eyes and recognized the man's astrakhan hat. He stopped.

"You again!" he cried, in a feverish voice. "You know Erik's secrets, but you don't want me to tell the others about him. Who are you?"

"You know who I am!" said the shadow. "I'm the Persian!"

Timothy II

Chapter Twenty
The Vicomte and the Persian

Raoul suddenly remembered that one night, during an intermission, his brother had pointed out to him the mysterious character, about whom nothing was known, except that he was a Persian and lived in a small, old apartment on the Rue de Rivoli.

The man with the dark complexion, the jade-green eyes and the astrakhan hat bent over Raoul.

"I hope, Monsieur de Chagny," he said, "that you have not betrayed Erik's secret?"

"Why should I hesitate to betray that Monster, Monsieur?" Raoul replied haughtily, trying to rid himself of the intruder. "Is he one of your friends?"

"I hope that you said nothing about Erik, Monsieur, because Erik's secret is also Christine Daae's, and to talk about one is to talk about the other!"

"You seem to know many things that interest me," said Raoul, becoming increasingly impatient, "but I don't have time to listen to you now, Monsieur!"

"Once again, Monsieur de Chagny, where are you going in such a hurry?"

"Can't you guess? To Christine's rescue!"

"Then, Monsieur de Chagny, you should stay here, because that is where she is!"

"With Erik?"

"With Erik."

"How do you know?"

"I was at the performance and no one in the world except Erik could pull off an abduction like that!" With a deep sigh he added, "Oh! How well I recognized that Monster's touch!"

"Then, you know him?"

The Persian made no reply, but Raoul heard him sigh again.

"Please, Monsieur," said the young man. "I don't know your intentions, but can you do anything at all to help me? I mean, to help Christine?"

"I think so, Monsieur de Chagny. That's why I spoke to you."

"What can you do?"

"I can try to take you to her–and to him."

"Monsieur! That's something I tried to do earlier myself, without success. But if you can do me such a service, my life is yours! Still, the Police Commissioner just told me that Christine was taken by my brother, Comte Philippe..."

"Oh, Monsieur de Chagny, I don't believe that for a second."

"It doesn't seem possible, does it?"

"I don't know if it's possible or not, but there are all kinds of ways of whisking people away, but Comte Philippe has never, as far as I know, *used any kind of magic*."

"Your arguments are convincing, Monsieur. I'm afraid I've been a fool! Please, let's hurry! I'm entirely in your hands! How can I not believe you, when you're the only one who believes me! You're the only one who doesn't snicker when I mention the Phantom of the Opera or the name of Erik!"

Spontaneously, the young man grabbed the Persian's hands. Unlike his own, which burned with fevered apprehension, they were ice-cold.

"Hush!" said the Persian, stopping and listening to the distant sounds of the theater. "We must never mention that name here. Let us say *he* or *him*–there will be less risk of attracting his attention."

"Do you think he is near by?"

"Quite possibly, unless he is, at this very moment, with his victim, *in his house by the lake*."

"Ah, so you know about that house, too?"

"If he's not there, he could be here, behind the wall, under the floor, in the ceiling! Who knows? He could be peering at us through a keyhole, or listening to us behind a wall!"

The Persian asked Raoul to walk as quietly as possible, then led him down corridors which Raoul had never seen before, even when Christine took him for walks through the maze that was the Opera.

"I hope that Darius has arrived!" said the Persian.

"Who is Darius?"

"Darius? My servant."

They were standing in the center of a seemingly deserted square, a large room poorly lit by a small lamp. The Persian stopped Raoul and, in the softest of whispers, so low that Raoul had difficulty hearing him, asked:

"What did you tell the Police Commissioner?"

"I said that Christine's abductor was the Angel of Music, a.k.a. the Phantom of the Opera, and that the real name was—"

"Hush! Did the Commissioner believe you?"

"No."

"He attached no importance to what you said?"

"None whatsoever."

"He took you for a bit of a lunatic?"

"Yes."

"Good!" sighed the Persian.

And they continued on their way.

After going up and down several staircases, which Raoul had also never seen before, the two men found themselves in front of a door which the Persian opened with a master-key that he pulled out of one of the pockets of his vest. Naturally, the Persian and Raoul both wore dinner jackets, but underneath, the Persian had on a colorful silk vest. While Raoul wore a top hat, the Persian, as I already mentioned, wore one made of astrakhan. That would normally have been interpreted as a violation of the Opera dress code, except that in France, foreigners are allowed a certain license to incorporate some of their native accoutrements in their dress: an Englishman, for example, could wear a plaid cap, and a Persian an astrakhan.

"Monsieur de Chagny," said the Persian, "your top hat will be in the way. You would be wise to leave it in the dressing-room."

"Which dressing-room?" asked Raoul.

"Christine Daae's."

And the Persian, letting Raoul through the door which he had just opened, showed him the singer's room opposite.

Raoul had no idea that it was possible to reach Christine's dressing-room by any other route than the one he usually took. They stood at the other end of the corridor up and down which Raoul had so often paced before knocking at Christine's door.

"I'm impressed by how well you know the Opera, Monsieur!"

"Not as well as *he* does!" said the Persian modestly.

Then he pushed the young man into Christine's dressing-room.

It was just as Raoul had left it only moments before.

The Persian, after closing the door, went to a thin partition that separated the dressing-room from a closet next to it. He listened and then coughed loudly.

At once, there was the sound of movement in the closet. A few seconds later, someone knocked at the door.

"Come in," said the Persian.

A man entered; he, too, wore an astrakhan hat and a cloak.

He bowed and took a richly-carved case from under his cloak, placed it on the dressing-table, bowed again and went to the door.

"Did anyone see you come in, Darius?"

"No, Master."

"Make sure no one sees you leave."

The servant glanced down the corridor and swiftly disappeared.

"Monsieur," said Raoul. "I just thought of something. What if someone sees us in here? It could prove embarrassing. I'm sure the Police will arrive soon to search this room."

"Pah! We've got bigger things to fear than the Police."

The Persian opened the case. It contained a pair of long pistols with beautiful carvings on their handles.

"When Christine Daae was taken, Monsieur de Chagny, I sent word to my servant to bring me these pistols. I've had them a long time and they can be relied upon."

"Do you mean to fight a duel?" asked the young man, surprised to see such an arsenal.

"It will certainly be a duel that we'll have to fight, Monsieur de Chagny," replied the other, examining the priming of his pistols. "And what a duel!"

Handing one of the guns to Raoul, he added:

"In this duel, we'll be two against one. But you must be prepared for everything, Monsieur, for we'll be fighting the deadliest enemy that you could ever imagine. But you love Christine Daae, do you not?"

"Of course I love her, Monsieur! But you, who do not, why are you so ready to risk your life for her? You must certainly hate Erik!"

"No, Monsieur," said the Persian sadly. "I don't hate him. If I hated him, he would long ago have ceased doing harm."

"Has he done you harm?"

"I've forgiven him the harm which he has done me."

"It's quite extraordinary," said the young man. "to hear you speak of him. You call him a Monster, you speak of his crimes, he's done you harm and yet, I find in you the same incomprehensible pity that drove me to despair when I saw it in Christine!"

The Persian did not reply. He had fetched a stool and set it against the wall facing the great mirror that filled the entire opposite wall. Then, he climbed on the stool and, putting his nose to the wallpaper, seemed to be looking for something.

"So? Any luck?" asked Raoul, stamping his foot with impatience. "I'm in a hurry! Let's go!"

"Let's go where?" said the other, without turning his head.

"Where? To the Monster's lair, of course! Down! You said you knew his secrets!"

"I'm looking."

The Persian continued to scrutinize every inch of the wall.

"Ah!" he finally said. "I think I've got it!" And, raising his finger above his head, he pressed against a small pattern in the wallpaper.

Then he turned around and jumped down from the stool.

"In 30 seconds," he said, "we'll be *in his domain*!"

Crossing the dressing-room, he began to feel around the great mirror.

"Hmm... It's not yielding yet," he muttered.

"Will we be leaving through the mirror?" asked Raoul. "Like Christine?"

"So you knew that Christine Daae got out behind the mirror?"

"She did it right in front of me! I was hidden behind the curtain in that alcove and I saw her vanish–not behind the mirror, but through it!"

"So, what did you do?"

"I thought it was some aberration of my senses, a hallucination or a mad dream!"

"Or a new trick of the Phantom!" chuckled the Persian. "Ah, Monsieur de Chagny," he continued, his hand still exploring the surface of the mirror, "would that he were a real phantom! We would then be able to leave our guns behind in their case. Put down your hat, please... Now, cover up the front of your white shirt with your jacket as much as you can... Just as I'm doing... That's right, pull the lapels forward, turn up the collar... We need to make ourselves as invisible as possible."

After a short silence while he leaned against the mirror, he added:

"When you press the spring on the other side of the room, it takes a little time for the counterweight to be released. It's different when you stand behind the wall and can manipulate it directly. Then the mirror turns right away and rotates at dizzying speed."

"What counterweight?" asked Raoul.

"Why, the counterweight that causes the whole of this wall to rotate on its axis. You don't think it moves by itself, as if by magic!"

The Persian grabbed Raoul and pulled him very close. His other hand–the one holding the gun–still rested against the mirror.

"If you watch closely, you'll see the mirror first rise an inch or two and then shift an inch or two to the left or to the right. It will then be on a pivot and will swing around. There are no limits to what can be achieved with counterweights. A child could rotate an entire house with his little finger. When a wall, no matter how heavy, is balanced on a pivot by a counterweight, it weighs no more than a whirling top!"

"But it's not turning!" said Raoul impatiently.

"Wait! This is not the moment to be impatient, Monsieur de Chagny! The mechanism may be a little rusty, or the spring could be broken, unless..."

The Persian's brow grew furrowed.

"Unless it's something else."

"What?"

"*He* may simply have cut the cable that supports the counterweight, thus stopping the whole mechanism."

"Why would he? He doesn't know that we're coming this way!"

"He might suspect it, because he knows that I know his system."

"Did he show it to you?"

"No! I followed him after each of his mysterious apparitions, and I've found most of methods! It's the simplest way to create secret doors, a mechanism as old as the hundred doors of the sacred palaces of Thebes, the throne room of Ecbatane and the Sybill's own chamber in Delphi."

"But it's not turning! Christine! What will become of her?"

The Persian said coldly:

"We'll do everything that it is humanly possible to do, Monsieur! But *he* may stop us on our very first step!"

"Is he the master of these walls then?"

"He commands the walls, the doors and the trap-doors. In my country, he was known by a name which meant the *trap-door lover* or the *trickster*."

"That's how Christine spoke about him as well... With that same sense of mystery, acknowledging the same terrible powers... But I still don't understand. It's all so unbelievable. Why do these walls obey him alone? He didn't build them!"

"Yes, Monsieur de Chagny, that is just what he did!"

Raoul looked at him in amazement; but the Persian gestured that he should be silent and pointed at the glass... There was a slight shimmer to their reflection. The image had been briefly disturbed, as in a rippling sheet of water, before returning to once again being static.

"You see that it isn't turning! We need to look for another route!"

"Tonight, there isn't one!" declared the Persian, in a singularly mournful voice. "Now, watch out! Be ready to fire."

He himself raised his pistol so it faced the mirror. Raoul imitated his movement. With his free arm, the Persian drew the young man close to his chest and, suddenly, the mirror turned in a blinding daze of light. It rotated like one of those revolving doors which have lately become part of the entrances of most restaurants. It revolved on its pivot, carrying Raoul and the Persian with it and suddenly hurling them from full light into the deepest darkness.

Fernando Calvi

Rich Faber

Chapter Twenty-One
In the Vaults of the Opera

"Hold your arm up, ready to fire!" repeated Raoul's companion quickly.

The wall, having completed its full circular rotation, closed behind them.

The two men stood motionless for a moment, not even daring to breathe.

At last, the Persian decided to move. Raoul heard him slip to his knees and grope around for something in the dark.

Suddenly, the blackness was dispersed by the light of a small lantern. Raoul instinctively stepped back as if to escape being spotted by their hidden foe. However, he quickly realized that the light belonged to the Persian, whose actions he watched closely. The little circle of reddish light was meticulously projected in every direction. Raoul saw that the floor and ceiling were made of wood, as was the wall to their left, the one to their right was masonry. Raoul told himself that this was the passage Christine had taken when she had followed the voice of the *Angel of Music*. This was the route taken by Erik when he came to abuse Christine's good faith and exploit her innocence. Remembering the Persian's remark, he also thought that the passage had been secretly built by the Phantom himself.

Later, he learned that Erik had found the secret passage already there; but its existence was known only to him for many years. The hidden corridor had been built in the time of the Paris Commune to enable the jailers to take their prisoners straight to the cells that were located in the vaults of the Opera. For the *Communards* had taken over the Opera immediately after March 18. They had used its roof to launch hot air balloons, which carried their incendiary proclamations to the rest of the country, while they turned its vaults into a state prison.

The Persian, still kneeling, set his lantern on the ground. He seemed to be doing something to the floor. Suddenly, he turned off his light.

Raoul heard a faint click and saw a square of pale light appear in the floor of the passage. It was as if a lit window to the vaults of the Opera had just been opened. Raoul no longer saw the Persian, but he felt him by his side and heard him whisper:

"Follow me and do everything that I do."

Raoul was gently pushed towards the bright aperture. Then he saw the Persian, who was still on his knees, hang by his hands from the edge of the opening and, with his pistol between his teeth, slide into the space below.

Strangely enough, the Vicomte had absolute confidence in the man, even though he knew nothing about him, and his words had only increased the mystery he felt about his adventure. He didn't hesitate for a second to believe that, in this crucial hour, the Persian was his ally against Erik. The man's emotion when speaking of the "Monster" had struck him as sincere. The interest he had displayed did not seem suspect. Finally, if the Persian truly had any sinister designs against him, he would not have armed him with his own guns. Besides, Raoul refused to allow anything to prevent him from finding Christine. He did not have the luxury of choosing his allies. If he had wavered for even a second, even if he had doubts about the Persian's intentions, in his own eyes he would have been the most cowardly of men.

Raoul, therefore, got down on his knees and hung from the trap-door with both hands.

"Let go!" he heard.

He did and dropped into the arms of the Persian, who told him to lie flat. The man then closed the trap-door above them, without Raoul being able to detect how he did it, and crouched down beside the Vicomte.

Raoul tried to ask a question, but the Persian's hand darted to his mouth to silence him and he heard a voice which he recognized as that of the Police Commissioner.

Raoul and the Persian were hidden behind a wooden partition. Near them, a narrow staircase led to a small room where Commissioner Mifroid walked back and forth while conducting his interrogations. They could hear the sound of his pacing as well as that of his voice.

The light was very faint, but after the total darkness that reigned in the secret passage above, Raoul was able to make out the shapes of things around him.

That caused him to make a whispered cry: *he had seen three corpses lying there*!

The first was on the narrow landing of the small staircase that led to the door behind which the Commissioner conducted his interrogation. The two others had rolled to the bottom of the stairs. Raoul could have touched the hands of the two poor wretches by sliding his fingers through the partition which concealed them.

"Hush!" whispered the Persian.

He, too, had seen the bodies and his explanation was a single word:

"*He*!"

The Commissioner's voice grew louder. He was asking the stage manager for information about the lighting system. He must have been standing near the "organ." Contrary to what one might think, especially in connection with an opera house, the "organ" is not a musical instrument.

In those days, electricity was only used for a few onstage special effects and for the bells. The vast building and the stage itself were still lit by gas. Hydrogen was still used to regulate and modify the lighting of a scene. This was all done by means of a special contraption which, because of its numerous pipes, was known as the "organ."

A seat next to the prompter's box was reserved for the head gaffer who, from there, issued orders to his assistants and saw that they were carried out. That man, Mauclair, stayed in this box during all performances.

But on that night, Mauclair had not been in his box, nor had his assistants been in their places.

"Mauclair! Mauclair!"

The stage manager's voice echoed through the vaults like the roll of thunder. But Mauclair made no reply.

I explained earlier in this narrative that a door opened onto the narrow staircase that led to the second level. The Commissioner tried to open it, but it was stuck.

"See here," the policeman said to the stage manager, "I can't seem to open this door. Is it always this difficult?"

The stage manager forced it open with his shoulder. He saw that, besides the door, he was also shoving a human body and was unable to suppress a cry, because he immediately recognized the body:

"Mauclair!"

Everyone who had accompanied the Commissioner on his visit to the organ stepped forward in alarm.

"Poor devil! He's dead!" moaned the stage manager.

But Commissioner Mifroid, who was surprised by nothing, was already bending over the tall body.

"No," he said, "he's dead drunk, which isn't quite the same thing."

"If that's true, it'd be the first time," said the stage manager.

"Then someone drugged him. That's certainly possible."

Mifroid walked down a few steps and said:

"Look!"

By the light of a small red lantern, they saw the other two bodies at the foot of the stairs. The stage manager recognized Mauclair's assistants. Mifroid went down and listened to their breathing.

"They're sound asleep as well," he said. "What an odd business! We can no longer question the fact that someone interfered with the lighting during the performance. That person, or persons, unknown was obviously in cahoots with the abductor... But what a bizarre idea to abduct a performer from the stage! They couldn't have made it more difficult if they tried, I'll be bound! Send for the theater doctor, please."

And Mifroid repeated:

"Odd business! Very odd business indeed!"

Then he turned towards the small room, addressing people whom Raoul and the Persian were unable to see from their hiding place.

"What do you say about all this, gentlemen? You're the only ones who haven't given your views. Yet you must have an opinion of some sort."

At that, Raoul and the Persian saw the two startled faces of the Directors appear above the landing–one could hardly notice anything else–and they heard Moncharmin's agitated voice say:

"There are things happening here, Monsieur le Commissaire, which we are unable to explain."

And the two faces disappeared.

"Thank you for your opinion, gentlemen," said Mifroid sarcastically.

But the stage manager, who held his chin in his hand in a sign of deep thought, said:

"It's not the first time that Mauclair has fallen asleep backstage. I remember finding him snoring in his chair, sitting next to his snuff-box, one night."

"Was that long ago?" asked Mifroid, carefully wiping his glasses, for the Police Commissioner was near-sighted, as occasionally happens with even the most beautiful eyes in the world.

"No, not so very long ago... Wait! It was the night–yes, of course!–it was the night when Mademoiselle Carlotta–well, you know, Monsieur le Commissaire–when she delivered her famous croak!"

"Really? The same night as Carlotta's famous croak?"

Mifroid replaced his now-clean glasses on his nose, then fixed his gaze on the stage manager, as if trying to read his mind.

"So Mauclair takes snuff, does he?" he asked with a tone of false indifference.

"Yes, Monsieur le Commissaire... Look, his snuff-box is there on the shelf... He's a great snuff-taker!"

"So am I," said Mifroid, and grabbing the snuff-box, he put it in his pocket.

Raoul and the Persian, themselves unobserved, watched as several stagehands carefully removed the three bodies. The Police Commissioner left and everyone else followed him. For a few more minutes, the sound of footsteps echoed on the stage above.

When they were sure that they were finally alone, the Persian made a sign to Raoul to stand up. The young man obeyed, but in so doing, he forgot to keep his hand high, in front of his eyes, ready to fire, as the Persian had asked him to do. His companion told him to resume that position and to maintain it, no matter what happened.

"But it tires the hand unnecessarily," whispered Raoul. "If I do need to fire, I won't be sure of my aim."

"Then shift your pistol to the other hand," said the Persian.

"I can't shoot with my left hand."

The Persian then made this strange reply, which was certainly not likely to dispel the confusion that reigned in the young man's mystified brain:

"It's not a question of shooting with the right hand or the left. It's a question of holding one of your hands with your arm bent as if you are about to pull the trigger of a pistol. As for the gun itself, all things considered, you can put that back in your pocket!"

He added:

"This needs to be clearly understood, or I won't be responsible for what happens. It's a matter of life and death. Now stay silent and follow me!"

They were on the second level of the fabled vaults of the Opera. The light of a few scattered lanterns, flickering behind their prisons of glass, enabled Raoul to see only a tiny portion of the extravagant, sublime and marvelous kingdom, which could be, in turn, as thrilling as a toy box or as terrifying as the deepest of chasms

The vaults of the Opera are enormous and are comprised of five underground levels. Large, horizontal beams support the entire structure. Huge columns, anchored on foundations of stone and iron, give each level the appearance of a cathedral. They are spaced widely enough apart that even the most elaborate set pieces can be moved with ease between them. Virtually every combination of stage settings required above, including built-in trap-doors, trompe l'oeils and special effects, are stored down in the vaults. Entire forests, farms and castles, tempestuous seascapes and rosy clouds are all there, side-by-side. Everything moves smoothly through a system of tracks and counterweights. Everywhere one looks is a dizzying array of cables, ropes, pulleys, drums, hooks and chains. Once these are put in motion by the stagehands, a *décor* can appear and disappear as if by magic, here one day, moved to another location the next, suddenly whisked out of the depths to appear sparkling new on stage, all according to the needs of the Opera. The architectural chroniclers Messrs. X***, Y*** and Z***, who so brilliantly studied the wonderful palace designed by Monsieur Garnier, concluded that it was in the vaults that all the magic of the Opera had its roots, in the vaults that a hunchback suddenly turned into a radiant prince, in the vaults that witches and fairies worked their magic. Satan, when summoned to the stage, rose up from the vaults—before being once again banished back to its depths. It was in the vaults that the fires of Hell were stoked and where the demons sang their infernal chorus.

...And where, apparently, Phantoms made themselves at home!

Raoul followed the Persian, obeying his instructions to the letter, without trying to understand why he was being asked to perform certain actions, telling himself that this man was his last hope.

What would he have done without his companion in the awe-inspiring maze?

Would he have been stopped at virtually every step by the mind-boggling jumble of cables, ropes and pullies? Would he have become trapped forever inside the mammoth web?

And, even if he could have made it through the mesh of chains and counterweights that constantly obstructed his path, wasn't there the danger of falling into one of the trap-doors that suddenly sprang up beneath his feet, its bottom hidden in a darkness that no eye could penetrate?

They descended ever deeper...

Until, at last, they reached the third level.

Their way was still lit by some far-off lamp.

The lower they went, the more precautions the Persian seemed to take. He kept turning around to look at Raoul and make sure the young man was holding his arm properly, showing him how he himself carried his hand as if always ready to fire, even though the pistol was in his pocket.

Suddenly, a loud voice made them stop. Someone above them shouted:

"All door-closers to the stage! The Police want to talk to you!"

They heard shambling footsteps. They saw shadows glide through the darkness. The Persian drew Raoul behind a set piece. They watched as dozens of old men, bent by age and the burden of having once labored hard, moving the heaviest set pieces, pass before and above them. Some could barely drag themselves along; others, with stooping bodies and outstretched hands, still looked for doors to close purely from habit.

They were the door-closers, old, worn-out stagehands on whom a charitable management had taken pity, giving them the job of closing doors, above and below the stage. They went about ceaselessly, from the top of the Opera to the bottom, closing doors. They were also called the *draft-killers*, at least at that time, as I have little doubt that, today, they are all long dead and gone.

This was done because it is known that drafts are very bad for the voice, from wherever they may come.[20]

In an *a parte*, the Persian and Raoul applauded their luck. as this coincidence relieved them of any potential, inconvenient witnesses. For, some of the door-closers, having nothing better to do and with no real fixed abode outside the Opera, spent their nights in the vaults, either due to idleness or necessity. They might have stumbled over them, woken them up and caused someone to question their presence. For the moment, Commissioner Mifroid's investigation had saved them from such undesirable encounters.

But they could not enjoy their solitude for long. Other shadows began to descend by the same routes the door-closers had used to go up above. Each of these shadows carried a small lantern and moved it up, down and all around, as if looking for something or someone.

"Damn!" muttered the Persian. "I don't know what they're looking for, but they could easily find us... Let's get out of here, quicklly! Keep your hand high, Monsieur, ready to fire! Bend your arm–more–that's it! Keep your hand at eye level, as if you were about to fight a duel and were waiting for the command to fire! You might as well leave your pistol in your pocket. Quick! Come on, downward! (He dragged Raoul down to the fourth level) At eye level, I said! It's a matter of life or death! Here! This way! Take these stairs!" (They had reached the fifth level.) Oh, what a duel, Monsieur de Chagny! What a duel!"

Once at the bottom of the fifth level, the Persian stopped to catch his breath. He seemed to exude a greater sense of security than that which he had displayed when they were on the third level. But he still never altered the position of his hand.

---

[20] Monsieur Pedro Gailhard himself told me that he created a few additional positions as door-closers for old carpenters whom he was unwilling to dismiss from the Opera. (*Note from the Author*.)

Raoul was still puzzled–although this time, he said nothing, because he thought it would have been out of place– by this rather extraordinary notion of self-defense that consisted of keeping one's gun in one's pocket, while keeping one's hand at eye level, ready to fire, just as if it had been holding said gun in the commonly accepted position of the duellist!

Reflecting upon this, Raoul remembered the Persian's earlier observation: "I know these pistols can be relied upon."

Thus, he logically wondered why anyone should be so pleased at being able to rely upon a pistol which one did not intend to use!

But the Persian interrupted his vague attempts to try to sort the whole thing out. Gesturing that the young man should stay where he was, he ran a few steps up the staircase which they had just taken, then returned just as quickly.

"How stupid of me!" he whispered. "In a few minutes, we won't have to worry about the shadows and their lanterns. They're the firemen doing their rounds." [1]

The two men cautiously waited five minutes longer. Then, the Persian again led Raoul up the stairs. He suddenly stopped him with a gesture.

In front of them it seemed as if the darkness itself was moving.

"Get down!" whispered the Persian.

The two men lay flat on the floor.

They were only just in time.

A shadow, this time carrying no lantern, just a shadow among shadows, passed by.

---

[1] In those days, it was still part of the firemen's duties to watch over the safety of the Opera outside the performances, but since then this service has been eliminated. I asked Monsieur Pedro Gailhard the reason, and he replied: "It was because the management was afraid that, due to their utter lack of knowledge of the Opera's vaults, the firemen might actually set fire to the building!" (*Note from the Author.*)

It passed so close to them it could have touched them.

They felt the warmth of its cloak upon their faces.

For they were able to observe it enough to see that it was shrouded in a cloak from head to foot. On its head, it wore a soft felt hat...

It moved away, gliding along the walls, sometimes giving them a soft kick when it turned a corner.

"Whew!" said the Persian. "We had a narrow escape. That shadow knows me and twice before it took me back to the Directors' office."

"Is it someone from the theater police?" asked Raoul.

"It's someone much worse than that!" replied the Persian, without providing any further explanation.[22]

"It's not–*him*?"

"*Him*? No! If it was him, unless he approached us from behind, we would see his infernal, blazing, yellow eyes! That, at least, is our trump card in the darkness. But if he comes

---

[22] Like the Persian, I, too, can provide no further explanation regarding this mysterious "shadow." Whereas, in the course of this historical narrative, everything eventually will be explained, no matter how incomprehensible it may have seemed at first, this is one area where I cannot elucidate for the reader what the Persian meant by the words: "It is someone much worse than that!"–"that" meaning the theater police. The reader will have to try to guess for himself, for I promised Monsieur Pedro Gailhard, the former Director of the Opera, to keep the identity of that extremely interesting and useful cloaked "shadow" secret. Said "shadow," was assigned to wander through the vaults of the Opera. It has rendered too many immense services to those few who, on gala nights for example, have risked their lives by attending a performance *above*, to be exposed casually. I am speaking of state secrets and, upon my word of honor, I can say no more. (*Note from the Author.*)

behind us, stealthily, we're dead men—that is if we don't keep our hands high, at eye level, ready to fire!"

The Persian had barely finished repeating his instructions, when one more fantastic vision appeared.

It was a whole face, not just two blazing eyes!

But an entire face with every feature on fire!

Yes, a head of fire was moving towards them, at the height of a man, *but without any body beneath it*!

That face radiated fire.

In the darkness, it looked like a man-shaped flame, a floating, burning mask.

"Oh," said the Persian, muttering between his teeth. "I've never seen this before! So Papin wasn't crazy after all: he did see it! What can that flame creature be? It is not *him*, but maybe *he* sent it! Careful! Careful! Keep your hand at eye level, for God's sake! At eye level!"

The fiery, bodiless apparition, which seemed to have come straight up from Hell—a genuine fire demon if ever there was one—was still advancing towards the two awestruck men.

"*He* may have sent us that thing from the front to better catch us from behind, or from the sides! With *him*, one never knows! I know many of his tricks, but not this one! Let's get away! It's safer, isn't it? Much safer! And keep your hand at eye level!"

And they fled down the long passage that opened before them.

After a few seconds that seemed to them like long minutes, they stopped.

"Still, *he* doesn't come here often," said the Persian. "This section doesn't interest him. It doesn't lead to the lake nor to his house by the lake. But perhaps he knows that *we are after him*? Even though I promised I'd leave him alone and never again meddle in his affairs!"

So saying, both he and Raoul turned their heads.

Once again, they saw the fiery head behind them. It had followed them. And it, too, must have run, perhaps faster than they, for it seemed to be closer.

At the same time, they began to perceive a strange sound, the nature of which they were unable to not guess. They noticed only that the sound seemed to move along, and come closer, with the fiery face. It was a grinding, grating noise, as if thousands of nails were being scraped against metal. It was the same unbearable sound that chalk sometimes makes when it screeches against a blackboard.

They continued to retreat, but the fiery face also moved forward and still forward, gaining on them. They could now see its features clearly. The eyes were round and staring, the nose a little crooked and the mouth large, with a dangling lower lip. It looked like the eyes, nose and mouth of the Man in the Moon, when the Moon is blood-red.

How did that blood-red Moon manage to glide through the darkness, at the height of a man, with nothing apparent beneath to support it? And how did it travel so quickly, straight ahead, with its staring, staring eyes? And what was that scratching, grating, grinding noise that accompanied it?

At one point, the Persian and Raoul could no longer retreat; they flattened themselves against the wall, not knowing what would happen to them as a result of their encounter with this mysterious fiery face. And they feared the noise, that furious, swarming, living, "many" sound, for it was definitely made up of hundreds of smaller sounds that moved along in the darkness, beneath the fiery face.

And the fiery face was almost upon them! Almost! With its noise! And now it was here!

The two companions, flat against the wall, felt their hair standing on end with horror, for they at last knew what the thousand noises were. They came as an army, a multitude wrapped in shadows, countless tiny sudden waves, faster than the waves that rush across the sands at high tide, tiny waves of night creatures, foaming under the blood-red Moon, the fiery head that was like a Moon.

And the tiny waves passed between their legs, climbed up their legs, unstoppably. Raoul and the Persian could no longer suppress their cries of horror, panic and pain.

They could no longer hold their hands at eye level–as if they were about to engage in a duel. Their hands went down to their legs to push back the small, shiny things, the sharp rolling waves full of little legs and nails and claws and teeth.

Yes, Raoul and the Persian were ready to faint, like Papin the fireman before them. But the fiery head, upon hearing their screams, turned towards them, and spoke:

"Don't move! Don't move! Whatever you do, don't follow me! I'm the rat catcher! Let me pass with my rats!"

And the fiery head disappeared, vanished into the darkness, while the passage in front of it suddenly lit up, as a result of a change that the rat catcher had made to his lantern. Before, in order not to scare the rats in front of him, he had turned his lantern on himself, lighting up his own face. Now, to hasten their flight, he lit the space in front of them. And he ran along, dragging with him the waves of screeching rats, all the thousand sounds.

Raoul and the Persian, free of the horror, breathed again, though they were still shaking.

"I should have remembered that Erik told me about the rat catcher," said the Persian. "But he never told me that he looked like that. It's strange that I never met him before." [23]

---

[23] Monsieur Pedro Gailhard, former Director of the Opera, told me one day, when we were both attending a party at the home of Madame Pierre Wolff on the Cap d'Ail, about the enormous ravages caused by rats beneath the Opera. That sorry state of affairs continued until management made a deal–on rather expensive terms, I was given to understand–with a man who claimed that he would get rid of the vermin by going through the vaults every two weeks. Since then, there are no longer any rats in the Opera, other, of course, than the *petits rats,* as the little girls of the *corps de ballet* are colloquially dubbed. Monsieur Gailhard thought that this man had discovered a secret scent that attracted rats, not unlike the "*coq-levent*" that some fishermen put on their legs to attract fish before getting into the water. He then led the drugged rats to some dark cellar

"I thought it was another of the Monster's devilish tricks!" he sighed. "But as I said, he never comes to this section."

"Are we still far from the lake, Monsieur?" asked Raoul. "How long till we're there? Please, take me to the lake, to the lake! Once we're there, I can call for her, shake the walls, shout! Christine will hear us! And *he*, too, will hear us! And, since you know him, we can talk to him!"

"Poor child!" said the Persian. "We'll never get into his house by the lake by going through the lake!"

"Why not?"

"Because that's where he has built all his defenses! Even I never set foot on the other bank–the bank where his house is. You'd have to cross the lake first, and it's very well-guarded! I fear that more than one man–retired stagehands, old door-closers–who has never been seen again disappeared because they tried to cross the lake... It's too terrible... I would have been nearly killed there myself, if the Monster hadn't recognized me in time! Let me give you one piece of advice, Monsieur de Chagny: never go near the lake. And, above all, block your ears if you ever hear the *Voice that sings under the water*, the siren's voice!"

"But then, what are we here for?" asked Raoul, in a burst of fevered impatience and rage. "If you can't do anything to rescue Christine, at least let me die for her!"

The Persian tried to calm the young man.

"There is only one way of rescuing Christine Daae, believe me! It's to enter the house unnoticed by the Monster."

"Is there any hope of that, Monsieur?"

---

where he drowned them. I have already recorded the terror that the vision of this figure caused fireman Papin, terror which made him faint–still according to Monsieur Gailhard. There is no doubt in my mind that the fiery figure that Papin encountered was the same man that frightened the Vicomte de Chagny and the Persian, a description of whom I found in the Persian's own papers. (*Note from the Author.*)

"Ah! If I didn't have that hope, I wouldn't have offered my help!"

"But how can one enter the house by the lake without crossing the lake?"

"Through the third level, from which we were so unluckily driven away. We'll go back there now. I'll tell you," said the Persian, with a sudden change in his voice, "I'll tell you the exact place, Monsieur: it's between a country farmhouse and a bit of discarded scenery from *The King of Lahore*, exactly at the spot where Joseph Buquet died..."

"That stagehand who was found hanging down there?"

"Yes, Monsieur! Then the rope that strangled him disappeared... Come along, Monsieur de Chagny, be brave and follow me! And don't forget to hold your hand at eye level! Let's see where we are exactly..."

The Persian lit his lamp and shone its rays down two enormous corridors that crossed each other at right angles and then disappeared in the darkness.

"We must be near the waterworks," he said. "I can't see any of the flames coming from the furnaces."

He walked in front of Raoul, progressing cautiously, stopping abruptly when he was afraid of meeting a waterman. Then, they had to hide from the glow of a sort of underground forge, which some men were tamping down. There, Raoul recognized the "demons" that Christine had seen on her journey during her first captivity.

In this way, they gradually arrived in a huge subbasement area perpendicularly below the stage.

They must have been standing at the very bottom of the area called the "*tank*," deep below the surface. One must remember that, when they built the Opera, they excavated the earth *50 feet below the aquifers* that existed under that entire section of Paris. All the water had to be drained. To give an idea of how much water had to be pumped out, the reader should picture in his mind a volume as wide as the Louvre courtyard and as high as one-and-a-half of Notre-Dame's tow-ers. Still, the engineers were forced to leave a lake at the bottom.

Just then, the Persian touched a wall and said:

"If I'm not mistaken, this wall might easily belong to the house by the lake."

He was knocking on a wall of the *tank*, and now would perhaps be a useful time for the reader to learn how the bottom and the walls of the *tank* had been built.

In order to prevent the water that remained at the site from coming into contact with–and thus weakening–the foundations, the supporting walls of the entire theater and the timberwork, metalwork, sculptures, frescos and *objet d'arts*, which all had to be preserved from dampness, *the architect was obliged to build double walls everywhere.*

The work of building these double walls took an entire year. They consisted of a thick stone wall designed just like an embankment or dam, then a brick wall, then a huge layer of cement, then yet another stone wall, several yards thick. It was that inner wall that the Persian had struck when speaking to Raoul of the house by the lake. To anyone understanding the architecture of the Opera, the Persian's action would seem to indicate that *Erik's mysterious house had been built inside the double walls.*

At the Persian's words, Raoul had flung himself against the wall and listened eagerly.

But he heard nothing, nothing except the echo of distant footsteps on the stage, carried down from the upper portions of the theater.

The Persian darkened his lantern again.

"Careful now!" he said. "Keep your hand high! And silence! We're going to try to find a way in."

And he led him to the little staircase they had previously taken when they had fled to the lower levels.

They walked up, stopping at each step, peering into the silent darkness... Thus, they eventually reached the third level.

There, the Persian motioned to Raoul to get down on his knees. In this way, crawling on both knees and one hand—for the other was still held high before them—they reached the end wall.

Against this wall stood a large piece of discarded scenery from *The King of Lahore*.

Next to it was a column.

And between the piece of scenery and the column, there was just enough room for a body.

The body of the man who had, one day, been found hanging there. The body of Joseph Buquet.

The Persian, still kneeling, stopped and listened.

For a moment, he seemed to hesitate and looked at Raoul. Then, he turned his eyes upward, towards the second level, where they could see the faint glow of a lantern through a space between two boards.

This glow seemed to confuse the Persian.

At last, he tossed his head and appeared to have made up his mind.

He slipped between the column and the scenery from the *The King of Lahore*, with Raoul close upon his heels.

With his free hand, the Persian felt the wall. Raoul saw him push heavily against it, just as he had done in Christine's dressing-room.

Suddenly, a stone gave way!

There was now a hole in the wall.

This time, the Persian pulled his pistol out of his pocket and made a sign to Raoul to do the same. He cocked the gun.

Then, resolutely, still on his knees, he wiggled through the hole in the wall.

Raoul, who had wished to go first, had to be content to follow him.

The hole was extremely narrow. The Persian stopped almost at once. Raoul heard him feeling the stones around him. Then, the man again took out his lantern, stooped forward, examined something beneath him and immediately turned the lantern off. Raoul heard him whisper:

"We'll have to drop a few yards without making any noise. Take off your boots."

The Persian took off his shoes and handed them to Raoul.

"Leave them outside the wall," he said. "We'll find them when we come out."[24]

Then, the Persian crawled a little further on his knees, before turning around and coming face-to-face with Raoul. He said:

"I'm going to first hang by my hands from the edge of that stone and then let myself drop *into his house*. You must do exactly the same. Don't be afraid. I'll catch you in my arms."

The Persian did just as he had planned and Raoul soon heard a dull thump, evidently made by his fall. The young man was worried that the noise might betray their presence.

Still, more than the noise itself, for Raoul the absence of any other sound was the cause of great anxiety. How could that be since, according to the Persian, they had succeeded in penetrating the very walls of the house by the lake? Where was Christine? Not a cry, not a whisper, not even a moan! Were they too late?

Crawling forward on his knees, grating against the stone, clawing it with his nervous fingers, Raoul, too, let himself drop.

At once, he felt himself caught in a hug.

"Hush! It's only me!" said the Persian.

They stood motionless, listening.

Never had the darkness been so total around them...

Never had the silence been more heavy and terrible...

---

[24] As far as I know, no one ever found those two pairs of boots which, according to the Persian's papers, had been left next to the scenery from *The King of Lahore*, where Joseph Buquet had been found hanging. They must have been taken by some stagehand or door-closer. (*Note from the Author.*)

Raoul buried his nails in the palms of his hands to stop himself from shouting: "Christine! I'm here! Answer me if you're still alive! Christine!"

Then the Persian again turned on his lantern and, with its beam, examined the wall above their heads, looking for the hole through which they had come, but failing to find it:

"Oh!" he said. "The stone has closed by itself!"

Then, the light of the lantern glided down the wall and across the floor.

The Persian bent down and picked up something. It was a thin rope which he stared at for a second then flung away with horror.

"*The Punjab wire!*" he muttered.

"What's that?" asked Raoul.

"That," replied the Persian with a shiver, "might very well be the rope that killed Joseph Buquet, which they tried to find for so long."

Suddenly, seized with a new fear, he moved the small reddish beam of his lantern over the walls. By so doing–and oddly–he revealed the trunk of a tree, which still seemed alive with all its leaves. Its branches ran right up the walls and disappeared into the ceiling.

Because of the narrowness of the beam, at first it was difficult to make out the shape of the thing. They saw the corner of a branch, then a leaf followed by another leaf and, next to that, nothing at all, nothing but the beam of light that seemed to reflect upon itself. Raoul passed his hand over that bit of nothingness, that reflection of light.

"How odd!" he said. "The wall is a mirror!"

"Yes, a mirror!" said the Persian, in a tone of deep emotion. And, wiping the sweat from his forehead with the hand that held the pistol, he added:

"We have dropped into the torture-chamber!"

Ron Sutton

Eric Shanower

Chapter Twenty-Two
Interesting and Enlightening Tribulations of a Persian in the Vaults of the Opera

The Persian's Journal [25]

It was the first time I had entered the house on the lake, *wrote the Persian*. I had often begged the *Trickster*–as we used to call Erik in my country–to open its mysterious doors to me. He always refused. So I, who had once been paid to learn his secrets and tricks, had tried using subterfuge to ignore his wishes in this matter. Ever since I had renewed my acquaintance with Erik in the corridors of the Opera, where he seemed

---

[25] The Persian himself told us how he had tried, in vain until that night, to enter into Erik's house by going through the lake, how he had discovered the secret entrance on the third level and, finally, how he and the Vicomte de Chagny, grappled with the Phantom's diabolical imagination in the torture-chamber. Here is the journal which he left us (I will explain later under what conditions) and of which I have not changed a word. I am reproducing it here verbatim, because I did not feel I had the right to censor the Daroga's adventures inside the house by the lake, after he entered it in the company of the Vicomte de Chagny. If this brief introduction has taken the reader away, for a few, brief minutes, from the torture-chamber, it is only to return him there after having explained these very important facts, so that he will better appreciate certain attitudes and mannerisms of the Persian, which otherwise might have seemed rather incredible. (*Note from the Author.*)

to reside permanently, I had been spying on him, above ground as well as below, even to the very banks of the lake, when he thought himself alone and climbed aboard his small boat to cross to the other side. But once there, the shadows that surrounded him were simply too dense for me to clearly see the exact spot on the wall where he had hidden the mechanism that opened the secret entrance into his house.

One day when I, too, thought myself alone, I remembered something the Monster had said and that, along with my own curiosity, compelled me to make a perilous attempt. I stepped into the boat and rowed towards that part of the wall through which I had seen Erik disappear. It was then that I came into contact with the siren who guarded the approach and whose charm very nearly proved fatal to me.

I had no sooner left the bank and started rowing than the silence amidst which I floated was disturbed by a sort of whispered song that hovered all around me. It was, at the same time, both breathing and music. It rose softly from the waters of the lake and surrounded me by some artifice I cannot explain. It followed me, moved alongside me and yet was so soft that it did not frighten me. On the contrary, in my longing to approach the source of that sweet, enticing harmony, I leaned out of the boat and over the water, for there was no doubt in my mind that the singing came from the water itself. By this time, I was alone in the middle of the lake. There was no one else in the boat but me. The voice–for it was now distinctly a voice–was next me, on the water. I leaned over, further still. The waters of lake were perfectly calm. A moonbeam falling from above, having passed through a vent in the Rue Scribe, showed me its empty, deserted surface, which was as smooth and black as ink. I shook my head to clear what I thought was a buzz, but soon realized that there was no buzzing in my ears–only that harmonious singing whisper that followed and now attracted me.

Had I been superstitious, or easily swayed by folk tales, I would certainly have thought that I had met with some siren whose business it was to confuse any traveler who might venture onto the waters of the house by the lake. Fortunately, I come from a country where we are too fond of the fantastic not to understand it intimately. I, myself, had experience in such matters. I knew very well that, with a few simple tricks, a skilled illusionist can work his victim's imagination into a fevered pitch.

I had no doubt that I was face-to-face with some new invention of Erik's. But it was so perfect that, as I leaned out of the boat, I was moved less by a desire to discover the trick than to enjoy its charm.

I leaned over, leaned over–until I almost overturned the small vessel.

Suddenly, two monstrous arms sprang forth from beneath the waters and, seizing me by the neck, dragged me down into the depths with irresistible force. I would certainly have perished if I had not had time to utter a cry, by which Erik recognized me.

For it was he. And, instead of drowning me as had certainly been his intention, he swam with me and laid me gently on the bank.

"How careless of you!" he said, as he stood before me, dripping with that hellish water. "Why would you try to enter my house? I never invited you! I don't want you there, nor anyone else! Did you once save my life, only to make it unbearable afterwards? However great the service you rendered him, Erik may eventually forget it, and you know that nothing can stop Erik, not even Erik himself."

He spoke, but my only desire at that point was to know what I already called the *trick of the siren.* He was willing to satisfy my curiosity, for Erik, who is truly a monster–I call him this having had–alas!–many occasions to see him at work in Persia–is also vain and conceited like a child. There is nothing he loves more than, after astonishing someone, to display the truly miraculous ingenuity of his mind.

He laughed and showed me a long reed.

"It's one of the simplest tricks you've ever seen," he said, "but it's very useful for breathing and singing under water. I learned it from the pirates in Tonkin, who could stay submerged and hidden for hours in the riverbeds." [26]

I spoke to him severely.

"It's a trick that nearly killed me!" I said. "And it may have been fatal to someone else!"

He did not reply but stood above me with that almost innocent air of menace I knew all too well.

But I would not let him bluff me that way and sharply rebuffed him.

"You remember what you promised me, Erik? No more murders!"

"Have I really committed murders?" he asked, putting on his most amiable air.

"Wretched man!" I cried. "Have you forgotten the *rosy hours of Mazenderan*?"

"Yes," he replied, suddenly in a sadder tone. "I prefer to forget them. I used to make the little Sultana laugh, though!"

"All that is in the past," I declared. "It's the present now, and you owe me for even having a present, because, if I had wished it, you would have had none. Remember that, Erik: I saved your life!"

And I took advantage of the turn of conversation to ask him something that, for some time had been preying on my mind:

"Erik," I asked, "Erik, swear that..."

"What?" he retorted. "You know I never keep my oaths. Oaths are for fools."

"Well, then, tell me... You can tell me this, at least..."

"What?"

"The chandelier... The chandelier, Erik?"

"What about the chandelier?"

"You know what I mean."

---

[26] An official report from Tonkin, received in Paris at the end of July 1909, relates how our soldiers pursued the famous pirate chief De Tham and his men, and how they all managed to escape by using this exact trick. (*Note from the Author.*)

"Oh, the chandelier" he snickered. "I don't mind telling you about the chandelier! *It wasn't me*! It was just quite old and worn." He laughed.

When Erik laughed, he was more terrifying than ever. He jumped into his boat, chuckling so horribly that I could not help but tremble.

"Quite old and worn, my dear Daroga! [27] Quite old and worn, was that chandelier! It fell all by itself! It came down with a smash! And now, Daroga, take my advice. Go and get dried off, or you'll catch a bad cold! And never take my boat again. And, whatever you do, never try to enter my house. I'm not always there to prevent accidents, Daroga! And I would hate to have to dedicate my *Requiem Mass* to you!"

So saying, and still cackling, he stepped onto the back of the boat and pushed off with a pole, swinging back and forth like some otherworldly demon. He looked just like Charon, the ferryman of Hades, but with blazing yellow eyes. Soon, I could only see the light of his eyes before he totally vanished in the darkness of the lake.

From that day, I gave up all thoughts of trying to get inside his house by the lake. That entrance was obviously too well-guarded, especially since he had realized that I knew about it. I suspected that there must be other entrances, for more than once, I had seen Erik disappear from the third level when I was watching him, though I could not figure out how he had done it.

I cannot repeat it enough. Ever since I had renewed my acquaintance with Erik and found him living beneath the Opera, I lived in perpetual terror of his ghastly tricks, not as far as I was concerned, but I feared what he might to do to other, innocent people.[28] And whenever I heard about some accident,

---

[27] Persian for Chief of Police. (*Note from the Author.*)

[28] Here, the Persian might have admitted that Erik's fate was also of some concern to him, for he was well aware that, if the Persian government in Tehran had learned that Erik was still alive, they might have stopped paying the modest state pen-

or some fatal event, I always thought to myself: "That could be Erik's doing!" just as others said: "It's the Phantom!"

How often did I hear people utter that phrase with a chuckle! Poor devils! If they had known that, indeed, the Phantom existed in the flesh, and was far more terrible than the ghostly apparition they imagined, I swear they would not have laughed! If only they had realized what Erik was capable of, especially in a domain like the Opera! And if only they had known the extent of my darkest fears!

I could not find peace! Even though Erik had solemnly told me that he had changed and that he had become the most virtuous of men *since he was loved for himself*–a sentence that, at first, perplexed me most terribly–I could not help shuddering when I thought of the Monster. His horrible, unparalleled and repulsive ugliness put him beyond the pale of humanity. Because of this, it often seemed to me that he no longer believed that he had any responsibility towards the human race. The way in which he spoke of his love only increased my alarm, for I foresaw that this phenomenon, to which he so boastfully alluded, would cause new and more hideous tragedies. I knew to what degree of sublime and disastrous despair Erik's pain could take him and the words he had spoken–vaguely prophetic of some unspeakable catastrophe–never left my mind.

On the other hand, I soon discovered the strange moral compact that existed between the Monster and Christine Daae. Hiding in the closet next to the young singer's dressing-room, I had listened to the wonderful musical lessons that had obviously cast their spell over Christine; but, all the same, I never thought that Erik's voice–which can be as loud as thunder or

---

sion that he still received as a retired Daroga. It is only fair, however, to add that the Persian had a noble and generous heart. I do not doubt for a moment that the possibility that Erik might cause some horrible harm to others must have greatly preyed on his mind. His conduct throughout this business proves it and is irreproachable. (*Note from the Author.*)

as soft as the whispers of angels–could enable her to overlook his ugliness. I realized what was going on when I understood that she had not yet seen him! I had an opportunity to enter her dressing-room and, remembering what he had once taught me, I had no difficulty in discovering the trick that made the wall mirror pivot; I also discovered how he used hollow bricks and hidden tubes to make his voice sound to Christine as if he was standing next to her. That way, too, I discovered the route that took them to the fountain and the *Communards'* cells, and also the trap-door that enabled Erik to go straight to the sub-basement just below the stage.

A few days later, I was amazed to discover that Christine Daae had seen Erik. I chanced upon the Monster while he was sprinkling water on the forehead of Christine Daae, who had fainted near the fountain in the *Communards'* passage. A white horse, the horse from *The Prophet*, which had disappeared from the Opera's stables, stood quietly beside them. I showed myself. It was terrible. I saw sparks fly from those blazing yellow eyes of his and, before I had time to say a word, I received a blow on the head that stunned me.

When I came to, Erik, Christine and the white horse had vanished. I felt sure that the poor girl was now a prisoner in his house by the lake. Without hesitation, I resolved to return to its banks, despite the danger of such a foolhardy enterprise. For 24 hours, I lay on those dark shores, waiting for the Monster to appear, convinced that he had to go out sometime, if only driven by the need to replenish his supplies. And, speaking of such mundane matters, I should say here that, when he went out in the streets of Paris or ventured to show himself in public, he wore a false nose with a mustache beneath it, instead of his own horrible hole of a nose. This did not quite disguise his macabre appearance and I learned that he had been nicknamed *Père Trompe-la-Mort* [29] behind his back by some in the neighborhood. But it did make him almost–I say almost–bearable to look at.

---

[29] Father Death-Cheater.

Therefore, I watched the banks of the lake, looking for Erik. Weary of this long wait, I began to think that he may have gone through another door, perhaps the door on the third level, when, suddenly, I heard a small splash in the dark. I saw the two blazing yellow eyes shining like lanterns. Soon, the boat touched shore. Erik jumped out and walked up to me:

"You've been here for 24 hours," he said. "You're starting to annoy me. I'm telling you that all this will end very badly. And you will have brought it upon yourself. I have been extraordinarily patient with you. You think you're following me, you great oaf (*sic*!), but I'm the one who is following you. I know everything that you've learned about me. I spared your life yesterday in *my Communards' road*, but truthfully, don't let me catch you there again! I swear, this is exceedingly reckless of you! Do you understand nothing, Daroga?"

He was so furious that I did not dare to interrupt him for even a moment. After blowing off some steam, he put his horrible thought into words, echoing my own inner fears:

"Yes, you've got to understand, once and for all–once and for all, I say–what's at stake here! I tell you again that, because of your recklessness, you've twice been caught by the shadow in the felt hat, who, not knowing what you were doing in the vaults, took you to the Directors, who've looked upon you only as an eccentric Persian interested in stagecraft and backstage gossip. Yes, I know all about it, I was there, in their office, I'm everywhere! I'm warning you that, with your recklessness, someone will end up wondering what you're really after down here... They'll find out that you're after Erik... Then, they'll be after Erik, too... And they'll discover my house by the lake... And then, it'll be too bad, my friend, too bad! I won't answer for what happens then."

Again, he huffed and puffed.

"I won't answer for what happens then! If Erik's secrets cease to be Erik's secrets, *too bad for a goodly number of the human race*! That's all I have to say! And unless you're a great oaf (*sic*!), it ought to be enough for you! Now, you understand, don't you, Daroga?"

He was sitting on the stern of his boat and was kicking his heels against the planks, waiting to hear my answer. I simply said:

"It's not Erik that I'm after here!"

"Who then?"

"You know as well as I do: it's Christine Daae!"

"I have every right to see her in my own house," he replied. "I am loved for myself."

"That's not true," I said. "You've abducted her and are keeping her locked up."

"Listen," he said. "Will you promise to never meddle in my affairs again if I prove to you that I am loved for myself?"

"Yes, I promise you," I replied, without hesitation, for I felt convinced that, for such a Monster, such proof was impossible to obtain.

"Well, then, it's quite simple... Christine Daae will leave here as she pleases and will return!... Yes, will return because she wishes... of her own free will... because she loves me for myself!"

"Oh, I doubt that she will return! But it is your duty to let her go."

"My duty, you great oaf! (*sic*!) It is my wish–my wish to let her go. And she will return, because she loves me! All this will end in a marriage... A marriage at the Church of the Madeleine, you great oaf! (*sic*!) Do you believe me now? My wedding mass is already written... Wait until you hear its *Kyrie*...*"

He beat time with his heels on the planks of the boat while singing: "*Kyrie... Kyrie... Kyrie Eleison...* Wait until you hear my mass!"

"Listen," I said. "I'll believe you if I see Christine Daae leave your house by the lake and return there of her own free will."

"And you won't meddle in my affairs anymore? Very well! You'll see her tonight. Come to the masked ball. Christine and I plan on dropping by. Go and hide in the closet next to her dressing-room and listen. You'll hear her agreeing of her own free will to return to the vaults by the *Communards'* route."

"Agreed!"

If I saw all this, then indeed, I would have no choice but give up; after all, a beautiful person has the right to love an ugly one, especially when, like Erik, he has at his command the seduction of music and the beautiful person is a distinguished singer.

"Now, be off, for I have shopping to do!"

I left, still concerned about Christine Daae, but primarily experiencing a sense of deep foreboding, reawakened by the Monster's remarks about the terrible consequences of my recklessness.

I asked myself: "How will this all end?" And even though I was a fatalist by nature, I could not let go of a vague feeling of anxiety caused by the enormous responsibility that I had, one day, taken upon myself when I spared the life of the Monster who, today, threatened *a goodly number of the human race*!

Still, to my intense astonishment, things happened just as he had foretold. Christine Daae left the house by the lake and returned to it several times, without, apparently, being forced to do so. I tried, then, not to think anymore about that bizarre love story, but it was difficult for me to let go of Erik because of that sense of deep foreboding which I mentioned. However, I resolved to be extremely prudent and did not make the mistake of returning to the shores of the lake, or of taking the Communards' passage.

But the idea of a secret entrance located on the third level obsssessed me. I went there repeatedly, because I knew it was deserted for most of the day. I waited for hours, endlessly twiddling my thumbs, hidden behind the scenery of *Le Roi de Lahore*, which, for some unfathomable reason, had been stored there, since they didn't play it very often.

At last, my patience was rewarded. One day, I saw the Monster crawl towards me on his knees. I was sure that he did not see me. He passed between the scenery behind which I was hidden and the column, went to the wall and pressed on a spot, the location of which I carefully noted. A spring released a stone which revealed a secret passage. He entered and the stone closed behind him. Now I knew the Monster's secret, the secret that, someday, might gain me entrance to his house by the lake.

I waited for at least a half-hour and then I, too, pressed the spring. Everything happened as it had with Erik. But I was careful not to go through the passage because I knew that Erik was still inside. Also, the idea that I might be caught by him suddenly made me think of Joseph Buquet's death. I had no desire to jeopardize the advantage of such a great discovery, which could prove useful to many people, to *a goodly number of the human race*, so, after carefully replacing the stone according to a mechanism I had known in Persia, I left the third level.

As you may imagine, I continued to be greatly interested in the relationship between Erik and Christine Daae, not from mere morbid curiosity, but because of the deep foreboding which never left me. "If Erik discovers that he is not loved for himself," I thought, "anything could happen."

I cautiously continued to wander around the Opera and soon learned the truth about the Monster's sad love story. He controlled Christine's mind by fear, but the dear child's heart belonged entirely to the Vicomte Raoul de Chagny. While they innocently played at being an engaged couple in the upper sections of the Opera, always fleeing from the Monster, little did they suspect that someone else was watching over them. I was prepared to do anything: even kill the Monster if necessary, and then explain it to the Police afterwards. But Erik did not show himself, and yet that did not leave me feeling any more comfortable.

I must take a moment to explain my chain of thought. I believed that the Monster, driven from his house by jealousy, would enable me to go inside, without danger, through the passage on the third level. I thought it was important for everyone's sake that I should learn exactly what was inside. One day, tired of waiting for an opportunity, I moved the stone and, at once, heard the sound of astounding music. The Monster was working on his *Don Juan Triumphant*, with every door in his house wide open. I knew that this was the work of his life. I was careful not to move and prudently remained in my dark little corner. He stopped playing for a moment and began pacing about the place like a madman. Then he said loudly, at the top of his voice:

"I must finish it *first*! Completely finished!"

This speech was not calculated to reassure me and, when the music started again, I very softly closed the stone. But despite that, I still heard the faint harmonies of his song seemingly rising from the bowels of the Earth, as I had heard the song of the siren coming up from below the waters. I remembered the words of some of the stagehands at the time of Joseph Buquet's death–words that had caused many to smile incredulously–that they had heard *music that came from nowhere surrounding the corpse... Music that reminded them of the Dance of the Dead*!

On the day of Christine Daae's abduction, I did not come to the Opera until rather late in the evening, trembling lest I should hear some awful news. I had spent a horrible day, for, after reading the announcement of the forthcoming marriage of Christine and the Vicomte de Chagny in the morning paper, I wondered if, after all, *it would not be better to denounce the Monster*. But reason returned to me, and I became convinced that this action would only precipitate a possible catastrophe.

When my cab let me out in front of the Opera, I was, in truth, almost astonished *to see it still standing*!

But, like most Persians, I am something of a fatalist and I went inside, *ready for anything*!

Christine Daae's abduction during the Prison Act, which naturally surprised everybody, found me prepared. I was quite certain that she had been spirited away by Erik, the King of Magicians. And this time, I thought that this was the end for Christine and *perhaps for everybody else*.

I was so convinced of it that, at one point, I thought of advising all who were inside the theater to leave while they were still able. But again, I thought that such a denunciation would certainly make everyone think I was certifiably insane and I refrained. Also, I thought that if I screamed "Fire!" for example, to force an evacuation of the theater, I might cause a panic that would result in people being trampled, suffocating, or being crushed to death while trying to escape–a fate almost worse than the catastrophe I sought to avoid.

So, I resolved to act alone, without further delay. The timing was excellent, I thought. There was a fairly good chance that Erik, at that very moment, was thinking only of his captive. It was a propitious time to get inside his house via the third level. I resolved to take with me the poor, desperate, young Vicomte, who, at the first suggestion, accepted my offer with so much confidence in me that I was deeply moved. I had sent my servant for my pistols. I gave one to the Vicomte and advised him to hold it as if he was ready to fire, for, after all, Erik might be waiting for us behind the wall. I had planned to take the Communards' passage and, from there, reach the third level through the trap-doors.

Upon seeing my pistols, the Vicomte asked me if we were going to fight a duel. I said: "Yes, and what a duel!" But, of course, I had no time to explain anything to him. The Vicomte had a brave heart, but he hardly knew anything about our enemy and it was much better that way!

What would a duel with even the deadliest swordsman be, compared to a battle with the King of Magicians? Even I found it difficult to reconcile myself to the notion that I was about to fight a man who was visible only when he wished it, but who, on the other hand, saw everything, even when you, yourself, were plunged into darkness! To fight a man whose weird science, subtlety, imagination and skills enabled him to control all the forces of nature and combine them to cast a deadly spell over your eyes and ears! Then, to fight that man in the vaults of the Opera, that is to say in the very Kingdom of Magic! Could anyone even conceive of this without trembling? Could anyone conceive of what might happen to their own senses if a savage and mercurial Robert Houdin, who would sometimes laugh and other times hate, sometimes steal and other times kill, was locked inside the Opera–five underground levels and 25 upper floors–24 hours a day for years? Think about that! To fight a man who was known in my Kingdom as the *Trickster*? Gods! How many trap-doors did he install in our palaces, those clever little rotating trap-doors of his? To fight the *Trickster* in the very Kingdom of Trap-doors!

If my hope was that Erik had not left Christine Daae's side in his house by the lake, where he had probably carried her, unconscious after her abduction, my greatest fear was that he was already somewhere near us, preparing to strike with his *Punjab wire.*

No one knows better than he how to throw the Punjab wire, for he is the King of Stranglers just as he is the King of Magicians. When he had finished making the little Sultana laugh, at the time of the *rosy hours of Mazenderan*, she herself used to ask him to amuse her by giving her a thrill. It was then that he introduced the sport of the Punjab wire.

Erik had lived in India and there, had acquired a phenomenal skill in the art of strangulation. He would have them lock him inside an arena to which they brought a warrior–usually, a man condemned to death–armed with a long pike and broadsword. Erik had only his small, thin rope. And it was always just as the warrior thought that he was going to slay Erik with a tremendous blow that we heard the rope whistle through the air. With a turn of the wrist, Erik tightened the noose around his adversary's neck and, in this fashion, dragged him before the little Sultana and her women, who sat looking from a window and applauding. The little Sultana herself learned to wield the Punjab wire and killed several of her women and even friends who visited her.

But I prefer to drop the terrible subject of the *rosy hours of Mazenderan*. If I mentioned it, it is only to explain why, upon arriving with the Vicomte de Chagny in the vaults of the Opera, I felt I had to protect my companion against the ever-threatening danger of death by strangulation. Once underground, I knew that my pistols would be of little use to us, for I was certain that if Erik had not fought us to stop us from entering the Communards' passage, then he was not likely to show himself, but he could still strangle us from behind. I had no time to explain all this to the Vicomte. And even if I had had the time, I do not know if I would have wasted it by telling him that somewhere in the shadows, there might be a Punjab wire lurking, ready to kill us.

I simply told Monsieur de Chagny to keep his hand at eye level, his arm bent, as if waiting for the command to fire. If someone stands in that position, it is virtually impossible, even for the most expert strangler, to throw his cord with accuracy. It catches not only the neck of its intended victim, but also his arm or hand. This enables one to easily loosen it, rendering that deadliest of weapons perfectly harmless.

After avoiding the Police, the door-closers and the firemen, after having encountered the rat catcher and the mysterious shadow in the felt hat, the Vicomte and I reached the third level without further incident. There, between the column and the scenery from *Le Roi de Lahore*, I found the stone, worked the spring and we landed inside the house which Erik had built for himself in the double walls of the Opera's foundation.

(*And this was the easiest thing in the world for him to do, since Erik was one of the main subcontractors employed by Philippe Garnier, the architect of the Opera; and he continued to work alone when the works were officially suspended during the war, the siege of Paris and the Commune.*)[30]

----

[30] The attempted invasion of Germany by Napoleon III in July 1870 came to a quick and disastrous end. On September 2, the Emperor was captured by Bismarck's army near Sedan in Eastern France. In Paris, mass demonstrations demanded the overthrow of the Second Empire. A new Government of National Defence was quickly installed. Soon, German troops encircled Paris and besieged the city. An armistice was signed on January 28, 1871. However, the workers of Paris refused to

I knew Erik too well to feel presumptuous enough to believe that I might have uncovered all the tricks he might have installed during all that time. So I was not at all comfortable when we entered his house. I knew what he had made of a certain palace at Mazenderan. From the most honest building in the world, he had made a devilish castle where one could not utter a word that could not be overheard or repeated by an echo. How many bloody tragedies and family dramas the Monster had created with his fiendish tricks. Also, in those palaces that he had rigged, one could never know exactly where one was!

He had come up with some astonishing inventions. Of these, the most curious, horrible and deadly was the so-called *torture-chamber*. Except in special cases, when the little Sultana amused herself by inflicting pain on some hapless citizen who had offended her, no one was let into it but wretches condemned to death. It was, in my opinion, the most ghastly invention devised during the *rosy hours of Mazenderan*. Also, when the unfortunate visitors of the *torture-chamber* had *had enough*, they were always free to put an end to their suffering with a Punjab wire left for their use at the foot of an iron tree.

My alarm, therefore, was great when I saw that the room in which Monsieur le Vicomte de Chagny and I found ourselves was an exact copy of the *torture-chamber of the rosy hours of Mazenderan*!

---

accept defeat and seized control of the city on March 18. They established a socialist government called the Paris Commune, after the government of Paris during the French Revolution (1789-1795). However, with Prussian support, the French army reconquered Paris and executed tens of thousands of *Communards* during the "Bloody Week" (May 21-28). France was obliged to cede its Alsace-Lorraine region and to pay a war indemnity of 5,000 million francs to Germany. German troops remained in parts of France until 1873. The 1870 war embittered Franco-German relations and eventually led to World War I.

At our feet, I found the Punjab wire which I had been dreading all night. I was convinced that this rope had already killed Joseph Buquet who one night, like myself, must have caught Erik entering or leaving his secret entrance on the third level. He probably tried to open it, succeeded and fell into the torture-chamber. He left it hanging by his neck.

I could well imagine Erik, to get rid of the body, dragging it behind the scenery of *Le Roi de Lahore*, and hanging it there as an example, or to increase the *superstitious terror that helped him guard the entrances to his lair*!

Then, upon reflection, Erik must have gone back to fetch the Punjab wire, which is made, rather strangely, out of catgut, and which might have excited the curiosity of the investigating magistrate. This explains the disappearance of the rope.

And now, I had discovered the very same rope, at our feet, in the torture-chamber! I am no coward, but a cold sweat coated my face.

Despite the shaking of my hand, I moved the red beam of my lantern over the walls.

Monsieur de Chagny noticed my condition and asked:

"What is the matter, Monsieur?"

I made a violent sign for him to be silent, for I thought I could still hope–foolishly!–that we were in the torture-chamber but that the Monster knew nothing about it!

And even that hope meant very little, for I was able to consider the possibility that the torture-chamber was meant to protect the entrance on the third level, *and could do so automatically*.

Yes, the tortures could begin *on their own*.

Who could say which of our gestures might trigger the deadly mechanism?

I asked the Vicomte to stay completely still.

A crushing silence now lay heavily upon us.

And the red beam of my lantern continued to glide across the mirrored walls of this accursed chamber which I knew so well...

Denis Rodier

Chapter Twenty-Three
Inside the Torture-Chamber

The Persian's Journal (continued)

We stood in the center of a small, six-sided room of perfect hexagonal shape, the inside walls of which were covered with mirrors from top to bottom. In the corners, we could clearly see the mirror-plated hinges, the small parts intended to rotate on their axis. Yes, I recognized them just as I recognized the iron tree in the corner, the accursed iron tree with its iron branch for hanging men.

I grabbed my companion's arm. The Vicomte de Chagny was trembling, overly eager to shout to his fiancée that he was coming to her rescue. I feared that he would not be able to contain himself.

Suddenly, we heard a noise on our left.

At first, it sounded like the opening and closing of a door in the next room. There was a low moan. I clutched Monsieur de Chagny's arm even more tightly. Then we distinctly heard these words:

"You must decide! It's either the *wedding mass* or the *requiem mass!*"

I recognized the Monster's voice.

There was another moan, followed by a long silence.

I was now convinced that the Monster was unaware of our presence in his house, for otherwise he would have certainly taken steps to prevent us from spying on him. He would only have had to close the small, invisible window through which a torture-lover outside could look inside the torture-chamber without being seen.

303

Furthermore, I was sure that, had he known of our presence, the torture would have already begun.

We had, therefore, a major advantage over Erik: we were near him and he knew nothing about it!

The important thing was to keep him from finding out. What I most feared was the impulsiveness of the Vicomte de Chagny, who wanted to rush through the walls to rescue Christine Daae, whose moans we continued to hear at regular intervals.

"The requiem mass is not particularly joyful," Erik's voice continued, "whereas the wedding mass–you can take my word for this–is magnificent! You've got to make up your mind and choose! As for me, I've decided that I can't very well continue to live like this, like a mole in a hole! My *Don Juan Triumphant* is finished. Now, I want to live like everyone else. I want to have a wife like everyone else and take her out on Sundays. I have invented a mask that makes me look normal. People won't even turn around and look at me in the streets. You'll be the happiest of women. And we'll sing, just the two of us, to our heart's content. What? You're crying! You're afraid of me! I'm not really a bad man, inside. Love me and you'll see! *All I ever needed to be good was to be loved for myself.* If you loved me, I would be gentle as a lamb, and you would be able to wrap me around your little finger."

Soon, the moans that accompanied that strange declaration of love grew and grew in volume. I had never heard such despair. Monsieur de Chagny and I realized that this terrible wailing came from Erik himself. On the other side of those mirrors, Christine must have been standing dumb with horror, with no strength left to cry out, while the Monster was on his knees before her.

Erik's lament alternated between the roar of thunder and the droning of the ocean. Three times over, he bemoaned his fate, screaming hoarsely:

"You don't love me! You don't love me! You don't love me!"

And then, more gently:

"Why do you cry? You know it pains me to see you cry!"

A silence.

Each silence brought us renewed hope. We thought to ourselves: "Perhaps he has left Christine alone behind the wall."

We thought of the possibility of warning her of our presence next door, without letting the Monster know.

We could leave the torture-chamber only if Christine opened the door. That was the only way we could hope to help her, for we did not even know where on our side the door might be.

Suddenly, the silence in the next room was broken by the ringing of an electric bell.

There was the sound of a jump on the other side of the wall and Erik's thunderous voice:

"Somebody's at the door! Come in, gentlemen, come in!"

Then, a sinister chuckle.

"Who has come to bother us? Wait for me here! *I'm going to tell the siren to open the door.*"

We heard footsteps walking away, followed by the sound of a door closing. I had no time to think of what new horror was about to take place. I put out of my mind the fact that the Monster was leaving so that he could perpetrate a fresh crime. I understood only one thing: Christine was alone behind the wall!

The Vicomte de Chagny was already calling to her:

"Christine! Christine!"

Since we could hear what was said in the next room, there was no reason why my companion could not be heard in turn. Still, the Vicomte had to repeat his cry several times.

At last, a faint voice reached us.

"I must be dreaming!" it said.

"Christine, Christine, it's me, Raoul!"

A silence.

"Please answer me, Christine! In Heaven's name, if you're alone, answer me!"

Then Christine's voice whispered Raoul's name.

"Yes! Yes! It is I!" cried the Vicomte. "You're not dreaming! Trust me, Christine! We're here to save you... but you must be careful! When you hear the Monster return, warn us!"

"Raoul! Is it possible? Raoul!"

The Vicomte had to tell her repeatedly that she was not hallucinating, and that he, Raoul de Chagny, had managed to reach her, thanks to the help of a devoted companion who knew Erik's secrets.

But Christine's joy upon the realization that her fiancé had come to her rescue almost immediately gave way to an even greater terror. She wanted Raoul to get away as fast as he could. She feared that Erik would discover our hiding place, and if he did, she was sure he would kill the young man. She told us in a few hurried words that Erik had gone quite mad with love and had *decided to kill everybody, himself included,* if she did not consent to become his wife in a dual ceremony before both Mayor and Priest–the Priest of the Chuch of the Madeleine. He had given her until 11 p.m. the next evening to make a decision. It was the final deadline. Then, she must choose, as he put it, between the wedding mass and the requiem mass.

And Erik had uttered a phrase which Christine did not quite understand:

"Yes or no! If your answer is no, everybody will be *dead and buried*!"

But I understood that sentence perfectly well, for it explained in a most terrible manner my own sense of deep foreboding.

"Can you tell us where Erik is?" I asked.

She replied that he must have left the house.

"Could you make sure?"

"No. I'm tied up. I can't move."

306

When we heard this, neither Monsieur de Chagny nor I could repress a cry of fury. Our safety, the safety of all three of us, depended on the girl's freedom of movement.

"We must try to reach her... free her!" said the Vicomte.

"But where are you?" asked Christine. "There are only two doors in the room where I am, the Louis-Philippe room which I told you about, Raoul... A door through which Erik comes and goes, and another which he has never opened in front of me and which he has forbidden me ever to go through, because he says it is the most dangerous of the doors, the door to the torture-chamber!"

"Christine, that's where we are!"

"You're in the torture-chamber?"

"Yes, but we can't see the door."

"Oh, if I could only drag myself so far! I would knock on it and that would tell you where it is."

"Does the door have a lock?" I asked.

"Yes, it has one."

I thought: it opens on the other side with a key, like every other door; but on our side, it opens with a hidden spring and a counterweight, and they won't be easy to find.

"Mademoiselle," I said, "you absolutely must open that door!"

"But how?" asked the poor girl tearfully. We heard her straining, obviously trying to free herself from the bonds that held her.

"We've got to use a ruse," I said. "We need the key."

"I know where it is," she said, in a voice seemingly exhausted by the efforts she had made. "But I'm tied up so tightly! The wretch!"

And she began sobbing.

"Where is the key?" I asked, while gesturing to Monsieur de Chagny to stay silent and leave this whole thing to me, for we didn't have a moment to lose.

"In his room, near the organ, with another little bronze key, which he also forbade me to touch. They are both in a small leather bag which he calls *the bag of life and death...*

Raoul! Run away, Raoul! Run away! Everything is strange and terrible here. Erik has gone crazy and you are in the torture-chamber! Escape the way you came. There must be a reason why that room is called what it is!"

"Christine," said the young man, "we'll leave here together or die here together!"

"We *can* escape together, but only if we keep our heads," I whispered. "Why has he tied you up, Mademoiselle? You can't escape from his house and he knows it!"

"I tried to kill myself! The Monster went out last night, after carrying me here unconscious and chloroformed. He was going *to see his banker*, or so he said! When he returned, he found me with my face covered in blood. I had tried to kill myself by hitting my head against the walls."

"Christine!" moaned Raoul; and he began to sob.

"Then he tied me up. I'm not allowed to die until 11 p.m. tomorrow night."

This entire conversation through the wall was far choppier and full of hesitations than I can convey in this transcription. Often, we stopped in the middle of a sentence, because we thought we had heard a creak, a step or a strange noise. Then, she said: "No! No! It's not him! He did go out! I recognized the sound that the wall by the lake makes when it closes."

"Mademoiselle," I declared. "The Monster bound you and he shall unbind you. You only have to play the necessary part! Remember that he loves you!"

"Alas!" we heard. "How could I ever forget it!"

"Remember it then! Smile at him, be nice to him, tell him that your bonds are hurting you."

But Christine Daae said:

"Hush! I hear something in the wall by the lake! It's him! Leave! Leave! Leave!"

"We can't leave, even if we wanted to," I said, to impress the girl with the seriousness of our prediucament "We can't get out. We're trapped inside the torture-chamber!"

"Hush!" whispered Christine again.

The three of us fell silent.

We heard the sound of slow, heavy footsteps from behind the wall, they stopped, then made the floor creak once more.

Next came a tremendous sigh, followed by a cry of horror from Christine, and we heard Erik's voice:

"I beg your pardon for permitting you to see a face like this! I'm in quite a state, aren't I? It's the *other*'s fault! Why did he ring? Do I bother people in the street or knock on their doors? Well, he won't be bothering anyone else ever again, that's certain–thanks to the siren."

There was another sigh, deeper, larger still, coming from the abysmal depths of his soul.

"Why did you cry out, Christine?"

"Because I am in pain, Erik."

"I thought I had frightened you."

"Erik, loosen my bonds, please... Aren't I your prisoner?"

"You'll try to kill yourself again."

"You've given me until 11 p.m. tomorrow night, Erik."

Once again the footsteps dragged along the floor.

"Well, since we're going to die together... And I'm just as eager for it as you are... Yes, I've had enough of this life too, you know. Wait, don't move, I'll release you... You only have one word to say: '*No!*' And it will be over at once, *for everybody*! You're right, you're right, why wait until 11 p.m. tomorrow night? True, it would have been grander... I've always had a weakness for the grandiose, the magnificient... It's childish really! One should only think of oneself in life. Think of one's own death; the rest doesn't matter. *You're asking yourself why I'm all wet, aren't you*? Oh, my dearest, it's because I was wrong to go out. It's raining cats and dogs out there! Which reminds me, Christine, I think I'm having hallucinations... You know, the man who rang for the siren just now–go and see at the bottom of the lake if he's ringing now!– well, he looked rather like... There, turn round, are you happier now? You're free. Oh, my poor Christine, let me look at your wrists... Tell me, have I hurt them? That alone deserves death... And speaking of death, *I must sing him a requiem!*"

Upon hearing those terrible words, I felt an awful trepidation. I, too, had once rung at the Monster's door and, without knowing it, must have set off some alarm. And I still remembered the two arms that had sprung up from the inky waters. Who was the unfortunate man who had strayed to these fatal shores this time?

The thought of that poor man almost prevented me from rejoicing over the success of Christine's stratagem. The Vicomte de Chagny whispered in my ear these wonderful, magical words: "She's free!" but I wondered who the *other* was? For whom would we now hear a requiem mass?

Ah! That sublime and furious singing! The entire house by the lake shook with it! The very bowels of Earth trembled! We had put our ears against the mirrors to better hear Christine Daae's stratagem, the stratagem she employed to secure our freedom, but we no longer heard anything above the sounds of the requiem, the mass for the dead... Or rather a mass for the damned... It was like a dance of demons from the lowest depths.

I remember that the *Dies Irae* Erik sang broke over us like a storm. Yes, we felt battered as if by thunder and lightning. I had heard him sing before, naturally... He even had used his powers to make the stony faces of the man-bull sculptures adorning the walls of the palace of Mazenderan sing... But he had never sung like this! Never! He sang like the God of Thunder...

Suddenly, the singing and the organ stopped so abruptly that Monsieur de Chagny and I were astonished and stepped away from the wall. And his voice, suddenly changed and transformed, distinctly uttered these words in a raspy, metallic tone:

"Christine, what have you done with my bag?"

Mike Manley

Hilary Barta

Chapter Twenty-Four
The Tortures Begin

The Persian's Journal (continued)

The voice repeated angrily:

"What have you done with my bag?"

Christine Daae could not have been more terrified than we were.

"You only asked me to release you so you could take my bag!"

We heard hurried steps, Christine running back to the Louis-Philippe room, as if to seek shelter on the other side of our wall.

"What are you running away for?" asked the furious voice, which had followed her. "Give me back my bag! Don't you know that it's the bag of life and death?"

"Listen to me, Erik," sighed the girl. "Since it's now agreed that we are to live together, why does it matter to you? Everything that is yours belongs to me, too!"

That was said in such a quivering manner that it was pitiful to hear. The poor girl must have used whatever energy she had left to overcome her terror. But such childish reasoning, delivered through chattering teeth, would not fool the Monster.

"You know there are only two keys in it," said Erik. "What do you want to do with them?"

"I want to see that room," she replied, "which I have never seen and which you've always kept me from... It's a woman's curiosity!" she added, in a tone which she tried to make sound playful, but which only succeeded in increasing Erik's suspicions since it so obviously rang false.

"I don't like curious women," he retorted, "and you should remember the story of Bluebeard... Now, give me back my bag! Give it back! And leave that key alone, you nosy girl!"

Then he chuckled while Christine cried out in pain. Erik had obviously forcibly recovered the bag from her.

It was at that moment that the Vicomte could no longer contain himself and made a small cry of impotent rage that I barely managed to suppress on his lips.

"What? What was that?" said the Monster. "Did you hear that, Christine?"

"No, no," replied the poor girl. "I heard nothing."

"I thought I heard a cry."

"A cry! Are you going mad, Erik? Who do you think might cry out in your house? I cried! Because you hurt me! Otherwise, I didn't hear anything."

"You don't sound convinced! You're trembling. You're terribly excited suddenly... You're lying! That was a cry, it was! There's someone in the torture-chamber! Ah, now I understand!"

"There's no one there, Erik!"

"I understand!"

"No one!"

"Your fiancé, perhaps!"

"I don't have a fiancé, you know I don't."

Another nasty chuckle.

"Well, it won't take long to find out. Christine, my love, we don't need to open the door to see what's inside the torture-chamber. Would you like to see? Would you? If there is someone in there, if there really is someone in there, it's easy. See that small window near the top? We only need to turn off the lights in here, turn them on in there, draw the black curtain that covers it and we'll see everything inside while being totally invisible ourselves. Let's do it! Let's turn on the lights in there and turn them off in here! You're not afraid of the dark, are you? Not when you're with your future husband!"

Then we heard Christine's agonizing voice:

"No! I'm scared! I'm afraid of the dark! I don't care about that room anymore now! You're the one who's always scaring me, like a child, with your torture-chamber! So, yes, I became curious about it, that's true... But now, I don't care about it anymore... Not a bit!"

And that which I feared above all began–*automatically*. We were suddenly flooded with light! Yes, everything was ablaze on our side of the wall. The Vicomte de Chagny, who did not expect it, was so surprised that he staggered. And the angry voice on the other side yelled:

"I told you there was someone! Do you see the window now? The small window, right up there, all so brightly lit-up? The ones behind the wall can't see it! But you can! Climb up that stepladder–that's what it's there for!–you've asked me the question often enough!–well, now you've got your answer! It's there to enable you to peep into the torture-chamber you nosy girl!"

"What torture? Who is being tortured? Erik! Erik! Tell me you're saying this just to scare me! Say it, if you love me, Erik! There is no torture, is there? It's only a scary tale, isn't it?"

"Go and look through the little window, my darling!"

I don't know if the Vicomte heard the girl's hysterical voice, for he was too startled by the astounding spectacle that had now appeared before his bewildered eyes. As for me, I had seen that sight too often, through the little window, during *the rosy hours of Mazenderan*. I cared only about what was being said next door, looking for a clue to extract ourselves from our predicament or a direction for some action to take.

"Go! Go and look through the little window! You'll tell me... You'll tell me afterwards *what his nose looks like*!"

We heard the sound of the ladder being dragged against the wall.

"Climb up! You don't want to? Then, I'll go up myself, my darling!"

"No! I'll go! Yes, I'll go up. Let me go!"

"Oh, my darling, my darling! How sweet of you! How so very sweet of you to save me the effort at my age! Go up then. You'll tell me *what his nose looks like*. Ah! If only people knew the happiness there is in having a nose! A nice little nose that rightfully belongs on your face! Why then, if they just knew, they'd never wander about in my torture-chamber..."

At that moment, we distinctly heard these words above our heads:

"*There is no one there, darling!*"

"No one? Are you sure there is no one?"

"Of course, I'm sure. There's nobody there!"

"Well, that's all right then! What's the matter, Christine? You're not going to faint, are you? Since there's no one there? Here! Come down! There! Pull yourself together–there's no one there! You said so yourself! But, tell me, *how did you find the scenery inside*?"

"Oh, quite attractive!"

"Very good! Much better! You're better now, aren't you? Good, good! We don't want any strong emotions, now, do we? That was a funny room, wasn't it? With a rather unusual décor, wouldn't you say?"

"Yes, it was a little like the Hall of Mirrors at the Musée Grevin... But I didn't see any torture implements in there... You said that just to scare me, didn't you, Erik? Well, what a fright you gave me!"

"Why? Since there's no one there?"

"Did you design that room? It's very attractive. You're quite the artist, Erik."

"Yes, that's me, a great artist, *in my own style*."

"But tell me, why did you call that room the torture-chamber then?"

"Oh, it's quite simple. First of all, what did you see?"

"I saw a forest."

"And what's in a forest?"

"Trees."

"And what's in a tree?"

"Birds."

"Did you see any birds?"

"No, I did not see any birds."

"Well, what did you see? Think! You saw branches... And what did you see in those branches?" continued the terrible voice. "*Gallows*! That's why I call my little forest the 'torture-chamber!' You see, it's just a joke. It's all for laughs. I never express myself like other people. I don't do anything like other people! But now I'm tired of it! I'm sick and tired of having a forest that looks like a torture-chamber in my house! Of living like a circus freak in a house full of trap-doors! I'm tired of it! Tired of it! I want to have a nice, quiet apartment, with ordinary doors and windows and an honest wife inside, like anybody else! You need to understand that, Christine, and I shouldn't have to repeat myself all the time! A wife like anybody else! A wife whom I could love, take out on Sundays and keep entertained during the week... You'd never be bored with me! I've got quite a bag of tricks, all kinds of tricks, like card-tricks–shall I show you some card-tricks? It'll help us while away a few minutes, while waiting for 11 p.m. tomorrow night...

"My darling Christine! My darling Christine! Are you listening to me? You won't reject me anymore, will you? Tell me you love me! No, you don't love me... But no matter, you will! Before, you couldn't look at my mask because you knew what was behind. Now, you don't mind so much looking at it and you've managed to forget what is behind! And you're not pushing me away anymore! So, you see one can get used to anything, if one wishes. Plenty of young people who weren't in love before their marriage end up adoring each other afterwards! Oh, I don't know what I'm talking about! But you would have lots of fun with me. There's no one on Earth with my talents! I can swear to that before God, the same God who'll marry us–if you're reasonable. For instance, I am the greatest ventriloquist that ever lived, the best ventriloquist in the world! You're laughing? Perhaps you don't believe me? Listen."

The wretch (who really was the best ventriloquist in the world) was trying to divert the girl's attention (as I realized) from the torture-chamber. But it was a foolish notion, for Christine thought only of us! She repeatedly begged Erik, in the gentlest tones which she could assume:

"Turn off the light in the little window! Please, Erik, do turn off that light!"

For she realized that this light, which appeared so suddenly at the window, and the diabolical tone which the Monster had used when describing it, must mean that something terrible was about to take place. One thing must have reassured her for a moment: seeing the two of us, behind the wall, in the midst of that blazing, dreadful light, but still alive and well. But she would certainly have felt much relieved if the light had been turned off.

Meantime, Erik had already begun to play his ventriloquist games. He said:

"Here, I'm going to raise my mask just a little bit... Only a little bit! Now, do you see my lips, such lips as I have? They're not moving! My mouth–such mouth as I have–is closed, and yet you hear my voice. I speak 'from my stomach.' That's what ventriloquists do. That's why it's called 'ventriloquism.' Listen to my voice! Where do you want me to throw it? In your left ear? In your right ear? To the table? To those little ebony boxes on the mantelpiece? Are you amazed? My voice is now in those little ebony boxes! Do you want it distant? Close? Thundering? High-pitched? Nasal? My voice is everywhere! Everywhere! Listen, my darling–it's now in the little box on the right of the mantelpiece! Listen to what it's saying: '*Shall I turn the scorpion*?' And now, woosh! It's in the little box on the left! And listen again to what it's saying: '*Shall I turn the locust*?' And woosh again! Now, it's in the little leather bag! And does it say? It says: '*I am the little bag of life and death*!'...And now, woosh! It's in Mademoiselle Carlotta's throat, in her golden throat, in her crystalline throat, upon my word! What does it say? It says: 'I'm Mr. Croak, I'm the one singing: '...*Et je comprends cette voix solitaire* croak!

croak! *Qui chante dans mon* croak!' And now, woosh again! And this time, my voice is on a chair, inside Box No. 5, the Phantom's box and it says: '*Tonight, her singing is bad enough to bring down the chandelier*!' And now, woosh! Ha! Ha! Ha! Ha! Where is Erik's voice now? Listen, Christine! Listen, my darling! It's behind the door of the torture-chamber! Listen! I'm the one in the torture-chamber! And what do I say? I say: 'Woe to those who know the happiness of having a nose, a nice little nose that rightfully belongs on their face, and wander into my torture-chamber!' Ha! Ha! Ha!"

Oh, the accursed voice of the ventriloquist! It was everywhere, everywhere. It passed through the little invisible window and through the walls. It ran around us, between us. Erik was there, speaking to us! We even tried to grab it, but, swifter, more fleeting than an echo, his voice had already leaped back behind the wall!

Soon, we heard nothing more at all, for this is what happened:

"Erik! Erik!" said Christine's voice. "You're wearing me down with your voice. Please stop! Oh! Isn't it very hot here?"

"Oh, yes," replied Erik's voice. "The heat is unbearable!"

Then, Christine's voice again, hoarse with terror:

"What does that mean? The wall is getting hot! Burning hot!"

"I'll tell you, Christine, my darling: it is because of *the forest next door*."

"What do you mean? The forest?"

"*Didn't you see that it was an African forest?*"

And the Monster's laughter rose so loudly and triumphantly that we could no longer hear Christine's supplications!

The Vicomte de Chagny shouted and banged against the walls like a madman. I could not restrain him. But we heard only the Monster's laugh, and the Monster himself can have heard nothing else.

Then, there was the sound of a body falling onto the floor and being dragged along, a door slammed and then nothing–nothing more around us except the scorching silence of Noon in the heart of a tropical jungle!

Phil Yeh

Bret Blevins

Chapter Twenty-Five
"Barrels! Barrels! Any Barrels for Sale?"

The Persian's Journal (continued)

I have said that the room where the Vicomte de Chagny and I were trapped was a perfect hexagon, lined entirely with mirrors. Many rooms of the same type have since made their appearance, usually at exhibitions: they are called "house of mirages" or "palace of illusions" or some such name. But their invention was entirely due to Erik, who built the first room of this kind, before my very eyes, at the time of *the rosy hours of Mazenderan.*

A decorative object, such as a column, for example, was placed in one of the corners and immediately gave rise to a hall of a thousand columns; for, thanks to the mirrors, the real room was multiplied into six hexagonal rooms, each of which was, in turn, multiplied into infinity. Erik had once entertained the little Sultana with his "Infinite Temple" but she had soon tired of this childish illusion, whereupon Erik modified his invention to turn it into a "torture-chamber." For the architectural motif placed in one corner, he substituted an iron tree. This tree, with its painted leaves, was absolutely true to life. It was made of iron to resist all the attacks of the "prey" who was locked inside the torture-chamber. We shall see how the scene thus obtained was twice altered instantaneously and successively into two other scenes, by means of the automatic rotation of the drums or rollers in the corners. These were divided into three sections, fitting into the angles of the mirrors and each supporting a decorative scheme that came into view as the rollers revolved upon their axis.

The walls of this strange room gave the prey nothing to grab hold of, because, apart from the cast iron decorative object, they were simply furnished with mirrors, thick enough to withstand any onslaught from the intended victim, who was thrown into the chamber empty-handed and barefoot.

There was no furniture. The ceiling contained hidden lights. An ingenious system of electric heating, which has since been imitated, allowed the temperature of the walls and room to be increased at will.

I am providing all these exacting details about this perfectly remarkable invention, because with nothing more than a few painted branches, it was able to manufacture the supernatural illusion of an equatorial forest blazing beneath a tropical Sun. And I do not want anyone to doubt my sanity or feel entitled to say: "That man has gone mad," or "that man is taking us for a bunch of fools." [31]

If I had merely written this: "Having gone down into the vaults of the Opera, we landed inside an equatorial forest blazing under a tropical Sun," I might have managed to shock my reader, but I am not looking for such easy effects. My goal here is merely to record faithfully what happened to me and the Vicomte de Chagny during the course of that terrible adventure which, at one time, became a matter for the Courts of my adopted country.

I now return to the facts where I left them.

When the ceiling lit up and the forest became visible around us, the Vicomte's amazement was beyond description. The sudden manifestation of that seemingly impenetrable forest, with its innumerable trunks and branches that surrounded us *into infinity*, threw him into a dreadful state of consternation. Several times, he passed his hands before his eyes, as if

---

[31] It was quite natural that, at the time the Persian wrote this, he should take so many precautions against any incredulity on the part of those who may have read his narrative. Today, we have all seen this type of room and these precautions seem rather superfluous. (*Note from the Author.*)

to banish the nightmarish vision. He blinked like a man who, upon waking from a dream, has difficulties grappling with the reality of his surroundings. For a moment, he even *forgot to listen.*

I have already said that the sight of the forest did not surprise me. All my attention remained focused on listening–for the two of us–to what was happening next door. Also, I tried to concentrate not so much on the scene before us, but on the mirrors which produced it. I noticed that, in several places, these mirrors *were broken.*

Yes, they were scratched. In one place, someone had even managed to smash the glass hard enough, in spite of its soilidity, to produce a pattern of small, starry cracks. To me, this proved that the torture-chamber in which we now were *had already been used*!

Yes, some unfortunate man, whose hands and feet were not bare like those of the victims of the *rosy hours of Mazenderan,* had fallen into this "deadly illusion" and, insane with rage, had kicked the mirrors which, nevertheless, despite the small cracks he had caused, had continued to reflect his agony. And the branch of the tree where he had finally put an end to his suffering was located in such a way that, before dying, he had seen–final torment!–a thousand *himselves* writhing in the same agony.

Yes, Joseph Buquet had undoubtedly been here!

Were we to die as he had done?

I did not think so, for I knew that we had a few hours before us and that I could use them far better than Joseph Buquet had been able to do.

After all, wasn't I acquainted with most of Erik's tricks? Now or never was the time to use such knowledge.

To begin with, I gave up on the idea of escaping through the passage that had brought us to that accursed chamber. I gave up on the possibility of releasing the stone that closed the passage from this side. The reason why was that I felt it was beyond our abilities. We had dropped from too great a height into the chamber to be able to reach it. There was no furniture

325

to help us. Neither the iron tree, nor each other's shoulders were tall enough to be of any use.

There was only one possible escape route: the hidden door that opened into the Louis-Philippe room where Erik and Christine Daae stood. But, if that issue looked like an ordinary door on Christine's side, it was absolutely invisible to us. We had to try to open a door without knowing where it was, which was not a simple task!

When, after I heard the Monster drag Christine Daae from the Louis-Philippe room so that *she would not interfere with our torture,* I became quite sure that we could no longer hope or expect any help from her, I resolved to set to work without delay to locate that door.

But first, I had to calm Monsieur de Chagny, who was already walking about the "clearing" like a madman, uttering incoherent cries. The snatches of conversation which he had caught between Christine and the Monster had contributed to driving him a bit out of his mind. Add to that the shock of finding himself in the magic forest and the scorching heat, which was beginning to cause sweat to run down his face, and you will have no difficulty understanding that Monsieur de Chagny's sanity was beginning to crack. Despite all my admonitions, my companion had abandoned all caution.

He ran back and forth, rushing towards space that did not exist, believing that he could walk into an alley that stretched to the horizon but instead hitting his head against the glass after only a few steps, bumping into his own reflection rushing towards him from the other ends of that forest of illusions.

So doing, he shouted: "Christine! Christine!" and brandished his pistol, called out the Monster's name with all his strength, challenging the Angel of Music in a duel to the death, and throwing insults at the forest of mirages. Sadly, the torture was beginning to work its spell upon a mind unprepared for it. I did my best to fight its effects by reasoning calmly with the hapless Vicomte. I made him touch the mirrors, the iron tree, the branches and the rollers in the corners. I used the laws of optics to explain to him the origin of the luminous images that surrounded us, and emphasized that we should not become its victims, like ordinary, ignorant people.

"We are in a room, a small room; that is what you must keep telling yourself. And we shall leave that room as soon as we have found the door. Help me look for it!"

I promised him that, if he helped me, without disturbing my concentration by shouting and rushing back and forth like a madman, we would discover the secret door in less than an hour.

Then, he lay flat on the floor, as one would in a wood, and declared that he would wait until I found the door of the forest, as there was nothing better to do! And he added that, from where he was, "the view was splendid!" (The torture was working, despite all that I had said.)

Myself, *forgetting the forest*, I tackled a mirror panel and began to feel every inch of it, *looking for the weak point* on which to press in order to make the door rotate, as was always the case with Erik's system of pivots and counterweights. This *weak point* could be a mere spot on the glass, no larger than a pea, under which the spring lay hidden. I looked and looked. I felt as high as my hands could reach. Erik was about the same height as myself and I thought that he would not have placed the spring higher than suited his stature—it was merely a hypothesis, of course, but remained our only hope. I had decided to examine closely each of the six panels in turn, and then the floor.

While touching the panels with the greatest care, I tried not to waste any time, for I was feeling increasingly overcome by the heat and we were literally roasting in that blazing forest.

I had been working like this for a half-hour and had finished three panels, when, as bad luck would have it, I turned around upon hearing a muttered exclamation from the Vicomte.

"I'm suffocating," he said. "All those mirrors are sending out an infernal heat! Are you any closer to finding that spring? If you are much longer, we'll be roasted alive in here!"

I was not sorry to hear him talk like this. He had not said a word about the forest and I hoped that my companion's sanity would continue to hold against the torture. But he added:

"What consoles me is that the Monster has given Christine until 11 p.m. tomorrow night. If we can't get out of here and rescue her, at least we'll be dead before her! Then Erik's requiem mass can serve for us all!"

And he gulped down a breath of hot air that nearly made him faint.

As I did not share the Vicomte's despair and acceptance of impending death, I said a few words of encouragement and returned to my work. But I had made the mistake of taking a few steps while talking to him and, in the tangle of the illusionary forest, I was no longer able to find my panel for certain! I had to start all over again, at random. I could not help but swear at such stroke of bad luck and the Vicomte understood that my earlier work had been in vain! That caused him a relapse.

"We'll never get out of this forest alive!" he moaned.

And his despair kept growing. And as it grew, it increasingly made him forget that we were dealing with mirrors and increasingly believe that we were lost in a real forest.

I had begun to feel, fumble and grope again. The fever laid hold of me in my turn, for I found nothing, absolutely nothing. In the next room, all was silent. We were truly lost in a forest, without an exit, a compass, a guide or anything. Oh, I knew what fate was in store for us if nobody came to our rescue—or if I did not locate the hidden door! But, search as I might for that spring, I found nothing but branches, beautiful branches that stood straight up before me, or spread their leaves gracefully over my head. But they gave no shade! And this seemed natural enough, as we were in an equatorial forest, with the tropical Sun right above our heads... A forest in the Congo...

Monsieur de Chagny and I had repeatedly taken off our coats and put them on again, sometimes because they made us feel hotter, at other times, because we felt that they protected us against the heat.

I was still fighting valiantly against the power of the illusion, but it seemed to me that Monsieur de Chagny had surrendered. He claimed that he had been walking in that forest for three days and three nights, without rest, looking for Christine Daae! From time to time, he thought he saw her behind the trunk of a tree, or gliding between the branches; and he called to her with words of supplication that brought tears to my eyes.

"Christine! Christine!" he cried. "Why do you run away from me? Don't you love me anymore? Aren't we affianced? Christine, stop! You must see that I'm exhausted! Christine, have mercy! I'm going to die in this forest! Far from you!"

"Oh, how thirsty I am!" he finally added, in a delirious voice.

I, too, was thirsty. My throat was on fire.

And, yet, squatting on the floor, I went on searching, searching, searching for the spring of the invisible door... Especially since it was dangerous to remain in the forest as night was about to fall. Already darkness was beginning to envelop us. Nightfall happened very suddenly, as is the case in tropical countries, with hardly any twilight.

Now night, in the equatorial forests, is always dangerous, especially when, like ourselves, one does not have materials to make a fire to keep away the beasts of prey. At one point, I abandoned my search for the spring to try to break off a few branches to make a fire for my lantern, but I knocked myself against the mirrors and remembered at that point that there were no branches, but only images of branches.

The heat had not gone away with the daylight. On the contrary, it was now even hotter under the blue light of the Moon. I urged the Vicomte to hold our weapons ready to fire and to not stray away from the camp, while I kept on looking for the spring.

Suddenly, we heard the roar of a lion only a few yards away, so loud that it almost burst our eardrums

"My God!" whispered the Vicomte. "He must be very near! Do you see him? There! Through that tree... in that thicket! If he roars again, I'll fire!"

And the roar sounded again, louder than before. And the Vicomte fired, but I do not think that he hit it. However, he smashed a mirror, as I discovered the next morning, at daybreak.

We must have covered a good distance during the night, for we suddenly found ourselves at the edge of a desert, an immense desert of sand, stones and rocks. It was really not worth leaving a forest to come upon a desert! Exhausted, I flung myself down beside the Vicomte, for I was too tired to keep looking for springs which I could not find.

I was quite surprised (and I said as much to the Vicomte) that we had encountered no other dangerous animals during the night. Usually, after the lion came the leopard and sometimes the buzz of the tsetse fly. These were easy effects to achieve. I explained to Monsieur de Chagny, while we were taking a break before crossing the desert, that Erik imitated the roar of the lion on a long tambourine with an ass's skin on one end only. Over this skin was strung a string made of some animal gut, fastened in the middle to another string that passed through the whole length of the tambourine. Erik had only to rub this string with a glove smeared with colophene. According to the manner in which he rubbed it, he could imitate to perfection the roar of a lion or a leopard, or even the buzzing of a tsetse fly.

The idea that Erik was probably in the room next to us, working his tricks, made me suddenly decide to enter into a dialogue with him, for we obviously had to give up any thought of catching him by surprise. By now, he must have known who the occupants of his torture-chamber were. So I called out to him:

"Erik! Erik!"

I shouted as loudly as I could across the desert, but there was no answer. All around us lay the silence and the bare immensity of that *stony desert*. What was to become of us in the midst of such awful solitude?

Literally, we were beginning to die of heat, hunger and thirst... Of thirst especially. Then, I saw Monsieur de Chagny raise himself on his elbow and point to a spot on the horizon. He had discovered an oasis!

Yes, far in the distance, there was an oasis... An oasis with water... Clear water like a mirror... Water which reflected the iron trees! Ah! *It was the mirage painting*! I recognized it at once! The worst of all! No one had ever been able to overcome it–no one! I did my utmost to keep my sanity *and not hope for water*, because I knew that, if a man hoped for water, the same water that reflected the iron tree, and if, after hoping for water, that man struck the mirror, then there was only one thing left for him to do: to hang himself on the iron tree!

So I cried to Monsieur de Chagny:

"It's a mirage! It's a mirage! Don't believe in the water! It's another trick of the mirrors!"

But he flatly told me, as they say, to go and get lost with my tales of mirrors, springs, revolving doors and palaces of illusions! He angrily declared that I must be either blind or crazy to think that all that beautiful water flowing over there, between those magnificent trees, was not real water! And the desert was real! And so was the forest! And it was no use trying to fool him! He was an experienced traveler... he had been all over the world!

And he dragged himself forward, muttering: "Water! Water!"

And his mouth was open, as if he was drinking.

And my mouth, too, was open, as if I was drinking.

For we not only saw the water, *we heard it*! We heard it flow, we heard it–gurgle! Do you understand that word: *gurgle*? *It's a word which you hear with your tongue*! You put your tongue out so that you can better hear it!

Finally–and this was the most merciless torture of all–*we heard the rain*–even though it was not raining! This was his most diabolical invention! Oh, I knew well enough how Erik achieved that effect! He filled with tiny stones, a very long, narrow box that was broken up inside with wooden and metal partitions. The stones, when falling, struck the partitions and bounced from one to the other, exactly mimicking the scattering sounds of pouring rain in a storm.

You should have seen me and Monsieur de Chagny putting out our tongues and dragging ourselves towards the gurgling river! *Our eyes and ears were full of water, but our tongues were stiff and dry as old leather!*

When we reached the mirror, M. de Chagny licked it... and I, too, licked the glass.

It was burning hot!

Then we rolled on the floor with a hoarse cry of despair. Monsieur de Chagny put the one pistol that was still loaded to his temple. I stared at the Punjab wire at the foot of the iron tree.

I knew why the iron tree had returned, in this new change of scenery!

It was waiting for me!...

But, as I stared at the Punjab wire, I saw a thing that caused me to tremble so violently that Monsieur de Chagny postponed his suicide attempt. But already, he was whispering: "Goodbye, Christine!"

I immediately grabbed his arm and took the pistol away from him. Then, I dragged myself on my knees towards what I had seen.

I had spotted, near the Punjab wire, in a groove in the floor, a small black-headed nail, the use of which I knew too well!

At last, I had discovered the hidden spring! The spring that would release the door! The door that would give us our freedom! That would lead us to Erik!

I felt the nail. I showed Monsieur de Chagny a radiant face... The black-headed nail yielded to my pressure...

And then...

And then, we saw not a door open in the wall, but a trapdoor released in the floor.

At once, cool air came up from the black hole below. We bent over that square of fresh darkness as if over a clear well. With our chins in its cool shade, we drank it in.

And we bent lower and lower over the trap-door. What could there be in that cellar which had opened before us?

Could there be water, perhaps?

Water to drink?

I thrust my arm into the darkness and came upon a stone, then another... It was a staircase... A dark staircase leading into the cellar.

The Vicomte wanted to rush down the hole!

Down there, even if there was no water, one could at least escape from the murderous blaze of the abominable mirrors.

But I, fearing some new trick of the Monster's, stopped the Vicomte. I turned on my lantern and went down first.

The stairs led down into pitch-black darkness in a winding spiral. But oh, how deliciously cool were that darkness and those stairs!

That coolness likely came less from the ventilation system that Erik had had to install than the dampness of the earth itself, which must have been saturated with water at the depth where we were, because of its proximity to the lake.

We soon reached the bottom. Our eyes were becoming accustomed to the dark. We saw shapes around us, round shapes... I turned the beam of my lantern towards them.

Barrels!

We were in Erik's cellar!

It was here that he must keep his wine and, perhaps, his drinking water as well.

I knew that Erik was a great lover of good wine. Ah, there was plenty to drink here!

Monsieur de Chagny patted the round shapes and said, tirelessly:

"Barrels! Barrels! So many barrels!"

Indeed, there were quite a number of them, arranged in two symmetrical rows, one on either side of us.

They were small barrels and I thought that Erik must have selected them in that size to make it easier to carry them through his house by the lake.

We examined them successively, to see if one of them had a funnel, showing that it had been tapped at some time or another.

But all the barrels were hermetically sealed.

Then, after half lifting one to make sure it was full, we went on our knees and, with the blade of a small knife which I carried, I prepared to loosen the bung-hole.

At that moment, I seemed to hear, coming from very far away, a sort of monotonous chant which I recognized, for I had often heard it in the streets of Paris:

"Barrels! Barrels! Any barrels for sale?"

My hand stopped from its work. Monsieur de Chagny had also heard the song. He said:

"It's funny! It sounds as if the barrel itself was singing!"

The song started again, from farther away:

"Barrels! Barrels! Any barrels for sale?"

"Oh!" said the Vicomte. "I'd swear that that song is going away *into* the barrel!..."

We stood up and went to look behind the barrel.

"It's inside," said Monsieur de Chagny, "it's inside!"

But we no longer heard anything and were reduced to blaming our nerves and our abused senses.

We returned to trying to loosen the bung-hole. Monsieur de Chagny put his two hands together underneath the hole and, with a last effort, I burst the bung.

"What's this?" cried the Vicomte at once. "This isn't water!"

The Vicomte brought his two hands full close to my lantern. I bent down to look–and at once threw away the lantern with such violence that it broke and went out, leaving us in total darkness.

What I had seen in Monsieur de Chagny's hands was not water or wine... *but gun powder!*

Manuel Garcia

gallagher

John Gallagher

Chapter Twenty-Six
The Scorpion or the Frog?

The Persian's Journal (concluded)

Thus, by heading into that damp cellar, I had reached the object of my deep foreboding! The wretch had not lied to me when he had uttered his vague threats towards *a goodly number of the human race*! Judging himself outside of Humanity, he had built himself a lair, far from the eyes of men, underground, like that of a beast. And he was fully resolved to blow it all up in a shattering catastrophic explosion if those who dwelled upon the surface of the Earth came down after him into that lair where he hid his unpeakable hideousness.

The discovery that we had just made threw us into a state of alarm that made us forget all our past torments and present sufferings... The extraordinary peril of our predicament, even though such a short while ago we were ready to commit suicide, had not even begun to dawn on us in all its stark horror. We now understood all that the Monster had said and meant to say when he had spoken these words to Christine Daae:

"Yes or no! If your answer is no, everybody will be *dead and buried*!"

Yes, buried under the ruins of what was once the Paris Grand Opera! Could anyone imagine a more horrible crime, to leave the world in such an apotheosis of horror? Once set up to protect the peace of his retirement, the catastrophe would serve to avenge the spurned love of the most awful monster who ever walked upon the Earth!

The Monster had given her until tomorrow night, 11 p.m., for her final deadline. Ah! He had chosen his time well.

337

There would be many people celebrating above... *A goodly number of the human race*, up there, in the magnificent upper floors of the theater. What finer retinue could he desire for his funeral? He would go down to his grave escorted by the prettiest shoulders in the world, adorned with the richest jewels. Tomorrow night, 11 p.m.! We were to be blown up in the middle of the performance–if Christine Daae said no... Tomorrow night, 11 p.m.! And what else could she say but no? Would she not choose to marry Death itself rather than that living corpse? Did she know that the horrible fate of *a goodly number of the human race* depended on her acceptance or refusal! Tomorrow night, 11 p.m.!

We dragged ourselves through the darkness, running away from the terrible barrels of gun powder, feeling our way to the stone steps, for above our heads, the trap-door that led to the room of mirrors had gone dark, its once-blazing light now extinguished. And we repeated to ourselves:

"Tomorrow night, 11 p.m.!"

At last, I found the stairs. But, suddenly I stopped on the first step, for a terrible thought had come to my mind:

"What time is it?"

Yes! What time was it? What time? For, after all, tomorrow night, 11 p.m. might be today, might be now! Who could tell us the time? We felt as if we had been imprisoned in that hell for days and days... for years... since the beginning of time. Maybe the explosion was imminent? I heard a sound! A creak!

"Did you hear that, Monsieur de Chagny? There! In that corner... Gods in Heaven! It sounds like some kind of machinery! Again! Ah! If only we had a light! Perhaps it's the machinery that will trigger the explosion? I tell you, I heard a creak–are you deaf, man?"

Monsieur de Chagny and I began to yell like madmen. Fear spurred us on. We rushed up the stairs, stumbling as we went, fearing that the trap-door overhead had closed and that that was the reason we were in the dark! Yes! To leave the darkness! Leave the darkness and return to the deadly light of the room of mirrors!

When we reached the top of the stairs, we found the trap-door still open, but it was now as dark in the torture-chamber as it had been in the cellar. We exited the damp basement and dragged ourselves along the floor of the torture-chamber, the floor that separated us from the powder-keg. What was the time? We shouted, we called. Monsieur de Chagny yelled with all his renewed strength: "Christine! Christine!" And I called Erik, reminding him that I had once saved his life. But there was no answer, other than that of our own despair, our own madness.

What was the time? Was it "Tomorrow night, 11 p.m." already? We argued, we tried to calculate the time which we had spent there, but we were incapable of figuring it out. If only we could see a watch! Mine had stopped long ago, but Monsieur de Chagny's was still going... He told me that he had wound it before dressing to go out to the Opera... We could tell by its tick-tock that it was still working, but we could not see its face in the dark. We had no matches... And yet we had to know... We had to hope that we had not yet reached those last, fatal minutes...

...The least noise we heard coming from the cellar–the trap-door of which I had tried in vain to close–caused us new fits of panic. What time is it? We must find out! Monsieur de Chagny finally broke the glass of his watch and felt its two hands. There was a long silence during which he groped the watch delicately in the dark... He questioned its hands with his finger-tips, going by the position of the ring and the winding mechanism on the dial. Judging by the space between the hands, he thought it might be just about 11!

But perhaps it was not the 11 p.m. of which we stood in dread, but 11 a.m. Perhaps we had still 12 hours before us!

Suddenly, I exclaimed:

"Hush!"

I thought I had heard footsteps in the next room.

I had not been mistaken. I heard the sound of a door opening, then a rush of footsteps. Someone knocked on the wall. Then we heard Christine Daae's voice say:

"Raoul! Raoul!"

Ah! We were now all shouting at once, on both sides of the wall. Christine was crying for she did not know if she would find Monsieur de Chagny alive. She explained that the Monster had behaved terribly, raving, waiting for her to give him the "yes" which she refused. And yet, she had promised him that "yes," if only he would take her to the torture-chamber. But he had obstinately refused, and had uttered hideous threats against all the human race! Finally, after hours and hours of that hellish torment, he had left, leaving her alone to consider her choice one last time...

"Hours and hours? What time is it now? What time is it, Christine?"

"It is almost 11! Five minutes to 11!"

"Which 11? 11 a.m. or p.m.?"

"11 p.m.–the hour that will decide between life or death! He told me so just before he left," continued Christine in her hoarse voice. "He's in a frightful state. He's gone quite mad. He tore off his mask and his yellow eyes are ablaze! He laughed like a drunken demon and said to me:

" 'Five minutes! I'll leave you alone because I know you're shy! I don't want you to blush like a virgin bride when you say "yes" to me later. What the Hell! I know women!' I told you he was just like a drunken demon!

" 'Here,' he added, taking a key from the little *bag of life and death*. 'Here is the little bronze key that opens the two ebony boxes on the mantelpiece in the Louis-Philippe room. In one of these, you will find a scorpion, and in the other, a frog, both very cleverly imitated in Japanese bronze. They will say yes or no for you. That is to say that you will only have to turn the scorpion around on its stand in the opposite direction in which you found it, and that will tell me, when I return, that you have said "*yes!*" and the Louis-Philippe room will become our bridal room. The frog, if you turn it instead, will mean "*no!*" and when I return, the Louis-Philippe room will become our funeral room!'

"And he laughed like a drunken demon, while I only begged him on my knees to give me the key of the torture-chamber, promising to be his wife forever if he granted me that request... But he told me that we would never need that key ever again and that he was going to throw it into the bottom of the lake! And he again laughed like a drunken demon and left me, telling me that he would be back in five minutes, because he knew that gallantry required of him that he show proper consideration towards a lady's feelings. Ah, yes, also he told me:

" 'The frog! Be careful of the frog! A frog does not only turn: it also croaks! It croaks! *As we might all croak when all is said and done!*' "

I am trying to reproduce here with full sentences, half-completed words and exclamations the meaning of Christine's delirious declarations. For she, too, during those last 24 hours, must have reached the deepest point of human despair... And perhaps, she had even suffered more than we! At almost every instant, Christine stopped, or stopped us, to inquire:

"Raoul? Are you in pain?

And she felt the walls, which had now grown cold, and wondered how they could have been so hot earlier. The five minutes had nearly elapsed and the images of the scorpion and the frog were scratching at my brain as if their live counterparts were trying to claw their way out.

Nevertheless, I had enough lucidity left to understand that, if she turned the frog, we would all *croak*, along with *a goodly number of the human race*! There was no doubt that the frog controlled an electric switch intended to blow up the powder-keg! Quickly, Monsieur de Chagny, who seemed to have recovered all his moral strength once he had again heard Christine's voice, explained to her, in a few hurried words, the dramatic situation in which we, and all the Opera, found ourselves. *He told her to turn the scorpion at once.*

The scorpion, which corresponded to that "*yes!*" so desired by Erik, must be something that could prevent the catastrophe from occurring.

"Go, Christine! Go, my love!" encouraged Raoul.

There was a long silence.

"Christine," I cried, "where are you?"

"Near the scorpion."

"Don't touch it!"

The idea had occurred to me–for I knew my Erik!–that the Monster had perhaps deceived the girl once more. Perhaps it was the scorpion that would blow everything up. Because, after all, why wasn't he here? The five minutes were long past, and he still was not back. What if he had taken shelter and was waiting for the explosion? Perhaps that's what he was hoping for! He could not realistically expect that Christine, willingly, would ever consent to become his victim! Why had he not returned? "Don't touch the scorpion!" I said.

"Here he comes!" cried Christine. "I hear him! Here he is!"

It was indeed him. We heard his steps approaching the Louis-Philippe room. He walked over to Christine, but did not say a word.

Then I raised my voice:

"Erik! It is I! Do you know me?"

At once, with extraordinary calmness, he replied:

"*So you're not dead in there?* Well, then, see that you keep quiet."

I tried to speak, but he said so coldly that, behind the wall, I felt ice in my veins:

"Not a word, Daroga, or I will blow everything up."

And then, he added:

"The honor to decide our fates rests with Mademoiselle Daae. Mademoiselle Daae has not touched the scorpion..." (how calmly and deliberately he spoke!) "Mademoiselle Daae has not touched the frog..." (and with such composure!) "But it is not too late to do the right thing. There, I open the caskets, without a key, for I am the Trickster and I open and close whatever I please however I please. I open the little ebony boxes. Look, Mademoiselle, at what is inside these little ebony boxes... Two little brooches shaped like animals... Aren't they pretty? And don't they look harmless? But appearances can be deceiving..." (All this spoken in the most banal, uniform tone possible.) "If you turn the frog, Mademoiselle, we shall all *croak*, all be blown up. There is enough gun powder beneath our feet to destroy this entire section of Paris. If you turn the scorpion, Mademoiselle, all that powder will be drowned in the waters of the lake. Mademoiselle, to celebrate our wedding, you shall make a very handsome present to the few hundred Parisians who are, at this moment, above our heads, applauding a rather poor composition by Meyerbeer... You shall make them a present of their lives... For you shall, Mademoiselle, with your own fair hands..." (his voice sounded very tired.) "You shall turn the scorpion... And merrily, merrily, we will be married!"

A pause; then:

"If, in two minutes, Mademoiselle, you have not turned the scorpion–by this watch," added Erik's voice, "this very fine Swiss watch–I, myself, shall turn the frog... And it will croak, *as will we all*!"

The dreadful silence began anew, more terrible than anything that had come before. I knew that, when Erik had spoken in that calm and composed, and tired, voice, it was because he was figuratively at the end of his rope, capable of the most colossal crime as well as the most slavish sacrifice, and the merest unpleasant syllable could trigger him.

The Vicomte de Chagny, on the other hand, realizing that there was nothing left to do but pray, had gone down on his knees to do so. As for me, my heart beat so fiercely that I had to grasp my chest with both my hands, lest it should burst. We felt the awful dilemma that, during these fateful seconds, tore apart Christine Daae's frenzied spirit. We understood her hesitation to turn the scorpion. Again, what if it was the scorpion that would trigger the explosion? What if Erik had resolved to bury us all together?

At last, we heard Erik's voice, soft an an angel's:

"The two minutes are past... Goodbye, Mademoiselle. Let's us all croak together..."

"Erik!" cried Christine, who had rushed to stop the Monster's hand. "Do you swear to me, Monster, do you swear to me on all your abominable passion that the scorpion is the one to turn?"

"Yes, if you wish to have a blast."

"Ah, you're toying with me! We're all going to die!"

"A blast–at our wedding, you gullible child! The scorpion opens the ball. But that will do, now! If you won't turn the scorpion, I'll turn the frog!"

"Erik!"

"Enough!"

I was crying out in concert with Christine. Monsieur de Chagny was still on his knees, praying.

"Erik! *I have turned the scorpion!*"

Oh! The awful second that we experienced!

Waiting!

Waiting to find ourselves blown into pieces, amidst thunder and ruin!

Waiting for something to happen beneath our very feet, waiting for things–things which might be the heralds of an apotheosis of horror–to crawl out from that yawning chasm... For, through the open trap-door, a dark mouth in the darkest night, we heard an appalling hiss, a hiss like the first sounds a rocket makes...

It came softly, at first, then louder, then very loud.

I listened and listened, grasping my chest in both my hands, lest my heart should explode–along with *a goodly number of the human race.*

But it was not the hiss of fire.

It was more like the hiss of water.

Listen! Listen!

And now it became a gurgling sound! Gurgle... gurgle...

To the trap-door! To the trap-door! To the trap-door!

What coolness!

344

Cool! Damp! Water! All our thirst, which had vanished with the terror of discovering the gun powder, now returned with the sound of lapping water.

Water! The sound of water, water rising!

Water which rises in the cellar, to the barrels, above the powder-barrels. (*"Barrels! Barrels! Any barrels for sale?"*) Water in which we kneel, bending our heards with parched throats to drink. Water which rose to our chins... to our mouths...

And we drank. At the bottom of the cellar, we drank straight from the floor.

And we went up the stairs again, in the darkest night, step by step; the same stairs that we had rushed down to seek the water, we now climbed back up, water at our heels.

Indeed, the powder kegs were now well below water, their deadly contents submerged and useless. It had all been done very efficiently. Water was not in short supply at the house by the lake. But if the level kept rising, the entire lake would soon fill the cellar.

For truthfully, we did not know when the tide would stop...

We were now outside the cellar but the water continued to rise...

It came out of the cellar and spread over the floor of the room. If this went on, the whole house by the lake would be flooded. The floor of the torture-chamber itself had become a small lake in which our feet splashed. There was enough water now! Erik must turn off the tap!

"Erik! Erik! That's enough water for the gun powder! Turn off the tap! Turn off the scorpion!"

But Erik did not reply. We heard only the sound of the water rising... It was halfway to our waists!

"Christine!" cried Monsieur de Chagny. "Christine! The water is up to our knees!"

But Christine did not reply... We heard only the sound of the water rising.

There was no one, no one in the next room, no one to turn off the tap, no one to turn off the scorpion!

We were all alone, in the dark, with the dark water that gripped us, suffocated us and froze us!

"Erik! Erik!"

"Christine! Christine!"

By this time, we had lost our foothold and were twisting around in the water, carried by an irresistible whirl, for the water turned with us and dashed us against the dark mirrors, which pushed us out again... And we screamed with our mouths raised above the whirlpool.

Were we to die here? Drowned in the torture-chamber? I had never seen that before. Erik, at the time of the *rosy hours of Mazenderan*, never showed me that trick, through the little invisible window.

"Erik! Erik!" I cried. "I saved your life! Remember! You were sentenced to death! You were going to be killed! And I helped you escape! Erik!"

Ah! We twisted around in the water like so much wreckage.

But, suddenly, one of my straying hands grabbed the trunk of the iron tree! I called out to Monsieur de Chagny, and soon, we both clung to its branch.

But the water rose ever higher.

"Ah! Ah! Can you remember? How much space there is between the branch of the tree and the dome-shaped ceiling of the mirror room? Let's try to remember! After all, the water might stop, if it finds its level!... There, I think it's stopping! No, no! It's horrible! Swim! Swim for your life!"

Our arms became entangled in the effort of swimming. We began to choke. We struggled in the dark water. It was already hard enough to breathe the dark air above the dark water–the air which was escaping, which we could hear escaping through some vent-hole or other.

"Let's turn around until we find the air-hole; then, we'll stick our mouths to it!"

But I was starting to lose my strength. I tried to grab hold of the walls! How those glass walls were slippery under my clawing fingers! We kept twisting around and around! We were beginning to sink! One last effort! One last cry:

"Erik!"

"Christine!"

"Gurgle, gurgle, gurgle," answered the water in our ears. At the bottom of the dark water, our ears heard only: "Gurgle, gurgle!"

And, before losing consciousness entirely, I seemed to hear, between two gurgles:

"*Barrels! Barrels! Any barrels for sale?*"

Francesco Mattioli

Chapter Twenty-Seven
The End of the Phantom's Love Story

The previous chapter marks the conclusion of the *written* journal entrusted to me by the Persian.

Despite the horrors of a situation which definitely seemed fated to cause their deaths, the Vicomte de Chagny and his companion were saved by the sublime devotion of Christine Daae. I heard the end of the story from the lips of the Daroga himself.

When I went to see him, he was still living in his tiny apartment on the Rue de Rivoli, opposite the Tuileries. He was very ill, and it required all my fervor, both as a reporter and a historian pledged to reveal the truth, to persuade him to relive that incredible tragedy for my benefit.

His faithful old servant, Darius, showed me in. The Daroga received me at a window overlooking the Tuileries gardens, sitting inside a comfortable armchair, struggling to hold his once-valiant body upright. His eyes were still magnificent, but his poor face looked extremely worn. He had shaved the whole of his head, which was usually covered with an astrakhan. He was dressed in a long, plain coat and amused himself by unconsciously twiddling his thumbs inside his sleeves. But his mind was sharp as ever.

He could not evoke the memories of those past torments without shaking all over and I had to wrest the surprising conclusion of that strangest of tales from him in bits and pieces. Sometimes, I had to beg a long time for him to answer any of my questions; at other times, he felt exalted by his memories and spontaneously described to me with uncanny details, the frightful image of Erik and the terrible hours that Monsieur de Chagny and he had endured in the house by the lake.

349

The tremors that seized him when he told me how he woke up in the Louis-Philippe bedroom after almost horribly dying from drowning were painful to see...

Here is the conclusion of that terrible tale, as told to me by the Persian in order to complete the written journal that he had already entrusted to me:

When he opened his eyes, the Daroga found himself lying on a bed. Monsieur de Chagny was on a sofa, besides the wardrobe. An angel and a devil were watching over them.

After the mirages and illusions of the torture-chamber, the precision of the bourgeois details of that quiet little room seemed to them to have been designed with the purpose of adding to the confusion of the mind of any mortal rash enough to stray into that realm of living nightmares. The wooden bed, the waxed mahogany chairs, the chest of drawers, the brass decorations, the care with which little squares of lace were placed on the backs of the chairs, the clock on the mantelpiece and the harmless-looking ebony caskets at either end... And, lastly, the shelves filled with shells, red pin-cushions, mother-of-pearl boats and an enormous ostrich-egg... All of this discreetly lit by a shaded lamp standing on a small round table... This collection of banal, mundane belongings, so friendly, so rational, and yet sitting *at the bottom of the vaults of the opera*, bewildered the imagination more than all the fantastic events that had occurred before then..

The shadow of the masked man seemed all the more formidable in this old-fashioned, neat and proper apartment. It bent over the Persian and whispered in his ear:

"Are you feeling better, Daroga? You're looking at my furniture? It's all I have left of my poor unfortunate mother."

He said more things, which the Persian no longer recalled; but—and this seemed rather strange to him—he remembered very precisely that, during this vision of the old-fashioned Louis-Philippe room, only Erik spoke. Christine Daae did not say a word. She moved about noiselessly, like a Sister of Charity who had taken a vow of silence.

She brought a cordial and a cup of hot tea. The man in the mask took it from her hands and gave it to the Persian.

Monsieur de Chagny was still sleeping.

Erik poured some rum into the Daroga's cup and, pointing to the Vicomte lying on the couch, said:

"He came to long before we knew *if you would still live another day*, Daroga. He is quite well and merely sleeping. We mustn't wake him."

Erik left the room for a moment, and the Persian raised himself on his elbow. He looked around him and saw Christine Daae, sitting by the fireplace. He spoke to her, called her, but he was still very weak and fell back on his pillow. Christine came to him, laid her hand on his forehead then went away again. The Persian remembered that, as she went, she did not even glance at Monsieur de Chagny, who, truthfully, was sleeping peacefully. As she again sat down in her chair by the fireplace, she remained silent as a Sister of Charity who had taken a vow of silence.

Erik returned with some small bottles which he placed on the mantelpiece. And, again in a whisper, so as not to wake Monsieur de Chagny, he said to the Persian, after sitting down and feeling his pulse:

"Both of you are now safe. Soon, I'll take you back up to the surface of the Earth, *to please my wife*."

Thereupon, he rose and, without any further explanation, disappeared once more.

The Persian now looked at Christine's quiet profile under the lamp. She was reading a small book with gilded edges, not unlike a religious book. There are editions of *The Imitation* that look like that. The Persian still had in his ears the very natural tone in which Erik had said, "to please my wife."

Very gently, he called her again; but Christine must have been *very absorbed* in her reading for she appeared to not hear him.

Erik returned, mixed the Daroga another drink and advised him not to speak again to "his wife" nor to anyone else, *because it might prove very dangerous for everyone's health.*

From that point on, the Persian remembered Erik's dark shadow, and Christine's white silhouette which glided silently through the room, occasionally checking on the Vicomte. The Persian was still very weak, and the least noise, for example the door of the dresser which creaked as it opened, gave him a headache. Eventually, he fell asleep, like M. de Chagny.

This time, he did not wake up until he was in his own room, nursed by his faithful Darius, who told him that, they had found him, the night before, propped against the door of his apartment. He had been brought there by a stranger, who had rung the bell before leaving.

As soon as the Daroga had recovered his strength and his wits, he sent Darius to Comte Philippe's home to inquire after the Vicomte's health.

The answer Darius brought back was that the young man had not been seen again and that Comte Philippe was dead. His body had been found on the banks of the lake beneath the Opera, on the side by the Rue Scribe. The Persian then remembered the requiem mass which he had heard from behind the wall of the torture-chamber, and had no doubt concerning the crime and the criminal.

Knowing Erik as he did–alas!–he easily reconstructed the tragedy. Believing that his brother had run away with Christine Daae, Philippe had rushed after him on the Brussels Road, where he knew that everything had been prepared for the elopement. Failing to find the two lovers, he had hurried back to the Opera. He had remembered Raoul's strange confidence about his fantastic rival and had learned that the Vicomte had made every effort to enter the vaults of the theater. He had found out that Raoul had subsequently disappeared, leaving his hat in the singer's dressing-room next to an empty pistol-case. And the Comte, who by then was pretty certain that his brother was insane, had in his turn rushed into that infernal underground maze.

This was enough, in the Persian's eyes, to explain the discovery of the Comte de Chagny's corpse on the banks of the lake, where a vigilant watch was kept by the siren's song, Erik's siren, the guardian of the lake of the dead.

Consequently, the Persian did not hesitate. Terrified by this new crime, not wanting to remain in the dark as to the ultimate fate of the Vicomte and Christine, he resolved to inform the Police.

The case was now in the hands of Monsieur Faure, the investigating magistrate, and it was to his door that he went. One can easily guess how a mind as skeptical, lacking in imagination and rather shallow as Monsieur Faure's (I'm being quite candid) was utterly unprepared to receive such a confidence. Monsieur Faure took down the Daroga's deposition but otherwise insisted on treating him as a madman.

The Persian, despairing of ever obtaining a fair hearing, sat down to write his story. Since the Law was not interested in his evidence, perhaps the Press would be glad of it. And, one night, as he had just written the last line of the journal I faithfully quoted in the preceding chapters, Darius announced the visit of a stranger who refused to tell his name, who would not show his face and declared simply that he would not leave until he had spoken to the Daroga.

The Persian guessed at once who his mysterious visitor might be and ordered that he be shown in.

The Daroga was right.

It was the Phantom! It was Erik!

He looked extremely weak and leaned against the wall, as if he were afraid of falling. Taking off his hat, he revealed a forehead white as wax. The rest of his face was hidden by a mask.

The Persian rose to his feet.

"Murderer of Comte Philippe, what have you done with his brother and Christine Daae?"

Erik staggered under this direct attack, kept silent for a moment, dragged himself to a chair and fell into it, heaving a deep sigh. Then, speaking in short sentences and gasping for air between words, he said:

"Daroga, don't talk to me about Comte Philippe... He was already... dead... when I left my house... he was already... dead... when... the siren sang... It was an... accident... a sad... a tragic... accident. He fell... clumsily... but by himself... naturally... into the lake!"

"You lie!" shouted the Persian.

Erik bowed his head and said:

"I have not come here... to talk about Comte Philippe... but to tell you that... I am dying ..."

"Where are Raoul de Chagny and Christine Daae?"

"I am dying."

"Raoul de Chagny and Christine Daae?"

"...Of love... Daroga... I am dying of love... That's how it is.... I loved her so much! And I love her still, Daroga... since I'm dying of love for her, I tell you! If you knew how beautiful she was when she let me kiss her... *alive*... It was the first time, Daroga... the very first time I ever kissed a woman... alive! Yes, I kissed her alive... and she was as beautiful as if she had been dead!"

The Persian got up and dared touch Erik. He shook him by the arm:

"Will you tell me at last if she is alive or dead?"

"Why are you shaking me like that?" asked Erik, making an effort. "I told you that I'm dying... Yes, I kissed her alive..."

"And now she is dead?"

"I tell you I kissed her just like that, on her forehead... And she did not draw it away from my lips! Oh, she is a brave girl! As to her being *dead*, I don't think so, but that no longer has to do with me... No, no, she is not dead! And I'd better not find out that anyone dared harm even a hair of her head! She is a brave, honest girl, and she saved your life, too, Daroga, when I would not have given two francs for your Persian skin. In fact, no one else cared about you. Why were you there with her young man? You were both about to die, and it served you right! But how she kept begging me for her young man's life! I told her that, as she had turned the scorpion, she had, by that very fact, and of her own free will, become engaged to me and that she did not have two fiancés, which if you think about it, was reasonable enough. As for you, you did not matter, you had already ceased to matter, as I just told you, and you were going to die with the other fiancé!

"Only, listen well to my words, Daroga, just as you were screaming like so many devils because of the water, Christine came to me with her beautiful blue eyes wide open, and swore to me, upon her eternal salvation, that she would consent to be *my living wife*! Until then, Daroga, I had always seen in the depths of her eyes, that she intended to be *my dead wife*. It was the first time that I saw *my living wife* there. She was truthful, upon her eternal salvation. She would not kill herself. That was her offer. Half-a-minute later, all the water was back in the lake; and I was pulling on your tongue, Daroga, for upon my honor, I thought you were done for! However, you made it! And that's the whole story. It was agreed that I would take you both back up to the surface of the Earth. And, after clearing the Louis-Philippe room of your presence, I returned alone..."

"What have you done with the Vicomte de Chagny?" interrupted the Persian.

"Ah, you see, Daroga, I couldn't carry him back up to the surface of the Earth like that. He was a hostage. But I could not keep him in my house by the lake either, because of Christine. So I locked him up comfortably, chained him up nicely (the perfume of Mazenderan had rendered him limp as a rag) in one of the Communards' cells, in the most deserted and remotest part of the Opera, beneath even the fifth level, where no one ever goes and no one can ever hear you. Then, I came back to Christine. She was waiting for me."

At this part of his story, I'm told that Erik rose with such solemnity that the Persian, who had again sat down in his armchair, had to rise too, as if following the Phantom's cue, and feeling that it was impossible to remain sitting at such a solemn moment. (He told me that, even though he had shaved his head, he felt compelled to take off his astrakhan.)

"Yes, she was waiting for me," said Erik, shaking like a leaf, but with real, solemn emotion. "She was waiting for me, erect and alive, like a real, living bride, upon her eternal salvation... And, when I stepped forward, more shy than a little child, she did not run away... no, no... she stayed... she waited for me... I even believe, Daroga, that she put forward... Oh! not much!... But a little, like a living bride... her forehead... And... and... I kissed her! I! I! I! And she did not die! And she stayed naturally at my side after I had kissed her... on the forehead! Oh, how good it is, Daroga, to kiss somebody on the forehead! You can't know! But I! I! My own mother, Daroga, my poor, unfortunate mother would never let me kiss her... She used to run away... and throw me my mask! Nor any other woman... ever, ever! So, as you can understand, my happiness was so great that I cried. And I fell crying at her feet... And I kissed her feet, her tiny feet, crying. I see that you're crying, too, Daroga... As she cried also... The angel cried!"

As he told his tale, Erik sobbed aloud and the Persian himself could not restrain his tears in the presence of that masked man, who, with his shoulders shaking and his hands clutching at his chest, was moaning with both pain and love.

"Oh! Daroga... I felt her tears flow on my forehead... My own forehead! Mine... mine! They were warm... they were sweet! They trickled under my mask... they mingled with my own tears from my own eyes... they flowed between my lips... Ah! To feel her tears on my face! Listen, Daroga, listen to what I did next... I tore off my mask to not lose a single one of her tears... and she still did not run away! And she still did not die! She remained alive, crying over me, crying with me. We cried together! God in Heaven! I have tasted all the happiness the world can offer!"

And Erik collapsed into a chair, choking for breath:

"Ah! I'm not going to die yet... not right away... Let me cry!" he said to the Persian.

Then, after a moment, the masked man continued:

"Listen, Daroga, listen well to this... While I was at her feet, I heard her say: '*Poor, sad Erik*!' *And she took my hand*!

Then, I became no more than, you know, a poor dog ready to die for her... That is the truth, Daroga!

"I held in my hand a ring, a plain gold ring which I had given her... which she had lost... and which I had found again... a wedding-ring, if you will... I slipped it into her tiny hand and said: 'There! Take it! Take it for you–and him! It shall be my wedding-present, a present from *your poor, unfortunate Erik...* I know you love that young man... don't cry any more! She asked me, in a very soft voice, what I meant... Then I made her understand, and she understood at once, that, where she was concerned, I was only a poor dog, ready to die for her... and that she could marry her young man when she pleased, because she had cried with me!... Ah! Daroga... know that, as I told her what I just told you, it was as if I was cutting out my own heart, but she had mingled her tears with mine, and called me her *poor, sad Erik!...*"

Erik's emotion was so great that he had to ask the Persian to avert his eyes, for he was choking with tears and had to take off his mask. The Daroga told me that he went to the window and opened it. His heart was full of pity, but he took care to keep his eyes fixed on the trees in the Tuileries gardens, lest he should catch a glimpse of the Monster's face.

"I went and released the young man," Erik continued, "and told him to come with me to Christine... They kissed before me in the Louis-Philippe room... Christine wore my ring... I made her swear to return, one night, after I am dead, crossing the lake from the entrance on the Rue Scribe, and bury me in the greatest secrecy with the gold ring, which she was to wear until that time. I told her where she would find my body and what to do with it. Then, Christine kissed me, for the first time, herself, here, on the forehead (don't look, Daroga!) here, on the forehead... on my own forehead (don't look, Daroga!) and they went off together. Christine had stopped crying... I, alone, cried... Daroga, Daroga, if Christine keeps her promise, she will come back soon!"

And Erik stopped talking. The Persian asked him no more questions. He was quite reassured as to the fate of Raoul de Chagny and Christine Daae; no *goodly numbers of the human race* could have, after hearing him, doubted the word of the weeping Erik that night.

The Monster put his mask back on and gathered his strength to leave the Daroga. He told him that, when he felt his end to be almost there, he would send him, in gratitude for the kindness which the Persian had once shown him, that which he held dearest in the world: all of Christine Daae's papers, which she had written for Raoul's benefit and left with Erik, together with a few objects belonging to her, such as two handkerchiefs, a pair of gloves and a shoe-buckle.

In reply to one last question from the Persian, Erik told him that the two young lovers, as soon as they were free, had resolved to go and look for a priest in some lonely spot where they could hide their happiness and, with that in mind, they had started their journey at the *Gare du Nord*–appropriately to travel to the *Far North of the World*. Lastly, Erik relied on the Persian, as soon as he received the promised relics and papers, to inform the young couple of his death. To do this, he was supposed to insert an obituary notice in the newspaper *L'Epoque*.

That was all.

The Persian saw Erik to the door of his apartment, and Darius helped him down to the street. A cab was waiting for him. Erik stepped in. The Persian, who had returned to the window, heard him say to the driver:

"Place de l'Opera."

And the cab drove off into the night.

The Persian had seen the poor, sad Erik for the last time.

Three weeks later, *L'Epoque* published this obituary:

"*Erik is dead.*"

Mark Bodé

Douglas Carrel

Epilogue

Such is the true story of the Phantom of the Opera. As I said at the beginning of this book, it is no longer possible to deny that Erik really lived. There are, today, too many proofs of his existence within everyone's reach for us to be unable to *reasonably* re-trace Erik's actions through the whole Chagny tragedy.

There is no need here to repeat how greatly the case excited the capital. The abduction of the singer, the death of the Comte de Chagny under such extraordinary conditions, the disappearance of his brother, the drugging of the Opera's gaffer and his two assistants! What tragedies, what passions, what crimes had surrounded the idyll of Raoul and the sweet, charming Christine! Whatever became of that wonderful, mysterious singer of whom the world was never, ever to again hear? She was made out to be the victim of a rivalry between the two brothers, but no one ever suspected what had truly happened. No one understood that, since both Raoul and Christine had disappeared, it meant that the two lovers had withdrawn, far from the world, to enjoy a happiness which they did not care to make public after the unexplained death of Comte Philippe... One day, they had embarked on a train and gone to the *Far North of the World...*

Maybe someday, I, too, shall take that train to go and look around the lakes of Norway, silent Scandinavia, for traces of the presence of Raoul and Christine, who are perhaps still living, and also of Madame Valerius, who disappeared at the same time! Maybe someday, I, too, shall hear the lonely echoes of the North repeat the singing of she who knew the Angel of Music!

Long after the case was closed, due to the unintelligent ministrations of Monsieur Faure, the newspapers made occasional efforts to solve the mystery, and continued to ask what monstrous hand had planned and executed so many amazing catastrophes! (Crime and abductions.)

One evening paper alone, which knew all the gossip of the Opera, had written:

"That hand is that of the Phantom of the Opera."

And even that was written as a display of irony.

Only the Persian, whom no one wanted to hear, and who, after Erik's visit, did not go back to the Police, knew the whole truth.

And he held the main evidence, which came to him with the pious relics promised by the Phantom.

It fell to me to complete that evidence with the aid of the Daroga himself. Day by day, I kept him informed of the progress of my inquiries, which he directed. He had not been to the Opera for many years, but had preserved the most accurate recollection of the building and there was no better guide than he to help me discover its most secret corners. He also told me where to gather further information, whom to ask. He is the one who sent me to call on Monsieur Poligny, just when the poor man was nearly drawing his last breath. I had no idea that he was so very ill, and I shall never forget the impact that my questions about the Phantom produced upon him. He looked at me as if I were the Devil himself and answered me only with a few incoherent sentences, which showed, however–and that was the most important thing–the extent of the perturbation which *P.O.* had, in his time, brought into his already rather agitated life. (Monsieur Poligny was what people call a *man of the world*.)

When I came and told the Persian the poor results of my visit to Monsieur Poligny, the Daroga gave a faint smile and said:

"Poligny never suspected the extent to which that amazing scoundrel Erik (The Persian sometimes spoke of Erik as a god and other times as a banal criminal) had swindled him. Poligny was superstitious and Erik knew it. Erik also knew many things about the public and private business of the Opera.

"When Poligny heard a mysterious *Voice* tell him, in Box No. 5, the use he made of his time and of his partner's confidence, he did not wait to hear any more. Thinking at first that it was a voice from Heaven, he believed himself damned. Then, when the *Voice* began asking for money, he realized that he and Debienne were being victimized by a shrewd blackmailer. Both of them, already tired of managing the Opera for various reasons, decided to leave without trying to inquire further into the identity of that mysterious *P.O.* who had forced such a singular rulebook upon them. They bequeathed the whole mystery to their successors and heaved a sigh of relief when they were rid of a business that had puzzled them greatly, without amusing them in the least."

Thus spoke the Persian about Messrs. Debienne and Poligny. I then spoke of their two successors and stated my surprise that, in his *Memoirs of a Director*, Monsieur Moncharmin should describe the actions of the Phantom of the Opera at great length in the first part of his book, then hardly mention them at all in the second. In reply to this, the Persian, who knew said *Memoirs* as thoroughly as if he had written them himself, remarked that I would understand the reason if I just took the time to reread the few lines which Moncharmin devotes to the Phantom in said second part. I quote those lines below, as they are particularly interesting because they describe the simple manner in which the famous matter of the 20,000 francs was finally resolved:

"*As for* P.O., (wrote Moncharmin) *some of whose curious tricks I related in the first part of these* Memoirs, *I will only say one thing: that with one beautiful gesture, he redeemed himself for all the trouble which he had caused my dear colleague and, I have to confess, myself. He felt, no doubt, that a practical joke can only be carried so far, especially when it is such an expensive joke. After the Police Commissioner was on the case, just as we had made a second appointment in our office to tell Monsieur Mifroid the whole story, that is to say a few days after the disappearance of Christine Daae, we found, on Richard's desk, a large envelope, inscribed, in red ink:* 'With P.O.'s compliments.' *It contained the large sums of money which he had succeeded in playfully prying out of the Opera treasury. Richard was immediately of the opinion that we should be satisfied with that and drop the entire business. I concurred with him. All's well that ends well, isn't it, my dear* P.O.*?*"

Of course, Moncharmin, especially after the money had been restored, continued to believe that he had, for a short while, been the butt of Richard's sense of humor, whereas Richard, for his part, remained convinced that Moncharmin had amused himself by inventing the whole of the affair of the Phantom of the Opera, in order to seek revenge for a few jokes.

Wasn't it the moment to ask the Persian to tell me by what trick the Phantom had taken the 20,000 francs from Richard's pocket in spite of the safety-pin? He replied that he had not researched this little detail, but that, if I myself cared to investigate the spot where it had taken place, I would almost certainly find the solution in the Directors' office. I should remember, he added, that Erik had not been nicknamed the *trap-door lover* or *trickster* for nothing. I promised the Persian to do so as soon as I had time. I may as well tell the reader now that the results of my investigation were completely satisfactory. I hardly believed that I could ever discover so many undeniable proofs of the authenticity of the feats ascribed to the Phantom.

It is good for people to know that the Persian's manuscript, Christine Daae's papers, the statements made to me by the people who used to work under Messrs. Richard and Moncharmin, by Little Meg herself (the worthy Madame Giry, I am sorry to say, having passed away) and by Mademoiselle Sorelli, who is now living in retirement in Louveciennes, it is good for people to know, as I said, that all these pieces comprise the total documentary evidence relating to the existence of the Phantom, and that I plan to deposit them in the archives of the Opera. Further, this evidence is supported by several major discoveries of which I am justly proud.

I have not been able to locate the house by the lake, Erik having definitely walled up all its secret entrances. Even so, I am convinced that it would be easy to reach it by draining the lake, as I have repeatedly asked the Ministry of Fine Arts to do.[32] On the other hand, I have discovered the secret passage of the Communards, the wooden boards of which are falling to pieces in some sections; I have also found the trap-door through which Raoul and the Persian entered the vaults of the Opera. In one of the Communards' cells, I noticed a number of initials carved into the walls by the unfortunate people jailed there; among these were an "R" and a "C"–for Raoul de Chagny. The letters are still there to this day.

Of course, I did not stop there. On both the first and the third levels, I found two of Erik's own hidden trap-doors, the existence of which was completely unknown to the staff of the Opera.

Finally, I can tell the reader, with a great deal of certainty: "Go and visit the Opera and ask for permission to wander about alone, without some inane tour-guide, go inside Box No. 5 and knock on the enormous column that separates it

---

[32] I was discussing this very topic only two days before the publication of this book with Monsieur Dujardin-Beaumetz, our very convivial Under-Secretary of Fine Arts, who left me with some hope that such a thing might yet happen. I told him that it was the duty of the Government to put an end to the legends about the Phantom of the Opera and to establish once and for all, on an indisputable basis, the strange story of Erik. For that, it would be necessary, and that would be the crowning of my personal efforts, to locate the house by the lake, in which there might still be some undiscovered musical treasures. For no one any longer doubts that Erik was a peerless musician. Who knows if the score of his *Don Juan Triumphant* might not be discovered in the house by the lake? *(Note from the Author.)*

from the *avant-scène*; knock on it with your fist or a cane and listen...Up to about a man's height, *the column sounds hollow*! After that, don't be surprised anymore that it might have been occupied by the Phantom's voice; there is room enough inside that column for two. And if you are still surprised that, when the various incidents occurred, no one turned around to look at that column, you must remember that it presented the appearance of solid marble, and that the Voice within seemed to actually come from the opposite side of the Box, for, as we have seen, the Phantom was an expert ventriloquist. The column was elaborately carved and decorated with a sculptor's chisel. I do not despair of some day discovering that the carving could be raised or lowered at will, in order to make room for the Phantom to carry out his correspondence with Madame Giry as well as their little gift exchanges.

However, all these discoveries, which I have seen with my own eyes and touched with my own hands, are nothing compared to what a prodigious and fabulous mind like Erik's was able to create in the mystery of a monument such as the Opera. Still, I would not trade all of these discoveries for that which I was able to make in the very presence of the Assistant Director in the Directors' office. Only a few inches away from the desk chair, there was a trap-door, the width of a floor board and the length of a man's forearm, a trap-door that shut silently like the lid of a box, a trap-door through which I can easily imagine a hand reaching out and dexterously searching the pockets of a coat.

That is how the 40,000 francs disappeared! And that is also how, through some trick or other, they were returned.

When I spoke about this, with understandable emotion I said:

"So Erik was simply having fun with his rulebook, since he eventually returned the 40,000 francs he stole?"

"Don't you believe it!" he replied. "Erik needed money. Thinking himself outside of humanity, he had no scruples and he used his extraordinary gifts of manipulation and fantasy, which he had received by way of compensation for his extraordinary hideousness, to prey upon his fellow men, often in the most artistic fashion possible. If, of his own free will, he gave the 40,000 francs back to Messrs. Richard and Moncharmin, it's only *because he no longer had any use for them*! He had given up on his marriage to Christine Daae. He had given up on all things from the surface of the Earth."

According to the Persian's account, Erik was born in a small town not far from Rouen. He was the son of a master mason. He ran away from his father's house at an early age, because his ugliness was a subject of horror and terror to his parents. For a time, he exhibited himself in fairs, where a showman introduced him as the "living corpse." He seems to have crossed the whole of Europe, going from fair to fair, and completing his strange education as an artist and magician from the very sources of art and magic: the Gypsies.

That entire period of Erik's life remained rather obscure. He was seen at a fair in Nijni-Novgorod, where he displayed himself in all his hideous glory. Already, he sang like no one else on Earth. He practiced ventriloquism and did magic tricks that were so astounding that caravans returning from Asia talked about them during the whole length of their journey.

In this way, his reputation reached the walls of the palace of Mazenderan, where the little Sultana, the Shah-en-Shah's favorite, was bored to death. A fur dealer, returning to Samarkand from Nijni-Novgorod, told her of the marvels which he had seen performed in Erik's tent. The trader was summoned to the palace and the Daroga of Mazenderan questioned him. Next, the Daroga was ordered to go and find Erik. He brought him back to Persia, where for some months, Erik's will was law. He was guilty of quite a few horrible deeds, for he seemed not to know the difference between good and evil. He assisted in a few political assassinations as calmly as he fought the Emir of Afghanistan, who was at war with the Persian empire, with his diabolical inventions.

The Shah took a liking to him. This was the time of *the rosy hours of Mazenderan*, of which the Daroga's narrative has given us a glimpse. Since Erik had some very original ideas about architecture, and he thought of a palace much as a magician would think of a trick-casket, the Shah ordered him to construct an edifice of this kind. Erik did so, and the building was so ingenious that His Majesty was able to move about it unseen and vanish without anyone being able to know how how had done it.

When the Shah-en-Shah found himself the possessor of such a marvel, he ordered, like a Czar had once done to the architect of a church on *Krasnaya Ploschad* in Moscow,[33] that Erik's yellow eyes be put out. But, he reflected that, even blind, Erik would still be able to build an equally remarkable palace for a rival sovereign; and also that, as long as Erik lived, someone other than he would know the secret of the wonderful palace. Erik's death was then decided upon, as well as that of all the laborers who had worked under his orders. The Daroga of Mazenderan was put in charge of the execution of this abominable decree. Erik had done him several favors and had entertained him on many occasions. So he saved his life by providing him with a means of escape, but almost paid for his generous indulgence with his own head.

Fortunately for the Daroga, a corpse, half-eaten by birds of prey, was found on the shore of the Caspian Sea, and was mistaken for Erik's body, because the Daroga's friends had dressed the remains in clothing that belonged to Erik. The Daroga was released with the loss of Imperial favor, the confiscation of all his property and exile. As a member of the Royal House, however, he continued to receive a monthly pension of a few hundred francs from the Persian treasury; and on this, he came to live in Paris.

As for Erik, he went to Asia Minor and from there, to Constantinople, where he entered the Sultan's service. By now, the services he was able to provide to a monarch haunted

---

[33] The word "red" does not refer to the color of the bricks or to Communism. In Russian, the word *krasnaya* means both *red* and *beautiful*, and the term *Red Square* originally referred to St. Basil's Cathedral, located at the southern end of the square.

by perpetual terrors were obvious. Erik designed all the famous trap-doors, secret chambers and mysterious safes which were found at Yildiz-Kiosk after the last Turkish revolution. He also invented those automata which, dressed like the Sultan, resembled him in every respect, and which were made so that people would believe that the Commander of the Faithful was awake in one location, when, in reality, he was asleep elsewhere.[34]

Of course, Erik had to leave the Sultan's service for the same reasons that had forced him out of Persia: he knew too much. At last, tired of his adventurous, extraordinary and monstrous life, he longed to become someone *just like everybody else*. And he became a contractor, an ordinary contractor, building ordinary houses with ordinary bricks. He tendered a bid for parts of the foundations of the Opera, which was accepted. When he found himself in the vaults of that enormous theater, his artistic, fantastic and *magical* nature took over. Besides, wasn't he as hideous as ever? He dreamed of building himself his own house, hidden from the eyes of the rest of humanity, where he could hide forever.

The reader knows and can guess the rest of the tale. It has already been revealed through the course of this incredible, yet true story. Poor, sad Erik! Should we pity him? Should we curse him? He only asked to be someone *just like everybody else*. But he was too hideous! And he had to hide his genius *or play tricks with it*, when, if he had had an ordinary face, he would have been one of the most noble representatives of the human race! He had a heart big enough to embrace the whole world, and, in the end, he had to content himself with a cellar. Ah, yes, we should pity the Phantom of the Opera!

---

[34] See the interview of the special correspondent of *Le Matin* with Mohammed-Ali Bey, the day after the entry of the Salonika troops into Constantinople. (*Note from the Author.*)

Despite his crimes, I have prayed over his remains that God might show him mercy. After all, why did God make a man as hideous as he?

Yes, I am sure quite sure that I prayed over his body, just the other day, when they dug it from the same spot where they were burying the phonographic records I mentioned in my foreword. It was his skeleton. I did not recognize it by the hideousness of the head, for all men are hideous when they have been dead as long as that, but by the plain gold ring which he wore and which Christine Daae had certainly slipped on his finger when she came to bury him, as she had promised him she would do.

The skeleton was lying near the small fountain, at the spot where the Angel of Music first held the fainting Christine Daae in his trembling arms, the night when he carried her down to the vaults of the Opera.

And, now, what are they going to do with that skeleton? Surely, it should not be thrown into some common potters' field! I say that the proper place for the bones of the Phantom of the Opera is at the archives of the National Academy of Music. In the Opera. For they are no ordinary bones, but the bones of the *Angel of Music*.

THE END

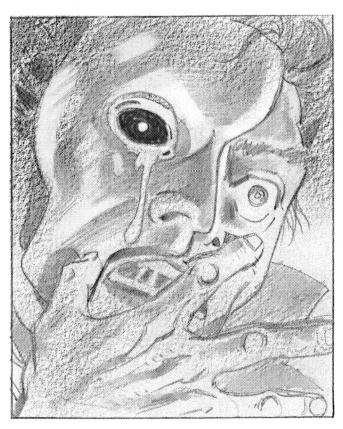

Paolo Ongaro

Alfredo Macall

His Father's Eyes

by

Jean-Marc & Randy Lofficier

Stephen R. Bissette

Rosemary spent a horrible night curled up on her miserable cot. She almost thought she could hear the vermin writhe inside the filthy mattress that she had found in the least damp corner of the shack. She could barely sleep and the night went on, endless, suffocating. With an implacable regularity, tiny drops of water dripped between the timbers of the roof and fell on the wet muddy floor of her prison, marking time like a grandfather clock. Outside, the Scottish wind howled. A storm was approaching from the North Sea and the wailing of the wind managed to whistle its way through the maladjusted wooden planks of the walls, bringing the girl what seemed in her nightmares to be the echoes of ancient curses.

She turned and turned on her cot in fits of impatient anguish. Even though she was wracked by exhaustion and fear, she could not find a merciful refuge in sleep. After a couple of hours of slow combustion, the torch *he* had left in its holder by the door fizzled out, and she was plunged into total darkness. She thought she would go mad from the faint rustling sounds— field mice or a rat, or perhaps, more horrible yet, the labor of the spiders who infested the beams above her.

Rosemary could not guess how much time elapsed before she again heard the sound of *his* footsteps. It was not yet dawn, for no light struck through the thin wooden walls. Her senses, finely attuned to everything that happened inside or outside the shack, felt *his* presence before she heard the steps.

He had returned.

Rosemary's breath sped up. Her heart thumped in her chest. She heard *him* remove the beam that kept the door secured. She steeled herself to once more face *his* terrifying presence and his evil yellow eyes.

375

The beam fell to the ground. The door, which only hung by one hinge, was pushed open.

He appeared on the threshold, holding a new torch, with which he replaced the one that had burned out. His face was inscrutable, but a tiny detail managed to extract a small whimper of fear from Rosemary in spite of her resolution to be brave. There was a small trickle of blood at the corner of *his* mouth.

He remained completely still, a ghastly living waxwork, looking at *his* captive, perhaps pondering her fate.

Long minutes passed.

Suddenly, without showing any emotion, *he* turned around and vanished into the darkness–without closing the door.

Dawn came and with it a day of new terrors. Rosemary did not dare cross the open threshold for fear of being confronted by her awful jailer. She occasionally heard *his* footsteps outside and knew that *he* was close by.

Was *he* playing with her? Like *he* had "played" with Maggie before... She shook her head, not wanting to remember the awful moments when *he* had come out of nowhere during her peaceful afternoon walk on the Scottish Highlands and seized her after brutally killing her brave Shetland collie who had tried to protect her mistress from the assault of her attacker.

The blood on the corner of *his* mouth was a sign of some other atrocity that he had no doubt perpetrated during the night.

She thought she too would end up like Maggie, her throat slit by his razor-sharp teeth, her bloody carcass dismantled and thrown away.

But despite the fear that gripped her entrails, the cold sweat and the shaking she could not stop, she was still alive. So there was still some hope left, wasn't there?

Her head hurt. Why had *he* spared her? Why not kill her and put an end to the hellish torments that she had endured? She welcomed the death that *he* seemed to refuse her...

Hours went by. Rosemary lay on her cot, exhausted. She finally mustered all her remaining strength to take some cautious steps towards the open threshold. Could she walk out of this shack that otherwise might become her coffin?

Why had *he* left the door open? Was *he* so sure that she would not try to escape?

During the last hour, Rosemary had not heard any footsteps or other sounds to indicate that *he* was nearby. The torch on the wall was starting to flicker.

She strained to hear as far as she could. There was no sound.

Perhaps *he* had gone at last.

She had not had any food since the day before and she felt light-headed. The cold and the damp gnawed at her body more efficiently than the rats would have done. She knew that soon she would have no strength left.

If she were to act, it had to be now.

She thought of running away, very fast, running through the moors towards her father's house and the safety of the village...

But could there be any safety with one such as *he*? What if *he* followed her? Didn't she risk bringing *his* awesome wrath down the heads of those she loved? How could her aging father ever prevail against one such as *he*? What about the innocent folk of the village...

With a deep sigh, she stepped back, away from the beguiling opening and again lay down on her cot, her eyes closed.

She fell into a near-comatose state of almost complete apathy. She could not move. She could only see and hear–and wait for *him*.

And then she heard *his* footsteps again.

He stepped inside the shack and approached the cot. Rosemary closed her eyes even tighter and held her breath.

She had no intention of screaming or struggling. She prayed for a quick, merciful death.

Through her eyes were closed, she felt *his* almost supernatural presence close to her, the burning of *his* evil yellow eyes upon every inch of her body.

He was there... so close. Seething with rage and yet totally still. What was *he* waiting for to finish his foul job? she thought.

In her mind, she silently begged for *him* to kill her as she could no longer stand this torture. Her eyes tightly shut, she imagined that she felt *his* breath near her throat... Something rustled gently past her breast... Was it *his* hand?

Suddenly, with blinding clarity, a revelation appeared in her fevered mind. Why had she not thought of it before?

He didn't want to kill her. *He* wanted her to stay with *him*.

He wanted her to be *his* mate.

When *he* had first seized her, *he* had mentioned in his ramblings the island of Cround, one of the Orkneys off the mainland. *He* had been raging, almost like a madman. Something had happened to *him* there that had upset *him* greatly. *He* muttered dark, murderous promises of revenge on someone close to *him*. Rosemary shuddered, and thought that, even though she had reached the bottom of despair, she still would not trade places with that other man, for if *he* could do to her, a complete stranger, what he had done, what even more horrible fate had he in store for the other?

She feared *his* foul touch, she was sure that would be next. Her eyes were still closed, her eyelids ached from being held so tightly shut. She strained to hear *his* every move over the wild beatings of her heart. She heard the creaking of the floorboards. She guessed that *he* had just kneeled down next to the cot.

Then she again felt *his* breath upon her face. It smelt like withered flowers, old, decaying, but not unpleasant. *His* lipless mouth, a mere slit in his taunt, corpse-like face, moved inexorably towards hers. She was trapped.

Rosemary's fingers contracted, gripped the cot nervously, then balled up into fists. She could no longer bear the horror. It was pointless to feign unconsciousness.

Abruptly, she pulled her legs up and sprang forth. She found herself upright, standing up breathlessly, hey eyes wide open, next to *his* terrifying figure. As she had guessed, *he* had been kneeling by the cot. With a speed defying imagination, however, *his* hand had grabbed a corner of her dress when she got up and *he* now held a piece of torn fabric in *his* hand. Her left shoulder was bare.

He sprang to his feet and, with a couple of steps, moved between her and the door.

She stood facing *his* ghastly, dead face where only the evil yellow eyes shone forth, and the dirty strands of long, black, matted hair quivered under the outside wind.

Any animal would have lunged forward. But *he* merely opened his arms to block her way and waited.

Then, he began to slowly step forward, all too slowly, fixing her with his evil yellow eyes.

A low growl came out of nowhere. It may have been an unconscious manifestation of triumph. For she was entirely at *his* mercy. Far from the eyes of God and Men, *he* would at last satisfy his vile desires.

She stood paralyzed, less than two yards away from *him*, reflecting that if she could have, at this very moment, found a way to kill herself, she would have done so, even at the cost of eternal damnation.

He took another step and seized her with *his* hands. *His* fingers dug painfully into her delicate shoulders. Rosemary tried to scream but found she could not. She still had the strength to cry, however, and tears silently ran down her face.

His image grew fuzzy. Only the burning amber flames of *his* evil yellow eyes shone before her. She perceived, more than heard, another, louder growl. Then, she felt her dress torn from her body. Purely by instinct, she brought her arms up to

379

cover her chest. She heard a rhythmic sound and realized it was her teeth chattering.

She suddenly felt herself pulled forward by *his* unshakeable grip, crushed against *his* powerful chest and, finally, all her senses obliterated by horror, she slipped into merciful oblivion.

When Rosemary woke up, she was in her bed, at home. Her father was by her side and, after the doctor had gone, he told her that she had been found naked, bloodied and mud-covered in an abandoned shack at the western end of the moors. Of *him*, there was no trace.

She recovered in time, somewhat, taking comfort in the notion that her sacrifice had saved her family, and perhaps the entire village as well, from *his* anger.

But the horror began again, first a fleeting dark thought, quickly banished, then a horrible premonition, too dreadful to face, and finally an inescapable truth...

She discovered that she was pregnant.

Her faith was too strong for her to take her own life, and she would never have sacrificed the innocent she now bore. However, due to her father's position in the village, she could no longer remain when her situation would become known to all.

Her father sent her to live with his brother, who was a mason in the city of Rouen in Normandy. Being childless, Rosemary's uncle and his wife had agreed to raise the child as their own.

So it came to pass that, one grey winter morning, Rosemary left Scotland and embarked for France.

Six months later, she prepared to give birth to the child.

The midwife–a robust Norman woman of considerable experience and utmost discretion–had loudly expressed her concerns over the mother's health, which had been declining throughout the pregnancy. Rosemary had been plagued by nightmares, reliving the dreaded hours she had spent in the shack, where the child had been conceived. She had told no one about the true horrors of that night, making up a story about an ordinary vagrant instead. She had tried to hide the truth, even to herself, but now it plagued her nights in the form of nightmares, each more terrifying than the last.

Finally, after long hours of painful labor, the midwife pulled the mewling infant from his mother's womb–reporting him to be a healthy baby boy–and cut the umbilical cord. Rosemary, still panting, exhausted, drenched in sweat, asked to take the baby to put him to her breast. The midwife, concerned about the mother's excessive bleeding, did as requested and handed her the child.

When Rosemary grabbed the newborn, she looked at his face, his taut, pallid skin, and she shuddered. She began to shake violently. Then the baby, for the first time, opened his eyes and looked at his mother.

Rosemary lifted up her head. Two tears ran slowly down her livid cheeks. Then she screamed the scream of the damned and her very life essence seemed to drain from her body as she exclaimed:

"He's got *his* father's eyes! *His* evil yellow eyes!"

Rosemary was buried at the Cemetery of Saint-Sever near Rouen. They named the baby Erik, after his grandfather. On his mother's side, naturally.

"Shall each man find a wife for his bosom, and each beast have his mate, and I be alone? I had feelings of affection, and they were requited by detestation and scorn."

The Monster. Mary Shelley, *Frankenstein*, Chapter XX.

Paul Pope

Index of Illustrators

Printed in the United States
47609LVS00001B/18